...heart.

...ht her

...desire.

"ARE YOU COMPLETELY MAD?" GUY DEMANDED.

"Coming to my room in the middle of the night? If you do not leave in the next minute or so, I think you have a very good idea of what is going to happen, as I am no monk. You must know that I have wanted you for a very long time. And if you don not leave right this minute, I will not answer for the consequences. Is that clear enough?"

Joanna considered for all of two seconds. "I—I know I am violating every last principle I ever believed in, but if the memories of a few months of happiness with you are what I will have to carry me through the rest of my life, then I am willing to sacrifice those principles."

Guy did not wear anything close to an appropriately appreciative expression at her willingness to become a fallen woman for his sake.

"Unless, of course," Joanna added, "I have misunderstood you and you do not want me for your mistress after all."

"I believe that you have most definitely misunderstood me," he said, looking down into her eyes. "Did I not mention that I'm in love with you? I want to marry you."

Dell books by Katherine Kingsley

Katherine Kingsley

✳

✳

The Sound of Snow

✳

A DELL BOOK

Published by
Dell Publishing
a division of
Random House, Inc.
1540 Broadway
New York, New York 10036

ISBN: 0-440-22389-X

Printed in the United States of America

Published simultaneously in Canada

April 1999

10 9 8 7 6 5 4 3 2 1
OPM

To Joanna Mary Verey,
whose inner light touches everyone she meets.
Shine on, lovely girl!

Acknowledgments

The author would like to extend thanks to Peter Dress, for providing the music and inspiration for the title, and to Garrett Fitzgerald, for supplying many valuable facts about Italy.

Thanks also go to the entire Verey family, who so graciously open their home and their hearts each summer in England to their lunatic cousin and patiently answer ceaseless questions for the rest of the year about flowers and snowdrifts and Norman towers. This time I stole directly not only from their village but straight from their household, in which case I should also profusely thank Margaret and Bill Watt, Wendy Donelan, and Shelley Collins, for lending me their first names and allowing me to borrow freely from my observations for the purposes of this book. No resemblance to anyone living or dead, I, ahem, swear.

Thanks as always go to my dear friends Francie Stark and Jan Hiland, who patiently read the pages thrown at them and make soothing noises, as does my husband, Bruce, who also cooks dinner. There's a man.

To the readers: Please do write me at **P.O. Box 37, Wolcott, CO 81655**, with your thoughts and comments. I always answer letters that include an SASE. You can also e-mail me at kkingsley@compuserve.com and visit my Web page at **http://ourworld.compuserve.com/homepages/kkingsley** for updates.

Happy reading and all best wishes,

Katherine Kingsley

The poet's eye, in a fine frenzy rolling,
Doth glance from heaven to earth, from
     earth to heaven;
And, as imagination bodies forth
The forms of things unknown, the poet's
     pen
Turns them to shapes, and gives to airy
     nothing
A local habitation and a name . . .
That is, hot ice and wondrous strange snow.

WILLIAM SHAKESPEARE, *A Midsummer Night's Dream*

1

*G*od certainly had an interesting way of turning the world upside down when one least expected it, Joanna thought angrily. Why did He have to deal poor Lydia such a low blow over such a simple pleasure? She really didn't see what point it served. If He'd felt the need to strike someone ill on this day, it should have been Joanna He'd chosen, for she wouldn't have minded nearly so much contracting the measles. But as she'd already had them and wasn't going to succumb again, all she could offer Lydia was comfort.

"Lydie, my love, you must calm yourself," she said, wringing out the cloth in water that she'd scented with lavender and placing it on Lydia's hot brow. "Getting worked into a state will do your fever no good, and it certainly won't change the situation."

A tear rolled out of Lydia's red, swollen eyes, but she still managed to glare defiantly at Joanna. "I am not in a state," she said, her voice thick. "And I *will* go to my own birthday dance. Nothing you or anyone else says is going to stop me."

Joanna sat down on the side of the bed and took her cousin's hand in hers. "Surely you must see that going downstairs this evening is an impossibility. Not only are you unwell, but you cannot risk exposing anyone else to your illness. You heard the doctor—you are highly contagious. Do try to be reasonable."

"Reasonable?" Lydia snatched her hand out of Joanna's grasp. "There is no reason or fairness to any of this, and I won't stand for it! I've waited all year for this night, Jo, you know I have. What terrible thing have I done to deserve being struck down on my eighteenth birthday, the very night that was supposed to be my personal triumph?" She scowled. "Anyway, there's no proof I have measles. I have no rash, have I? You cannot be absolutely sure unless there's a rash. Doctor McFadden said so; you were standing right there when he said it."

"I was, and I also heard what the doctor said directly after that," Joanna replied gently. "The Tuppford boys both came down with measles last week, and you did sit next to them in church last Sunday. You have all the other symptoms, Lydia, and Doctor McFadden told you the rash would be the last thing to appear."

Lydia's face crumpled and she turned it into the side of the pillow. "It's all right for you," she said on a sob. "You can go ahead and revel without me. It's supposed to be your birthday celebration too, even if your twenty-first birthday was really a fortnight ago. Why should you want me there when everyone is bound to make a huge fuss over you for having reached your majority? You'll probably have a whole handful of proposals while I lie here in the dark, alone and suffering, turning eighteen all by myself."

Joanna had to stifle a laugh. Lydia was prone to dramatics. "I cannot imagine that anyone will make much of a fuss over me," Joanna replied, wringing out the cloth again and reapplying it to Lydia's brow. "It is you who always draws the attention, beautiful creature that you are."

"And now you compliment yourself," Lydia said with a sniffle and an annoyed look. "We might be sisters instead of second cousins, everyone says so. The only real difference between us is age—well, that and my substantial dowry, but that's not what people actually see on the surface, is it? They look at me and just as well might be looking at you."

"We might share some family traits, Lydie, but my personality is a much paler version of yours," Joanna said with complete truth. "I have none of your sparkle or your allure, and that's what makes someone beautiful. People gather round you like moths to a flame, wanting to bask in your light, whereas I only bore them to tears."

"That's because of the way you behave. People must think you'd rather spend time with your silly paintings than with an eligible man," Lydia said with disgust. "Really, Jo, you might be older, but sometimes I think you haven't the least bit of understanding of what it takes to get on in life. A watercolor isn't going to put pretty clothes on your back or a wedding ring on your finger. It certainly isn't going to fill your heart and soul with passion or love."

Joanna just smiled. Lydia would never understand the joy Joanna took from translating color and light and form to paper or canvas any more than Lydia would ever understand why she wasn't interested in rushing into marriage with the highest available title. She'd be wasting her breath if she tried to explain yet again. Unlike her cousin, she was not inclined to fall in and out of love every other day of the week. If she ever did fall in love, it would be once and for a lifetime.

Despite the physical similarities she and Lydia shared, they were as different as night and day. Lydia's interests revolved around her appearance, her social standing, and making the best possible match as soon as she could. As far as Joanna was concerned, society could go hang for all she really noticed or cared, and she doubted that society held her in any higher regard, since she had neither position, money, nor charm.

"I suppose you'll finally have to accept someone now

that you've reached your majority, and it's bound to be Lord Holtingham," Lydia said flatly.

"Lord Holtingham?" Joanna said, surprised. "What on earth are you talking about?"

"You know perfectly well of whom I am speaking. Charles Maitland, Viscount Holtingham, heir to the Earl of Dunleigh and one of the more eligible men in Britain," Lydia replied. "He might not be a duke, but he has a large fortune and he's exceptionally attractive. Anyway, Clara Codrington told me that her father told *her* that Holtingham's father has made it clear to Charles that he must marry this year. He has it in mind to marry you, hasn't he?"

"Lydia," Joanna said patiently, "I cannot see why you think my attaining my majority would suddenly make a difference to him or anyone else. Most people think me on the shelf by now." Never mind that Holtingham was one of the biggest rakes in Christendom who had no interest in marrying anyone, no matter his father's wishes.

"Don't be silly. Everyone knows you had to do a year's mourning for Uncle Edward and Aunt Amanda when they died, and that was right in the middle of your first season. By the time you'd put off your mourning clothes, you'd missed the better part of two seasons, and I don't think you can be considered on the shelf until you've had at least three proper seasons in which to fail."

"Really?" Joanna replied dryly, suppressing the stab of pain that any reminder of her parents' death always brought. "Tell me, do you make up these rules and regulations yourself, or are they written down somewhere?"

Lydia made a rude sound in the back of her throat, then coughed heavily. "The point is that you *have* reached your majority," she said when she'd recovered. "You are free to make your own choice with no one to object, including Mama and Papa, not that they'd object to anyone you chose, since they wish only for your happiness—I even heard them discussing Henry Warnock as a suitable prospect since he is so obviously taken with you, although I personally would die before I'd marry him, but never mind that."

"Exactly. Never mind that," Joanna said, hoping to stem the tide of Lydia's speech.

Lydia ignored her. "I feel sure that is why Mr. Warnock has been included in the house party—Mama and Papa think that with strong encouragement he might succumb, despite your lack of a decent dowry. You know how anxious we all are for you to marry well, and he *does* have a rich uncle with no one else to leave his money to, so he has good prospects, even if he will only be a baron when his father dies and have very little else until the uncle dies. He's presentable nonetheless, don't you think, at least in a masculine sort of fashion?"

"My dear Lydie," Joanna said, trying to make sense out of those last two sentences with no luck, "has it ever occurred to you that I might not wish to marry?"

Least of all marry the unfortunately bacon-brained Henry Warnock, who forever trailed after her like a dog waiting for a scrap to be thrown his way. "Or at least I do not wish to marry without love," she amended.

"Oh, not that again. Love is a luxury for the rich, although I myself would wither away into nothing should I be forced to marry without it, which fortunately I need not." She raised a finely etched eyebrow. "You and I both know that you can't afford *not* to marry."

"I am not in the poorhouse just yet," Joanna retorted. "My inheritance might be meager, but it is enough to scrape by on."

"Mama says spinsterhood is not a sensible notion for a person in your position, not if you have happier options, and you are nothing if not sensible, even if you don't have romantic sensibilities."

"I thought you consider me hardheaded and intractable," Joanna said with amusement.

"You are certainly stubborn, for I am sure you are only holding out for a better arrangement," Lydia said, sniffling again. "I know you: You like being mysterious."

"Do I?" Joanna said, even more amused by that piece of nonsense.

"Yes," Lydia replied darkly. "Furthermore, I saw the way you secretly looked at Holtingham when we were in London."

"And how was that?" Joanna asked.

"From the corner of your eye when you thought no one was watching. You have it in mind to accept him, I feel sure of it, and there's no use denying it. Come, Jo, we are accustomed to confiding *everything* in each other, are we not?"

Joanna shook her head, exasperated. She did indeed watch Holtingham from the corner of her eye, but only from a sense of self-preservation, so that she could escape before he advanced on her. More than once he had attempted to grope her in the garden, but Joanna did not think it wise to enlighten Lydia further.

"Oh, very well then, you have me," she said lightly, determined to put an end to the ridiculous conversation with a tease. "I think I just might make up my mind to accept him if it will satisfy you, since you take such a great interest in my matrimonial status or lack thereof. You know I can deny you nothing."

"Now you are funning with me," Lydia said, but not looking entirely certain that was the case.

"Am I?" Joanna said, trying to keep a straight face. "I confess, I hadn't realized how dire my predicament was, but now that you've pointed it out to me, I think perhaps you are right. I should seize any opportunity that presents itself lest I do find myself on the shelf. Holtingham might do nicely after all."

Lydia's mouth dropped open. "No—you cannot mean it," she gasped, staring at Joanna as if she'd just announced that the moon really was made of green cheese and she intended to eat the whole of it.

"Why not?" Joanna said, unable to resist teasing her. "As you said, he's handsome enough, and he comes with a large fortune and an acceptably impressive title and estate. Perhaps he won't mind that I have very little to offer him in return, including clever conversation."

"I knew it! I just knew you have been playing him along, making all of us wait and wonder—oh, Jo, how *could* you?" To Joanna's dismay Lydia burst into tears. "You might at least have said something to me about your intentions. I thought you and I were the dearest of friends," she sobbed.

"Lydia, I honestly hadn't realized my marrying meant so much to you," Joanna said, suddenly ashamed of herself for teasing her cousin about a subject so close to the girl's heart.

"It's just that I thought—I wasn't entirely sure of your feelings, and now—oh, never mind!" She stopped abruptly and buried her face in her hands.

"And now?" Joanna prompted, determined to discover the cause of Lydia's distress. "Do tell me what upsets you so."

Silence came from the direction of the pillow.

"Perhaps you really are concerned that if I don't marry now that I have reached my majority, I will be condemned to a life of misery?"

Lydia shook her head.

"No?" Joanna thought hard, accustomed to playing this guessing game. For someone who chattered as much as Lydia, she could be surprisingly reticent when it came to revealing her innermost thoughts.

It occurred to her that perhaps Lydia was more aware of Holtingham's unfortunate reputation than she'd realized. "Then it must be the opposite—you decided Lord Holtingham was going to ask me to marry him, and you've been worried that I might accept him? Could that be it?"

A tiny nod and another sob.

Joanna's heart ached with love for her cousin. As frivolous as she could be, Lydia always found time to worry about the people she loved. That she had thought for even one moment Joanna would be foolish enough to accept Holtingham made Joanna want to laugh, but perhaps Lydia saw nothing beyond her steadfast conviction that every woman secretly wanted to be married to someone of good position no matter what his reputation.

"Lydie—do listen," she said, covering Lydia's trembling fingers with her own. "You mustn't worry so about me, really you mustn't." She stroked Lydia's damp hair. "You should be concentrating only on making a full recovery, certainly not upsetting yourself over my situation. In any case, I strongly doubt Holtingham has any intention of offering for me. Unlike you, I am not all the rage."

Lydia looked up at her from between her fingers. "I d-do not b-believe you," she said, hiccupping. "You are only—only trying to make me feel b-better."

"Well, yes—I suppose I am," Joanna said, "if reassuring you means that I can put your mind at ease. You know that I love you better than anyone on this earth, and I cannot bear to see you unhappy, especially on my behalf."

"Then do nothing to make me so," Lydia said, wiping her eyes with the back of her hand. "I do love you, Jo, but sometimes I think you believe me nothing more than a silly little girl. I assure you that is not the case: I am perfectly grown, even if I might not seem so to you, and I have eyes in my head. I have not missed the way Holtingham follows you about."

"Forgive me if I was insensitive," Joanna said, dropping a kiss on her brow. "I did not mean to imply that you are unobservant in any way. You notice many things that entirely escape my attention." Indeed, Lydia was awake on every suit when it came to the ins and outs of courtship and had already accurately predicted seven matches in the four short months since she'd been presented at court, although in this case she had gone badly astray in her assumption.

"That is exactly my point," Lydia said. "You hardly notice *anything* important, including Holtingham's regard. I wish that I'd never brought the subject up, for you are bound to accept him now that you do know his intentions, and that would break my very heart."

An entirely different thought suddenly occurred to Joanna. "Lydie, my love," Joanna asked gently, "is the problem perhaps that you might want Holtingham for yourself? Please, you can tell me if that is the case."

"Don't be absurd," Lydia said impatiently. "Why would I want him? He's much too old for me. I am only worried for you, darling Jo. I feel that you must marry soon, just not him—he would make you very unhappy and—and I could not bear it." More tears trickled down her cheeks. "You have had too much unhappiness these last three years, with your parents dying in that awful accident." She wiped at her eyes. "It was so unfair."

Joanna decided that fever and disappointment were making Lydia overwrought far more than the idea of Holtingham marrying her spinster cousin. What Lydia needed was rest.

"Listen to me, my pet," she said gently as she stood up. "You must put the very idea of my marrying anyone out of your head, for it will only make it ache the more. I really must go if I'm to prepare to greet our guests. I do not want to keep them waiting."

"No—please do not leave me," Lydia cried, clutching at Joanna's hand. "Please do not, not yet!"

"Very well then," Joanna said, not wanting Lydia to work herself back into hysterics. "I'll stay just a little while longer until you feel you might sleep, but you must promise me you will close your eyes and make the effort."

Lydia sighed heavily, but she nodded and closed her

eyes. Joanna sat back down and with her free hand began to stroke Lydia's hair rhythmically, idly rearranging the shining strands, admiring the way the deepening light turned the brown to gold.

She could only imagine the poor girl's frustration. Houseguests had been arriving all day, and various estates around the county accommodated those lesser lights who had been invited for the dance alone.

Joanna's name might be co-listed on the invitation, but she knew perfectly well that was only for politeness's sake; Lydia, only child of Sir Quentin and Lady Oxley, was the light of their lives and they longed for her to make a brilliant match. Joanna was no more than an obligation, one the Oxleys had taken on after her parents had died and a duty they would be just as happy to discharge.

Fortunately, Lydia remained blissfully unaware that this was the case, believing in her romantic fashion that Joanna was considered a second and much-loved daughter, just as she considered Joanna her beloved sister.

Had Joanna been cut from a different cloth or perhaps had a different upbringing, she would have been happy to marry if only to oblige her aunt and uncle, but she was the product of two people who had loved each other fully and completely, and Joanna could not bear the thought of settling for anything less.

She had witnessed a loveless marriage firsthand: Her aunt Alice had brought a sizable dowry and a respectable if insignificant name to the match, and Uncle Quentin had provided the requisite estate and baronetcy. The combination of money and title had given both parties what they desired, but the marriage had given neither pleasure, as evidenced by their constant bickering.

Now Alice dearly wished to further elevate her position in society through her daughter, and her ambitions knew no limits. Her reaction to the doctor's order that Lydia be confined to her room for the next two weeks with no exceptions had been nothing short of hysterical. Joanna had spent a full hour trying to pacify her, with little success. Only the fact that the evening's festivities could not be canceled at this late date had kept her aunt from taking to her bed and her laudanum bottle.

As soon as Lydia's breathing had slowed and her grip on Joanna's hand relaxed, Joanna stood, knowing if she didn't leave now, she'd never get away.

"Must you really go?" Lydia asked in a small voice.

"Yes, I really must, but you must remember that my very presence downstairs will remind everyone how much they miss you, not that they will need reminding," Joanna replied. "You are the heroine who has been martyred by measles, and I am merely the messenger who conveys the news of your tremendous courage and poise in the face of such misfortune. Everyone adores you, as you know perfectly well."

"I suppose," Lydia said, her face a picture of misery. "Oh, Jo, *why* did it have to be me? I don't mean that I would wish this on you, but if it *had* been you, you wouldn't have felt it a tragedy, whereas as far as I'm concerned, my life is over."

"I am so sorry. I'll come up and check on you later, how is that? I expect you'll be sound asleep, so I won't disturb you if you are, but should you be awake I will give you a progress report."

"No—you are kind to think of me, but you can tell me all about it tomorrow. I do not want you to interrupt your evening for me, and I confess, I am exhausted; I think I will sleep after all." She turned on her side and tucked one hand under her cheek. "Good night. Have a lovely time. And, Jo? Don't forget about Holtingham. He wouldn't do for you at all, as much as he is enamored of you."

Joanna smiled down at her. Lydia was like the sky in March: one minute filled with thunder and lightning, the next calm and clearing with the promise of sunshine. "You are a brave girl," she whispered, bending to press a kiss to Lydia's temple. "Sleep well, and I'll see you in the morning."

Joanna had done no more than touch the door handle to her room across the hall when the door flew open and Bunch pounced from within, grabbing her by the arm and dragging her inside, her bright blue eyes flashing out from their sea of wrinkles.

"'It's about time. Here I am waiting with everything laid out for you, the hot water long gone cold, and where are you but coddling that Lydia. It's already coming up to eight and you're expected downstairs in only half an hour, or did you forget?" Her flushed face betrayed her uncharacteristic agitation, for not much really rattled Bunch, as much as she liked to complain.

"Not to worry, Bunch—we'll manage. We always do, don't we?" Joanna patted her shoulder.

"We? You mean me. You always say the same no matter what the disaster and expect me to work wonders," Bunch replied tartly as she swiftly began to unbutton Joanna's dress. "You've been the same from the time you were a little girl, coming in with your clothes torn and your hair in tangles with no care to what anyone might think. 'Not to worry, Bunch,' you'd say. 'You can fix it, Bunch.' I don't know why I didn't go to live with my sister when I had the chance."

"Because you know I couldn't have done without you. Ouch, have a care!" Joanna winced as Bunch jerked the dress over her head, catching a strand of hair in one of the hooks.

"Have a care? It's you who might have a care, my girl. I've held my tongue until now, but tonight is your last opportunity, certainly the last chance those Oxleys are going to give you to snare a husband. If you *don't* have a care you are going to find yourself living under Lady Oxley's thumb for the rest of your life, the poor relation relegated to the corner, and it will be a cold one at that—and don't think I plan to share it with you. I'm your old governess, not your mother, and I can pick up and leave anytime I choose."

She pulled Joanna over to the washbasin and started to scrub her down as if she were still a child of five. "If I were you—and I'm not, thank the good Lord—I'd get on with it."

"You needn't go on, Bunch—I've already heard it all from Lydia," Joanna said, shivering as the cold water ran in rivulets over her naked skin. "If I don't marry by tomorrow I'll be forever alone and penniless to boot, the rest of my life nothing but a gray and parched wasteland."

"That's the first sensible thing that girl has said this month."

"Don't be rude, Bunch. It's not Lydie's fault that her parents brought her up to believe her only assets are her looks and her dowry, any more than it's her fault that her parents didn't think giving her an education was important. She has a good head on her shoulders despite a lack of formal training."

Bunch exhaled noisily through her nose. "It's not good for any child to think the world revolves around her, no matter how pretty she might be. Good looks never turned *your* head, my girl."

Joanna grinned. "If they had, you would have thrashed me until I couldn't sit down for a week. Anyway, I'm not really pretty, not like Lydie—she's growing into a real beauty, don't you think? She makes me think of a pixie dancing about dispensing moon dust and enchanting everyone who meets her. I have no doubt that she'll get what she wants—a handsome, highborn man who will give her everything her heart desires and worship the ground she walks on."

"It wouldn't hurt for you to think along the same lines, Joanna. Your father was a good man and a clever one, but he didn't have the first notion of what it meant to live within his means, and your mother, God rest her soul, didn't have any more common sense than he. You can stretch out the income on the scrawny inheritance they left you, but it's not much to live on, my dear—I can tell you that from my own experience. Why do you think I had to give up my lovely little house in Yorkshire and come to look after you? It's not an easy life, being an impoverished gentlewoman."

"I am sorry for you that it worked out that way, but every day I thank God for sending you to me, dear Bunch. We've had sixteen happy years together, haven't we, despite the ups and downs?"

"You're changing the subject, as you always do when you don't like what I'm saying," Bunch said, vigorously rubbing her down with a towel. "I may have tried to teach you to be practical, but you've inherited your father's artistic nature and your mother's soft heart. There's nothing wrong with either, but it can be a troublesome combination when one is without the means to support oneself properly. Idealism doesn't put food on the table."

Joanna frowned, reminded once again of Lydia's words of warning. *Why* did everyone press her to marry for expediency when a loveless marriage would make her miserable above all things? Did they care more for the state of her pocketbook than the state of her heart? Obviously, although she couldn't fault either Lydia or Bunch for loving her enough to care about her financial welfare. "If worse comes to worst," she said, stepping into the flimsy underskirt Bunch held out, "there's always the villa my grandmother left me. It costs much less to live in Italy than England—and I must confess, I've always wanted to see it."

Bunch snorted. "And how do you think the place has fared in these five years since that good woman died? No money has gone into it; your grandmother assumed your father would take care of that for you, but then unfortunately she assumed a great many things about your father's state of affairs, because your mother was too proud to tell her how things really were. You might find yourself living in an Italian villa, but with no roof over your head."

Joanna shrugged. She doubted that was the case— Bunch always painted the bleakest picture possible.

"Lift your arms—really, Joanna, you might try to be a bit more graceful about it. You're not a circus performer."

Fifteen minutes later Bunch gruffly pronounced Joanna marginally fit for company. "You'll have to do as you are," she said, giving Joanna's dressed hair one last critical look and a final pat. "Keep your hands from fiddling with it or you'll crush the roses I've threaded through. A show of nerves is not attractive. Do remember to smile, and for goodness sake use your fan to good effect, will you? It's not there for swatting flies."

"I'll do my best." She leaned down and gave the older woman's cheek a tender kiss. "Thank you for your help, dearest Bunch. You see, you always do manage somehow."

"Heaven knows I try." She blinked, then pressed her fingers against her eyes and patted down her neat gray hair. "Terrible, the dust in this house. It's what comes of giving it a thorough clean only once in a blue moon, and that miserly Lady Oxley wouldn't have ordered that if it hadn't been for the guests she wanted to impress. Go on with you, child. Make me proud of you tonight. You look so like your mother just at this moment . . ."

"I'll try to make you both proud," Joanna said gently, touched by the tears Bunch was trying so hard to disguise. "Please don't wait up for me; I might be very late and you need your rest. I can manage on my own, believe it or not."

"I believe you can manage anything you put your mind to," Bunch retorted. "The question now is what it's going to be. Well, whatever it is will either be the making or the breaking of you, and it's not for me to say—I've done my best, and the rest is up to you."

* * *

Joanna stood in the hallway, her aunt and uncle next to her as they said their farewells to the last of the departing guests.

All in all the evening had been satisfactory, she judged.

Aunt Alice had recovered from her vapors and put on a splendid performance of a concerned mother who wished only to rise above her own trouble to see to her guests' pleasure. The dancing had gone well, although Joanna could have done without standing up for nearly every last one. Her feet ached from the various quadrilles and country reels they'd performed, and her face ached from smiling for five full hours.

She had to force herself to continue smiling when Holtingham appeared and bowed over her hand, his dark hair immaculately in place as ever, his gray eyes calculating.

"Miss Carew. You were the evening's shining star," he said, looking into her eyes with a conspiratorial smile.

"Not in the least," she said, wishing his thumb would leave the palm of her hand alone. What was it about him that always managed to imply that they both knew Joanna would like nothing more than to be taken to a dark room and ravished? "Good night, Lord Holtingham. My regards to your father." She pulled her hand out of his grasp.

A momentary hint of a frown crossed his brow, but he swiftly erased it, smiling smoothly. "Thank you, Miss Carew. I shall be sure to pass your regards on. I hope to see you again before too much time has passed—my life is dimmer when you are not about to grace it with your presence. I hope you will soon be married and free to grace me on a more frequent basis."

She managed to resist the urge to step hard on the toe of his highly polished slipper and instead gave him one last insincere smile before turning to the next guest.

Still, she expected that conduct from Holtingham. What she couldn't work out was Henry Warnock's peculiar behavior.

Halfway through the evening he had suddenly ceased to dog her footsteps and started to behave as if she were invisible—not that she had any cause for complaint. She'd been living in dread that he might embarrass them both by offering for her—she'd felt a proposal coming on all season, although she'd refrained from enlightening Lydia for fear of encouraging her on her relentless pursuit to secure Joanna's happy future.

Henry emerged into the hallway just at that moment and spoke briefly to her aunt and uncle. She cringed as he made a beeline to her side.

"Miss Carew," he said, making a bow, "such a splendid evening I have never before experienced. The food, the dancing, the company—ah, yes . . . the company. I go to my bed an inspired man." He looked deep into her eyes.

Puzzled anew by this next extraordinary shift in behavior, Joanna wondered if he hadn't been studying Holtingham's technique and trying to emulate it.

Poor Henry. He was attractive enough in appearance, he even had rather nice blue eyes, but he just didn't have Holtingham's rakish charm or the sophistication to be a convincing rogue. It wasn't that there was anything overtly wrong with him, it was just that he made her want to yawn.

"I am so pleased you enjoyed yourself, Mr. Warnock," she said, smiling politely. "I hope you sleep well. The country air is so refreshing."

"The country air becomes music when we breathe it together," he said, raising his eyebrow meaningfully. "Until we meet again, Miss Carew."

She sighed, thinking that she was going to have to find excuses to avoid his company for all of the next week or he'd corner her and propose for certain.

She finally dragged herself up the stairs after the last lingering guest had disappeared. Checking on Lydia, she found her sound asleep, her breathing deep and not too raspy. She softly closed the door. Joanna would give her every last detail she could remember in the morning, emphasizing that although the dance had been a success, it would have been far more so had Lydia been there.

That would please her hugely. And Joanna would be speaking the truth. She wouldn't be surprised if Lydia was engaged to be married by the end of the year, given how many gentlemen had appeared thoroughly crushed when news of her illness and confinement reached their ears. Lydia had made a huge success of her season, even if she had missed her own dance.

Joanna walked down the corridor to her own room, impatient for her bed. Bunch had thoughtfully left the candles burning, and Joanna quickly undressed and pulled on her night shift, slipping under the cool sheets. She only turned to blow out the last candle before settling her head on the pillow and falling into a deep sleep.

"Papa? Have you come to kiss me good night?" Joanna lifted her arms to receive her father's embrace—it had been so long, so very long since she'd felt his strong, reassuring arms around her.

"My darling, oh, my darling—I cannot believe I am finally holding you as I have always longed to do. Kiss me, Joanna, and seal our promise—"

Joanna's eyes flew open, her heart coming to a stop as she realized that the man in her cozy dream was not her father, and the dream was not a dream at all.

She bolted upright, shoving at Henry Warnock's bare chest with all of her strength. "What do you think you're doing?" she cried. "Are you mad?"

"But, my darling—I could not have misunderstood your intention?" he said, leaning forward and planting a wet kiss somewhere above her left ear.

"My *intention*?" Joanna sputtered, violently turning her head to avoid his attack. "What intention?"

"Oh, my dove, I do so love your modesty, but do not play

me false; there is no one here but ourselves. Let me declare my love in every way a man can to his beloved."

Joanna had just drawn breath with the intention of filling his ears with blistering invective when her door inched open. Joanna's heart froze in her chest as Lydia appeared, sleepily rubbing her eyes.

"Are you awake, Jo? I feel so feverish, I thought you might give me some more willow—" Her eyes opened wide as she took in the scene before her, and her mouth dropped open. A second passed before her ear-splitting scream filled the air and echoed down the corridor.

In an instant Henry had jumped to his feet, fumbling for his shirt and trousers. Joanna sat frozen in bed, the covers pulled up to her chest, incapable of speech or movement or even coherent thought.

She did, however, register Lydia's ongoing screams and Henry trying to push past her to escape, but in that he was too late. His exit was blocked by Sir Quentin, who had appeared out of the darkness, his nightcap askew, a shotgun in hand. Behind him Joanna spotted Aunt Alice, her mouth working like a landed fish, no words coming out of it, but her eyes wide with shock at what she saw in front of her.

The sound of doors opening farther away mingled with voices raised in excited question, and Joanna's heart sank straight down to the pit of her stomach. She could imagine how compromising the scene must look, despite how false the impression.

"Stand and deliver," bellowed Sir Quentin, "or I'll have your guts for garters!"

"I-I am unarmed, s-sir," Henry managed to sputter.

"Ha!" cried Alice. "The last thing I'd call you is unarmed, my man. What is the meaning of this disgrace?"

Joanna finally found her voice. "He—Mr. Warnock—he came into my room uninvited and attempted to assault me," she said, her voice shaking.

"And who do you think will believe that tale, missie? I can see with my own eyes exactly what has been going on."

"Oh, Mama," Lydia sobbed, "you must be forgiving to Jo—she didn't know what she was doing, I am certain of it. You know how she pays no attention to how one should go on in society. Please, please, Mama, Papa, do not punish her."

"I will take your daughter back to bed, Lady Oxley. She is unwell and should not be exposed to any more upset."

Bunch's voice spoke quietly from behind Sir Quentin, and for the first time Joanna felt a sense of reality emerge from the nightmare.

"Perhaps it would be best once all parties are dressed if this conversation was continued downstairs in the library, away from the eyes and ears of your other guests." Bunch shot a significant glance down the hallway, where Joanna knew a crowd of curious onlookers had formed.

"Yes," said Sir Quentin, jamming the business end of his shotgun in Henry Warnock's side. "An excellent notion, Miss Fitzwilliams. I am sure both Mr Warnock and my niece have a great deal of explaining to do. Joanna, make yourself decent at once. Mr. Warnock, come with me."

Joanna didn't know how she managed to survive the next two hours. It all seemed to pass in a haze—questions being fired at her from all sides, she protesting her innocence, Henry Warnock blathering senseless lies like the idiot he was.

"You say Miss Carew invited you to her bedroom, Mr. Warnock?"

"Yes, Sir Quentin, that is exactly what happened. She let me know my attentions would be welcome."

Joanna's mouth fell open. "I did no such thing!" she cried. "He is lying—he cannot possibly back up his claim.

I said a very proper good night and then went straight up-stairs to check on Lydia. Then I went straight to bed and went to sleep. The next thing I knew, Mr. Warnock was mauling me!"

Sir Quentin ignored her as if she hadn't spoken. "In what fashion did Miss Carew let you know your attentions would be welcome, Mr. Warnock?"

"Miss Carew, she—she allowed me to kiss her in the garden, sir. She told me that she had pined for me all of this year, knowing her situation was hopeless because of her lack of dowry. She—she said that she could no longer contain her passion and would rather give herself to me in love than suffer the agony of her heart any longer."

He mopped his damp brow with his handkerchief as Joanna stared at him in wonder. For someone with a brain the size of Henry Warnock's, this piece of fiction was most impressive.

Alice Oxley was apparently equally impressed, for she gazed at Joanna with an entirely new expression on her face, which Joanna might have interpreted as respect if the situation hadn't been so ludicrous.

"Can you not see how absurd his story is?" Joanna said, frustrated to the point of tears.

"So you decided to accept Miss Carew's desperate invitation," Alice said, ignoring Joanna's protest every bit as much as her husband had. "You cared nothing of her honor, of her reputation, let alone the heart you would leave broken, the child you might get on her?" Her voice quivered with indignation.

"You misunderstand me," Henry replied, his fingers fiddling nervously with the buttons on his waistcoat. "I intended none of those things. We planned to announce our engagement in the morning—tonight was to be ours alone." He hung his head. "Had I not been so overcome with passion I would have thought the situation through better, but I could not resist my baser feelings, most especially when Miss Carew was so—so enthusiastic in her response. I do swear to you that I planned to acquire a special license so that we might be married as soon as humanly possible."

Oh, that's very good, very good indeed, but none of it your idea from start to finish, was it, Henry? Joanna's eyes narrowed. She was convinced now that Henry must have consulted earlier with Holtingham on how best to achieve his goal of marriage, for this scenario was exactly the sort of thing Holtingham might have recommended, solely for his own amusement.

"I hope you will soon be married and free to grace me on a more frequent basis."

The next time she saw him she would have *his* guts for garters. "I repeat," she said with cold fury, "Mr. Warnock is fabricating this entire story, clearly to save his own skin. I have told you the full truth and hope you know me well enough to take my word over that of a near stranger's."

"You realize, Mr. Warnock," Sir Quentin said, once again behaving as if he hadn't heard her, "that through the extreme foolishness of your behavior you have no choice but to marry Miss Carew, and marry her as soon as it can be arranged. I personally doubt that you had any intention of offering for Miss Carew given your compromising action, but it is done now and we can only try to avert scandal by concocting a story about my daughter's illness—perhaps that you went to fetch Miss Carew, having heard Lydia's distress in the night, and were trying to rouse her from a deep sleep when you were discovered."

"No—oh, please, no, Uncle! You cannot be so cruel as to force me into a marriage I do not wish when I did nothing wrong."

Her uncle pursed his plump lips, his gaze fixed on Henry Warnock. "Naturally no one will believe a word of it, but the marriage will at least forestall the worst of consequences."

"Indeed, Sir Quentin," Henry said eagerly. "I am most happy to comply with your wishes. I understand your hesitation in believing me, but I assure you, it truly has been my most sincere desire to secure Miss Carew's hand in matrimony these long months since first I laid eyes on her. I had my doubts, naturally, as she is not possessed of fortune, but I soon overcame those, unable to deny the deeper calling of my—"

"I wish to hear nothing more on the subject, Mr. Warnock. My wife and I will make the announcement of your engagement in the morning to our guests, and the marriage announcement will be published in the papers immediately after the fact is accomplished." Sir Quentin stood, putting an end to the interview.

"Uncle Quentin, I'm afraid I must object." Joanna rose, her heart pounding in slow, heavy beats. "I will not marry Mr. Warnock."

All three turned their heads to stare at her.

Alice was the first to recover her voice. "Have you lost your senses, girl? You have no choice! Surely you cannot be so stupid that you cannot understand that."

"I do have a choice," Joanna said, surprised at how calm her voice sounded when she was shaking inside. "I cannot marry a man I do not love, no matter what the circumstances. I did nothing wrong: The story Mr. Warnock has concocted is just that—a concoction, and I will not be party to any further deceit."

"Deceit?" Henry roared. "How dare you! It happened just as I said it did—I will not have my reputation or word challenged, no matter your desire to protect your maidenly modesty." He visibly regained control of himself, but his hands shook at his sides. "I have offered you the protection of my name, and you now stand upon your pride and refuse it? Do not be such a little fool, beloved. You are cutting off your hand to spite your face."

"I believe you mean my nose, Mr. Warnock," Joanna said, quickly losing patience, "and I am cutting off nothing except this farce of a marriage concocted solely for the sake of satisfying sacred British propriety. Go and find someone else to compromise into marrying you, for it will not be me." She raised her chin and met his blazing blue eyes defiantly.

"Joanna," her aunt said, her voice suddenly soft and cajoling, "you are not thinking clearly, my dear. No doubt the distress of tonight's events have overcome your common sense. You need to sleep, you poor lamb. You will see everything more sensibly in the morning."

"I am truly sorry, Aunt, but I will see everything just the same," Joanna said, determined to stand her ground. If she didn't she might as well die now, for if she should be forced into marriage with Henry Warnock, her life would be as good as finished. "I cannot marry Mr. Warnock under any circumstances, and I can only pray that you will forgive me for my refusal."

Alice Oxley's eyes turned to steel, her voice turning just as cold and hard. "Forgive you? I think not, Joanna. We took you in when you had nowhere else to turn; we fed you and clothed you, reintroduced you to society, tried our best to make a match for you despite all your shortcomings. And this is how you choose to repay us, by disgracing us in a salacious manner under our very roof, your poor innocent cousin a witness to your misdeed?" She advanced across the room until her face was only inches away from Joanna's. "Defy us in this matter and you shall be cast from this house forever, your name never spoken again in polite society. This I will promise you."

Joanna gazed straight back at her aunt and made her decision without another moment's thought. "Then I will leave this house," she said. "I cannot stay on with people who doubt my word and would force me to marry against my will."

"Do not be stupid, Joanna," Sir Quentin said, his round face flushing red with anger. "You will regret your hot temper—you do not have much to live on and nowhere else to go."

"But I have," Joanna said, remembering her earlier remark to Bunch. "Now that I am twenty-one and independent I shall go to Italy. I shall go to the Villa di Camigliano and never darken your door again."

2

*J*oanna felt as if her teeth might rattle out of her head as the hired carriage swayed and jerked, the wheels catching in the deep, sodden ruts in the road. In the years she'd been away from England she'd made a new life for herself in Italy under the sun of the Marche. She'd married a wonderful man and then she'd lost him to a sudden death. But through all of the joys and sorrows the bright sun had warmed her and the beauty of the rolling Italian landscape had comforted her. She'd managed to forget how bleak and damp and nasty the weather generally was in England in November. The coming winter would be even worse.

Huddled inside her cloak, she tried desperately not to think of the cold, tried not to think at all. Thinking only invited pain. Far better not to feel.

She lowered her tired eyes, only to see the enameled chest that sat beside her, the chest that contained every last letter Lydia had ever written her. It was no use trying to avoid the truth.

Lydia was dead.

No matter how many tears Joanna shed, no matter the fury with which she berated God, Lydia was gone from this world and there was nothing Joanna could do to bring her back.

The cruelest blow of all was that Lydia had been dead a

full year and Joanna had not known. The letters had stopped coming, but Joanna assumed that Lydia had her reasons for not writing, had thought that perhaps she had decided to travel as she'd always wanted.

Lydia had been looking for an escape from her miserable marriage for years, and it was only the fear of leaving her precious little boy in his father's hands that had held her back—that and her deep love for her child.

"My dear girl, you are looking far too pale—perhaps we should ask the coachman to stop at the next inn so that you may warm yourself by the fire and eat something sustaining?"

"No, thank you, Bunch—I'd like to get to Wakefield as soon as possible."

Joanna looked up at the older woman's own pinched face and felt an instant pang of remorse. She ought to have thought of Bunch's comfort instead of her own driving need to reach Wakefield. She'd put Bunch through enough as it was, tearing them both away from Pesaro with only a moment's preparation. "On second thought, perhaps that would be a good idea. We'll stop for the night if rooms can be had."

"For the Contessa di Capponi I am sure there will be no trouble finding rooms, child. The question is whether there is any point if you don't make use of the bed."

Joanna shivered involuntarily. Bunch knew her too well. She had not managed a decent night's sleep since learning of Lydia's death; she wondered if she ever would again. A hot mist filled her eyes. Lydia. Poor, poor Lydia.

Joanna had the most horrible apprehension in the back of her mind that Guy de Salis was somehow responsible for Lydia's death; she hadn't been able to shake the suspicion since she'd first read Sir Quentin's letter, as morbid and farfetched as the thought was. She realized she was probably being ridiculous—she didn't even know how Lydia had died. Influenza or some such other illness might easily have carried her away, and she was being unfair to lay Lydia's death automatically at her husband's door, even if he was a brute.

The black-edged letter she'd received from the Oxleys had told her little: It was cold and vaguely accusing, as if she were somehow responsible. She knew it by heart, having read it over and over, first in shock, then in denial, and finally in something approaching a numbed acceptance.

DEAR JOANNA

I enclose this token of Lydia's affection as she requested in her last will and testament. It has taken your aunt and myself a long while to come to the decision that we should honor her wishes. We did not encourage her correspondence with you, but she was a married woman with a life of her own and so we did not interfere. Therefore we pass on this locket that bears a likeness of her from her childhood, although we do so with great reluctance.

The sweetness and innocence intrinsic to our darling Lydia's soul caused her to continue in her mistaken belief of your virtue, and I feel sure that had it been you who had died, she would have mourned you to the very depths of her being and shown you every gesture of respect, deserved or not. Such is the mark of a decent woman.

However, Lydia's death November last was clearly of no great importance to you, as we have received no note of condolence or even an acknowledgment of her passing. I wonder if your cold-blooded nature allows you to feel any sorrow at all.

I beg you not to respond to this missive, as Lady Oxley and I have no wish for further communication of any sort with you.

YOURS, ETC.

QUENTIN OXLEY, BART.

She should have expected nothing kinder from them, but to have learned the news in such a manner had shaken her badly.

"I cannot see why we should stop now that we are so

close," Bunch said, interrupting Joanna's bleak thoughts, "as long as you feel you can go on. Do you suppose Lord Greaves received your letter?" she asked. "He might not be expecting us, in which case we probably should stop and send a message ahead."

"My letter will surely have arrived by now," Joanna replied with certainty. Of course it had. She'd sent it before they'd left, and they had traveled far more slowly than the mail.

"Even if it has, what the marquess will actually have to say about your appearing on his doorstep is another question, isn't it?"

"We'll have to deal with that when we come to it. I cannot see that sending notice ahead will make any difference now. He will have us turned away if that is his inclination, although I cannot believe that he is so much of a monster that he will refuse us hospitality after our long journey. I did explain about my promise to Lydia."

"He would have to care about such things as promises for that to make any impression, and according to your cousin he cares for nothing but himself and his own pleasures. I am sure that is why Lydia asked of you what she did."

"Yes," Joanna said, thinking how odd it was that Lydia should have been so insistent about her request, almost as if she expected something to happen. These words, too, she remembered by heart, words she'd thought had been nothing more than Lydia being melodramatic. She'd been young and healthy—what could possibly happen to her? Now Joanna realized the words had been prophetic.

Please, my dearest cousin, Lydia had written, *you must swear to me that you will do what you can for my sweet baby should I be taken from him. Guy cares nothing for Miles. Once he had his precious heir he felt no further responsibility and has now abandoned us both. My son needs love, someone who will look after his best interests. I can think of no one but you who would care for him as he needs.*

"I don't know what Lydia expects me to do, though," she said aloud. "I can't exactly walk into Wakefield and announce that I'm taking Greaves's son back to Italy with me. He'd never allow such a thing, and I cannot say I would blame him."

Bunch gave her a stern look. "As I have said to you from the moment you hatched this absurd scheme, you would have been better served to think first and act later. You have a habit of behaving in an impulsive and willy-nilly fashion, Joanna. A proper letter requesting guidance from Lord Greaves would have been better advised—we certainly would not be in this predicament now if you'd followed a sensible course."

"Perhaps not," she replied with a shrug. "I couldn't think what else to do—the poor child's been without his mother for a full year, and if Wakefield is as dismal and depressing as Lydia described, he can't have been living a very happy life. I cannot let Lydia down over so important a matter as her son. He's only five, Bunch, and he has no one to care for him but a hard-hearted father."

"And you, a perfect stranger, think you are going to step into his life and be mother and savior all rolled into one?"

"I think nothing of the sort," Joanna replied hotly.

"Ah," said Bunch, touching the tips of her gloved fingers together and pursing her lips in a manner that Joanna knew meant she didn't believe a word her former pupil was saying. "Then you plan to pay your respects and bow out of his life. That will surely make all the difference to the child."

"Bunch, *why* are you being so difficult?" Joanna glowered at the old woman. "I'm trying to do my best, and in any case, what is done is done—we are nearly there, and there is no turning back at this late date. As far as Miles will know, I am merely coming for an extended visit, after which I shall return to Italy. I see no harm in that, do you?"

"Who is to say where harm might be done? You know nothing of the situation at all."

"I know what Lydia had to say about it: Guy de Salis is a self-centered, maniacal monster who made her life a living hell. He's probably doing the same to his child, but I intend to see for myself. Then I'll decide what needs doing."

"If Guy de Salis is all the things Lydia claimed, then I strongly suggest you stay out of his way," Bunch said dryly. "In fact, if I were you I should be prepared to be greeted by an ax-wielding marquess at the front door."

"This is no time for funning," Joanna said, turning away. She was growing more annoyed with Bunch by the moment, for the truth was that Bunch was too close to the mark by far. Joanna was secretly terrified of what Guy de Salis's reaction might be. Lydia had written over and over that his violent rages caused her to fear for her life, that she never knew what might set him off, that there was no reasoning with him.

The first letter she'd received from her cousin after her marriage had told such a different story. Joanna's cold fingers fumbled with the clasp of the chest on her lap, and she removed that particular letter to reread it and remember a time when Lydia had been so very happy and the world still held promise for the charmed life she'd been determined to have.

Joanna scanned the page, remembering the pleasure she'd taken in hearing Lydia's news, the description of how she'd met her husband at a party in London, only months after Joanna had left for Italy.

> . . . *There he was, Jo, the most beautiful, magnificent man I'd ever seen, a god from one of those Greek mythology stories you always liked to read. He'd just come back from the Peninsula, having received a wound to his leg, and he had still not gained his bearings, only just recuperated and come out into society—hence our never having met before. Can you imagine? Our eyes met, and that was it!!*

I was not even aware of his identity at the time, so imagine my astonishment to learn he was a marquess, and an eligible one at that, possessed of an enormous fortune!!

We were married within the month! It is now April, and we have just come up to London. Such heaven, but I will write about the season another time—Guy, of course, knows everyone, so we are brilliantly received, and you cannot believe how different it is to be a married, titled woman—too blissful to be true, and on every front possible, but then, as I said, Guy knows everything. I should be blushing to write such things, but I am too happy to prevaricate or be modest!!

He is a man more perfect than I'd ever thought possible, kind and thoughtful and dear to me and, as I said, possessed of the most handsome countenance. He loves to buy me things. I have practically another entire trousseau on top of the trousseau that Mama and Papa provided!

Oh, Jo, and the jewels he has already given me are simply beyond belief. I have an entire set of emeralds and diamonds fit for a queen! Necklace, earrings, matching bracelets, a huge ring! I couldn't look more grand. Mama is beside herself with pride. I made the match of the year after all, even despite the disaster of my measles and missing my very own dance.

You should see Wakefield Abbey! A grander house I cannot imagine. It is the hugest thing I've ever seen, far too big for the two of us, although naturally there is an army of servants.

Of course I shall have to fill Wakefield up with constant guests or I shall rattle about with nothing to do between London visits. After all, what is the use of living in a place so impressive if one cannot impress one's friends and relations?

I do love being a marchioness and mistress of Wakefield, but far more than that, I love being Guy's wife. More later, dearest Jo—I have missed you so but was forbidden to write by Mama and Papa. You should hear the dreadful things they say about you!! They've spread terrible rumors all about town about your degenerate nature!

Never fear, I do not believe a word and never shall, and I defend you every chance I have. You know I adore you and that is how it

shall always be. Oh, Jo, I only wish you could be as happy as I am.
You might really think about marrying, it has so many benefits.

WITH LOVE FROM LYDIA

P.S. I think I might have a wonderful little secret!!!! I will let you
know in my next letter.

The secret, of course, had been her pregnancy. Joanna
refolded the letter and replaced it at the bottom of the
chest. So many letters over five years, letters that had pro-
gressively given Joanna a clear picture of Lydia's growing
disillusionment with her husband and her marriage.

Now here Joanna was, on her way to Wakefield Abbey.
She would finally meet the man she'd heard so much
about over the last few years—nearly all of it horrifying.

Although she had no idea of what she was embarking
on or how she would deal with what she found, she was
still bound and determined not to let anyone or anything
get in the way of her establishing a relationship with Lydia's son. It would be her final gesture to her dear cousin's
memory.

An hour later Joanna woke stiff and sore as the carriage
slowed and made a sharp turn to the right. Sitting up and
wrapping her scarf more tightly around her neck, she
leaned toward the window and peered out.

The heavy rain had stopped and the gray afternoon
light was nearly gone. Through the swirling mist she could
just make out the outline of a great house in the distance.
Smoke curled from only a few of its many squared chim-
neys, and most of the long windows that fronted what she
took to be an Elizabethan exterior looked dark.

"Expecting us, is he?" Bunch commented from the shadows. She used the corner of her cloak to clear a small circle

on the carriage window. "If we're expected at all, it must be through the back from the looks of it."

"We'll arrive at the front," Joanna said, setting her chin in steely determination despite the desperate pounding of her heart. "He might intend to insult, but I can play the contessa to his marquess any day of the week. We shall proceed, Bunch dearest, and we shall overcome any adversity thrown in our path."

Bunch threw her head back and crowed with laughter. "Ah, my girl, you never did have an ounce of sense in your head," she said when she'd recovered. "However, I have to admit that I admire your backbone, even if it is the most impractical gift God gave you. No man likes an intractable woman."

"I am *not* intractable," Joanna protested. "I simply know my own mind."

"I don't care what you call yourself; the truth is the truth." Bunch leaned back against the squabs. "Very well, contessa, proceed. We will see what is what. I wonder if it has occurred to you that his majesty might not be here at all. The lights are not lit, as would be the custom."

Joanna waved her hand in dismissal. "Don't be absurd; of course he is here. He will still be in mourning."

"Oh, and you think that someone in mourning is forced to stay in seclusion as the Oxleys made you do? I think not," Bunch said, crossing her arms. "Furthermore, this is the sixth day of November, and you have no idea as to which day in November Lydia actually died. Perhaps he is already out of mourning—perhaps he has already made plans to remarry. It is perfectly clear to me that he did not love his wife, so why shouldn't he have moved on with his life?"

"Because he just can't have," Joanna said stubbornly, as she pulled her scarf all the way up over her mouth to the frozen tip of her nose, which felt as if it might snap off her face if she touched it.

The carriage pulled up outside the massive edifice and came to an abrupt stop.

Nothing happened. Not a door opened, not a person appeared, there was no movement from any direction except for Joanna's furious lunge for the carriage door. She'd go and pound on the blasted front door, force them to let her in.

Bunch shot out a restraining hand, surprisingly strong for a woman of sixty-two. "Wait," she commanded.

"I will not," Joanna said. "They cannot treat us in such a fashion."

"You will wait," Bunch said in a voice that brooked no argument. "The servants come to the contessa, not the other way around. You never did learn the part well enough, my girl."

Joanna slumped against the carriage door, fuming.

Once again Bunch was right. Only a few minutes later the front door opened and a butler appeared along with two liveried footmen who trotted down the steps through the thick fog, lanterns in hand.

Sadly, Joanna had turned her head away and so did not see this development. One of the footmen obligingly opened the door Joanna was leaning on, and she had to rapidly readjust her balance as it swung open to keep herself from falling out.

This did not help her equilibrium. Contessas did not nearly tumble from carriages if they wanted to make the correct impression.

"May I help you, madam?" the butler inquired politely enough, although his tone rang decidedly stiff. "Your coachman has lost his way, perhaps? The inclement weather would make such a mistake understandable."

"He has found his way perfectly well," Joanna replied in the haughtiest tone she could manage, although she realized it might have been more effective had half her mouth not been muffled by scarf and she hadn't practically fallen in his lap. "I am the Contessa di Capponi. Lord Greaves is expecting me."

"I beg your pardon, your ladyship," the butler said with a bow. "However, I regret to inform you that his lordship expects no one. He is not in residence, nor has he been these last three months."

"What!" she exclaimed, refusing to believe him. "That's— that's impossible. I have come all the way from Italy to see him! He must be here, given that he is in mourning for his wife."

"His lordship has many matters of business to attend to that take him elsewhere, your ladyship. However, I do believe he will have put aside his mourning by now."

"I—I see," Joanna said in a low voice. Once again Bunch had been right. She ought to have thought ahead and not just presumed. "Well. It is clear to me that Lord Greaves did not receive my letter or he would have been here to greet me." She hesitated for a moment, then plowed on, deciding she had nothing to lose. "Could you just tell me if Lord Wycombe is in residence? I really came to see him."

"You came to see Lord Wycombe?" the man asked incredulously. "You do realize he is a boy of five?"

"Yes, of course," she replied, impatiently pulling away the scarf that kept sticking to her lower lip. "He must be so lonely with both his parents gone—or one of them gone and the other away," she amended.

The butler stared at her as if she had grown two heads.

"My—my lady?" he stammered. "Is it—it cannot be— oh, God help me . . ." He staggered back a number of steps.

The reason for his distress dawned on Joanna two seconds too late. She'd forgotten all about her resemblance to Lydia—in the bad light she must have given him the most terrible shock when she'd pulled her scarf away and revealed her face. How could she have been so thoughtless?

She clambered out of the carriage and approached him.

"Please, sir," she said in the same tone she used with

frightened animals. "Do not alarm yourself so. I am Lady Greaves's cousin, only her cousin. They always said we looked alike. I've honestly come to see Lord Wycombe. She wished for me to look after him should anything happen to her, so I came as soon as I heard. . . ."

"Oh, my. Oh, my goodness." The man raised the lantern and peered at her more closely and then at Bunch. "Forgive me, your ladyship," he said, returning his gaze to Joanna, "but for a moment I thought—never you mind what I thought. Her cousin, you say? Well, that explains it then." He slowly lowered the light and stood back, still visibly shaken. "I believe you and your companion would be more comfortable inside. If you will follow me? Dickson will bring your valises."

"Thank you," Joanna said, truly grateful, for she honestly didn't know what she would have done if they'd been turned away. She smiled and gestured to Bunch, who responded with nothing more than her usual pursing of the lips and a grunt, thereby acknowledging her own superior knowledge.

Joanna considered Bunch and herself fortunate. The staff obviously knew how to leap to attention, for not only was a roaring fire instantly set in the sitting room, but two trays of hearty pea soup, freshly baked bread, and thick slices of cold ham appeared only a half hour later.

"Forgive the simple fare, your ladyship," the butler said as he brought it in, "but we have only what Margaret, the scullery maid, prepared for the staff's evening meal. Chef Emile is away for the week."

"We are both grateful for a meal of any sort," Joanna replied. "It looks delicious."

It was, and they washed it down with an equally delicious bottle of French claret that the butler had kindly brought up from Lord Greaves's cellar.

Ambrose, as the butler was named, busied himself with

seeing that proper rooms were aired and fires lit. "One could catch one's death in this climate," he said before bustling off to look after the arrangements.

Joanna watched him leave, wondering if he hadn't just made a passing reference to the manner of Lydia's demise. But then he'd said nothing more about Lydia. Thinking about it, he'd said nothing further about the marquess and nothing at all about little Miles.

She wasn't quite sure how to go about posing the questions she burned to ask—the first being how Lydia had died. She couldn't just blurt that question out. She'd have to feel her way along, find the right time, the right person to approach.

Then there was the question of Miles. She couldn't wait to meet him, but she thought it might be wiser to request to see him first thing in the morning. The child was probably settled fast away in his nursery by now and didn't need to be disturbed by a total stranger.

As exhausted as she was, she still doubted she'd manage to sleep.

So many questions and thoughts swirled about in her mind, and one of the foremost was just where Guy de Salis was and why he wasn't at home attending to his young son.

3

Joanna hunched over the beautifully illustrated book that she'd taken from the library shelf. She didn't dare remove it entirely, so she sat perched high on the mahogany ladder and carefully turned the pages, admiring each piece of work. She had to say one thing for Guy de Salis: He had fine taste in reading matter, and his collection of art books was extraordinary. She'd availed herself of them for the last two weeks, lacking anything better to do.

Two long weeks and not a word from the high-and-mighty Lord Greaves. Two long, wasted weeks in which she'd found out nothing about the manner of Lydia's death. The servants looked at her blankly every time she mentioned their late mistress's name, and when she'd asked Ambrose how the marchioness had died, he had blanched.

"You had best ask the marquess," he'd said, and that was the end of that.

She'd made no progress with Miles either. Her frustration ate away at her, keeping her up at nights. She had no idea what to do, how she might reach out to him in a way he would respond to.

She sighed and glanced out the tall latticed window, where rain dripped down the glass and pooled on the sill.

Miles trudged along beside Mrs. Loppitt, his head down as usual, small hands hanging limply at his sides, his coat padding his thin frame against the cold.

Poor little boy; he led such a regimented life that his nanny took him out at precisely twelve o'clock no matter what the weather, walking him like a dog on a leash.

She imagined that his eyes held their usual lifeless expression. His eyes had been the first thing about Miles to alarm her—that and the way he cowered away from physical contact. Just as alarming had been her next discovery: Mrs. Loppitt herself.

She'd never forget the afternoon following her arrival when Mrs. Loppitt finally saw fit to present the boy in the drawing room. Joanna had waited all day, the request to visit Miles that she'd sent via a footman first thing in the morning refused. The return message from the nursery was firm: Lord Wycombe would be presented at four o'clock and not a moment sooner.

Joanna nearly choked at the audacity of the nurse, but she'd had no choice—she had no authority over Miles, certainly none over his despotic keeper.

When Mrs. Loppitt brought Miles in, Joanna's first impression was that of a sweet little boy with knobby knees beneath his frock and pinafore. His dark hair had been wet down and combed relentlessly into order, and his rounded cheeks were pink from a recent scrubbing, she guessed. His cheeks aside, the rest of his body looked far too thin.

Poor child—little wonder. Lydia had been his entire world.

Miles's huge brown eyes opened wide as he took her in. "Mama?" he said, stumbling backward, a flicker of what she could have sworn was fear in his eyes.

"No, darling, not your mama," she said gently, kneeling before him, wishing she'd remembered the resemblance that had caused the same reaction in Ambrose. Obviously it had grown far stronger over the years. "I am your cousin Joanna. Perhaps your mother mentioned me to you? We were great friends, she and I, and I imagine you must miss her very much. I certainly do."

He gave her such a piercing look that she had the odd feeling he saw straight into her. Then he averted his eyes and looked down at the floor. One finger went to his mouth.

Joanna's heart squeezed in her chest at the sight of him. He looked so small and vulnerable, so lost somehow. Examining him more closely, she could see that he was like Lydia only in his eyelashes, which were as long and sooty black as hers had been, and in the dark eyebrows that traced the same gentle arch. The line of his mouth was unfamiliar to her, the bottom lip slightly fuller than the top, and at the moment it trembled. Only his chin showed a certain determination in its squared shape; everything else about Miles indicated trepidation.

"I've waited a long time to meet you," she said, tentatively stretching her hand out to him.

Miles responded by inching away until his back pressed against the edge of a chair behind him.

She threw a questioning glance at Mrs. Loppitt, who just shrugged. "The boy is impossibly shy," the woman said in a voice as rigid as her posture. "At least he behaves himself, don't you, my little lord?"

"Has he—has he always been so withdrawn?" Joanna asked, rising and drawing Mrs. Loppitt away, not wanting Miles to hear them talking about him.

"As I said, he's shy. What the child needs is strict discipline and a strict routine—that's how he'll get over it. He'll have to, won't he, if he's to be the marquess one day."

Appalled by the cold brutality of that speech, Joanna said nothing. If this was the sort of caretaker Lord Greaves had chosen for his small son, who obviously still suffered from losing his mother, she could scarcely imagine what the man himself was like. *Heartless* was too good a word.

"I—I would like to see Miles each day, if you please. Perhaps I could read to him or play with him in the nursery—anything to give him a little pleasure," she said, forcing firmness into her voice.

"I am sorry, your ladyship, but his routine is not to be disturbed," Mrs. Loppitt said, her tone brooking no argument. "I have no objection to bringing him downstairs at this time each day; this is his lordship's usual fifteen minutes for visiting with the marquess when he is at home. Other than that, we maintain our schedule without fail. That is what Lord Greaves wishes." She turned, her back ramrod straight, her stiff black dress crackling as if to emphasize her point.

That had been that. Miles was marched back out of the room, and the only times Joanna had seen him thereafter had been at the appointed daily hour for the appointed fifteen minutes.

Since Miles did not wish to converse, Joanna decided that she'd read to him—she'd had to go into town to the local bookshop to find her childhood favorites.

Each afternoon she read to Miles as Miles sat on the sofa next to her, his gaze fixed on his dangling feet, his hands motionless in his lap. He never looked her in the eye, never said a word, not even in greeting or farewell. With each passing day, Joanna's concern grew.

This was not the child Lydia had described so glowingly—a little boy filled with mischief, the precocious son who showed signs of a keen intelligence and promising physical prowess despite his tender age. Joanna recognized absolutely nothing about the Miles of Lydia's letters in the Miles she found before her now.

Joanna massaged one knuckle hard into her forehead, wishing she could think of a way to break through the barrier Miles had created between himself and the world. She knew how it felt to be so overwhelmed by grief that one willed oneself into numbness. She also knew what had brought her back to life and to hope, both after her parents' untimely deaths and, later, her husband, Cosmo's: Bunch.

Bunch and her never-ending pragmatism. Bunch, who refused to allow her to isolate herself once Bunch had decided that Joanna's allotted time for grieving was up.

Bunch had practically forced her to return to the business of life.

Perhaps, Joanna thought, one finger tapping the corner of her mouth, perhaps that was what Miles needed. Someone to remind him that life was a joyful thing. The question was, how? What might entice a child of five back to the land of the living?

She glanced back down at the book spread in her lap. This illustration showed a marble relief of Orpheus and Eurydice. . . . she remembered their story well, it being one of Bunch's favorites.

She traced her finger lightly over the figure of Orpheus, the great poet and musician, who married his true love, Eurydice. And here, the lovely Eurydice, who was tragically bitten by a serpent and died.

Joanna smiled, hearing Bunch's voice even now. *"Silly man that he was, in his grief Orpheus journeyed down to Hades, hoping somehow that he might bring his Eurydice back. So charming a man was he that he was given a chance to rescue his beloved, and he proceeded to do so . . ."*

Joanna quickly turned the page, for the ending was not so pretty. Typical of Bunch to read her young charge stories with cautionary overtones. Just on the brink of the rescue, Orpheus lost his wife to the underworld forever by breaking the rules he'd been set.

No, Bunch never left her with any illusions at all if she could help it. On the other hand . . . Joanna lifted her head, a sudden thought occurring to her. The underworld— Orpheus had charmed his way in, hadn't he, through his gifts of music and poetry. Well, she was certainly no poet, and God help her if anyone ever heard her sing, but she did understand the medium of painting. Better yet, it was a silent art, fit for a silent child.

Maybe, just maybe, this might at last be a way into Miles's world and a way to let him out into the light, to let him breathe the air the rest of the world breathed.

She covered her face with one hand and drew in a deep breath, then released it. *God, please let me be worthy of this task*, she prayed with everything she had in her. *I have nothing else to give, no better understanding, no other road I know how to follow. Please, oh, please, will You show me the way?*

For one shocking moment she thought God had actually deigned to reply, for a voice boomed like thunder through the silence of her meditation.

"I do not wish to hear it—nothing, do you understand? Leave me in peace, will you!"

Joanna's head shot up and she blinked. Surely God wouldn't be quite so harsh, not if He bothered to answer—and that she highly doubted.

She needn't have worried. It wasn't God but the devil himself in the form of Guy de Salis, Marquess of Greaves. He stormed into the library and slammed the door behind him.

"Bloody cursed fool," he muttered, throwing a folder of papers onto the ormolu desk in front of the window and flinging himself into the chair behind it, oblivious to her presence.

Joanna, who had frozen with horror in her spot high on the ladder, thanked not only God, but all the gods and goddesses that she'd ever heard of for that one piece of luck. She thought that maybe, if she stayed as still as a statue, she might go undetected. Maybe he was just depositing his papers and then he would leave. . . .

Holding her breath, she barely opened the eyes she'd squeezed shut and peered at his imperial magnificence through tiny slits, trying to get an impression of what the devil actually looked like in human form.

She couldn't help herself. Her eyes shot wide open, completely of their own accord. Dear heaven, but he was the finest-looking man she'd ever laid eyes on in her life, and that was saying something. Italy was filled with men who might have been models for Michelangelo's "David."

Not one could compare to Guy de Salis.

It wasn't that he looked anything like the "David." It was simply that he possessed an innate grace and power that she'd seen in no one else.

His face had strong character in its own right, yet its symmetry made it beautiful at the same time. A natural wave of thick dark hair rose from his brow and fell back to sweep behind one well-shaped ear. Straight brows slashed over his lowered eyes, which she guessed were probably the same dark shade of sherry as his son's. His nose, the bridge narrow, ran in a straight line to the tip, the nostrils finely drawn.

His mouth was Miles's—wide, the lower lip slightly fuller—but oh, how different the shape looked on this man. There was no softness here, no innocence, and the firm, square chin indicated a will of iron.

Joanna shivered as if a cold wind had just run down her back.

He suddenly stood and turned to the window, his head slightly bowed, one hand pushing back his coat and resting on his hip. Joanna's gaze traveled with a practiced, un-embarrassed ease over the broad shoulders that created a perfect triangle when drawn in geometric proportions down to his lean waist and hips. Strong thighs finished off the entire impression of symmetry, once again the proportions just right compared to the more slender but equally muscular length of calf.

She had to forcibly push away the automatic awe that her artist's eye induced—he was a cad and a blackguard, and on top of that a terrible father, she reminded herself firmly.

For the first time Joanna understood why her cousin had fallen head over heels in love at first sight: Guy de Salis was just the sort of man Lydia had been looking for, the prince among princes, dark and powerful, vaguely dangerous.

Lydia had just forgotten about the darkest and most dangerous of princes when she'd gone seeking, and Joanna wished to heaven that she'd been there to warn her.

Exhaling loudly, he moved back to the desk and slumped into the chair, the heel of his hand pressed against his forehead.

If Joanna hadn't known better, her heart probably would have gone out to him; he looked so defeated and miserable that any person with an ounce of compassion would have been tempted to comfort him. But anger also showed in the tight line of his mouth, the tense set of his shoulders.

He picked up the heap of paper in front of him, staring down at it, then abruptly tossed it down again, his fist striking the pile as if he wished to pound it into oblivion.

"Damn you, Lydia!" he roared. "Dear God, will you *never* leave me in peace?"

Joanna stared, horrified. If she'd needed confirmation that Lydia's husband despised his wife, he'd just given it to her. Fury surged through every fiber of her being until she, too, shook from head to toe. If she'd had a gun in her hand, she'd probably have shot him dead on the spot.

"How *dare* you?" she cried, forgetting in her rage that she was supposed to be hiding from him. "I ought to throw this book directly at your head, but I have too much respect for good artwork!"

His head shot up and he looked straight at the bookcase, his hands gripping the edge of the desk as he half-rose, his gaze steadily climbing until it settled full on her face.

Joanna was prepared for anything but what happened next.

First came the impact of his eyes when they met hers. Dark as a moonless night, they lacked no inner fire. For one suspended second of time she thought they might burn straight through her, consume her with their intensity. She felt utterly stripped, as if his gaze had peeled away her skin, turned her bones to ash, exposing her unwilling soul to his view.

Next came the realization that she'd imagined it all—the truth was that he'd turned white as a sheet and looked as if he might be sick.

"Lydia?" The single word came out in a ragged whisper. He rose and moved over to the bookshelf, his eyes never leaving hers. "Oh, God—Lydia? It cannot be. . . . I—I must be dreaming." He clutched the bottom of the ladder with both hands.

She managed to resist the temptation to play Lydia's ghost, despite how instructive it might have been. "No, Lord Greaves," she said from her seat. "Not Lydia."

"Not Lydia? Then who?" His eyes, glazed with shock, remained fixed on hers, an expression of appalled question in them.

"I am Lydia's cousin Joanna, Joanna di Capponi. That is what your butler was trying to tell you when you arrived, had you only been willing to listen. My companion and I arrived a fortnight ago." She paused, then forced the apology out. "I—I understand there is a striking resemblance between your late wife and myself. I beg your pardon if I alarmed you."

He closed his eyes for a long moment and rested his brow against the step. "Alarmed me," he said, his words muffled against the sleeve of his coat. "Oh—not at all. Please do not concern yourself in the least." He lifted his face, still pale, and glared up at her. "You might, however, explain what the *bloody* hell you're doing here, not just in my house but perched in my library like a—like an eagle spying from its aerie."

"I was reading," she replied defensively, wondering if he was habitually this rude to complete strangers. "What else does one do in a library?"

"Tresspass? Poke about, perhaps?"

She returned his glare, furious at the insinuation that she'd been doing anything dishonorable. "I *like* to read. You have *books* in your library. You cannot possibly be so selfish as to think that they were written for your pleasure alone."

He gazed at her, his face expressionless. "You would be well-advised to climb back down to earth. Perhaps you can summon up a semblance of manners by the time you land?"

Manners? He had the gall to accuse her of lacking in manners? She did, however, summon up every bit of discipline she'd ever possessed and carefully closed the precious book, sliding it back into its place. She then made her way down the steps with as much grace as she could manage.

He stepped back with an exaggerated bow and sweep of his arm as she reached the ground. "If the contessa would be so kind as to take a seat?" he said, planting himself behind his desk without bothering to pull out a chair for her.

She refused to rise to the bait, taking the chair opposite for herself. Placing her hands in her lap, she calmly regarded him. "So you do know who I am."

"Oh, yes. I know all about you. Doesn't everyone?" One corner of his mouth lifted in clear derision.

Joanna colored hotly. She should have remembered that the Oxleys had spread nasty stories about her; after all, Lydia had warned her. Society was the same everywhere, eager for rumor, ready to accept innuendo regardless of truth. God only knew what they'd actually said, but she could just imagine, given the expression of disdain on Guy de Salis's face.

Fine. Let him think whatever he pleased. She would not lower herself to explain anything to him. "I see," she said, trying to maintain her composure. "Then Lydia told you of our relationship."

"She mentioned it." He clasped his hands in front of him. "Which leads me to wonder why you are here. Your cousin died a year ago this month. Did you suddenly feel the need to pay your respects at her grave? Or perhaps some other sort of belated remorse overcame you and caused you to come rushing to Wakefield uninvited."

Joanna jumped to her feet in outrage, any shred of tolerance she'd had for this man vanishing. He'd just finished cursing Lydia, and now he had the nerve to accuse *her* of lacking proper feeling?

She planted both hands on his desk and leaned forward over them. "See here," she said, "I came the very minute I learned of Lydia's death. I came for no other reason than to see to Miles's welfare—you *do* remember him, your little boy? He's five years old, dark hair, on the undernourished side, doesn't smile or talk or do much of anything except allow himself to be hauled around by that dragon of a nanny you picked—"

"Enough!" Guy stood, planting his own hands on the opposite side of the desk. He leaned toward Joanna from his greater height until his face hovered only inches away, his eyes flashing with black fury. "Don't you ever speak of Miles as if you have any right to it—I am his father! I will decide what he needs and doesn't need, and no one—most especially not you—will dictate to me! Have I made myself clear?"

Joanna smiled coldly. "Oh, perfectly, my lord. You have decided that your son needs no love, no nurturing, that he will flourish far better on a ceaseless regimen of harsh discipline administered by a woman who would be better directed to bullying helpless inmates in Bedlam!" She paused only to draw breath. "I hope you do realize that your precious heir is well on his way to becoming so hopelessly withdrawn that he might very well end up in a place like that."

Guy abruptly sat down. "What makes you say such a vile thing?" he asked.

"If you bothered to spend any time with him, you'd know exactly what I speak of," Joanna replied, sitting to face him. For Miles's sake she would put aside her anger and her distaste for his father. For Miles—and for Lydia—she would do anything. "Your son might have been a happy and normal child at one time, or at least he was according to my cousin, but he is now severely troubled."

"Tell me, contessa, are you usually this melodramatic?"

She sucked in a slow breath, forcing herself to remain calm. "I assure you, I have no tendency toward melodrama."

He snorted.

Rising abruptly, he said, "If you'll excuse me, I have business to attend to. Good day, contessa."

Stunned by his terse dismissal, she didn't move for a moment. Then she quickly stood and turned on her heel, letting herself out into the hall, closing the door behind her with what she considered to be great restraint.

Once out of his presence, though, she dropped her pretense of composure, wanting to cry with frustration. She rubbed her temples, not knowing what more she could say or even if there was any point. What difference would another speech make to a man who didn't care to begin with?

Amazing, she thought, what structural rot a beautiful facade could hide.

4

The minute he heard the door shut on Joanna di Capponi's unwelcome back, Guy breathed a sigh of relief.

He'd used every ounce of discipline he had to conceal his raging emotions for the twenty minutes she'd been in the room, and he had no intention of turning into a wreck now that she was finally gone.

Shaken to his very core, he was amazed he hadn't made even more of a fool out of himself in front of the blasted woman. The shock of seeing what he'd believed to be Lydia's ghost had practically undone him—for one bad moment he'd thought he was going to faint dead away.

He was already haunted nearly every night by tortured dreams of his wife—Lydia as she had been, Lydia as she was the last time he saw her. It had been a bit much to be wide awake and see her suspended in the air, more beautiful than ever.

He shuddered. He wished she *had* been a ghost. Ghosts went away; they didn't insinuate themselves as unwanted houseguests, or at least not in the flesh. How could God possibly be so unkind as to have cast another woman practically in Lydia's exact mold and then place her directly under his nose in his own house, where the memories of Lydia were already a torment to him?

And yet there was a subtle difference between them, at least when it came to the physical. Once he'd overcome his immediate shock and she'd climbed down from her perch and walked into the better light, he'd seen that she had a softer look about her. Something slightly more ethereal, as well as a maturity of expression that Lydia had never had.

The same beauty was there, the same honey-colored hair coupled with large, slightly slanted hazel eyes and elegant cheekbones, the same bowed mouth, but somehow it all looked quieter on Joanna di Capponi, more subtle. More beautiful.

Rolling his neck in a circle to ease the tension that made it feel as if it might break, he rubbed the tight muscles with his fingers.

Far more important than the contessa's resemblance to his dead wife was his son. Could Miles really be missing his mother as much as she'd implied?

To be fair, every now and then Lydia had shaken off the indifference she'd shown to Miles from the time of his birth and suddenly had a fit of maternal devotion, returning to Wakefield to smother the child half to death. However, she usually did that only when other people were around to watch.

He rolled his neck in the other direction. Then there were the times when she'd have another one of her tantrums and go flying off to the nursery to weep over her "darling little boy, the only person in the world who truly loves me." God, but he'd heard those words often enough. So had Miles.

Other than that she'd generally ignored Miles in favor of the constant social diversions that took her away from home.

And yet . . . and yet it was true that the boy had been unusually quiet when Guy had last been home. The new nanny—what was her name? Oh, yes. Mrs. Lippett. Or was it Lappitt?

He pressed his fingers against his aching temples. Anyway, something to do with rabbits.

He vaguely remembered hiring her—what, eight months ago now? She'd seemed firm but kind, steady as the day was long, a complete change from the ridiculous woman Lydia had insisted on hiring to coddle Miles when he'd been old enough to move on from the care of his wet nurse.

What had that blasted interfering cousin meant by calling his personal choice of Miles's caretaker a dragon who was better suited to bullying helpless inmates?

And what the *hell* did she mean by saying that his son was seriously troubled? He was just a tiny boy—he hadn't had time to become troubled, for the love of God. The contessa was clearly overexcitable. Hardly surprising, given her family background. He'd go up to the nursery right now and prove her wrong.

"Lord Greaves!" Good heavens, you did give me a turn. I didn't hear you come in." Mrs. Loppitt practically dived into a curtsy when she turned to see him standing in the nursery door. "I had no idea you were home, my lord."

"I'm not surprised, as I only just arrived," Guy said, his attention focused on his young son, who sat on the window seat staring out. He hadn't even turned his head when Guy spoke.

Frowning heavily, Guy walked over to him and cleared his throat. "And how are you, young man? Did you miss your father?"

Miles turned to look up at him, then blinked and looked back out the window.

"Have you been behaving yourself for Nanny, then?" he asked, hoping for a more appropriate reaction.

He received nothing, just the back of Miles's head. He didn't like this, he didn't like it at all. Perhaps there really was something after all to Joanna di Capponi's story. He prayed to God that was not the case. He found himself actually praying that Miles was simply being bad-tempered and sullen.

"Tell me, Mrs. . . . er, Nanny," he said, moving across the room to where the woman was standing, her hands folded neatly on her apron. "How has my son been in my absence?" He guided her into the night nursery as he spoke and closed the door behind them.

"The veriest angel, my lord. He does exactly as he's told, never causes any trouble—quite a change from the early days. Oh, we had some crying spells in the beginning and a bit of temper, but that's all over with now. A firm hand, that's all his little lordship needed to bring him into line."

"A firm hand? And how firm a hand would that be?" Guy inquired in a neutral voice.

"Firm enough for little boys to understand. It's no good letting them think they can get away with nonsense, for they will try it on every time. As we discussed, my lord, a strict schedule and strict rules will turn the most undisciplined of children into little lambs."

"Spare the rod and spoil the child, would that be the philosophy?" Guy asked, trying not to show his mounting concern.

"You understand me exactly," she replied with a self-satisfied smirk. "There's not a thing wrong with a swift cane to the hands or backside, begging your pardon, to get quick results."

"Ah," Guy said, fury building within him. No one caned his child. No one. "I believe I do understand you exactly," he continued, determined to drag out the rest of the details. "Tell me, what other methods of discipline do you employ? They have clearly taken effect."

"Thank you," the woman said, smiling primly. "Well, let me see . . . I had some trouble with his little lordship walking about in the night, but restraining children in their beds is highly effective—it prevents them from getting up to mischief and teaches them that bedtime is bedtime and there is no argument about that."

"Do you mean to say that you—you tied him to his bed?"

"Oh, yes, my lord. You see, that way they also soon learn not to wet themselves in the night." She nodded wisely. "I had that trouble with his little lordship too, but a few nights of lying in his own soiled sheets and a cane to his bottom in the morning broke him of the habit fast enough."

Guy curled his hands into fists at his sides, his stomach churning sickly. He could scarcely believe what he was hearing. A child of only five, caned? Tied to his bed and left to lie in soaking sheets for hours on end? God in heaven, it was a wonder poor Miles hadn't taken a knife to the woman. He felt like it himself.

"Thank you," he said, his voice cold as the ice in his heart. "You have told me everything I need to know."

"Not at all, my lord. It is unusual for a father to take such interest in a young child still in the nursery, I will say, but I'm not like some who insist on the parents keeping away. I'm sure it does the boy good to see you after all this time."

"Yes, and it will do the boy a great deal better never to see you again. You will pack your bags and leave this house within the hour. Expect no reference from me, madam."

The woman stared at him, her mouth hanging agape. "But, my lord, you—I—I have done exactly what you required of me! I have produced a beautifully behaved child who never speaks back, who—"

"Who never speaks at all, from what I understand," Guy snapped. "Do you consider that normal behavior?"

"It's that—that woman, isn't it? She's already been telling you stories. Believe me, my lord, they are all lies—the contessa does not like to be denied in anything, but if I had bowed to her constant requests, she would have pampered his little lordship in no time and undone all my good work, I am sure of it! I only followed your instructions, sir. You said that you did not want any pampering, that you wanted your son disciplined, and that is what I did!"

"What I wanted was a child who had some structure and consistency in his life. I wanted a comforting female presence to guide him after the loss of his mother," he continued, his voice rising. "I did *not* ask for you to turn him into a wooden puppet, nor did I ask you to abuse him day and night!"

"But I—but I—ohhhh!" She burst into tears, producing a square of linen from her apron pocket and dabbing it delicately all over her face. "I should have expected no less," she sobbed. "They say in the village that you made your wife's life a misery, and I can believe it. They say before she died that—"

"Be gone!" he roared, outraged that she'd dared to bring up such a personal subject. "I do not wish ever to lay eyes on you again, woman!"

She fled without a backward glance, the door to her quarters banging like the report of a shotgun.

Guy released a long breath. How could he have been such a complete idiot, his judgment gone so badly astray that he missed all the warning signs of an unbalanced tyrant?

He walked quickly back into the day nursery, where Miles still sat in the window.

Lowering himself down beside the boy, Guy laid one hand awkwardly on his son's tiny arm. "Miles, you won't have that nasty nanny looking after you anymore, not from this minute on. Someone else will be taking on her duties, so you are not to worry. I will see that your new nanny is nice and kind and will never once tie you to your bed—I am sorry for all the things this last one did," he finished ineptly, not knowing what more to say.

Miles pulled away from his touch.

"See here, my boy, you must let bygones be bygones. This nanny did many things she ought not to have, but that's all finished now. You have a nice supper and a good sleep and it will all look better in the morning."

Miles ignored him, his hand creeping to his ear as if to drown out the sound of his father's voice.

"Very well, you needn't speak to me if you do not wish, but by tomorrow I expect you'll have thought it all over and seen that there is no more reason for this silence. You've made your point, rude as it might be, and I am doing my best to oblige you. No more vile nannies, and that's a promise."

Miles stuck his finger in the corner of his mouth and pressed his forehead against the windowpane.

Guy had no idea what to do next, so he stood up and shoved his hands onto his hips. "Well, then. I shall say good night. I will see you tomorrow."

Since Miles didn't bother to respond, Guy decided to do the dignified thing and take himself off. He really didn't know what else to do. He had no training in the management of children: In his experience they were presented, briefly admired, and taken away again. Anything beyond that was taken care of by nurses and governesses.

Oh, *God*, he wished he did know. He'd give both his arms to make Miles feel happy and secure.

Once back in the safety of his library, Guy poured himself a large glass of sherry from one of the decanters on the side table and tried to be logical about the situation. He'd have to instruct Ambrose to go about the task of finding another nanny. Guy would then interview the prospective candidates, and this time, by God, he'd make sure he got it right.

The trouble was that the process might take weeks. In the meantime, poor little Miles might well continue to spend his days and nights sitting in a window, staring out at nothing.

"I came for no other reason than to see to Miles's welfare. . . . I hope you do realize that he is well on his way to becoming hopelessly withdrawn . . ."

Joanna di Capponi's words echoed in his head, pounding like a hammer, over and over.

"Oh, very well," he finally shouted, thumping his fists down on the arms of his chair. "To hell with it! Let the woman earn her keep whilst she's here—she says she's so concerned. Let's see what the precious pampered contessa has to say about that, shall we? Ha! That will be a measure of her sincerity."

"Will you stop your endless fidgeting?" Bunch demanded, glaring at Joanna from over the edge of her reading spectacles. "Anyone would think you'd been infested by fleas."

"I'm sorry," Joanna replied, putting down the crystal paperweight she'd picked up from the writing desk. "I just can't seem to relax—I know that I'm going to receive a summons any moment, and that will be that. We'll be tossed out the door by that monster, and that will be the end of any help for Miles."

"If I've said it once, I've said it a hundred times: If you'd only thought—"

"I know, I know. If I'd only thought before I acted, we wouldn't be in this predicament," Joanna said in a singsong voice, mimicking Bunch. "Lecturing me now doesn't do Miles any good, though, does it, and it certainly doesn't help us. I haven't much money left, Bunch, unless I write to Mr. Frobisher and ask him to sell some funds. I am reluctant to use capital, though, when we rely so heavily on the income from it."

"Humph. You wouldn't have these problems if you had listened to me three years ago." Bunch scowled at her. "I've never known such an impractical girl as you. A fortune at your fingertips and what did you do—"

"Please, let us not go back over that ground again," Joanna said, quickly cutting her off. "We have enough to deal with. Oh, Bunch, just wait until you meet the marquess—if you ever get the chance, that is. He's singularly the most dreadful-tempered, arrogant man I've ever had the misfortune to meet."

"That's saying something," Bunch replied dryly.

"It's not saying nearly enough." Joanna nearly jumped

out of her skin when a knock came at the door. Her hand slipped to her throat. "Oh, no—here it is," she whispered. "The eviction notice."

"Answer the door, girl, or you'll never know, will you?"

"Very well, send me to the hangman," she retorted over her shoulder, pulling the door open.

Dickson stood there in his red and gold livery, his poker expression telling her nothing. "His lordship requests your immediate presence in the library, your ladyship."

"Does he?" Joanna said coolly. "I suppose his lordship always gets what his lordship wants."

The corner of Dickson's mouth twitched upward, but he instantly controlled it. "He is accustomed to being obeyed, yes, your ladyship."

"Tell me, have you been employed in this house a long time, Dickson?"

"Long enough to know his lordship does not like to be kept waiting," the man replied with a bow. From his lowered position he murmured, "My advice would be to accommodate him as soon as humanly possible." He coughed, then straightened as if he'd said nothing at all.

"Thank you," Joanna said with a smile, appreciating Dickson's tactfully delivered precaution. "I shall be down directly. There is no need to inform his worship—his lordship, I mean."

She could have sworn that she heard Dickson chuckle as he vanished down the corridor.

Naturally, Joanna took her time. She wasn't about to have the monster marquess snap his fingers at her as if she were a dog, although she did truthfully need a few minutes to compose herself. It wouldn't do to let Guy de Salis see how unnerved she felt at the prospect of being in his presence, let alone see how upset she was at the prospect of her imminent expulsion from the premises. The thought of abandoning Miles broke her heart.

Smoothing her hair in front of the glass, she decided that she would have to do as she was. She didn't have five dresses for every other hour of the day, and why should she? She lived a simple life, with no need for that sort of extravagance.

Bunch unbent far enough to give her a reassuring squeeze of her hand as she left, but Joanna still felt as if she were walking straight into the lion's den unarmed, without a single feminine wile to help her further her cause.

Lydia would have known just what to do, she mused as she nervously made her way down the endless hallway, around the corner to the next endless hallway, and finally down two endless flights of grandiose stairs that were interminably lined with portraits of the marquess's narrow-nosed predecessors.

Or maybe not. Apparently even Lydia's charm hadn't been enough to soften her hard-hearted, haughty husband.

She straightened her back as she reached the cavernous grand great hall, marched past the yellow drawing room, the red drawing room, turned right at the ivory and gold dining room, and proceeded to the library, where Dickson stood guard outside the massive door.

He inclined his head as she approached, then tapped lightly, opened the door, and intoned, "The Contessa di Capponi, your lordship."

She rolled her eyes. "Joanna's good enough for me," she said softly, then walked past Dickson into the room.

He sat behind his ornately gilded desk, his back to the window, his attention fully on a letter he was in the process of writing. His dark eyes slowly lifted as she presented herself in front of him, and he replaced his quill in its stand, his gaze raking her up and down as if she were a serving girl beneath his contempt.

Had she thought him haughty? Insolent was a better

description, she decided, her hands curling into fists at her sides as the color rose from her neck and washed into her cheeks.

"You wished to see me?" she said, willing her voice to remain steady despite the rapid pounding of her heart and the earnest desire to ram his quill and its stand down his throat.

Not bothering to stand, he gestured at a chair. "Sit, if you please."

She lowered herself into the seat, but typical of her luck, one stray ray of sunshine had managed to penetrate the thick gray cloud cover and beamed directly into her eyes, forcing her to squint at him.

He regarded her with eyes as hard and cold as onyx. "So good of you to spare a few moments of your time. I do hope I have not taken you from anything too pressing."

That did it. Her pride refused to let him toy with her any longer like a cat with a mouse. "Nothing more pressing than packing my belongings, my lord," she said, lifting her chin.

His eyes sharpened, and for the first time she had the impression that he was truly looking at her. "Packing your belongings? May I ask why?"

She shrugged. "You made it clear at our first meeting that I am unwelcome here. You also made it clear that you feel Miles has no need of my help or my companionship. I will not stay where I am not wanted. I never intended to impose myself."

"To the contrary, contessa. You have second-guessed me rather badly." He folded his hands in front of him. "I do not wish for you to leave."

She stared at him blankly, certain she must have heard him wrong. "You do not—you do not wish for me to leave?"

"As I said. If you will listen to me and try not to interrupt every other word, I shall explain." He stood and strolled over to the bookshelves, leaning one broad shoulder against the mahogany paneling.

She twisted in her chair to look at him, still numb with shock. "Please," she said, her head spinning with confusion.

"I went to the nursery to see my son. What I discovered there alarmed me." He looked down at the tip of his shoe, and she could no longer see his face. "I must thank you for alerting me to the situation," he said, his voice stiff.

"I—I am only relieved that you noticed for yourself that things were amiss."

His head jerked up. "You are relieved that I *noticed*? Do you take me for a complete imbecile, contessa, or merely an unobservant and irresponsible fool?"

"I take you for nothing, not knowing you," she retorted, lying through her teeth. Better that, though, than telling him what she really thought—that he was a cold-hearted devil with a temperament to match.

"Wise," he said. "To return to the matter at hand, I dismissed that wretched woman who was supposed to be looking after my son. She will be gone directly." He crossed his arms and looked back down at the toe of his shoe. "I need someone to take her place. Given your professed concern for my son and taking your rather . . . ambiguous position here into consideration, I though you might do. If you agree, naturally."

He glanced up and shot her a skeptical look that clearly indicated he thought her concern for Miles nothing more than an excuse for insinuating herself as a permanent houseguest.

Her hands shaking in her lap with relief at his willingness to let her try to help Miles, Joanna bowed her head. The last thing she wished for him to see were the tears that suddenly filled her eyes. Miles. She would have a chance after all, and nothing—nothing—mattered more than that. For that she would ignore the marquess and his misguided assumptions, his despotic attitude, the miseries he had heaped upon his wife.

Lydia—it's a beginning. At least it's a beginning. I swear I will move heaven and earth to help your little boy.

She turned her head and brushed away the tears that threatened to spill over. When she was more certain of her composure she looked up, although not at him. Least of all at him. "I would be happy to look after Miles. Do I take it to mean that you wish me to act in the capacity of nanny?"

"I wish for you to look after him; what you call your role is of little significance to me."

"I beg your pardon, my lord, but it is of significance to me. I need to know my standing in this house. It does not do to confuse the servants." She spoke with as much dignity as she could muster.

"Oh, for the love of God!" he roared. "Very well, then. I suppose I can hardly have a contessa acting as nanny." He shoved his hands on his hips. "Since you are my late wife's cousin and therefore related to my son, you will be his . . . his—"

"I will still be his cousin, my lord," she finished for him. "However, also to serve as his governess would not be an inappropriate position. Many dependent relatives have taken on the role—not that I consider myself the least dependent."

"Very well, his governess, then," he said. "On a trial term of three months, let us say. If I see no change in my son by then, I expect you take yourself back from whence you came."

"Agreed." Lord, but she prayed she could make a difference by then. She turned to look back at him, her composure back in place. "Where do you wish for me to stay? In the nursery?"

"Where do you stay now?"

"In one of the guest suites, my lord," she replied demurely. "Not the state apartments, you'll be happy to know, but nevertheless, the upstairs accommodations are far grander than a governess would be accustomed to."

"Do not push me," he said, casting a warning glance at her. "If you think to throw your status as the widowed wife of an Italian count about, I can assure you I am not impressed. However, I see no reason why you should not stay where you are."

"How kind. And my companion, my lord? What would you have me do with her? Miss Fitzwilliams is not a young woman, and she *is* entirely dependent on me."

"Oh, a governess with a companion." He shook his head. "I don't mind what you *do* with her. Lock her in the wardrobe if you like; just keep her out of my way."

Joanna narrowed her eyes. "Lock her in the wardrobe? Is that your idea of a joke? If it is I do not find it at all amusing."

"What you find amusing and what you do not is of absolutely no interest to me, contessa. All I require of you is to look after my son and try to draw him out of his shell. Beyond that, I think we would both be best served by avoiding each other as much as possible."

"That would be my pleasure. I take it that you wish for Miss Fitzwilliams and myself to have our meals in our suite? It is the Red and Black Suite, by the by," she added, deliberately needling him. Personally, she didn't give two figs where she stayed, although she did worry about Bunch.

"Contessa, take your meals standing on your head on the dining-room table. I doubt I will be at home often enough to notice either where you eat or where you sleep. Or care."

"Very good, my lord," she said, rising. "In essence, then, I am to do as I please, go where I please, sleep and eat where I please and with whom I please, and all of this as long as I look after Miles and avoid you. Is that correct?"

She waited for his reaction with bated breath. She didn't think she'd ever been so evil in her entire life, but she just couldn't help herself.

It took less than three seconds and exactly six long strides for him to cover the distance between them. She knew, because she counted each one with growing alarm.

She hadn't been aware of his commanding height until he towered over her, a thunderous expression on his face.

"You are everything and more that I have heard told over the years," he hissed down at her. "Trusting one minute of my son's life to you is probably the worst mistake of judgment I have ever made, barring my—"

He stopped abruptly, but Joanna had no trouble filling in the blank. Barring his marrying Lydia. Did he think she didn't know how he'd treated his wife? Still, she'd keep her silence on that subject, not willing to jeopardize her position. Instead, she said, "If you feel that way, Lord Greaves, then why do you give me the chance at all? Why *do* you entrust your child's care to me?"

"Because I am . . . I am desperate," he said, the lines around his mouth strained. "The resemblance you bear to my late wife is alone enough for me to wish you away, for it—I find the reminder difficult." He paused for a moment, then continued, his voice shaking slightly. "I have no idea whether that likeness makes Miles more receptive to you or terrifies the life out of him, since he chooses not to speak at the moment."

"He has shown no signs of terror. I would hardly put him through any further distress if I thought I was the cause."

"Yes, well, I am hoping that he will find you a comfort, as he was—he was fond of his mother and he has been upset enough by the events of the last year. So regardless of what I think of you, if you can help my son in some way, I will be grateful. Do as you see fit."

He released a heavy sigh, then stepped back and turned abruptly away.

Joanna swallowed hard, surprised by this display of emotion from a man who had shown no feeling of any sort until now. She had to dig deep to find the words that were so important to say for Miles's sake.

"It matters not what you think of me, my lord," she said softly. "The only issue either of us needs to be concerned with is your son's welfare. I thank you for giving me this chance—I thank you from the bottom of my heart. I will do everything in my power to help Miles through this difficult time."

Incapable of saying another word, she fled the room.

5

"My dear child, I see no reason why I should stay here at Wakefield another moment," Bunch said, folding a snowy-white nightdress and laying it in her case. "You don't need me, and there's nothing for me to do here except listen to your endless worries about that little boy and your grumblings about his inattentive father."

"I'm sorry," Joanna said, truly contrite. "I didn't mean to bore you—I do know that I've been going on rather a lot about them both, but I haven't anyone else to talk to. I certainly didn't mean to drive you away."

"Who said anything about your driving me away? Don't be so thin-skinned, Joanna. It's a failing of yours that you must try to curb." She looked up from her packing. "I told you, my sister wants me home for Christmas—it's been six long years since I've seen her, so you have no call to be selfish. I've already wasted five weeks of my time in this miserable place, and you know I can't bear to be idle."

Joanna knew that Bunch was right—it was just that she'd never been without her, or at least not in the last twenty-two years. For so long Bunch had been her teacher and adviser, and Joanna honestly didn't know what she'd do to fill the void. She was being selfish, she knew that, and she had no right to try to make Bunch stay.

"Of course you must go, dearest," she said. "It's only that you caught me by surprise. I thought we'd have Christmas together."

"You have plenty to occupy you, never mind spending day and night with the boy. Lord Greaves is giving his big yearly party on Christmas Eve, and someone needs to put the staff in order. They're running about in every direction like chickens with their heads cut off. I've never seen anything so silly." She pursed her lips. "That Mrs. Campion might be a fine housekeeper when it comes to keeping a place of this size running smoothly, but she clearly doesn't know how to manage these large affairs without direction. What do you think I trained you for but to oversee just this sort of thing?"

"They won't listen to me," Joanna said with a bitter laugh. "As far as they're concerned, I'm nothing but a nuisance."

"The problem is that they don't know where you stand, girl. How many times do I have to tell you that social order means everything? All you've done since you arrived is to upset it—you start out a contessa and their late mistress's cousin. All well and fine and just as it should be." She put a careful fold into a dress and lined it with tissue paper.

"All well and fine?" Joanna said indignantly. "I don't see your point, Bunch."

"My point is that the next thing they know you're the new nanny—"

"Governess," Joanna said firmly.

"Semantics. Nanny, governess, it makes no difference. You take all your meals in the nursery, ignoring everyone and everything except the little boy, myself included. You even move yourself up there into the vacant bedroom next to his—even though I understand your reasons, with the poor lad and his sleepwalking, but what, may I ask, do you expect them to think?"

Joanna opened her mouth to answer, but Bunch didn't give her a chance.

"I'll tell you—they think Lord Greaves banished you, that's what they think. They think he banished you as far as he could without being entirely unseemly and tossing you out altogether. Why else would you never show your face anywhere else?"

"But Bunch, that's not fair—Miles needs me, he needs all the attention I can give him!" Joanna protested. "He's made a little progress, anyway. At least now he lets me bathe him and dress him and tuck him up in bed, and he's staying dry at night, even if he still does wander, but wouldn't you if you had bad dreams about your mother? At least that's what I assume they're about."

"Humph," Bunch said, turning to glare at Joanna. "If you ask me, which you haven't, what that boy needs is for you to stop coddling him. It's one thing to abuse a child and another to bend over backward to indulge him."

"I'm not indulging him; I'm trying to get through to him."

Bunch slammed down the top of her case and snapped the latches into place. "Fresh air and exercise, that's what I say—give Miles de Salis a normal life full of vigorous and enjoyable activity coupled with a steady routine. You treat him as if he were made of Venetian glass."

Joanna frowned. She hadn't thought of it before this moment, but Bunch might be right: In trying to avoid all of Mrs. Loppitt's dreadful strictures, she had gone to the opposite extreme and had been treating Miles as if he were broken and in need of fixing. Maybe, just maybe, what he really needed was to be treated as if he were already healthy.

"Bunch, you are brilliant," she said, skipping over to the old woman and giving her a huge hug. "I think you've hit on the solution, I really do! I'm going to start straightaway—the first thing is a new wardrobe. No more frocks and pinafores, but proper little boy's clothes. And—and he needs a dog. Yes, that's it, a puppy—I've been wondering what to get him for Christmas, and it's perfect, isn't it? Much better than another storybook, which is what I planned."

"A dog will do nicely," Bunch said, nodding in approval.

"It will give him something to think about other than himself."

Joanna clapped her hands together in delight. "Good! And he must learn to ride, of course—heavens, I was jumping my pony over everything in sight by his age. I'll go down to the stables and speak to the groom, see what he can arrange—I'll need a mare of my own as well so that I can ride with him. Maybe the groom can organize a puppy too—there must be a recent litter somewhere about?"

Bunch shook her head. "You're so much like your father that you worry me at times. Put an idea in your head and you're off and running without ever considering the consequences. Next thing I know you'll have the child leaping off cliffs to improve his confidence."

Joanna crowed with laughter. "Dear Bunch. I only wish you'd pointed me in this direction three weeks ago."

"You needed time to make your own mistakes," Bunch replied dryly. "Otherwise you'd never have listened. While we're on the subject of listening, you might consider befriending the staff. If you want to know what happened to your cousin, they'll be the ones to tell you the truth of the matter, but you won't get a word out of them until you show you can be trusted. Call a footman, if you please? My carriage awaits my departure."

Joanna considered that last piece of advice and knew she'd mull it over later, then obediently pulled the bell rope. Dashing through the connecting door to her old room, she retrieved a package she'd hidden away for Christmas Day.

It was a small oil she'd painted of her calico cat sitting on the west-facing veranda of the Villa di Camigliano, looking down over the rolling hills beyond. Joanna had it framed in Pesaro, never dreaming then that she'd be presenting the painting to Bunch in England, and at the moment of Bunch's departure.

"Bunch?" she said, handing it to her. "Before you go, put this in your luggage. Don't open it until Christmas, but when you do, know that I love you very much and will always be grateful to you for everything you have ever done for me. Do come back, won't you?"

Bunch smiled. "Don't be absurd. Of course I'll be back—what would you ever do without me? Mind you, I'll take my time about it—my sister does deserve the pleasure of my prolonged company after all this time."

Joanna pressed a swift kiss to Bunch's soft cheek and dashed out of the room before she burst into tears.

It was just her luck that as she barreled down the final flight of the staircase, Guy de Salis happened to be coming up.

He grabbed her hard around the waist, somehow preventing them from tumbling backward and breaking both their necks.

"Urgent business?" he inquired mildly, his grip relaxing and his hands moving up to her arms as he steadied her.

Joanna turned a deep red, the heat of his palms burning through the material of her sleeves directly into her flesh.

She wished she might vanish in a puff of smoke. She'd barely spoken to him since their interview three weeks before. He had not requested her to bring Miles down for a daily visit, as Mrs. Loppitt said was his habit, but he often came to the nursery door and silently observed them, leaving just as abruptly, very rarely saying anything at all beyond the most curt of polite greetings, if he even bothered with that.

She acknowledged him with a nod of her head and a tentative smile, always alerted to his presence by an odd prickling up the back of her spine, as if her body had more awareness than the rest of her to his nearness.

Now that prickling ran not just down through her spine but through every nerve ending, a massive heat that flooded her entire body and sent her senses to spinning. Not even Cosmo, whom she'd loved dearly, had ever had such an alarming effect on her physical being. His had been a comforting touch, not a sensual one—he had never made her knees turn weak. But why on earth was she thinking of Cosmo now?

Her breath caught in her throat and she glanced up at Guy, alarmed by the smoldering look in his dark eyes, a look she couldn't begin to interpret.

"Have you lost your tongue?" he asked softly, his warm hands smoothing down to lightly grasp her wrists. "I wouldn't have thought it possible."

Stepping back and attempting to hang on to a shred of dignity, she bowed her head. "I—I was going out, my lord," she stammered, wondering what was wrong with her. Her knees felt as if they might give out, and her heart felt as if she'd just run all the way up the stairs instead of down them.

"Out? In this weather? You do realize it is raining cats and dogs?"

She hadn't, so distressed was she over Bunch's sudden announcement that she hadn't ever bothered to look outside. "I had a thought and wanted to see if it was viable," she murmured.

"I am intrigued by what kind of thought could possibly drive you out with no shred of protection against the raging elements. I don't suppose the hired carriage that stands outside would be yours?" He released her wrists as if reluctant to let her go. "Do you flee us, contessa? Perhaps you find the challenge of the nursery too great?"

His teasing tone of voice unsettled her. "I do not," she replied properly, but her face flamed nonetheless. "The carriage is for my companion, Miss Fitzwilliams. It is she who leaves, no longer wishing to burden you with her presence. As for myself, I would not abandon your son under any circumstances, save for your dismissing me."

He raised one dark eyebrow. "How reassuring. And how fortunate Miles is to have such a protector, although I cannot help but wonder if he does not offer you equal protection from me. I am obviously the devil in the piece."

Joanna looked away from his piercing gaze. "I do what I can, my lord," she said, wishing herself a hundred miles away, anywhere that might relieve her from this terrible discomfort she couldn't even identify. "I beg your permission to continue doing what I can to aid your son's recovery."

Guy glanced away, his expression shielded from her gaze. "As you say. Do what you can."

"Then will you permit me to order him new clothes? He is outgrowing the ones he has." Joanna risked a glance up at him and immediately decided it was a mistake. He was far too handsome for his own good, and clearly too handsome for hers, given her reaction to his closeness. Heat moved into her cheeks and she had to look down at her feet.

"Order whatever you please. I've already told you that you need not consult me on such trivial issues."

"What is it that you do expect me to consult you on, my lord?" she replied, gazing up at him. "Or perhaps I should more appropriately ask what you do *not* consider trivial. You come to watch us in the nursery, and yet you have not once inquired as to your son's progress. Does that fall into the category of the insignificant?"

"You are a proper little hellion, aren't you?" he said, his amused tone raising her ire. "I do not wonder at the reputation you have earned for yourself."

"And I do not wonder at your reputation, my lord, for indeed you have earned yours also," she shot back, wishing she didn't feel so flustered.

"Oh, did Lydia confide in you what a brute I am?" He shrugged one shoulder. "Typical. Although you do have a far finer wit than your cousin ever had, I must admit." He looked her up and down with interest. "Tell me, contessa, were you born to it, or is clever sparring an acquired talent you have learned via your brief marriage into the Italian aristocracy?"

"It you refer to my marriage to Cosmo di Capponi, I can assure you that my husband married me for what I was and not for what I might become," she replied coolly. "If I have any wit at all, I must have learned it from my parents."

She had to admit, she rather enjoyed fencing with him. If anyone had a sharp wit, it was he—she was not accustomed to finding that quality in the men she'd known, and she appreciated his obvious intelligence.

So unnerved that she couldn't bear his presence for one more moment, she said, "If you will stand aside, I have business to attend to."

One corner of his mouth lifted in a half smile. "Now I really *do* wonder what business could be so pressing as to take you out in this weather, and in such a tremendous hurry. Ah, well. Whomever he is, you had best not keep him waiting."

One swift push and he would have toppled straight down the steps, but somehow she managed to restrain herself. "You are quite right, my lord," she said with a toss of her head, forcing herself to assume an unpertubed expression. "I am off to meet with your head groom. He is such a fine-looking man."

Guy considered, then scratched the tip of his nose. "Toomsby is indeed a fine man, although fine-*looking* might be stretching the point," he said. "Do give him my regards— and, contessa, please, do try to go easy on him? At seventy-three he hasn't the stamina he once had, and his joints trouble him in the cold weather."

He moved past her, and Joanna could hear him chuckling as he continued up the stairs.

Joanna couldn't help but grin. She really had met her match in Guy de Salis.

6

Wakefield Abbey
Christmas Eve, 1818

Carriages started to arrive at eight, pouring out hordes of the chattering, fashionably dressed ton, all there to celebrate not only the advent of Christmas, but also the Marquess of Greaves's formal putting aside of his mourning.

Joanna, hidden in the shadows of the upper landing, couldn't resist watching them enter in their elaborate finery, fans fluttering, hands gesticulating, bows and curtsies being exchanged right and left.

She also couldn't help feeling resentful, not because she hadn't been invited: God forbid. She couldn't imagine a worse fate. No, her resentment stemmed from the way they behaved, as if Lydia might never have lived in this house, might never have been the marchioness, might never have existed at all.

Guy de Salis stood in the great hall, which was festooned with boughs of holly and garlands of fir, a Yule log burning brightly in the huge fireplace. He smiled as he greeted his guests, he, too, behaving as if he hadn't a care in the world. She couldn't hear what he was saying above all the hubbub, but he exhibited a charm that clearly enchanted his guests and astonished her. *Charming* was the last word that came to mind when she thought of him. And yet in his black knee breeches and evening coat, his snowy-white linen shirt and neckcloth providing the perfect contrast to his dark good looks, he was unbearably handsome.

She could see why he had mesmerized Lydia, drawn her into his orbit. Joanna saw his power, felt its impact even from her place high above. That didn't surprise her—hadn't she felt the impact of his physical presence that day when he'd caught her alone on the stairs?

No wonder Lydia had fallen straight into his arms.

In evening dress, laughing and joking with his guests, he really did look and behave like a prince.

"Oh, thank heavens, there you are, your ladyship—I've been looking everywhere! I tried the nursery, but Margaret said she hadn't seen you since you put Lord Wycombe to bed, and Mrs. Campion is worried that the aspic will not hold long enough—the heat from the chandeliers is making it limp already!"

Joanna turned to see Wendy, the most efficient of all the chambermaids, breathlessly patting her bosom.

"Then we'll just have to put it outside to cool it down," Joanna said, reluctantly dragging herself away from her position on the landing and the scene below.

She quickly followed Wendy down the back stairs to the kitchen, where another scene, this one of near pandemonium, reigned.

"Contessa! Where 'ave you gone?" Emile, his chef's hat practically falling off his balding head, leapt at her the moment she appeared in the door, agitation combined with heat causing rivulets of sweat to drip down his red face. " 'Ow am I to finish this—this what-you-call-it? Risotto, yes? I cannot put the prawns on just like so under the fire—they will be burned!"

Joanna hurried to his side and murmured instructions into his indignantly quivering ear, then moved over to the pastry chef to put out the next fire.

She silently thanked the good Lord for all the experience she'd gained during her years in Italy in dealing directly with the kitchen, hands right in the food, her *cuoco* guiding and teaching her as she went. She then added a quick thanks to Bunch for the good advice she'd dispensed just before she left.

Joanna had had to steel herself to take it, overcoming her innate shyness and facing down the staff, but in the end her unobtrusive efforts had been worthwhile.

At least she thought they had. A fortnight ago, when she'd hesitantly gone to Mrs. Campion and offered up her services, she thought she might have made a terrible error in suggesting that she take some of the burden of preparing for the Christmas Eve party from the older woman's shoulders.

"If you feel you must give advice, your ladyship, then indeed it had best come through me," Mrs. Campion had said curtly, her tone decidedly lukewarm.

"I thought I might just be an extra pair of eyes," Joanna replied diffidently. "I realize you must know far more about managing a house this size than I do, but from my own experience in trying to run a household, I found that having someone else watching over the smaller bits and pieces was a tremendous help."

"Oh, very well, if you insist," Mrs. Campion replied, already looking weary. "I have enough on my hands dealing with the decorations. See what order you can put into the kitchen. I don't suppose you speak any French?"

"Oh, but I do," Joanna said brightly. "Fairly well, as it happens."

"Then you can tell that Emile person to get on with his job and stop his whining!" Mrs. Campion tugged at one of the pins holding her cap in place. "He's a right bother, he is, and does nothing but upset the others. How they're to manage a full supper for a hundred when they've done next to nothing at all this year save for cooking for the few of you upstairs, I just don't know, I really don't!"

Mrs. Campion covered her face with one hand and shook her head over and over. "His lordship cannot expect to appear out of nowhere after such a long absence and announce a dance to be held in a month, with the house only marginally staffed and no time for proper preparation."

"Never mind," Joanna said in the most soothing voice she could muster. "We'll see it all to rights together. Why don't we start with a reasonable menu, and then go from there. I've always found two heads are much more useful than one. . . ."

For some reason her approach worked in the end, probably because Mrs. Campion was at such loose ends that she didn't have time to argue.

To her surprise Joanna found the experience of working with people she'd never even seen before not at all difficult. They demanded nothing of her in terms of conversation, and she only asked that they carry out her orders with a minimum of fuss.

Which they had. Here they were on Christmas Eve, working side by side, looking to Joanna for guidance, but on the whole managing to carry out their orders. Even Mrs. Campion looked relatively less frazzled, although she, too, turned to Joanna without hesitation when something or someone needed sorting out.

Joanna felt ridiculously pleased.

Three hours later the midnight repast was completed and laid out. Looking around, Joanna decided that she was not needed for the moment. She took her cloak from the hook by the kitchen door where she habitually kept it and slipped outside into the night air.

Walking briskly to ward off the cold, she made her way by the tiny sliver of moon down to the stables, where she knew she was guaranteed to find some badly needed peace and quiet. She had a good excuse too.

Toomsby, dear man that she'd found him to be— despite her mortification to discover him just as Guy de Salis had described, bowed legs, stiff joints, and all—had been true to his word. He'd organized not a puppy, as there were none to be had locally that he knew of, but a dog only two years of age and of sound character.

"Aye, missus," he had said when Joanna had approached him that cold afternoon two weeks before, dripping with rain and indignation from her encounter with Guy de Salis. "I do know of a good un. His master's going to India on army commission, and he be looking for a good home for the dog—gentle as the day is long, that Boscoe, and smart as a whip. I myself've been out as beater with the cap'n, and the dog's got a mouth as soft as you could hope for with the birds, and he do answer well to commands."

His brow wrinkled, and he pulled off his cap and scratched his head. "But, er . . . the boy, missus. Will he be a good un for the dog is my question. He's been a bit queer since his poor mother passed over, if ye know what I'm saying?"

"I think Master Miles will be just fine, Toomsby. I think they'll both be fine. You wait and see. They'll do each other a world of good."

Toomsby lifted his cap and scratched his balding head, then nodded. "Right you are, missus. "I'll take yer word and tell the cap'n his Boscoe has a home. He'll be right pleased, he will, since he was that worried—and to know Boscoe'll be right here at the Abbey, well, so much the better."

"Thank you," Joanna said, delighted with how easy it had been to implement her idea. "Now, about a pony for his lordship and maybe a nice mare for me. I plan to teach his lordship to ride, but I'd like to make it a surprise for his father, so please do be careful not to give our secret away. . . ."

Boscoe, who had turned out to be a large golden retriever, lifted his head as Joanna entered the tack room through the side door of the stable. He padded over from the bed Toomsby had made for him out of an old blanket and a sack of hay and gave her a halfhearted swipe of his tongue in recognition.

"Tomorrow," Joanna said, kneeling and scratching behind the soft felt of his ears. "Tomorrow you will meet your new little master, Boscoe. I'm sure you've been wondering why you've been here the last three days all on your own, and you must be missing your old master terribly, but I promise that you are going to do Miles a great deal of good."

She pulled out a large, meaty bone that she'd brought along and handed it to him. "He's a bit shy, mind you, and you'll have to be very patient, but I feel certain that together we can make all the difference to him."

Boscoe ignored her, his concentration now fully on devouring his beautiful joint of beef.

She closed the door behind her and moved down to the row of stalls. The mare Toomsby had picked out saw her immediately and nickered gently in greeting. A dappled gray with an alert but sweet temperament, she was beautifully put together, her legs long and graceful, her head delicately molded.

Joanna felt sure that she had a good portion of Arabian blood; she certainly looked as if she'd been bred for speed, although Joanna had yet to take her out and get a feel for how she moved. They were still becoming friends—but oh, how Joanna itched to mount her and see what she could do. She missed riding almost more than she missed her villa, but Toomsby had yet to give the word that Joanna might take her out, and Toomsby ruled the stables and everything that went on in it, including who rode what and when. She wondered if even Guy de Salis, despite all his arrogance, ever argued with the little man.

The mare softly blew through her nose as Joanna approached. Stretching her neck out over the stall door, she pushed her nose against Joanna's cloak, parting the woolen folds. Laughing, Joanna produced the apple she'd hidden inside. She'd been bringing little treats each day as a way of earning the mare's confidence.

"You are a clever girl, aren't you," she said, stroking the velvety muzzle as the mare delicately took the apple from her hand and crunched down on it. "Toomsby said your name was Callie. I can't imagine why you were given such a common name when you're clearly an aristocrat. Never mind; if Toomsby has as good an eye for finding the perfect pony as he had for choosing the perfect mare, we'll have Miles off and running in no time."

Joanna froze as the main stable door creaked open and the sound of muted voices drifted over to her. Callie's ears pricked back and forth and she whinnied softly, shaking her head and turning around in the stall as if suddenly uneasy.

Joanna had no idea who could possibly be needing the stables or anything in it at that hour—whomever they were, they weren't familiar to the horses, for Joanna heard them begin to stir restlessly in their stalls farther down the row. Boscoe whimpered from behind the tack-room door, probably wanting to investigate for himself.

"Shhhh, darling," said a distinctly female voice from around the corner. She giggled as her companion kicked over a bucket. "You're going to set all the animals to braying."

"Horses don't bray, they winnow—whinny, I mean," replied the darling in a well-bred if slightly slurred accent. "Donkeys bray."

"Well, whatever horses do, you don't want them to start, do you? You know how Greaves is about his horses. You'd think they were his children, the way he carries on about them. And do be careful with the lantern—you don't want to set the place on fire and burn up the precious beasts."

"Never mind Greaves and his horses. I didn't bring you here to talk, sweeting."

Joanna rolled her eyes. She'd had enough experience in Italy not to be surprised by this sort of extramarital intrigue, but she'd also had an equal amount of experience to tell her it didn't do either party any good to be discovered. In this case discretion was definitely the better part of valor, so she settled herself down on the ground, leaned her back against the stall door, and prayed they'd get their pawing over with quickly. She really didn't feel like waiting, and being forced to be a reluctant eavesdropper on an amorous adventure was definitely not her cup of tea.

"Lambkin, what are you doing?" the woman suddenly shrieked. "Your hands are freezing!"

Lambkin? Oh, Lord, it was going to be a long night.

"Come closer, you lovely creature, and show me your charms. I've been staring at the swell of those creamy breasts all night, and guess what's been getting hot and hard as a poker?"

Joanna put her head in her hands.

"A poker?" the woman tittered. "You do yourself a great injustice. I was thinking more of a battering ram myself."

Lambkin guffawed. "Such a way you have with words, my petal. And speaking of petals, show me yours? I'm going to burst the buttons of my breeches with lust, I swear, with just the thought of those plump, rosy folds overflowing with passion's dew. Lift your skirts and spread your legs, I beg you. Let me gaze upon the wonder of your feminine flora; let me adore and adorn you with my eyes, my hands, my mouth, the very heart of my being. Let me bestow the gift of Adam upon his Eve and take you to heights of pleasure known only to the Garden itself."

Joanna couldn't believe what she was hearing. Lambkin clearly fancied himself a poet. What an ill-advised career that would be.

"You won't see a single thing until you find me a clean and comfortable place. I refuse to soil my dress or have my backbone ground into dust as you did the last time."

"My pet! I have never done any such dreadful thing. Here, look, this anteroom is more private, and this pile of hay will do nicely. I shall lay my cloak upon it, and then I shall lay you."

He wheezed with laughter at his own joke. Some rustling, grunts, and moans came from the side room, and then more conversation.

"Nothing like hay to make a bed on, eh? Ah, God, that's good. Yes, stroke it just so. Spread your legs just a little wider, my Petalfold of the Sahara." More groans. "Oh, God. Oh, God. That's it. Oh, let me plunge and pillage you with my rod, let me sack you until you are nothing more than ashes in a wild wilderness. Oh, *God!* Yes, yes, yes—succor me, take me to your bosom like a lamb about to be sacrificed. I will gladly die your slave. Ahhhhhh."

Joanna covered her mouth with both hands, trying not to burst into laughter. She had never, but *never* heard such awful hyperbole in her life.

A few minutes later a loud groan from Lambkin and some halfhearted wails on the part of Petalfold, and all went silent.

Good, Joanna thought with relief. *Maybe now they'll get back to the dance. It's been long enough that they'll be missed if they delay any longer.*

She was wrong.

"Bet your boring husband never took you on a hay pile," Lambkin said, panting hard.

"My boring husband never takes me anywhere at all," Petalfold replied with another coquettish giggle. "That's what Lydia used to say."

Joanna's spine stiffened at the mention of her cousin's name. She sat upright, for the first time straining to listen.

"For God's sake, no more talk about Lydia," Lambkin said impatiently. "She's dead and buried, and thank the Lord for it. That's all I've heard about tonight—whispered voices going on about Lydia this, Lydia that, as if she's still fodder for the same gossip. Greaves put her to rest in her grave a good year ago, and that should be an end to it. Greaves—grave . . . ha! That's good. Must remember that."

"She was my friend," Petalfold protested. "I think you're

being horribly cruel. You know how unhappy she was with him—he was beastly to her."

"He was a saint, you silly woman. Must you all take the same cockeyed line? Look here, what are you doing? You can't just get up like that. The night is still young—round two awaits."

"I won't let you near me ever again if you insist on speaking of Lydia in such a way. How can you be so callous, so cold-blooded, especially considering the way she died?"

Joanna had to resist the temptation to crawl closer and eavesdrop in earnest. She *still* didn't know how Lydia had died, and she could hardly ask Guy de Salis . . . or could she? *Could she?*

"I don't see why I'm being cold-blooded just because I refuse to beatify her now that she's dead," Lambkin said with annoyance. "She was a spoiled child."

"She was an angel! A dear, darling angel who tried everything to make her husband happy until it became obvious that he wanted nothing to do with her. Why do you think she spent so much time away from him? It was torture, sheer torture for her to be in his presence and be completely ignored." Petalfold released a small sob. "I think you are as awful as he is. I shall warn anyone who is stupid enough to set her cap at you that she will end up just like Lydia—heartbroken, abused, and alone. I never want to speak to you again!"

Joanna heard the rustling of skirts and then a moment later the slam of the stable door. She could hardly contain her disappointment—she knew nothing more than she had before, save that Guy de Salis's male friends sided with him, hardly surprising.

Everything that Petalfold had said only confirmed the miserable marriage Lydia had written about. Although she had been given one clue: Petalfold had said "especially considering the way she died," which implied that Lydia's death had not been peaceful.

Joanna shuddered. Dear Lord, but she hoped that wouldn't prove to be the case. She would infinitely prefer to discover that Lydia's health, always on the delicate side, had been her undoing, that she had gone quietly to her Maker in her sleep.

Joanna would just have to summon up her courage and ask Guy de Salis the truth as soon as she could find an appropriate opportunity. For some absurd reason she hadn't been able to bring herself to ask him before now, perhaps because she was afraid to learn what really had happened, perhaps because she hadn't felt comfortable enough with him to allow herself to be vulnerable in his presence. Whatever the reason, her delay had been no more than cowardice on her part. She made an inner vow that she would discover the truth as soon as humanly possible. She'd kept her silence far too long as it was and had no one to blame but herself for that.

"Bitch," Lambkin shouted. "See if I ever pleasure you again. Go back to your damned husband. He's not likely to ram you the way you like, not at his age."

Another slam of the stable door.

Joanna breathed a sigh of relief. Two of the most disagreeable people she'd ever had the misfortune to overhear had finally taken their leave. She hoped she'd never have the further misfortune of meeting them face to face— although, she reflected, she had no idea of what their faces actually looked like and no idea of their actual names.

She gave them both a good ten minutes to make their separate ways back to the house, then slipped out the side door after a final good-night pat to Boscoe.

Hurrying back toward the house, her mood grim, she pulled the hood of her cloak up over her head, warding off the frigid chill of the night. The stars shone crisp and bright, clustered like millions of diamonds in the black heavens, yet hanging so close that she felt as if she might reach out and touch them.

One in particular gleamed with a special brilliance, serving to remind her that Christmas Day had arrived, the celebration of the birth of the Christ child and the message of glad tidings He had brought.

She paused, tilting her head back, and smiled up at it. The star somehow managed to banish the dark, tainted feeling that Petalfold and Lambkin had left her with.

If she tried hard enough she imagined she might even be able to hear the angels singing.

Peace and good will. She sighed. All she'd ever wanted in life was that, and yet both had proved so elusive—at least after her parents had been killed. Before that awful day life had been entirely idyllic. Since then she had struggled to find a semblance of peace; good will—with the exception of ever-loyal Bunch and, briefly, Cosmo—had been in short supply.

She was so tired of struggling, so tired of forever trying to make sense out of a world that became increasingly complicated. At least she had her art, which gave her a respite from the harsh demands of daily life. She wished she'd been more successful with giving Miles the same outlet, but to date he was not interested in the pad and pencils she'd put in front of him. The window still held his full attention, although she doubted he saw the world beyond it.

Joanna focused the full force of her prayers on that one brilliant star. She pressed the palms of her hands together, then took a deep breath and released it.

Please, Lord, on this day of Your miraculous birth, give Miles back the joy of life. Let him be a little boy again, remind him how to play, how to be silly, how to receive love and give it in turn. Please banish the darkness he has drawn down on himself; show him the way back to light. And, Lord—please give me the knowledge to aid him in his journey and the strength to see him through.

She crossed herself, then pulled her hood up and moved on her way.

She had no idea that Lambkin stood staring at her in horror from the shelter of the bare rose bower, the cheroot he'd stopped to smoke smoldering, forgotten, in his fingers.

7

"Greaves—Greaves, for God's sake, I must speak to you!"

Guy turned abruptly from his conversation at the hushed voice that came from over his shoulder. Malcolm Lambkin stood behind him, white as a sheet and trembling all over.

"Good heavens, man, what's happened?" he asked with concern, excusing himself and drawing Malcolm away.

"Not here," Malcolm hissed. "Somewhere—somewhere private. God, I need a drink."

"Of course," Guy said, for once agreeing with him. Malcolm, usually the epitome of insouciance, looked shaken to his marrow. "Come, we'll go into the library, where we won't be disturbed."

Once he'd shut the door Guy immediately poured them both a brandy from the side table. "Here you are," he said, turning to hand Malcolm the snifter. "What are you staring at?" he asked, wondering why Malcolm was peering out the window into the pitch black.

"She's out there," Malcolm said, his voice shaking.

"Who is out there?" Guy asked curiously. Malcolm might not be the brightest fellow, but he was steady as the day was long and not prone to flying up into the boughs over nothing.

"Just a moment," Guy said, the obvious suddenly occurring to him, "you're not referring to Sally Neville, are you? She's not out there, I can assure you—I saw her reappear not ten minutes ago, and she looked in a proper snit over something." He grinned. "Did she threaten to tell her husband about your little liaison? Don't worry, Malcolm, she'd never go through with it—she's up to her ears in gambling debts and can't afford to annoy him. Don't let her upset you."

"It's not Sally who upset me, you idiot," Malcolm said, spinning around, his eyes wide and frightened. "It's your wife!"

"My wife is dead," Guy quietly reminded him, thinking that perhaps Malcolm was deeper in his cups than he'd realized.

"I know she's dead, you bloody fool! That's the point!"

Guy considered, trying to untangle this statement. Sally Neville and Lydia had been bosom buddies, both of them cut from the same cloth. He wondered if Sally hadn't accidentally let slip one of Lydia's secrets to Malcolm, who was now determined to tell Guy but was terrified of his reaction. Guy's mood was not at its best when the subject of Lydia and her incessant peccadilloes came up—as they had a habit of doing even now.

"Obviously I am being stupid," Guy said as patiently as he could manage. "Perhaps you would be kind enough to explain just what you mean?"

"Lydia might be dead, but she's come back from the grave. She was gliding around out there the way ghosts do, you know, like they're floating, all gray and misty."

Guy stared at him, speechless. *"What?"* he finally managed to sputter, sure he must have misunderstood. "Say that again?"

"Lydia," Malcolm said urgently. "Her *ghost!*"

"Where was this?" Guy asked, scratching his cheek, not sure whether to be shocked or amused. "You weren't conducting your tryst in the chapel, of all places?"

Many people had claimed to have seen ghosts in the chapel over the centuries, not surprising considering that the remains of generations of de Salises were interred there, Lydia included. To date there had been no report of a sighting of Lydia's ghost, or at least not that he'd heard about. Surprising, considering how hungry Lydia had always been for attention, he thought cynically.

"Not in the chapel. I saw her on the path leading up from the stables, and I tell you, it made the hair on the back of my neck stand up. She was wearing a cloak, the hood pulled up like—like a monk's cowl, but I could see her face clear as day. It was Lydia, I am certain of it." He wiped the remains of brandy from his mouth with the back of a shaking hand.

"Ah," Guy said, the light dawning. Joanna di Capponi, if he knew anything about it, although he couldn't think what she was doing in the dead of night, prowling around in the freezing cold.

"*Ah?* What do you mean by that?" Malcolm demanded. "Don't tell me you've seen her yourself? Do you think she's come back to torture you?"

"I imagine that's her intention," Guy said, thinking of Joanna. "But that was Lydia's style," he said, more to himself than to Lambkin. "She swore that one day she'd make me pay for her misery." He attempted a smile. "I wish she knew that I pay every single day as it is. I never meant her a moment's unhappiness, but that's all I ever seemed to give her. Now she's gone, and I have no way to tell her how sorry I am that I couldn't be the man or the husband that she wanted."

"You've always been too hard on yourself," Malcolm said glumly, scratching at his collar and idly picking a piece of straw out from under it. "I've never known a man to shoulder the blame for other people's follies the way you do. You did it when we were boys—always protecting your friends, taking the responsibility when we got ourselves into some coil or other."

"Only because I was the largest," Guy said with a laugh.

"And the smartest by far," Malcolm said, nodding. "You always did manage to get yourself and the rest of us out of nearly any pickle. Look at what you did in the Peninsula that time when we were in the worst pickle of all, backs against the wall, facing sure death."

"Please, Malcolm, spare me the memory," Guy said with bitter distaste. Those years were not a time in his life he cared to remember, and his last battle and its aftermath not one that bore thinking about at all.

"Nonsense. You spare me the modesty—I will never forget what you did so that what was left of the regiment could get safely away. Never seen the likes of it. No wonder you were mentioned in dispatches."

"It's kind of you, my friend, but I should more probably have been given a court-martial for the sheer stupidity of my actions," Guy said, trying desperately to sound casual, and even more desperate to change the subject. "I thank God I'm no longer young and foolish."

Malcolm waved a careless hand. "You're alive. We're alive, or at least those of us who didn't die in the slaughter," he added nonsensically. "I don't see what is so foolish about that. Gallantry is gallantry, Guy, and it's no good trying to hide your light under a bushel. Your wife never appreciated that about you. Thinking about it, she never appreciated much of anything about you except your title and your money."

"Yes, she did appreciate my wealth. I discovered only last month that shortly before her death she'd sold the de Salis emeralds."

"No!" Malcolm's jaw fell open. "But—but that's—those are famous! Practically priceless!"

"Mmm. I probably still wouldn't know, since I'm not in the habit of going to the safe-box to check on them, but I saw Olivia Crankishaw wearing them when I passed her on her way to the theater. Unmistakable."

"That parvenue," Malcolm said with disgust. "I suppose she doesn't realize how gauche she is—shows what too much money and no breeding will do. Did you get them back?"

"Not yet, although I am about to. You wouldn't have believed the negotiations. My solicitor, her solicitor, offer, counteroffer. I ended up paying twice what Lydia sold them for—a king's ransom doesn't cover it."

"What d'you suppose Lydia did with the money?"

"God only knows," Guy said, running his fingers through his hair. "She must have had some unbelievable debts that she didn't want me to know about—you know how much trouble Sally Neville led her into."

"Oh. Right you are," Malcolm said, sinking back into gloom. "Lucky for Sally that Neville's rich as Croesus."

"He won't be for long unless he reins her in."

"If you're referring to me," Malcolm said, attempting to look dignified, "I have finished it with Lady Neville. She is spoiled, selfish, and vapid. I pity the next man who is taken in by her charms, for he shall only suffer to the deepest depths of his being. I intend to write a poem about it—I might even have it published."

"Good idea," Guy said with a straight face. "Get it out of your system and all that, although I'd be a little careful about naming names. Look what happened to Byron."

"I shall disguise all the parties involved, naturally," Malcolm said, standing and pulling his evening coat into place. "I am a gentleman after all."

"Indeed you are," Guy said, fondly grasping his old friend's shoulder and leading him to the library door. "Speaking of which, we should get back; I don't want my guests to think I've deserted them. Merry Christmas, Malcolm."

"Merry Christmas," Malcolm replied, and proceeded on his merry way.

Guy wandered over to the window, leaning his palms on the sill and looking out into the same night where Malcolm had seen what he'd fondly imagined to be Lydia's specter.

He stretched one hand out and traced a line down the

cold pane with his fingertips. The crescent moon hung high in the sky now, not much more than a punctuation mark among the stars. Odd how dependable the heavens were, never reflecting any of the madness beneath them. Still, silent, they were the one constant. They looked the same to his eye year in, year out, changing only in his perception as they rotated around the earth, their heavenly positions remaining fixed.

When he'd been fighting in the hellhole of the Peninsula, he would lie awake at night tracing the familiar constellations, drawing comfort from them. Later, in the makeshift field hospital, he had taken comfort from looking up through a torn piece of material in the tent and honing his gaze in on the few stars he could make out on the rare nights that rain didn't pour down.

He tried to imagine to which constellation they belonged, to trace the old, familiar lines in this mind, to remember the story behind each and every one. The exercise served as a distraction from the physical pain, although it didn't help nearly as much with the wracking emotional agony that twisted at his gut and tore at his heart every waking minute, leaving him weak and spent.

He'd far have preferred gangrene to guilt. One died of the former and lived forever with the latter.

Now all he could do was remember.

Guy took one last look at the enigmatic stars, then straightened and pressed his fingertips into both temples, rubbing in small circles.

He reached for his snifter of brandy and finished it, bracing himself to return to his guests.

Joanna yawned and stretched on the nursery window seat, where she'd left the draperies open to the night. Despite her exhaustion, she hadn't wanted to miss the breaking of dawn on this special day. Pushing back the shawl that covered her nightdress, she wandered over to the fading fire and sparked it into life, adding some more coal as an afterthought.

Miles might very well be up soon, given it was Christmas morning. More likely, though, she was indulging herself in wishful thinking. He'd shown no interest in the crèche she'd set up, no interest in the wreath of holly she'd woven and placed on the door. The truth was that Miles was not that much further along than when she'd taken him under her wing.

She returned to the window seat and resumed her position. Only one star remained in the heavens, the same star she'd earlier given up her petition to, still shining brightly as if it, too, didn't want to miss the dawning of Christmas.

Pressing one palm against the cold window, where frost clung to the edges of the glass in little starbursts, she sighed, knowing she could trust only in the power of prayer now, and in the healing magic of a young dog.

The slightest of sounds from the outer door made her start, and she sat up abruptly.

She drew in a quick, sharp breath as she absorbed the astonishing image of Guy de Salis, still wearing black breeches and white waistcoat, standing in the doorway, his coat in one hand, a candlestick in the other.

"Lord Greaves," she said in surprise.

He looked as surprised to see her as she was to see him. "Heavens," he murmured, moving into the room and placing the candle on the table along with a package that had been covered by his coat. "I must be seeing a specter. What else would be up at this hour?" He casually tossed the coat over the back of one chair. His gaze roved up and down her body, finally settling on her face. "Tonight you nearly frightened one of my friends to death. He saw you walking outside after midnight and believed Lydia had come back from the dead. Lambkin thought you were Lydia's ghost."

Lambkin? Not *the* Lambkin? Joanna pressed her hand

hard against her mouth to keep from laughing. "Oh," she gasped, her eyes tearing up with suppressed laughter.

"You find this amusing, do you?" he said in a dangerous tone, advancing toward her.

Joanna couldn't help herself. "I—oh, I—forgive me," she managed to say. "It is just that I was down in the stables seeing to Miles's Christmas present, and then I went to, to—" She doubled over, holding her aching sides.

"To what?" he demanded, a distinct note of curiosity in his voice.

"To—oh, dear, my lord, I really do not think I can say anything more, other than I can promise you that I kept well out of sight when your friend Lambkin came in." She released an enormous breath, fighting for control. "If he thought he saw any ghosts, he was simply seeing double. I was around the corner, hiding."

To her amazement, Guy sank down on the window seat next to her. "No, I cannot believe it," he said. "You must be making this up. You couldn't possibly have been there when—" He gazed over at her. "Were you?"

"I am afraid to say I was," she said, not able to meet his eyes. "I, um . . . I believe your friend fancies himself a poet of sorts?" Her face contorted again, and she clapped her hands over it. "His prose needs some work."

"Yes, I know," Guy said. "I, er, I beg your pardon on his behalf."

She risked a glimpse at him, amazed to see that he was smiling broadly, even more amazed by the transformation the smile made to his face. He looked practically friendly. "Are you begging my pardon for your friend's bad prose or his illicit . . . um . . . his nocturnal activities?" she asked.

He cocked an eyebrow, but the dark eyes beneath were amused. "You shock me."

"I doubt it," she replied tartly. "I doubt much of anything shocks you."

"What would make you say a thing like that? You shocked

the life out of me the first time I laid eyes on you, and you know it."

"Yes, I do know," she said. "I understand why now, but believe me, at the time I had no idea that the resemblance between Lydie and myself had grown so close. People used to say we looked like sisters, but no one ever actually mistook me for her before I came to Wakefield, you see." She shook her head, still puzzled. "Your butler did look a bit taken aback when I arrived, and Miles, of course, when I first met him, but no one else seemed surprised by my appearance, not until you appeared."

"Most of the staff is new," he said, looking down at her. "I kept Ambrose on because he's been with the family since my father's time, as has Toomsby. The others I found positions for elsewhere."

"Why?" she asked, wondering if the old staff had all turned against him when Lydia had died.

"I suppose I let them go because I didn't want any reminders. The situation was difficult enough as it was, and I thought it best to start afresh."

"That does explain why nearly everyone was at sixes and sevens over organizing this evening. Of course, I was happy to be able to assist Mrs. Campion with tonight's festivities," Joanna said, more to herself than to him.

"You assisted Mrs. Campion?" he asked, surprised.

"She didn't know what she was doing. Neither did anyone else, or so it seemed."

"Thank you—thank you for stepping in."

"I didn't mind at all," Joanna replied, thinking with an inner chuckle that he sounded as if he might choke on his own words. "I much prefer being on that side of the entertainment. To tell you the truth, I've never been very good at mixing in society."

He scratched his cheek. "Is that so. You surprise me, contessa."

"Why?" she said, pushing herself to her feet and trying to

arrange her shawl more modestly over herself. "Surely Lydia must have told you a little bit about me? She was eternally exasperated by my social ineptness. You might think I look like her, but I assure you, I have none of her grace or charm—yet another reason why I would not make a convincing ghost. You might have also pointed out to your friend that ghosts are not known to haunt stables. Do they not customarily wander through hallways or hover about graveyards where their mortal remains are interred? In Lydia's case, that would be the chapel, of course." She winced, realizing that she was suddenly treading on treacherous ground.

He stood and abruptly looked away, his gaze moving back to the fire. "Yes. She lies in the chapel."

"Did you—did you have a full funeral service for her?" she asked in a small voice, desperately wanting to know.

He nodded. "Yes. If it is any comfort, the place was filled to overflowing. All her favorite hymns were sung, hothouse flowers stood in every available space. She would have liked it."

Joanna swallowed hard, then summoned all her courage. She'd opened the door, she might as well walk through it.

"Lord Greaves, forgive me for asking, but could you possibly tell me how Lydia died?"

8

$\mathcal{G}$uy slowly lifted his head and even more slowly turned to face her. "You cannot be saying that you do not know?"

His face looked tight and drawn, a sudden pallor marking it, and for the first time Joanna saw a completely different side to Guy de Salis. This was a man who did suffer over Lydia's death, whatever his reasons.

"I do not," she said, moving slightly toward him. "I only received a brief letter from her parents this last October, enclosing a locket she'd bequeathed to me." She fumbled at the neck of her nightdress and pulled the locket out as if it might offer proof of her words.

"They assumed I already knew and so offered no details. I—I have so wanted to know. Please, my lord, will you not tell me?" She tucked the locket away again. "Did she take ill? Her constitution wasn't as strong as it might have been, and she often suffered from chills."

He blew out a long breath, his hand moving to the back of his neck. "I think it would be best if you sat down," he said, gesturing at the sofa with his free hand.

Her eyes widened in alarm. "What—what happened? Was it an accident?"

"Yes," he said, his voice grim. "An accident. A terrible accident." He lowered his gaze and looked down at his hands.

"What sort of accident?" Joanna said, sinking onto the sofa. "Please, do not keep me in suspense!"

"I—I don't know how to tell you except to say it directly. Lydia died in a fire. I'm so sorry." He passed one hand over his face.

"A fire." She hardly managed to get the words out. She

wasn't even sure she had—she felt as if all the air had left her body in a great rush, all words gone with it. No. Oh, no. He was mistaken, surely. It wasn't possible. Not Lydia, lovely, lovely Lydia. And there were no signs of fire anywhere about. She shook her head back and forth, back and forth. Not possible. Not possible.

As if he'd read her mind he spoke again, his voice very low and slightly hoarse. "It didn't happen here, in case you were wondering. She'd left to visit friends in Cornwall and stopped at an inn on the first night of the journey. The place went up in flames sometime after midnight."

"What happened?" Joanna cried.

"A dirty chimney lit the roof, they say. She was asleep on the second floor, and the place burned so fast that there was no time to get her out."

Joanna pressed her hands against her face as if she could block out his words, the horrifying images they brought that branded themselves into her brain—Lydia waking in terror, fighting her way through the flames as she tried to save herself, crying out for help that never came.

"No," Joanna cried. "God, please, no! Oh, God, not Lydia!"

Sobs shook her helpless body; she doubled over, rocking, her arms folded against her middle as if she could somehow shield it from the knife of pain that sliced through her over and over again. She couldn't catch her breath, but it didn't seem to matter. Nothing mattered but the thought that Lydia had died alone and in terrible agony.

She vaguely registered arms coming around her, lifting her up and carrying her somewhere. The next thing she knew a gust of icy air blew into her face, so incredibly cold that the shock forced her to take a deep breath and then another.

"That's good," a voice murmured in her ear. "Go on, Joanna. Keep breathing. Nice even breaths now. Focus on that—only that. In and out. Good. That's good."

A blanket came around her shoulders and large hands

briskly rubbed her arms, then folded around her, holding her steady. As her breathing eventually slowed she realized that the hands belonged to Guy de Salis. Of course they did. She was in the nursery of Wakefield, making an utter ass out of herself, held in the arms of the man she despised more than anyone on earth.

Or did she?

For some reason his strong arms around her felt so good, so comforting, his hard chest pressing against her back like a refuge in a storm.

And he smelled so nice, so clean, and—and spicy, somehow, a deep, rich, lovely spice. Why hadn't she ever before noticed how *nice* he smelled?

That observance was enough to jolt her right back to her senses, even more effectively than the blast of cold air. What was she thinking?

She sat up abruptly, wiping at her face and nose with the sleeve of her nightdress. A handkerchief magically appeared in her hand.

"Th-thank you," she stammered. "Forgive me. I—I had a shock." She blew into the linen.

"I did manage to grasp that," he said. "Feeling a bit better now?"

She nodded and blew her nose hard again, then wiped at her eyes with one clean edge.

"You're right," he said with a little smile. "You have absolutely no regard for any of the social graces. All the women I know who had heard such terrible news would have misted over, dabbed carefully at their eyes so as not to disturb their complexions, made loud exclamations of despair, probably attempted a faint, but you—no. You're a proper caterwauler."

Joanna jumped to her feet and spun around, glaring at him. "How can you be so insensitive!"

"Actually, I was paying you a compliment," he said. "I admire anyone who can give such honest vent to despair.

I was trained from the cradle to suppress my emotions. Not the done thing, you know, to allow people to believe one might actually *feel* something."

She sank back on her bare heels and regarded him through swollen eyes. "You are actually admitting to having feelings?" she said.

"Do not misunderstand me." He took the handkerchief from her and gently wiped her chin with the remaining clean edge. "I am far too manly to admit anything of the sort. The point is that you have displayed a rather interesting array of feelings tonight, and not a single one meets the previous image I had of you—with the exception of your hair-trigger temper."

Joanna belatedly realized that he'd intentionally forced her out of shock, using the one thing he did know about her—her temper.

"You haven't met my expectations either," she admitted reluctantly. At least he hadn't in the last thirty minutes.

There were so many things she'd hadn't noticed about him before this—the way his dark eyes softened when he chose to be kind, and he *had* been kind to her, very kind. Or the way his lashes lowered when he tried to disguise his pain.

His immediate reaction to her own pain—his complete disregard of any propriety when he'd picked her up in his arms and practically hung her head out the window—had been such a departure from the stiff, insensitive man she'd previously encountered that she wanted to laugh.

"What are you grinning at?" he asked.

"I think you might actually be human after all," she said, managing a small laugh.

Guy tilted his head to the side and smiled. "Fair enough. I suppose I deserved that. Look here, Joanna—do you mind if I call you that?"

"You did before, and I far prefer it to your rather sour

rendition of 'contessa,' " she said. "I've always hated being called that."

"Have you," he said, regarding her thoughtfully. "Very well, I shall continue to call you Joanna, but only if you cease and desist calling me 'my lord' in that spiteful and vindictive tone you are prone to use. Guy will suffice."

Joanna scrubbed her nose with the back of her fist. She had the most terrible feeling he was trying to charm her the same way he'd charmed Lydia, but she didn't have the strength or the inclination to refuse such a simple request. "As you wish," she said reluctantly.

"Good. I am delighted to discover that you can be reasonable."

She was about to challenge him on that inflammatory remark, since she was nearly always reasonable, but before she could begin he stood and walked back to the fireplace, his fingers drumming against the mantelpiece for a long moment before he spoke.

"Tell me. How is Miles? How is he really?"

She realized in that moment, and for the very first time, that he really did care about his son. His voice held a softness, a vulnerability she'd never heard in it before.

"He is much the same, I'm sorry to report—he is completely obedient in all things, but I wish he wasn't. I wish he'd cry, or lash out, or do something, anything that told me he was living and feeling in the real world."

"I thought you said he was improving." Guy shifted to look at her. She noticed that his fist had balled into a tight knot.

"I said that I thought I was starting to get through to him, but the changes are so slight that they are probably not noticeable to anyone but myself. He—every now and then when I ask him to do something, I have the feeling that he looks at me out of the corner of his eye just as I'm turning my back, and the expression is rebellious. I never actually catch him at it; as soon as I turn around, he's bowed his head so that I cannot see his face."

Guy nodded. "I see. It is at least a small sign of hope if you are correct, though. I pray to God you are."

"My lord—Guy, that is," she amended awkwardly, not yet accustomed to the familiarity. "May I ask you why you have never inquired about your son's progress before this night? I can see that you do care, but you have almost always given the impression that you were indifferent. Why do you come to the nursery door every day and then not come in, not speak to him?"

He sighed heavily and sank onto the sofa. "I do not speak to Miles when I come to the nursery because I do not want to disturb him any further. I feel I must be a large part of the problem, so it is best if I do not force him to respond to me. The last time I tried, he made it very clear that he wished to have nothing to do with me. This is not his fault, but mine."

"But why?" she asked, desperate to understand.

He released a deep breath and looked down. "If truth be told, I always felt Miles to be his mother's child. Lydia protected him from me like a lioness keeping her cub away from a dangerous predator." He shook his head. "I never really had a chance to know him—much of that my fault as well. I spent as little time here as I could, and after she died I spent even less."

Joanna pressed her hands together in her lap. "Do you know your son at all?" she asked, her voice low.

He fixed her with a piercing gaze that unnerved her completely. "No. Not really. Not as I should. Are there any other knives you'd like to plunge into me tonight?"

She colored. "I beg your pardon. I didn't mean to upset you any further. I was just hoping that you might have some insight that I lacked into your son's character."

He exhaled. "Miles was always energetic," he said. "Bright, amusing, full of life. His mother, when she was home, tended to crush him with the tremendous amount of attention she gave him, although that attention was sporadic. Then it was gone altogether, as was she."

"You did explain to him about Lydia's dying, about what that meant?"

"I told him, yes. Of course I did. I told him that his mama had gone to heaven to be with the angels, that she wouldn't be staying with us any longer. He seemed to grasp the point."

Joanna jumped to her feet, outraged by Guy's insensitivity. "He seemed to *grasp* the point? He was only just four years old! How could a child of that age grasp anything other than that his mother had completely vanished from his life in the most inexplicable way?"

Guy's eyes flashed at her. "Do not presume to lecture me. I told him what I thought best for him to hear. I tried to protect him."

"You made it sound as if his mother had abandoned him for something more enjoyable, as if the angels were better company than he was! He needs to know that his mother's death was a terrible accident over which she had no control, that she never would have left him if she'd had any control over the situation. Can't you see that?"

"I am not a complete fool, contessa, as much as you persist in believing me one. We clearly have very different viewpoints, although I would remind you again that I am the boy's father, and my viewpoint is the only one that is important."

"How can you say that when you entrust his well-being to me? Am I to use my judgment only when you are not about to dictate yours? So far the latter has proved faulty, from everything I have seen and heard."

Guy glared at her, looking as if he could happily murder her. "You, madam, have just conclusively proved that your amazing likeness to your cousin is more than skin deep. I will take my leave of you, as I do not relish being treated to another show of your temper."

He strode over to the table where he'd left his candle, now sputtering low in the holder, and collected his coat. "The box is for Miles," he said, marching to the door and yanking it open. "And just so that you feel informed, I leave for town early this afternoon to take care of pressing business. I shall not return for at least twelve weeks. Probably I shall be longer."

"As you please, your royal worship," Joanna muttered as the door closed firmly behind him.

Christmas Day had gotten off to a shining start, thanks to Guy de Salis.

She'd been a fool to hope that this blessed day would also be a merry one.

9

*H*er emotions in shreds and her thoughts so jumbled that she couldn't sort one from the next, Joanna finally gave up any thought of peacefully watching the dawn approach. Changing into a warm day dress, she left the nursery, hoping to find someone, anyone, who might keep an ear out for Miles.

Luck was with her. She flagged down Dickson, who happened to have the misfortune of showing his weary face, furrows planted deep on both sides of his mouth.

"Please," she said, "would you mind keeping watch in the nursery for the next hour, Dickson? Miles is sound asleep—I just checked—but I sent Margaret, who's been helping me in the nursery, home hours ago to be with her family, and I don't want to leave him alone in case he might wake and be frightened. I'm—I'm going to the chapel should you need me."

Dickson didn't hesitate, didn't show any surprise. He merely bowed his head in acquiescence. "As you wish, your ladyship," he said quietly. "Do you perhaps need another candle to light you on your way?"

She looked down at what she held, seeing his point. The candle was already halfway burned. On the very edge of tears, she simply nodded.

"Here, take mine," he said, handing his candle to her with one hand and taking hers with the other. No question, no argument, simply "take mine."

"You will find a lantern already burning by the side door off the boot room," he continued, "and a heavy cloak that will be overlarge, but it will keep the chill off. I would guide you to the chapel myself, but as you requested, someone should look after his little lordship."

"Th-thank you," she managed to say through the tight, hot knot in her throat. "You are very kind. You have always been so kind."

One corner of this thin mouth lifted. "It is not I who is kind, contessa. God speed you to your purpose and bring you back with a lightened heart."

He moved quietly off toward the direction of the nursery.

Joanna covered her face with one hand, willing back a fresh onslaught of tears, then hurried on her way, already thanking God for the kindness not of strangers, but of a steady friend, however remote. "Contessa," he'd called her. She'd always hated the sound of that until now. Dickson had made it sound almost like an endearment.

The walk to the chapel, long familiar to her by now, caused her no trouble and certainly no fear. Joanna was not inclined to nerves, and unlike Guy's friend Lambkin, the idea of being confronted with ghostly apparitions, unlikely as it seemed, did not dismay her.

She'd always thought that if a ghost found her interesting enough to bother to manifest in front of her, she would do her best to be interesting in return.

The little chapel loomed up out of the darkness, the rich sepia stone muted. Silent. So silent. Not a sound was to be heard anywhere, not of any kind. Her own breath sounded loud in her ears.

She reached out to the door handle and it turned smoothly, the weight of the door easily swinging open.

She knelt at the side of Lydia's crypt for a moment, her hand pressed against the marble top that had Lydia's name and dates of birth and death inscribed. Joanna never drew any comfort from looking at the cold stone slab beneath which Lydia lay.

Instead, she went to the front of the chapel and said her prayers to Lydia there, where it always felt warmer, somehow, despite the frigid air.

This morning the simple altar was alight with a single candle that burned in the direct center. Someone had gone to the trouble of laying out a white altar cloth.

She walked quickly up the nave and sank to her knees at the altar rail, not so much to pray as to steady herself. Her fingers clung to the wood, and she bowed her head onto them.

Faith had always been a guiding force in her life, but never more so than when she'd been in crisis. She'd prayed tonight already, prayed for Miles and healing and peace.

Now she could only cry, a little for herself, but most of all for Lydia.

"Oh, God—how could you? How *could* you?" she sobbed, burying her face more deeply in her arms. "You gave Lydia to that dreadful man and caused her to suffer torment in her marriage, and then you chose to take her away in such a cruel fashion. You left her little boy motherless, God. You did that to Miles, and I don't understand why."

"God's will is not for you to understand, my child. It is only for you to accept."

Joanna's head shot up, and she frantically looked around for the person who had spoken, her heart pounding. "Who is it—who are you?" she cried, fear licking at her heart.

A man in a black cassock stood in the front pew, mostly hidden by the shadows. He moved slowly forward, holding his hand out to her.

The flickering light revealed his face, and Joanna saw that it was not only kind, but that it held a simple peace.

She hadn't seen peace like that in any face since Maria's, a blind woman who spun silk into magic in Pesaro's main square. She'd loved Maria for years, but hadn't thought of her for months. Somehow this man brought her immediately to mind, although he struck her more as a spinner of souls.

"Do not be afraid, my child. I intend you no harm. We are both here early this morning on God's work."

She shivered, then forced herself to relax. "Forgive me. I didn't expect anyone else to be here."

"At this hour? Why should you? Not many hold vigil in deserted chapels on the dawning day of Christ's birth. That work is usually done elsewhere and in grander places than this." He drifted slightly closer. "Tell me, why did you come? You are clearly in despair, and perhaps I can help."

"I—I don't even know your name," she said foolishly, as if an introduction at this time was a social necessity.

He laughed softly. "If it matters, please, call me Michael. Brother Michael. May I kneel down next to you?"

"I wish you would," she said, moving over on the cushion that ran below the rail. "I am Joanna."

"Yes . . . I think you are the cousin who has come from Italy. Such beautiful pietàs were created there, not to be rivaled anywhere else. I do so admire the earlier Italian artists. We haven't seen anything like them for sometime now. Soon, I hope—although what might rival the Sistine Chapel I can't quite imagine."

"You—you know Italy—Italian art?"

"Oh, indeed," he said, bestowing a smile on her that radiated warmth. "But then so do you, so let us not waste our time on something whose magnificence we are both in agreement with. Tell me, Joanna, what brings you in tears to this place at this cold and lonely hour before dawn?"

She pressed the palms of both hands hard against her knees. "I do not know if I can explain exactly."

"You mentioned Lydia," he said, folding his fingers together. "You need not explain, as I know all about her unfortunate story. It is her child, Miles—he is the one who gives you the greatest concern?"

"He does. He is so young and already so damaged. I very much want to help him. He doesn't speak anymore, and I can't love him any more than I already do, but even that doesn't seem to be enough."

"Yes. Yes, I do understand why you would be worried. I must tell you that I think he is a very fortunate boy to have found you. Love does work wonders, I have discovered, although I have also discovered that patience is very often the key."

Joanna looked up at him through blurred eyes. "Yes. Patience. I had forgotten about that these last few hours. Thank you for bringing it back to mind. I—I was distraught over some news, and I seem to have forgotten a great many things."

"You have forgotten nothing that you will not remember in the days to come. Be of good faith, Joanna, and believe in your heart that God always listens to those who believe in His wisdom and mercy. He does not fail those who do not fail Him, and even with those who do fail Him, His compassion and forgiveness are endless."

He took hold of her icy hands and held them tight in his. "I must go. This is only one of my ministries that I must see to over the next few days. I give you God's blessing and wish you peace in all your endeavors. And remember, love and patience heal many wounded souls, and not only those of children." He smiled at her, his peaceful eyes filled with such warmth and compassion that she suddenly wanted to cry afresh.

"Thank you," she said, swallowing hard over the tight knot in her throat. "I am so glad you were here."

"As am I, Joanna. I trust one day we will meet again."

Joanna stared after him as he left, his footsteps hushed on the stone floor.

She looked down at her hands and realized that they throbbed with heat, although she couldn't understand why.

Suddenly incredibly tired, she felt as if she could sleep deeply and easily for the first time in years.

As she made her way out, she barely noticed that the breaking dawn had flooded the chapel with light.

* * *

Not particularly rested but shaved, dressed, and with enough coffee in his system to carry him all the way to India, Guy walked into the stable yard.

"A happy Christmas to you, Toomsby," he said, with a quick inclination of his head in the old man's direction. "How does the Vicar look this morning? Ready for a romp?"

"Indeed, my lord," Toomsby replied, giving the gelding's gleaming black coat a last licking with his brush. "The Vicar senses you be leaving again for a time, and he's ready for his last good run. The question is more whether ye be ready, my lord. Ye look a bit done in."

"Don't you worry. The Vicar's carried me through worse a state in his time, and the cold air is bound to clear my head." He fondly ran his hand over the ring of white around the gelding's neck that had inspired his name.

Just about to mount, he noticed a dog cavorting in the corner of the yard. "I say, isn't that Charles Meekford's pup, Boscoe? What's he doing over here? Run away, has he?"

"No, my lord," Toomsby said, checking the girth. "That un's here to stay, he is. He be your son's Christmas present. Didn't ye know? The cap'n is off to India, and the lady governess took Boscoe for the boy. He just be waiting fer his red bow and his new master, and he'll be getting both this morning."

Guy shook his head, stunned. Joanna had chosen a dog for Miles? What a perfect present for a little boy—something he should have thought of himself, a live, playful companion rather than a box of inanimate toys. Miles needed as many reminders of life as he could get, and Joanna knew it.

Every time he thought he understood what she was really made of, she did something that changed his mind. The woman thoroughly confused him, and she also exasperated him, but he couldn't deny that he was drawn to her. Extremely drawn to her, in a fashion that mightily unsettled him. He also couldn't deny that his son was indeed lucky to have her as a governess.

He thrust one booted foot into a stirrup and mounted quickly. "Well, keep Boscoe out of the main house. No point in spoiling him," he said, turning the horse's head toward the stable-yard arch. "Oh, and be sure Bill Willowsby has the carriage ready to leave by two. I want to be in London by nightfall if possible."

"Aye. A Merry Christmas, my lord, and I hope ye find some way to take a piece of joy from it," Toomsby murmured under his breath, as Guy urged the horse into a canter.

Miles padded out of his bedroom, one little fist rubbing his eyes as Joanna gently led him along by the other hand.

"Look, darling," she said, showing him the wrapped box. "Your father has left you a present. Shall we see what is inside?"

He scratched at the bottom of his short gown, then nodded, his face as solemn as ever.

She sat him in his chair, then pushed the mysterious box toward him. He did nothing but look at it, so she leaned over and undid the paper. A simple, slightly battered, red tin box sat before them, giving no clue as to its contents.

"What do you suppose this could be?" She lifted the lid, expecting sweetmeats or some other offering devoid of any emotional context.

Inside, carefully nestled in tissue paper, lay a collection of toy horses, all shapes and sizes and colors, most beautifully crafted from metal and painstakingly painted. Here and there the paint had been worn off by constant handling.

She picked up the card that lay on top and read it aloud.

"*My dear Miles, I do hope you take as many hours of plea-sure from these horses as I once did. My own father added one new horse every year, and so I shall for you. Merry Christmas from your loving Papa.*"

Joanna couldn't help herself. Tears started to her eyes, and she had to swallow hard over the lump that had suddenly appeared in her throat.

Guy de Salis had given his son what was obviously his prized childhood possession. Here she had as good as accused him of being callous and insensitive about his son, and he'd gone to the effort of trying to find a Christmas present that would give his little boy pleasure.

That intention was what had brought him to the nursery, and she had driven him straight away from it with her sharp tongue and ready judgment. She groaned, feeling like an idiot—again.

"Look here, Milo," she said, using the pet name she'd given him. Reaching over, she took out one horse after another, turning each one around so that he could see the colors, the differences. "You can make a wonderful game out of them. Line them up so that they are ready to race each other, or put them together like this," she said, shifting them around, "and you can pretend that they're about to go on a fox hunt, just as your papa likes to do."

She kissed the top of his tousled head. "I think we must better acquaint you with horses so that you can grow up to be just as fine an equestrian as your father is, or at least as fine an equestrian as I think he must be. He certainly has the horseflesh in the stables to give that impression. Soon enough we'll have a pony for you as well, and you can ride it whenever you please. Would you like that?"

Miles reached over and pushed one of the horses with the tip of his finger, but just as quickly dropped his hand.

Joanna's gaze sharpened. Had that been an actual reaction to what she'd been saying? Hard to tell, she decided. Still, she refused to be pessimistic. It was Christmas, and anything might happen. Brother Michael had reminded her of that.

After breakfast, she helped Miles dress in the suit of clothes that she and Margaret had made together, Joanna took him out to the stables. Toomsby was waiting when Joanna arrived with Miles's hand tucked in hers. "Look, Milo, it's Toomsby," she said, bending down to whisper in his ear. "He looks awfully pleased about something, don't you think?"

"There ye be, missus, and a Merry Christmas to ye both. There's something here that's been scratching to say the same to the little lord."

Joanna knelt and lightly drew Miles back against her chest. "Let us have a look at this mysterious something," she said with a grin.

Toomsby pulled at the brim of his cap and vanished through the stable door. A minute later he reappeared, Boscoe leaping at his side, his pink tongue hanging out. "Now, you sit, dog," Toomsby commanded, and Boscoe obediently parked his hindquarters. "See here, Boscoe, this boy be your master now, so you listen to him when he tells you what to do."

Boscoe, who had already spotted Miles, started to wriggle, his golden feathered tail thumping frantically on the ground.

Joanna felt as if it were beating in time to her own pounding heart. She hadn't felt so excited about anything in years.

"Right, dog, go gently now and make yer greetings. Remember the boy's a mite smaller than ye be."

Boscoe jumped up and dashed over to Miles, coming to a screeching halt at his feet. His tongue came out and gave Miles's cheek a swipe, and then he dropped down on all fours and rolled over, exposing his belly.

Joanna felt Miles freeze in her arms as soon as Boscoe leapt forward, and his face recoiled from the enthusiastic washing it received, but he didn't show any other signs of fear.

On the other hand, he didn't display any delight.

Boscoe, realizing that no rubs were forthcoming, jumped back to his feet, then raced in mad circles around and around Miles, returning to face him, front paws lowered, rear end raised, inviting Miles to a game of tag.

Joanna couldn't help laughing, but Miles didn't move.

Boscoe whimpered, then put his head down on his paws and lowered his hindquarters, softly nudging at Miles's knees with his nose.

Joanna, amazed by the animal's acuity, watched in fascination as Boscoe went through his various maneuvers, sizing the child up. She lifted her gaze to Toomsby, only to have her heart give a jolt.

Guy stood a short distance away, leaning against the stable wall, his arms folded across his chest, a funny half smile on his face that looked positively tender as he watched Boscoe play with his son.

As if he felt her watching him, his gaze shifted from Miles and his eyes met hers. He straightened, his arms dropping to his sides.

Despite their recent argument and his thoroughly unreasonable behavior, she couldn't help smiling broadly at him.

"Merry Christmas," she said. "What do you think of Miles's new companion?"

"You couldn't have picked a finer dog," he said, strolling over to where she knelt. "I've been out with him in the fields, and he's as steady as they come."

"I didn't pick him; Toomsby did," she said, looking up at him. "But you're right, he is steady, and I think he will make Miles a wonderful friend, don't you agree, poppet?"

Milo sucked in his lower lip, then touched his finger to the dog's ear and looked up at his father.

Guy shot Joanna a look of surprise, and she smiled and

nodded at him in encouragement, her heart singing at this tiny but unmistakable reaction.

"Here, Miles, like this," Guy said, crouching down and scratching Boscoe's head. "He probably likes to be scratched behind his ears above all things, next to having his belly tickled." He ruffled Miles's hair. "Why don't you try?"

Joanna couldn't help wishing that he'd ruffle her hair too. She also couldn't help noticing Guy's spicy, slightly elusive scent, which now had a faint but lovely touch of horse added to it, or the glossy sheen of his dark hair. A lock had fallen over his forehead, and she had an absurd impulse to reach out and tuck it back behind his ear.

Oh, Joanna, my girl, you are heading for trouble, she thought, feeling a queer jerk in the pit of her stomach, which she interpreted as guilt. How could she have thoughts like that at all for Lydia's husband? It was—it was practically immoral, even if Lydia was dead

He glanced up at her. "I'm sorry. Did you say something?"

She blushed furiously. "I—I said nothing, but I did want to tell you that your present to Miles was wonderful. I think he will get real enjoyment from the horses."

"I hope so. I cannot tell you how many hours of pleasure they gave me. I was thinking earlier when Toomsby told me about the dog that I—well, that I wish I'd thought of it myself. Your intuition is far better than mine when it comes to what Miles needs."

"Nonsense," she said. "I'm just more practiced with him. You only need some practice of your own. In your own time, of course."

He nodded, then stood. "Would you mind? I'd like a private word. Toomsby can keep an eye on Miles and Boscoe, can't you, Toomsby?"

"Aye, my lord," Toomsby said with a grin. "I think I know my way around little boys and dogs."

"That you do," Guy said, holding out a hand to help Joanna up.

She took it, then wished she hadn't, for the feel of her hand in his only made her go all hot and flushed again. She had to stop this, she really did, she told herself firmly.

He led her a short distance away.

"Joanna," he said, rubbing the back of his neck, "I feel I owe you an apology. I lost my temper earlier, and I ought not to have. You . . . you touched a nerve."

"I beg your pardon for that, and I thank you for your apology. I think we were both a bit tired and overwrought."

He shifted his weight from one leg to the other and looked down at the ground. "Regarding what you said, I really do have to go to London. I have urgent business there this evening, and then I have to attend to some other matters, including the opening of Parliament. I won't be back until sometime in March."

"You needn't explain," Joanna said, although she couldn't help feeling a heavy disappointment that he would be away so long.

"Ah," he said with a smile and a raise of his eyebrow, "but I do not wish another tongue-lashing from you about neglecting my son, and I wish to assure you that is the last thing I intend."

"I realize that now," she said, returning his smile. Oh, she really was going to miss him, she thought with a sharp pang. Odd how one night could make all the difference in the way she felt about him. "We will look forward to your homecoming."

He reached out and took her hand in his, his fingers gently wrapping around hers. "Thank you. And thank you for giving Miles such a wonderful Christmas present. He is a lucky boy to have you in his life." His dark eyes held warmth and something else she couldn't define, but the intensity of his gaze made her knees turn to jelly.

Joanna couldn't help the shiver that ran down her spine. She forced herself to withdraw her hand from his, knowing that if she kept it there any longer he would feel the trembling of her fingers. "I am the one who is lucky," she said. "Safe journey, Guy, and Godspeed."

"Merry Christmas, Joanna," he replied softly. "Oh—I almost forgot. This is for you. I was going to bring it up to the nursery before I left, but since you are here I might as well give it to you now." He reached into his breast pocket and withdrew a small, slim package wrapped in the same colored paper as Milo's box had been. "Consider it my personal act of contrition. It is a small thing, but I hope you enjoy it."

He awkwardly placed it in her hands. Then he smiled one last time and quickly turned and walked away as if he didn't want to see her open it.

Astonished, Joanna watched him until he rounded the corner of the stables and disappeared from view. Sighing heavily at the thought that it would be spring before she saw him again, she looked down at the package, unable to imagine what it might be.

Her shaking fingers carefully opened the wrapping, and she drew in a quick, startled breath. In her hands lay a beautifully bound edition of Donne's poems. Guy had marked a page, and she turned to it and read.

> *Wilt thou forgive that sin, where I begun,*
> *Which is my sin, though it were done before?*
> *Wilt thou forgive those sins through which I run*
> *And do them still, though still I do deplore?*
> *When thou hast done, thou hast not done,*
> *For I have more.*

Her eyes stung with tears as she took in the meaning of his gift. He was apologizing not just for his outburst last night, but for their awkward beginning. Swallowing hard, she wiped a hand over her eyes, knowing she was equally to blame, but appreciating his generosity.

Guy de Salis was becoming more of an enigma by the moment.

"Merry Christmas, Guy," she whispered, then turned and walked back to Miles.

10

*S*omething tugged at her arm and Joanna came instantly awake.

Miles stood at the side of the bed, his hand gripping the flannel sleeve of her nightdress.

Every sense came alert. "Milo—my darling, what is it?" she said, shifting herself to a sitting position and placing her hand over his smaller one. "Did you have a bad dream?"

He shook his head and tugged even harder, urging her to come with him.

She didn't hesitate. Throwing the covers off, she reached for her woolen shawl and wrapped it over her shoulders.

"Show me," she said.

He hauled her through the dark nursery to the window seat.

Please, God—not the window again. I thought he'd finally given up watching for his mother.

Miles climbed up onto the cushion, but instead of staring out, he pointed down.

She looked but saw nothing. "I'm sorry, poppet," she said, her heart breaking for him. "What is it that I'm meant to be looking for?"

He kept pointing with one hand.

She looked again. And then she heard what Milo intended for her to hear.

A long plaintive whimper, followed by another.

Joanna leaned forward, peering down at the lawn.

Boscoe emerged from the shadow of an oak tree, pacing, his tail tucked between his legs, his head down. He lifted his head again and howled, directing his cry straight toward the nursery window.

Miles's hand tightened on Joanna's arm, and she tilted her head down and cupped his little square chin. He gazed up at her with an expression just as pleading as Boscoe's and just as unmistakable in intention.

"Oh . . . oh, Milo," she said, her heart constricting painfully in her chest. "How on earth did Boscoe get out of the stables? Toomsby made him such a nice place, and your father did say that Boscoe couldn't come into the house. . . ."

Her resolve fell apart, the pleading look on Milo's face ripping straight into her heart. Hadn't she been praying to see a reaction from him? Well, this was a reaction if she'd ever seen one, and the best possible sort.

To the devil with his father's wishes. He wasn't around to know any different, was he?

"Wait here," she said, flying into Milo's bedroom and fetching his shoes and coat. "We'll go right down and bring him in, poppet. Boscoe shouldn't be out in the cold, not when he so obviously has made up his mind that he belongs with you all the time and not just part of it."

As she helped him don his coat and shoes, Joanna wanted to cry with happiness. This was it, the first real sign of Miles opening up. He had tolerated Boscoe from the day of their first walk, but hadn't paid any more attention to the dog's frolics than he had to the magnificent pair of swans that Toomsby had guided them to. She'd begun to wonder if Miles really noticed Boscoe at all, even though they spent a good portion of the day together outside.

She didn't bother to walk him down to the kitchen door.

Instead, she scooped him up in her arms and planted him on her hip, stopping only to take a candle from the nursery mantelpiece.

Half-running, half-walking, she made their way all the way down to the deserted kitchen. Lowering Miles to the ground, she grabbed her cloak off the hook next to the door.

"Now, Milo," she said, giving him the gentlest push out the door, following along behind him. "Call him to you."

She knew she was taking the most tremendous chance, but if Miles cared enough for Boscoe to come and fetch Joanna in the middle of the night, then he might care enough for Boscoe to finally break his silence.

She waited. Miles stood, finger in mouth, his feet shifting back and forth.

And well they should, she thought, the frigid wind biting through her till her limbs threatened to turn to ice.

"Milo, Boscoe's not in the warm stable now," she said, rubbing her arms but leaving him entirely alone to feel the chill of the elements. "If you are cold with your nice thick winter coat wrapped around you, think about how cold he must be with only his fur to protect him. He is not accustomed to being outside late at night, so I can only imagine that he wanted to be with you so badly that he escaped from his cozy bed to let you know how lonely he is without you."

Miles glanced up at her, a strange, unreadable expression on his face that sharply reminded Joanna of his father.

And then Miles looked away and walked two paces forward.

"Boscoe! Boscoe, come!"

His high, clear voice, surprisingly loud, split the air.

Joanna's breath vanished completely. She had to fight to inhale. Every instinct in her propelled her forward to embrace him in his victory, but some greater wisdom held her back.

She concentrated on breathing, watching condensed clouds of air drift up from her mouth in place of words.

They reminded her of clouds. Heaven's clouds, little puffs ascending upward and upward, all unspoken intent, arriving in the hands of the Almighty. They reminded her of Brother Michael's words: *"Love and patience heal many wounded souls. . . ."*

Her arms stayed steady by her sides, her feet planted firm as Miles took another step and then another.

"Boscoe. Come, boy, come!"

Tears silently slid down her cheeks.

What occupied her full attention was the sight of Boscoe barreling around the corner of the west wing and hurling himself straight at Miles, whose arms had spread wide to receive him.

It didn't matter to either that Boscoe's weight knocked Miles to the ground. Miles's arms wrapped around the dog in a tight embrace, and Boscoe somehow rolled Miles back over, licking his face as if he were a load of laundry in need of a good wash.

The giggles that came from Miles as he tried to fend off the affectionate onslaught left Joanna shaking with a combination of sobs and laughter.

"Come, poppet," she said as soon as she'd regained control of her emotions. "Let's get you both inside. Up, Boscoe, there's a good boy."

Boscoe jumped to his feet and loped along behind her, staying right by Milo's side.

Joanna couldn't stop smiling.

Once she had Milo tucked up in bed, she rummaged about in a chest for a blanket and spread it out on the rug next to the bed. Milo watched every move.

"Here's a bed for Boscoe, poppet. If you should wake in the night, you'll know he's right there to protect you from anything—bad dreams, anything at all. I'm right next door as always, and you now you can come and fetch me just as you did tonight, clever boy, but now you have a first guard—like a sentry in the army."

Milo nodded. He rolled over and dangled his hand toward Boscoe, who had already made himself at home on his new bed. The dog lapped his fingers, then sighed and put his head on his paws. He raised his eyes and shot Joanna a look from under his brow as if to say, "You see? I knew where I belonged. It took *you* long enough to work it out, silly woman."

Joanna grinned, thinking of Bunch. Just what she would have said too.

"You will have to be up and dressed early to take Boscoe out, Milo—unlike us, he doesn't have the luxury of a chamber pot or a water closet."

Milo nodded again, but Joanna could have sworn she saw the faintest semblance of a smile as he turned his head into the pillow.

"Good night," she said, leaning over and giving Milo a kiss on his temple. "Sleep well, both of you."

She blew out the candle and softly closed the door.

Before she went to sleep, she dropped to her knees and gave her fervent thanks up to God and His angels for sending her a miracle, and another to Brother Michael for reminding her to be patient.

House of Lords, London
February 15, 1819

"Guy? Guy—wake up, man." Randolph Cato, Earl of Trevelyan, shoved his elbow into Guy's ribs. "You are due to speak next."

Startled out of his thoughts, Guy came to with a jolt. He hadn't been sleeping—not anything close to it. As usual his mind had been preoccupied with thoughts of Wakefield and how Joanna di Capponi and his son were getting on.

He brought his focus to bear, cleared his throat, then stood and began his speech, knowing perfectly damned well he was making a hash of it.

Randolph let him know all about it six hours later when they dined together at White's.

"Look here, Guy," he said, leaning back and wiping his mouth with his napkin. "I think you'd better come clean and tell me what is on your mind. Something has been plaguing you since you came up to London, and I know it cannot still be having to buy back those damned emeralds."

Guy fiddled with his piece of turbot, pushing it about his plate with his fork. He didn't have much of an appetite; he hadn't really had much of one since he'd arrived in London nearly two months ago. "There's nothing to tell," he said. "I made a cock-up today, that's all."

"You didn't make a cock-up; you just weren't your usual brilliantly eloquent self, something I find surprising since you've been diligently preparing your speech for the last month. Look, man, you need say nothing—I will not press you further. I am merely concerned."

Guy shrugged. "My mind is on other things, I suppose. Miles is not in the best of health."

"Good Lord, why did you not saying something earlier? You know how fond I am of my godson. What is it—not his lungs, I hope?"

"His lungs are fine. I wish he would put them to better use," Guy replied, putting his knife and fork down. "He doesn't speak, Ran. He doesn't speak, he doesn't play, he doesn't do much of anything except stare out of windows day and night, and there's not a damned thing I or anyone else can seem to do about it."

Randolph stared at him in horror. "Do you mean he's— he's gone—"

"No, he's not insane, if that's what you're thinking. He's just . . . removed. Silent. Distant. I think the loss of his mother must have been too much of a shock for him, and he hasn't recovered from it. You know how she was with him."

"Oh, yes. The poor boy was the victim of her constant hysteria—I don't see why he would miss that."

"Mmm," Guy said, turning his glass around and around. "I always thought he squirmed when she smothered him with overweening attention, but I must have been wrong. The bond was obviously as strong as she claimed."

"Begging your pardon, but your wife claimed a great many things that were not true."

Guy inclined his head in acknowledgment. "Still, I can think of no other cause for such withdrawn behavior—I did hire a nanny after Lydia's death, whom I recently discovered to have been a very poor choice, indeed a distressingly unsympathetic woman given to barbaric practices. It was during her tenure that Miles began this silence." He ran the edge of his thumb under his chin. "I cannot help but wonder if the abuse was even worse than I realized."

"Who looks after Miles now?" Ran asked, gesturing to the waiter to pour more wine.

Guy ran his hand over his face, not knowing how he could possibly present this part of the story in any sort of reasonable fashion.

"Guy?" Ran regarded him quizzically. "Why are you suddenly looking bilious?"

"Because you will not believe what I have to tell you, and I don't know how to make it believable." He ran his tongue over his lower lip, his mouth suddenly dry. "Do you remember the stories about my wife's distant cousin, a certain Joanna Carew, who was drummed out of England for scandalous behavior, landed in Italy, and married the Conte di Capponi?"

"Oh, yes . . . I do recall some talk—wasn't she the latter-day Borgia who was supposed to have poisoned him or some such thing?"

"She was," he said uncomfortably, unable to believe any longer that there was any truth in it.

"Remind me," Ran said, regarding him curiously.

Guy wished he'd never brought the subject up, but he was stuck now. He steeled himself and tried to look blasé. "The story circulated all over England what—three years ago," he said, remembering well all the fuss and Lydia's hysterical reaction. "As the story goes, Joanna married Cosmo di Capponi for the usual reasons and decided to dispose of him some months later for the same, only no proof ever surfaced. Lydia was mortified to be associated with her, naturally."

"Naturally," Ran said dryly, paring the rind off his cheese. "You're not trying to tell me that this cousin has anything to do with Miles, are you?"

"She's his new nanny—or governess, as she prefers to be called." Guy waited for the outcry. He had no idea how he was going to explain Joanna to his closest friend, when he couldn't even explain her to himself.

Randolph's jaw dropped. "You cannot be serious. Please, Guy, do not fun over such a thing."

"I tell you the absolute truth," Guy said, taking a very large sip of wine.

He quickly ran through the entire story, from the time Joanna had manifested on his bookshelf to the moment he had left the stables, his composure in ruins.

"So you see why I am slightly distracted," he said, finishing up the sorry story. He looked away.

Not a sound emanated from across the table. Randolph sat with golden head bent and meal forgotten, his forefingers forming a steeple in front of him. Unlike Malcolm, Randolph's ruminations could take some time but almost always resulted in a useful outcome.

Randolph finally lifted his head. "Guy," he said, one finger scratching at the corner of his mouth, "I have always known you to be a person of keen instincts and good judgment from the time we were young boys—in fact, the only time I have ever seen either go astray was when you married Lydia, but there were mitigating circumstances."

"Thank you for excusing me in that instance, but I take full responsibility," Guy said. "As I do in this as well."

Ran regarded his friend thoughtfully, his blue eyes keen. "Exactly. You would never have left Miles in the hands of someone you did not trust, not after what you just told me of his tenuous emotional condition."

"No. I wouldn't. That's not my point," Guy said in frustration. "Of course I trust her with Miles."

"Then what is your point?" Ran asked calmly.

Guy plowed his hands through his hair, struggling to erase the image of Joanna in her nightdress, tears streaming down her face as she sat in a heap on the floor, doubled over in hilarity, and then only minutes later doubled over in grief when he'd told her the manner of Lydia's death.

God, he'd been haunted by those memories ever since, the feel of her soft body in his arms as he'd tried to comfort her, the roselike smell of the soft hair that drifted against his cheek, the way she'd howled like a child, sobbing and gulping with complete disregard for her swollen eyes and streaming nose. She'd shown such a sweetness then, such a vulnerability . . . and later, when he'd watched her with Miles and the dog she'd given him, grinning as if it were Christmas ten times over and she was the one who'd been given the treat. And when he'd said his farewell to her, holding her hand in his, he'd found it very difficult to leave at all. He wondered what she'd made of his present. She was far too bright to have missed the point of Donne's poem, but he could only hope she'd managed to find forgiveness in her heart for his boorish behavior.

He drew in a deep breath. "My point is that I don't trust myself," he finally said. "My—my feelings have become engaged in a way I never expected."

"Ah. I think I begin to see," Ran said. "In which case my

suggestion to you is to go immediately back to Wakefield. You're doing no one any good here in the state you're in. You need to be with your ailing son for both your sakes, and you need to work out just what your feelings for Joanna di Capponi really are." He drained his glass. "The one thing you cannot do is stay here in town and carry on tormenting yourself or avoiding the issue."

Guy looked down at the table, mulling over Ran's words. Ran was right. He was wasting his time here in London when he really needed to be at Wakefield with Miles. With Miles *and* Joanna. By God, he missed them acutely, both of them. It was little wonder that he hadn't been able to concentrate.

He stood, filled with sudden resolve. "You are absolutely correct," he said, throwing his napkin down on the table. "I shall leave in the morning." The truth was that he could hardly wait to get home.

"That is the Guy de Salis I know," Ran said, clapping him on the back. "Firm and decisive. I will make your excuses for you."

"Thank you, my friend. I shall be in touch."

"I am counting on it," Ran said, leading the way out of the dining room.

Guy followed, already planning his return.

11

"Milo, what a fine picture you've made," Joanna exclaimed, picking up the piece of paper he pushed over to her. She examined it intently, admiring his complete disregard for form of any kind, but far more important, looking for clues to the state of the heart she was convinced had truly started to heal.

For well over a month now, Miles had been producing page after page of these wild drawings, his little hand clutching the brush as he furiously lashed paint all over. She and Margaret spent a good deal of time cleaning up after Milo was finished expressing himself.

The afternoon after his enormous breakthrough with Boscoe, he'd watched silently as she sat down at the table, not even offering him a chair or paper and colors as she had in the past.

This time she'd focused on her own thoughts and began to lash watercolors all over, big swirls of color, overlapping them, moving them in and out, over and around, thinking only of feelings—how did relief look on paper? Joy? Anger? The more she painted, the more she enjoyed herself.

She'd never let herself release in such a way, always before concentrating on method, on a fixed image, the proper balance of color and spatial proportion.

She kept on and on until Miles finally reached over and tugged at the pad, pulling it away. With no more than a smile, she handed him the brush and moved the paints toward him.

He hadn't stopped painting since, eager every day to grab the pad and paints as soon as he'd finished his breakfast.

Each picture, carefully examined, told her something, and she was now able to see a story emerging of what had been hiding inside Milo's troubled heart. That story might have broken her own heart if she hadn't been so happy to see him finally find a way to tell it.

A silent art fit for a silent child, she thought.

She was right about that. Milo's silent world thundered.

Joanna could only begin to imagine the anger he'd been holding inside and thanked God that he finally was beginning to release some of it.

Around the second week he also started to speak in little bursts.

The first time, Joanna had been startled out of a daydream about planting white and shell-pink roses along her villa steps.

"Jojo? More paper, please? It is all gone."

She sat upright, startled by the unexpected voice. Miles gazed up at her expectantly.

"More—more paper?" she stammered. "Yes. Yes, just wait a moment, poppet. I have a fresh pad in my bedroom."

Margaret looked up from cleaning the grate and met Joanna's eyes with an equally astonished expression. Joanna dashed out of the room, heart racing. Save for a few words directed at Boscoe, Miles had remained silent to the rest of the world.

Until now. Until now, Joanna thought, digging in her cupboard for the new pad. She had to stop her hands from shaking and her breath from racing before she took it next door into the nursery.

Miles smiled sweetly as she laid it before him. "Thank you, Jojo," he said, resuming his painting.

Margaret dropped onto the sofa, silently mopping at her streaming eyes, while Joanna went to the window and buried her face in her hands, trying very, very hard not to cry.

Only Boscoe, lying under the table in his usual position—rear toward Miles and nose poking out at the rest of the nursery—looked as unperturbed as Milo.

Even now, three weeks later, Joanna had to refrain from obvious reaction when he did anything she considered a milestone. If she'd learned anything, she'd learned that quiet praise and gentle attention worked wonders—he habitually shied away from anything that hinted of strong emotion.

Today, as she studied the piece of paper he'd just given her so deliberately, she wondered if he wasn't being as articulate as he could be, using the power of his hand instead of his voice.

"Such a good job, poppet," she said, admiring the blue and green swirls he'd made. "Good heavens!" She looked again, her heart quickening with excitement. "Milo, would this happen to be your pony?" she said, closely examining a fat brown blob that appeared to have four legs and two small upward projections that might be interpreted as ears.

He grinned and nodded vigorously. "Pumpkin," he said. "Pumpkin in the paddock, waiting for me."

"Of course it is Pumpkin. I don't know why I didn't see it at once. You did such a fine job." She wanted to jump up and crow with delight: This was the first time Miles had drawn anything lifelike. But she said only, "Let's put the paints away and clean up, shall we, and then we can go down to the paddock and you can ride Pumpkin. Toomsby will have him waiting for you, just as you drew it."

Miles speedily complied. He never could get down to the stables fast enough. Riding Pumpkin had become the highlight of his day, and Joanna took no little pleasure from it herself.

Oh, how she wished she could tell Guy how well Miles

was coming along—or better yet, show him. She squeezed her eyes shut.

Guy. Ever-present in her thoughts, she found it impossible to make him go away, even in her sleep, where he constantly invaded her troubled dreams.

Why couldn't she control herself any better? She'd never been obsessed by anything other than painting, certainly not a man. Indeed, the only other male who had ever occupied her thoughts so completely was Miles, and he *would* have to be Guy's son. One led to the other and straight back again so that the two were inextricably entwined in her mind.

She put the paints back into their special box and carefully gathered the paintings Miles had made that afternoon, all the while fighting off the image of Guy on the window seat Christmas morning, smiling down at her, not looking the least bit forbidding—anything but.

His hair had been rumpled, his shirt open at the collar. She'd belatedly realized that the handkerchief he'd handed her had in fact been his neckcloth. No wonder it had smelled so delicious. And his smile—she'd never forget how his eyes had lightened and the creases on the sides of his mouth deepened when he'd grinned.

She'd seen him smile a few times now, the most endearing when he'd watched his son with Boscoe. There had been such tenderness in his face, such a yearning that her heart squeezed tight even now, remembering it.

Almost eight weeks, and she couldn't help but miss him. The problem was that she didn't know what she was going to do when he did return. Somehow she would have to find a way to fend him off, for fend him off she must. She might not be able to help her unbridled thoughts of the feel of Guy's hard chest against her back, of the way his hands had moved over her arms, of how his warm breath had stirred at the hair just behind her ear, but she could surely manage to keep him well away from her.

She had no choice—her loyalty to Lydia had to be paramount, and her own feelings couldn't matter. She only wished that her chest didn't ache so much, that her belly didn't throb with a mysterious longing she'd never felt before and didn't know what to do with.

Joanna furiously wiped away a tear that had leaked from the corner of her eye, then dampened a cloth and started to wipe the table down with deliberate swipes, wishing she might erase Guy de Salis as easily as she could Miles's paint.

Toomsby's face split into a broad smile when Miles tore down into the stable yard. "There ye be, young man. Did ye remember Pumpkin's sweetie, then?"

Miles nodded and opened his hand, where a sugar cube lay inside. "Here!"

"Then let's be going out into yonder pasture. Pumpkin'll be wondering where ye be."

Miles took off, running as fast as his little legs would take him, Boscoe at his side.

Joanna and Toomsby walked behind, and Joanna told him all about the picture Miles had painted.

"Aye, he be coming right along, and not jest with his drawings and his speaking," Toomsby said. "He's got the way of it with the horses, like his father do."

"He plays at horses half the day," Joanna said. "I cannot express how much Pumpkin has done for him—and you, Toomsby. He worships you, you know."

"Mmph. Better he worship his father."

"That's not easy to do when his father's never here," Joanna said, stepping over a puddle. "Toomsby . . . has Lord Greaves always spent so much time away?"

"Well, not allus, at least not until he went away to fight. We didn't see hide nor hair of him for three years, and then he married. His wife didn't much care for this place—she liked city life. But then ye'll be knowing about that, being family and all."

"I know she wasn't happy here," Joanna said, "but I don't know how much of that had to do with Wakefield. I think—well, to be honest, Toomsby, I think that she and Lord Greaves were mismatched."

Toomsby scratched his cheek and gave her a sidelong glance. "Jest like pairing the horses, missus, ye can't have one with a steady temperament and hitch it next to one that's skittish. The next thing ye know, they both go crazy and pull the carriage right over."

Joanna had to smile at his analogy. Toomsby always managed to bring everything back to horses. "I see your point. Lydia—her ladyship, that is—was always high-spirited, but Lord Greaves isn't exactly mild-tempered, you know."

"Begging your pardon, missus, but his lordship's nerves was allus steady as the day is long until he came back from the war."

"What?" she said, her step slowing. "What do you mean?"

"I don't be knowing much about it, but he was mentioned in those 'spatches." He nodded proudly. "Mr. Ambrose up at the house told me about that—his lordship was a captain in the Grenadier Guards, and they thought highly of him, 'specially after what he did."

"And what was that?" she asked curiously.

"I don't rightly know the details. All I *do* know is he weren't quite himself when he came home. I can't say more, 'cause he wouldn't talk about it to no one. And then that wife o' his gave him nothing but a heap of trouble when what he was needing was some peace and quiet and time with his horses."

Joanna came to a full stop. "You're saying that my cousin made Lord Greaves unhappy?"

Toomsby tugged the brim of his cap. "Begging your pardon again, missus, but that be the truth, just as it's the truth that his lordship's wound might have healed nicely on the outside, but it left a big hole on the inside, to my way of thinking."

"He was—he was wounded in the leg, wasn't he?"

Toomsby nodded vigorously, warming to his story. "They said he was a hero right and proper, missus—I was that proud of my boy. Allus did have an unflinching way about him—he'd take any fence put in front o' him, providing he weren't putting the horse at risk." He pulled off his cap and scratched his head. "They say he saved many a man in Spain." He leaned toward her in a confidential fashion. "That Mr. Lambkin, he did tell me that he was one o' them, that his lordship put his life on the line for all his men."

Joanna pressed her hand against her mouth, suddenly feeling ill. How could she have misjudged Guy so badly? If all of what Toomsby had just told her was true, then Guy couldn't possibly be the selfish, self-indulgent monster Lydia had named him. A man willing to put his life on the line for his men was anything but selfish. She'd heard some of the stories about the conditions in the Peninsula, knew that life had been a misery to soldiers and officers alike and that the fighting had been vicious.

She trusted Toomsby; if he said that Guy had been wounded in spirit as well as in body when he returned from the war, she believed him.

In which case Lydia would have been the worst possible person for Guy to marry. As much as she loved her cousin, Joanna knew full well that Lydia had been spoiled and indulged all of her life; she would have had no way of knowing how to deal with a man as complex as Guy, who had obviously gone through some awful experience. No wonder Lydia had been so unhappy. . . .

Joanna felt as if a huge weight had been lifted off her

shoulders, that she finally had at least the beginning of a reasonable explanation for Guy and Lydia's troubled marriage.

"Thank you, oh, thank you, dear Toomsby," she said, taking him by both arms and planting a kiss on his astonished face. "You have no idea what insight you've just given me!"

He cleared his throat and shoved both hands onto his cap. "Glad to be of help, missus," he said gruffly. "Now, what be that lad doing, climbing all over the fence there? He'll break his noggin sure enough if he don't take some care."

Joanna, who had forgotten entirely about Miles, let out a cry of alarm and tore toward the paddock, shouting at him to stop dangling off the top of the railing.

Only later did she reflect that Miles had been behaving like a perfectly ordinary little boy.

Guy stood outside Wakefield's front door, his head tilted back as he took in some deep breaths of clean country air. God, but it felt good to be back home. He realized anew how much he'd missed not just Wakefield, but Miles and Joanna.

The first thing he planned on doing was going for a brisk ride. Then he would track down Joanna in the nursery and question her about his son.

If he was going to be a proper father, the only way to proceed with matters was to learn every detail possible about his child, which meant learning his schedule, his reading material, his inclinations and disinclinations. He didn't even know if the boy ate his vegetables.

Well, Joanna could tell him all that and more. Joanna . . .

He couldn't help the tightening in his chest at the thought that he'd be seeing her so soon now. She'd have her hair up, of course, although he much preferred it falling in loose waves about her shoulders and back. She'd probably be wearing that ghastly gray dress she chose as her governess costume.

He wondered if she'd be at all pleased to see him or whether she'd regard him with that singularly disagreeable expression she assumed when she deliberately wanted to annoy him.

God, he was happy to be home.

Walking down to the stables, he looked around as if he was seeing Wakefield for the first time in years. He hadn't realized just how much he'd missed it.

February—a time of such dormancy but of such promise as well. In another month kingcups and lady's-smock would be out, a lovely spread of yellow and pink amongst the green of field and riverbank, the blue of speedwell a nice punctuation. He'd already spotted celandine along the verge of the road, its brave yellow petals a sure harbinger of the coming spring. He imagined the snowdrops were already in bloom in the woods. He'd have to walk out and see.

Odd, he thought, that he hadn't noticed flowers for so long, had barely even thought of them, when once they had given him such pleasure. Once the seasons had held importance to him, his life revolving not around the social calendar but the natural rhythms of life.

A faint sound of laughter rippled over from the left field, catching his attention. Laughter was not commonly heard at Wakefield, or at least it hadn't been in years. Curious, he diverted his route.

He stopped dead in his tracks as he absorbed the unbelievable sight of Miles sitting bareback atop a fat Shetland pony, Joanna running in front of it, a lead rein in her hand, Boscoe loping alongside.

Miles's fingers clutched the pony's thick mane, high peals ringing through the crisp air as he bounced up and down on the pony's back, looking as if he didn't have a care in the world and never had.

"Faster, Jojo," he cried. "Faster!"

Guy didn't know what stunned him more—the sight of his son on a pony, looking and laughing like a perfectly normal, happy child—*speaking* like a normal child—or the astonishing sight of Joanna, hair caught back in a loose ribbon, cheeks flushed, tearing about the paddock with her dress bunched up in one hand and her bonnet dangling behind her as if she were a schoolgirl.

He had the oddest sensation that he'd just walked into someone else's life, for he surely didn't recognize it as his own.

"Papa! Papa, look what I can do!"

Guy hardly believed his ears. Miles had actually called to him. *Papa* . . . it seemed a lifetime since he'd heard Miles call him by name, and the sound felt like a balm to his heart.

"I see, Miles," he said, trying desperately to steady his voice. "You are riding all by yourself, and doing a fine job of it. How proud I am!"

Joanna shot around at the sound of his voice, the color draining from her cheeks. "Lord Greaves," she said, her hand slipping to her throat. "You've—you've come home."

"I have," he replied, moving toward her, not sure whether she was pleased or dismayed, but not really caring. He was so damned happy to see her that nothing else mattered. "I confess that I am astonished by what I see before me. Miles has come a long way in seven weeks."

Her face brightened. "Oh, he has, in so many ways. I've been longing to tell you everything—" She stopped abruptly. "That is, I knew you'd be pleased by his progress. But I thought you were away until late March."

"I was meant to be, but I decided I ought to be here instead." He cleared his throat, feeling absurdly awkward. "Joanna . . . I do not know what to say. I came back expecting to find Miles much the same as when I left, and he is— he is a different child entirely."

"Not entirely," she said gravely. "We still have work ahead of us. He's begun to speak, chatter even, but on occasion he will retreat into silence. He does have other eloquent ways of expressing himself, especially with watercolors, and through his drawings I have discovered so much about him and what he has been keeping bottled up inside."

"I would like to hear all of it. Perhaps you would dine with me tonight? We have much to catch up on."

Joanna looked as if he'd just asked her to swim with the crocodiles. "Dinner?" she said, staring at him, her beautifully expressive eyes filling with dismay. He watched with fascination as they suddenly turned from green to a bluish-gray.

"Yes. Dinner. You do eat dinner, do you not?"

"Naturally I eat dinner," she said with a twitch of her rosy lips. "However, I am accustomed to eating it in my sitting room. Alone."

He smiled, discovering that he'd missed her pointed barbs. "In other words, you prefer the pleasure of your own company to that of mine."

"I didn't say that," she said, looking thoroughly rattled. "I just meant—oh, never mind. I would be delighted to have dinner with you, my lord."

"Guy," he said. "My digestion suffers when I have to swallow stiff formality along with my food."

A fleeting smile lit up Joanna's face and he remembered anew her quick sense of humor, which made her so different from Lydia. "I would not be so cruel as to deliberately give you indigestion," she said. "Name the time and place, and I shall be there."

"You make dinner sound like a duel. Next you'll be asking me to choose my weapon and name my seconds."

"A knife and fork will do," she said with a broad smile. "As for seconds, you will have to make do with whatever Emile presents."

"In that case, the drawing room at seven," he said, sweeping her a bow, then walking past her into the paddock to meet Pumpkin and praise his son.

Yes, it was definitely good to be home.

12

Joanna, dressed only in her shift, scrambled through the dresses in her wardrobe, her fingers clumsy with nerves, her brain spinning so wildly that she couldn't keep her thoughts in any order at all. Dinner—what on earth was she going to wear for dinner?

She still hadn't recovered from the shock of seeing Guy standing outside the paddock, looking as if he'd never left. Could he *never* give a person due warning? This habit he had of appearing and disappearing made her stomach lurch every time. And he talked about formality giving him indigestion? He had no idea what his mere presence did to her insides.

She'd nearly keeled over at the sight of him. But, oh, how wonderful it was to see his pleased expression of surprise, the way his eyes had lit up when he'd seen his son's accomplishment.

The look on his face alone was worth the hard work of the last three months, not that she needed any more reward than Miles's slow but steady recovery.

Joanna reluctantly pulled out a silk evening dress, the most serviceable she owned, and held it up to the light. The net frock that covered the blue-green satin slip was still in good condition, although the dress itself wasn't particularly à la mode, having been made for her during her marriage to Cosmo.

A sharp pain tugged at her heart, for the dress reminded her far too acutely of those happy months, of Cosmo himself.

She could still hear the faint echo of his words as he'd admired her in it, his voice so soft and tender.

Come, bella, *turn around and let me admire you. How did I ever manage to capture such a beauty for my very own? Ah,*

Joanna, how happy you make me—any man would be proud to call you his own, and I am the most fortunate man on earth to have that honor. . . .

She bit her lip, willing back tears. Cosmo, such a gentle, good man. She ran her hand over the fine net of the dress, as if in touching it she might somehow touch him.

Cosmo's image formed unerringly in her mind, the thick white head of hair, the hawked nose, the heavy-lidded eyes, sharp with intelligence and warm with compassion. He'd been so wise and strong, always there for her, yet so understanding about her periodic need for solitude. His had been such a calm, undemanding presence.

He couldn't have been more unlike Guy de Salis.

A light scratch came at the door and it cracked open, Wendy's face appearing.

"I heard the news that you're dining with his lordship and thought you might need a bit of help dressing for the occasion," she said, marching into the room, both eyebrows lifting. "What's all this about, then?"

Joanna grinned. Wendy never minced words. Little wonder she was Joanna's favorite chambermaid. "Put away your salacious thoughts, Wendy, for there's nothing to tell. His lordship simply wants to know about Miles's progress, and dinner seemed the best time to go over it."

"That may be, but something tells me that there's a bit more to it than that from the look on your face, your ladyship."

"What's the matter with my face?" Joanna asked, hoping against hope that her nerves weren't showing. The last thing she needed was to have Wendy or anyone else read something into this dinner that wasn't really there.

"Nothing that wasn't wrong with it before," Wendy said smugly. "Just a bit more of it. Ooh, is that the dress you're wearing? Now that's a pretty thing indeed." She fingered the silk. "Italian, is it?"

"Yes," Joanna said, laying it on the bed.

"Mmm. A far sight better-looking than those other things you wear all the time. I'll bet my month's wages that his lordship's eyes pop out at the sight of you in that. Ooh, look at that neckline. That won't be leaving much to the imagination."

"Wendy, please," Joanna said in exasperation, digging in the chest of drawers for a pair of silk stockings. "If you really want to help me, then you might help me fasten my stays."

"Oh, if you're going back to wearing stays, you must be serious," Wendy said with a wink.

Joanna shook her head. "How, may I ask, am I to wear stays day in and day out without someone to lace me into the horrid thing? When Mrs. Fitzwilliams departed, so did the stays."

"Lift up then," Wendy said, pulling the corset off the bed where Joanna had tossed it. She wrapped it around Joanna's front and pulled hard at the laces at her back.

"Oof," Joanna said, wincing as the loathed corset tightened around her waist till she could hardly breathe. "That's enough, Wendy! I'll be fainting into my plate if you pull it any tighter."

"I know someone else who'll be fainting into his plate if I pull any tighter," Wendy said with a wicked snicker, but she loosened the stays slightly. "There you are."

She helped Joanna into her dress—a good thing, since Joanna could barely raise her arms over her head. "Very nice. For once you look like a contessa," Wendy said, standing back and admiring her. "Now let's get on with making something of your hair."

"And what would you know about doing hair?" Joanna said, taking a few shallow breaths.

"Nothing at all," Wendy replied with a self-satisfied smirk. "If you'll just wait two ticks, I happen to know someone who does." She went to the door and stuck her head out. "Shelley," she bellowed, "we're ready for you now."

Shelley? Joanna couldn't imagine what Shelley would know about dressing hair; she spent most of her time tending to the vast amounts of silver and brass about the place. Was she planning on using polish to shape Joanna's hair?

Not five seconds later Shelley appeared with a small case in hand that looked nothing like her housemaid's box. "Evening, your ladyship," she said cheerfully. "Let's have a look at you, then. Oh, my—aren't you a fine sight? Right, let's get to your coiffure. Best sit down at the dressing table or I'll have to fetch a ladder."

Joanna obediently sat, wondering what on earth was to become of her hair, but reluctant to hurt Shelley's feelings. She reckoned she could always undo the damage after the fact.

In truth, she couldn't help but be touched by Wendy and Shelley's concern over her appearance. It had been a long time since anyone fussed over her, and although she'd become comfortable with the staff, regarding them as part of an extended family, she hadn't realized that they were prepared to treat her with such relaxed affection.

The realization made her want to cry.

Shelley's fingers deftly arranged and rearranged Joanna's hair, while Wendy let fly a stream of unceasing commentary about what Shelley should and should not be doing. Shelley responded in kind, the two of them sounding like two sisters having a good-natured squabble.

Joanna, watching all of this in the looking glass, sighed with contentment, her nerves temporarily forgotten. Being part of a family meant more to her than anything in the world, and she had to count her blessings that in some small way she'd found one here in the staff at Wakefield. Between Toomsby, Wendy, Shelley, Dickson, Margaret, and Margaret's husband, Bill, down at the stables, who always had a kind word for her and a piece of peppermint candy for Miles, she really couldn't be more fortunate.

She felt nearly as much at home here as she did at her

little villa, where the minimal staff treated her like a child in need of guiding and nurturing. The way Wendy and Shelley were carrying on right now, she might never have left Pesaro, she thought with an inward smile.

"That's it then," Shelley declared. "I'm as finished as I'll ever be, and if that's not a head of hair fit for presenting to the King of England, then I don't know what is."

"Not bad," Wendy conceded grudgingly, one finger rearranging a pale pink rosebud just to have the last touch.

Joanna stopped watching their faces and, trying not to flinch, looked at what they'd managed to do to her. Her eyes widened at her image in the glass and her hands flew to her cheeks.

"What—how ever—Shelley? How did you *do* that?"

"Me mum was chambermaid up at Hauntsby Hall, first hand to her ladyship's personal maid," she said casually. "Mum watched everything and passed it on to me, hoping one day I might elevate myself."

"Consider yourself elevated," Joanna said, taken aback by the delicate arrangement of her hair, the simplicity of which could only be acquired by great skill. "Shelley, I shall speak to Mrs. Campion first thing tomorrow, for you are truly talented."

"Does that mean you need a lady's maid?" Shelley asked, eyes sparkling.

"I have no need of a personal maid, no," Joanna replied, "but if his lordship has guests—and he might well now that he is home and no longer in mourning—his female visitors might be in need of someone, and I feel sure that between you and Wendy, you can provide the ladies with everything they need—although you both will have to have a bit of extra training."

Both Wendy and Shelley squealed in delight and threw their arms around each other, their feet executing a rapid little dance.

Joanna burst into laughter. "Enough. I must get downstairs or I shan't be around to tell Mrs. Campion anything in the morning. My head will more likely be flying from the flagstaff." She hugged them both. "Thank you so much for coming to my rescue tonight. It's been so long since I've had to dress properly that I'd forgotten how complicated it can be."

"Right, come on, then, Shelley, time for a cuppa tea," Wendy said, taking Shelley by the arm and pulling her out of the room.

"Good luck, your ladyship," Shelley called over her shoulder.

"And don't let the governor put you off your dinner," Wendy added. "The chef has gone to a special effort—but don't you worry, Margaret told him to go light on those sauces of his. . . ." Her voice faded down the corridor.

Joanna took one last look at herself in the long looking glass, wondering what Guy saw when he looked at her—did he see her at all, or did he only see Lydia?

She peered at herself, her fingers running down her cheek, but all she saw was her usual face, which didn't remind her of Lydia's at all. Oh, the nose was the same—neat, but a trifle on the short side—and the shape of the eyes and arched brows very similar, but Lydia's eyes had been lighter in color, more of a sea green compared to her drab olive. And they had shone so much brighter, just as Lydia's full, bowed mouth had always been busy, laughing or pouting or chattering. Maybe that was it—Lydia's face had never been still, every single one of her emotions playing upon it, creating an ever-changing landscape.

Joanna's face really was so very dull in comparison.

She sighed. What difference did it make what superficial likeness Guy saw? She and Lydia were chalk and cheese, and her chalk made Guy want to choke. He'd made that clear more than once—although he'd found Lydia just as hard to swallow in the end.

In any case, she shouldn't care what he thought. She was there for Miles and only Miles, and his father was simply someone she had to put up with for the duration, however long that might be.

She did feel the most peculiar attraction to him, as if he were a lodestone and she the metal that couldn't resist its pull. She, Joanna Carew di Capponi, who'd thought she didn't have a passionate bone in her body and had been perfectly content with that state of affairs, was at the mercy of a male magnet.

How had life ever become so complicated? she thought in despair, turning away from the glass and picking up her silk shawl, her fingers straightening the tangled fringe as if that might somehow sort out her scrambled thoughts.

She'd never been more confused about anything or anyone in her entire life.

Dickson magically appeared at the bottom of the last stair of the last flight, his face perfectly sober, but his eyes smiling at her as he bowed his head.

"Your ladyship. Lord Greaves awaits you in the drawing room."

"Which one?" she asked dryly.

"The blue and silver," he replied with a twitch of his mouth, now so familiar to Joanna. "A fine choice of color scheme, which I am sure his lordship will soon realize. This way, if you please."

Guy had his back to the room when Dickson opened the door.

"The Contessa di Capponi," he intoned, and Joanna had to grin. She well remembered the last time Dickson had made the announcement—the day she'd thought she was being sent away from Wakefield.

"Joanna's good enough for me," she murmured to Dickson as she had then. He backed away, his face perfectly straight, but the amusement in his eyes answered her smile as he closed the door behind her.

"Good evening," Guy said. "Come over to the fire and warm yourself. This house is horribly drafty in the winter."

"Thank you," she said, moving into the pool of light cast by the lamps over the mantelpiece and drawing close to the glowing coals. "One would think that evening dresses would be more practically designed for this climate."

Guy didn't answer, and she peered through the shadows to where he stood. "Guy? Have you frozen in place?" He didn't move a muscle, his body still as marble, as still as his face.

"What is it?" she asked, her nerves now completely on edge.

"Nothing," he said, passing a hand over his eyes. "Nothing at all. Forgive me: I am tired from the journey, I think."

Joanna had the most ghastly feeling that once again she'd invoked a memory of Lydia that had taken him back in time, and from the agonized look in his eyes, not to a happy time.

She looked down at her hands. "I am sorry," she said.

"For what?" He moved toward her. "What can you possibly be sorry for?"

"Because I forever seem to bring up painful memories," she said in a low voice. "I cannot help it—I know I remind you of Lydia, I suppose especially so when I am dressed like this, but I cannot change my appearance."

"Actually," he said, his voice sounding slightly hoarse, "I wasn't thinking of Lydia at all."

She frowned. "You weren't? That's good, or at least I think it is."

A brief smile flashed across Guy's face, vanishing almost before she had a chance to register it. "You are not usually tongue-tied," he said.

"I am not usually half naked," she said without thinking,

then clapped her hand to her mouth in horror. "Ohhhh," she moaned, sinking into the nearest chair. "It is no good trying to pretend. I have never been accomplished at this sort of thing."

"What sort of thing would that be?" Guy asked, leaning his elbow on the mantelpiece and scratching the corner of his mouth with his finger. His expression remained unreadable.

She looked up at him, mortified. "*This* sort of thing. Making casual conversation, producing bon mots, flapping a fan, all the rest of the foolishness that society prizes so highly and I am sure you do as well."

He scratched the other side of his mouth. "Hmm. I see. Then what are you good at? Other than being utterly infuriating, and of course your singular talent for pulling miracles out of thin air for small, troubled boys."

She blinked. "I—I do not know whether you have just insulted or complimented me."

"Both, I should think," he said, moving over to a table and pouring her a glass of sherry. "You had better drink this if you're to survive the evening. There is a great deal I wish to know about you, Joanna di Capponi, and you might find the interrogation alarming."

She took the glass from him with shaking fingers, not because she was concerned about an interrogation, but because the light contact of his hand on hers sent a shiver through her body.

Oh, God, if You love me at all, give me strength, she prayed silently, then took a large sip of the amber liquid, savoring its nutty flavor and warmth—especially its warmth.

"Very well," she said, looking up at him, her nerves feeling slightly steadier, "you may interrogate to your heart's content, but only on one condition."

"And what might that be?" he asked, gazing down at her, his eyes gleaming with curiosity.

"You must allow me to interrogate you in my turn. Fair is fair."

Guy moved back to the table and poured himself a glass, apparently thinking her proposition over. "I reserve the right to refuse to answer," he finally said, facing her again.

"I don't mind, as long as you accord me the same right," she replied absently, admiring the way his long, finely shaped fingers curled around the crystal bowl. "However, we must both agree that we will answer any question to which we choose to respond with complete honesty."

"You strike a hard bargain," he said. "Still, very well. Agreed." He placed his glass on the mantelpiece and folded his arms across his chest, the black silk of his coat stretching across his broad shoulders. "Shall I begin?"

She nodded, watching him with as much trepidation as if he were a coiled snake about to strike but still managing to appreciate his beautifully proportioned physique.

"Why did you really come to Wakefield?"

Joanna's hand froze, glass halfway to her lips. "*What?*" she spluttered, nearly spilling sherry all over her front. "You know why I came! Why do you ask me such a peculiar question now, after all this time?"

"I thought it best to start at the end rather than the beginning and save myself time," he replied. "Come, Joanna, you established the agreement for complete honesty."

"I cannot see what more there is to be honest about. I came because I'd made Lydia a promise that I would see to her son's welfare should anything happen to her. I came as soon as humanly possible, once I learned of her death, but I've *told* you all this."

"Yes. Yes, you have. What I continue to wonder about is why you would leave the comfort of your own home, give up all the luxuries you were accustomed to in order to isolate yourself not only in a cold corner of England, but in my house and in the upstairs nursery."

"Because I loved Lydia with all my heart," she said simply, tears suddenly starting to her eyes. "Because I would never retract my promise to her for any reason. Now I have come to love Miles, and so I stay for his sake as well as Lydia's."

A knock sounded at the door, and Joanna jumped up and turned her back as Dickson appeared. She wiped her eyes with the corner of her shawl.

"Dinner is served, my lord."

"Thank you," Guy said. "We will need just a few moments." He moved over to Joanna and gently laid his hands on her shoulders, turning her to face him. "Joanna," he said softly, "I am sorry if I upset you, but I needed to hear your answer again, before we go any further."

She looked up into his face. "Do you still not believe me?" she whispered, willing him to with all her heart. She didn't know if she could bear being thought a liar, not by Guy.

"I think I do believe you," he said slowly, two furrows appearing between his eyebrows. "After what you have done for my son, I would be a cad not to believe you. There is so much else, though, that I need to understand."

"Then ask me, and I will answer," she said, swallowing against the painful tightness in her throat. "I—I can only imagine some of the things you might have heard, for Lydia kept me informed about the gossip."

He closed his eyes for the briefest of moments, as if her words pained him. "Let us go in to dinner," he said. "We can talk there."

He offered her his arm and she rested her hand on it, trying not to think about the little shocks that ran directly through her fingertips and straight down to her belly.

She really didn't know how she was going to survive the evening.

Guy turned the talk to inconsequential matters over the first course of turtle soup, trying very hard to put his objectivity back in place before he proceeded any further in his questions, fighting valiantly to regain his composure. He'd first been laid low by the stunning sight of Joanna when she'd appeared in the drawing room, looking like Aphrodite herself.

And then when she'd gone into her flustered speech about Lydia—he hadn't gone so far as to tell her that Lydia had been the furthest thing from his mind. Joanna took his breath away with her utter simplicity, her lack of feminine artifice, the classic beauty of which she seemed completely unaware.

Odd—he didn't know when he'd stopped associating Joanna with Lydia. To his eye now, Joanna looked only like . . . like Joanna. Unique, lovely, as forthright as she was puzzling.

And then when she'd made her comment about being half naked, he'd nearly choked. He hadn't missed the swell of her creamy bosom rising from her low-cut bodice, or the alluring shape beneath her flimsy dress, but what had sent a jolt of real delight through him was her absolute bluntness, followed by another jumbled speech about her social failings. How in God's name could he reconcile this woman to the one Lydia had described, the one that society had marked as a fallen woman, without morals or conscience?

The only thing that rang at all true was her apparent disregard for society itself. In which case he'd love to know why she'd married Cosmo di Capponi, head of one of the more influential families in Italy.

He watched her, her spoon delicately dipping into her soup as she talked with enthusiasm about Miles's first meeting with his pony. She had no trouble at all making conversation that he could see. Indeed, she had welcomed the opportunity with open arms and a burst of nonstop chatter.

At least her chatter had substance, unlike that of most women of his acquaintance—and so unlike Lydia's.

"You should have seen Miles's little face, Guy. I thought he might explode with excitement—he didn't say anything, mind you, at least not then, but he grabbed hold of my hand and dragged me right over to Pumpkin, then raised his arms, asking to be lifted up."

She smiled, her eyes misty as if she were still there in the moment, her spoon forgotten in her hand. "He never showed a moment's hesitation, as if he knew he'd been born to be on a horse. I remember so well how I felt the first time I mounted my own pony—I thought I must know why the angels liked heaven so much."

She glanced over at him with a sheepish expression that made his heart ache. So sweet, so utterly natural, so entirely unpredictable. "Go on," he said, longing to know what was coming next. "Tell me why."

She bowed her head. "You will think I am very silly."

"I doubt it, although I cannot know until I hear the rest. Please, Joanna, do not leave me hanging."

"Well . . . I decided that angels didn't have wings, they had steeds to carry them about, flying steeds, and then Bunch read me the story about Bellerophon and his horse, Pegasus, and that sealed that. I *knew* I was right." She grinned. "Pegasus was, after all, the symbol of immortality. He was also the symbol of flights of imagination, so I wasn't so far off. In any case, I thought that horses represented the ultimate freedom."

Guy held up a hand, trying very hard to keep a straight face. "Wait. Joanna, please, I can hardly keep up with you. First of all, who is Bunch?"

"Oh—Miss Fitzwilliams. You do remember about my companion? Well, really, she was my governess from the time I was five and just never left. I think she worried that if she did leave me after my parents died, I would revert to their artistic and impractical natures and that would be an end to me."

"Why do you call her Bunch?" he said, discovering that

he wanted to know so much more—he wanted to know every detail of her childhood, her time with the Oxleys, her life in Italy.

She didn't just like horses, she understood their very nature—he'd never have guessed. And she liked mythology. That, too, he hadn't realized, and both were interests dear to his own heart.

"I called her Bunch because I couldn't pronounce her name," Joanna replied. "What child of five can say Fitz-williams? In any case, every time she was displeased with me—and believe me, that was often—she would bunch up her face just so and regard me with what was meant to be terrifying disapproval. The trouble was, I could never help giggling, because she looked so silly."

"So you started calling her Bunch?" he said, highly amused. "Did that not irritate her even more?"

"No, I think she rather liked the endearment, which is what it really was—her own special name from me to her, rather the same way Miles calls me Jojo."

"That's right," he said, only now absorbing the implication of Miles bestowing a pet name on Joanna. Lord, but he had missed so much. "Tell me, why has Bunch really stayed on for so long when you are well past the age of needing a governess?"

"I don't exactly know, but I am so glad she has. She's been mother, father, friend, and adviser to me for the last nine years, and I'll never be able to show her my gratitude. Of course, she'd never listen to it—she's the most practical person you could meet, Guy, and the kindest."

Guy nodded. "Thank you for describing her to me, Joanna. I look forward to meeting this good woman when she returns. She is returning?"

"In her own good time," Joanna said, reapplying herself to her soup. "She went to visit her sister, but I think she decided I needed to be taught a lesson."

"What lesson would that be?" Guy said, enjoying himself more than he had in years.

"Mind you, I could be wrong, but Bunch was annoyed in the extreme with the way I picked up and moved us both from Italy without a moment's planning or thought or even your permission and then landed on your doorstep and proceeded to interfere." She absently toyed with a stray lock of hair that fell against her cheek. "So she decided to leave me to my just desserts and hoped that I'd learn my lesson. The thing is, I have learned a lesson, just not the one she intended."

"And what lesson have you learned?" he asked, waving Dickson straight back in the direction of the kitchen when he appeared, next course in hand.

"I've learned that when love is given freely and without condition, the way one might scatter seeds over barren ground and till and water with patience and hope, a garden grows, no matter the season."

Guy covered his eyes, forcing back a sudden sting of tears. Joanna had a way of ripping at his heart, and no barrier he tried to erect stayed up for very long.

"Guy," she asked in a small voice, her hand creeping over his. "Did I upset you?"

He looked down at the small, slim hand that rested on top of his, the bones so fine, the skin so pale and delicate—and yet this was the same hand that had gripped at a leading rein and hauled Miles about a paddock at a fast clip.

This was the hand that soothed his son to sleep, that now attempted to comfort the father in a moment of weakness—no, not weakness. Joanna had taught him that also. In a moment of emotion for which he should feel no shame.

Hadn't he admired her for her ability to express exactly what she thought, whether it be by furious tongue or a torrent of tears?

Dear God, but he felt as if all his carefully constructed

walls were tumbling down around him, faster than he could put them back in place.

"No," he said, forcing his voice back to steadiness. "You didn't upset me. You pointed something out to me that I'd forgotten. Where the devil is that blasted footman with our food?"

13

*J*oanna immediately lifted her hand from his and placed it in her lap, her mouth trembling with an attempt to keep a smile from appearing. She was beginning to understand Guy better by the moment, to understand why he so often behaved in a curt and unreasonable fashion.

Every time that she came anywhere close to touching his emotions, he fled like a fox going to ground. In that manner he was not unlike his son, she realized. How interesting that she'd never made the comparison before this—and yet now that she had, she realized that the same diversionary technique might work just as well on the father.

"I do believe," she said, touching her napkin to the corner of her mouth, "that Dickson was attempting to serve us when you dismissed him. No doubt Emile is in the kitchen having wild hysterics in the French manner, believing that you did not like the presentation of his duckling. You might want to summon Dickson back and avert catastrophe."

Guy cleared his throat. "Quite right," he said, then picked up the bell and rang it. "We cannot have the chef dulling his knives on animate objects." He shot her a quick look. "You seem to know everyone by name."

"I would hope so," she said. "I've been living side by side with the staff for over three months now, and I've become very fond of some of them. Did you know that the woman who helps me to look after Miles is the wife of your coachman, Bill Willowsby, and is as warm and tender as anyone could wish for? Or that Margaret and Bill have three children of their own, who are sweet as can be and more than willing to play with Miles when I take him down to the farm?"

He shook his head. "I am not accustomed to knowing the comings and goings of the servants. Why are you going on about them in such a fashion?" Guy demanded, glaring down at the plate of duckling that Dickson put in front of him as if he wished to kill it all over again.

"Because if you would only look, you would see an entire retinue of people who devote their time and their service to you. Many of them have nothing else but life at Wakefield, denied the opportunity to have families of their own. Did you treat the soldiers in your regiment as if they were invisible, as if their only reason for existence was to serve you?"

"Of course not," he snapped. "That is an entirely different matter."

"Why? They were under your command, were they not, their lives in your hand? Can you not see that your staff is in the same position? Their actual lives might not be in danger, but their livelihood is. You let go almost an entire staff with a sweep of your hand only a year ago."

"Well done, your ladyship," Dickson murmured in her ear, placing a plate of root vegetables next to her elbow. "The duck, just as you like it."

"Thank you." Joanna lowered her head and stared at the napkin in her lap, terrified she was going to burst into laughter. That would not be wise just at the moment.

"Are you deliberately trying to provoke me?" Guy asked.

"No. I am merely pointing out that you have very little idea of what transpires belowstairs between the time your valet wakes you and shaves you and dresses you and the time that he performs nearly the exact same maneuvers in reverse when you wish to go to bed."

Guy raised an eyebrow. "Why should I? I pay well to have my valet look after my needs. He does so without giving me an earful of foolish chatter about his aged mother, ailing sister, and the cousin who is in debtor's prison."

Joanna leaned forward with keen interest. "Has he told you that? Oh, the poor man, how trying for him on all counts."

"Very," Guy agreed dryly. "You might be happy to know, given your Homeric heart, that I not only pay him well but provide a bit extra on the side for the aged mother and the ailing sister. I had to draw the line at the cousin in debtor's prison. Tenning will have to buy his cousin's freedom out of his wages."

"How very democratic," Joanna said. "Socrates would be proud of you." She applied herself to her delicious duck, which for once Emile had not smothered to death in something thick and sticky.

"Joanna," he said, regarding her curiously, "tell me about your early life. I know nothing of your situation, only that you went to live with Lydia at the age of eighteen when your parents died."

Joanna very carefully put down her knife and fork, trying to maintain her composure in the face of Guy's unexpected question, one that she hadn't anticipated.

"My parents gave me the happiest years of my life, a childhood anyone might envy," she said, honoring her vow to be honest, as difficult as it was. She hadn't spoken of her parents in years, not since talking to Cosmo about them. "They loved each other enormously and completely, and they extended that same love to me after I was born." She pressed her hand against her mouth, trying not to cry. "They were killed in an accident."

"I am sorry," he said, his voice so gentle that she had to bring every ounce of strength to bear to keep her tears at bay. "If you do not find the story too painful to relate, what sort of accident?"

She drew in a deep breath, the memory of that dreadful night forever ingrained in her brain. "They were on their way back from a ball—so close, *so* close to reaching home.

A runaway carriage hit theirs, and the force of the impact threw their carriage over the embankment."

She closed her eyes as if she could block out the appalling image playing out yet again as it had for the last nine years. "I do not know if they suffered or if they were given the peace of instant death. I—I only was told that they were found in each other's arms."

"How dreadful," he said softly. "Forgive me for asking—I had no idea."

"No, forgive me," she said, looking over at him. "I am not usually so emotional, but the subject is still difficult for me, even after all this time." She attempted to smile. "We did have an agreement that we would answer each other's questions if possible."

"Then I thank you for your willingness. I know what it is to lose one's parents, although in my case, my mother succumbed to a long illness when I was twenty-two, and my father followed her not a year later, his heart giving out from what I always believed was grief. Theirs, too, was a love match—highly unfashionable but very rewarding for both of them," he added with a sad smile. "I had always hoped for the same sort of marriage, but, sadly, that was not to be."

Joanna looked down at her plate. "Did you ever love Lydia?" she asked in a small voice.

"Oh, yes," he said with a faint sigh. "Or at least I thought I loved her; perhaps I loved the person I believed her to be. We both slowly discovered that we were mistaken in each other's natures, and for that I blame myself. I should never have asked her to marry me."

"Why did you?" Joanna said, shifting in her chair and regarding him keenly. For the first time she felt as if she was getting closer to the truth.

He shook his head. "To be honest, I think I was being utterly selfish. I had just come out of a rather bad experience, and I suppose that when I met Lydia, she represented everything I felt I had lost. She was gay and amusing and so full of life, and I wanted desperately to drink in her warmth, her innocence. I was terribly wrong."

Joanna couldn't help but think of Lydia's first letter.

. . . There he was, Jo, the most beautiful, magnificent man I'd ever seen. . . . He'd just come back from the Peninsula, having received a wound to his leg, and he had still not gained his bearings, only just recuperated and come out into society. . . .

Only now she could see that encounter from a second perspective, that of a man who had been wounded far more deeply than Lydia realized, a man who thought that Lydia's bright light might bring him out of his own darkness.

And what Lydia had seen was a handsome, dashing marquess who showered her with attention as well as all the material goods she could ever want.

Unfortunately, Guy had needed a woman, not a child, and Lydia had needed a man who would cosset and coddle her every waking moment, not a man in need of healing peace and quiet understanding.

"What are you thinking?" he asked, his fingers toying with the stem of his wineglass.

She looked up. "I am thinking how sad it was for both of you that it all went so badly wrong, but that the tragedy happened long before I realized. Guy, what happened to you in the Peninsula?"

His hand jerked, and he had to steady his glass to keep it from falling over. "Why would you ask that?" he said, his brow snapping down.

Joanna saw that she'd touched an exposed nerve and immediately retreated before he could. "Only because Lydia mentioned in a letter that she'd met you shortly after your return and that you had just recovered from an injury," she replied, forcing a light tone into her voice. "From everything you just said, I have to assume the injury was more serious than she implied."

He shrugged one shoulder. "I took a bullet in the leg,

nothing more. As you can see, I am now perfectly well, but if you do not mind, I would rather pass on that particular subject."

She inclined her head in acknowledgment. "Of course. Perhaps when you trust me better, you will tell me."

He looked at her oddly, then averted his gaze. "Perhaps," he said, his voice thick with something she couldn't interpret.

He fell silent as Dickson appeared, removing their plates and replacing them with fresh ones. He placed a board of cheeses and a bowl of dried fruit on the table between them and refilled their glasses before quietly vanishing again.

As soon as Dickson left, Guy said, "I believe it is your turn now."

Joanna groaned. "I already feel drained dry. But very well, what is your next question?"

"Why did you refuse to marry Henry Warnock when you were found together in an extremely compromising situation—in bed, to be precise?"

Joanna stared at him in astonishment, unable to believe he would think any such thing after knowing her as he did. A choked laugh escaped her throat, and then another. "Oh—oh, forgive me," she said, wiping her eyes with her napkin.

"What so amuses you?" he asked, not looking the least amused himself. "The matter was serious enough to cause you to leave the country in disgrace and stay away all this time."

She made a valiant attempt to sober. "Guy. Please listen carefully and believe what I tell you. I left the country of my own volition because the idea of marriage to Henry Warnock was beyond any serious consideration. Trust me, I did *not* compromise myself. Henry managed to compromise us both all by himself."

"Perhaps you would go into a bit more detail?" Guy asked, offering her the cheese board.

"If you like," she said, cutting a slice of firm cheddar and another of crumbly Stilton. "I attended the birthday dance that Lydia's parents had arranged for both of us. Lydia, ill with measles, could not come down, so I played the reluctant hostess."

He waved his hand in dismissal. "I know all about that; I wish only to hear your point of view about the later part of the evening."

"Oh. Well, I went to sleep and woke to find Henry in my bed, half-suffocating me with a most unwelcome and unpleasant kiss. The next thing I knew, Lydia came in to ask for medicine, and she screamed the house down, thinking I was being attacked, which I was, I suppose, only not in the way Lydia thought."

"You are saying that you did not invite Henry to your bed?" he said, cutting himself some cheese and spearing it with more violence than was called for.

"Do I seem that stupid to you?" she replied tightly. "I loathe Henry and always have—in fact, I had been at pains to avoid him for months, knowing that he wished to marry me, which," she said, popping a piece of cheddar into her mouth, "is where the dastardly Holtingham comes in."

Guy's fork remained buried in the cheese, his attention fully concentrated on Joanna. "Holtingham? What does he have to do with anything?"

"Holtingham, blackguard that he is, made his intentions perfectly clear to me during all of that season, and they were not in any way honorable. He seemed to think if I was married—not to him, but to some poor fool like Henry—that I would then lose my sense of morality entirely and happily fall into his arms. So when Henry sought his advice as to how to win my hand—"

"Good God," Guy said, gazing at her in fascination. "He didn't."

"Oh, but I believe he did. He must have told Henry exactly what to do in order to realize both their fondest wishes and Henry did it, but the only thing that Holtingham hadn't counted on was my obstinate nature."

Guy crowed with laughter. "You, obstinate? Tell me it isn't so." His expression slowly sobered. "Do you know, this entire story is so unbelievable that I find it plausible, especially given the characters involved. What happened next?"

"Oh, then my aunt and uncle threatened to cast me out if I didn't obey, so I accepted their offer," she said with a tiny shrug. "I had some money of my own—not much, but just enough to get by on—and a small villa in Italy that my grandmother left me, and off I went." She brushed off her fingers with her napkin and placed it back in her lap with a determined sweep. "Better that than Henry any day."

"How very interesting," Guy said, leaning his chin on his fist. "How very, very interesting, and how very unlike the story I was told."

Joanna selected a dried apricot from the plate. "I am not at all surprised. Lydia said that half of England talked of nothing but the scandal for months, the details wildly embellished by her parents. At least Lydia tried to defend me."

"Is that what she told you?" He took a sip of wine. "Then again, why would she tell you anything else? Half-truths were always her way."

"You're not accusing her of lying to me?" Joanna said indignantly. "Lydia would never do that!"

"Wouldn't she?" he said dryly. "But I forgot—you conferred sainthood upon her."

"I did nothing of the sort," Joanna retorted, frowning at him. "I loved her with all my heart, but I knew her shortcomings. She was young and a little foolish and more than a little spoiled, but her heart was good and honest and she loved with great devotion."

Guy rubbed his hand over his mouth. "Does loving

with great devotion include maligning you to me and everyone else she met?"

Joanna sat back, feeling as if she'd just been kicked in the stomach. "What—what do you mean?" she whispered. "Lydia would never do such a thing. You must be mistaken."

"We swore ourselves to honesty tonight, Joanna, so believe that I am not lying now, nor am I mistaken. Brace yourself, for your beloved Lydia portrayed you as promiscuous, unfeeling, ambitious beyond belief, and determined to have your own way in every matter."

"No." Joanna shook her head back and forth, so stunned that she could barely absorb his words.

"Yes. She said you would accept a peer or no one at all."

"No," Joanna said quickly, "you see, you did misunderstand. She had it in her head that Holtingham intended to offer for me, which of course he didn't, and she thought I might be foolish enough to accept him. That is what she meant."

"Begging your pardon, but that is not what she meant. Trust me. She also told me that the only reason she corresponded with you was because she felt sorry for your disgraced state and it was her Christian duty as your cousin to support you, despite your lack of character."

"No, that is not possible," Joanna cried, certain that he was wrong, that he had somehow twisted her words. "Lydie loved me as much as I loved her—we—we were like sisters. You must have misunderstood her, you *must* have—she would never have said such things!"

He reached over and took her cold hand, holding it fast inside the warmth of his own. "And yet she did. She said all that and more. Can you see now why I reacted to you as I did when you first came here? I had nothing more to go on but Lydia's description of you, and since it matched almost every vitriolic thing her parents said, I believed her."

Joanna squeezed her eyes tightly shut. The searing pain

that stabbed through her heart was almost too much to bear. "No," she heard herself saying. "No, not true. Not Lydie. Not Lydie. She wouldn't betray me like that, she just wouldn't."

Guy moved from his chair, and kneeling, he wrapped one arm around her, pulling her to him and holding her shaking body close against his side. She dropped her face into his shoulder, unable to stem the tide of tears a moment longer. She wept as if her heart might break.

His hand stroked her cheek, his thumb running up the side of her throat and over her chin, cupping it in his palm, his head coming to rest on top of hers.

"Joanna," he murmured, "please, you mustn't upset yourself so. You obviously love so deeply that you cannot understand how other people, even those dearest to you, are not capable of the same devotion or the same ability to temper their judgment."

Her entire body shuddered. "It is not them, not their fault, it is mine," she said on a gulp. "I am too different, too difficult. I do not know how to change myself to fit the rules and regulations, nor do I want to. Lydia knew that about me—that must be what she meant when she said those things."

She dug her cheek harder into his shoulder, both hands reaching up to cling to his strong arm as if he could anchor her against the violent emotions tearing her apart.

"If you feel better thinking that, then I will keep my silence, but remember that I lived with Lydia for five years; you were not the only person she savaged. Think, Jo, think about all the dreadful things she wrote to you about me, which you believed without question." He tilted her chin up, his eyes gazing down at her as if he might look straight into her heart.

"Tell me," he said softly, "do you still believe them?"

She slowly shook her head inside the cup of his hand, tears dripping down her cheeks and pooling in his palm.

She couldn't lie, not to Guy. "How could I?" she said, her voice breaking. "How could I, now that I know you?"

"Thank you," he said, wiping her cheek with the pad of his thumb. "You have no idea how much that means. Or how much it means to know that you are none of the things Lydia described. I have been tearing myself up the last few weeks, trying to sort out truth from fiction."

She gulped. "I am some of those things," she said. "It is true that I—I am stubborn. That I do not care for the same things other people do. I am best off on my own, best living where I do not ruffle other people's sensibilities. I just have that sort of nature—I always seem to upset everyone when I open my mouth."

He smiled, a gentle smile. "But you don't, my sweet, you don't. Look at the happiness you have brought to Miles. He is a different boy since you came into his life. And the staff you described—I may seem impervious, but I am not entirely blind. Even in these last few hours since I've been home, I have noticed a difference about the place, as if some degree of contentment has returned, as if this is not just a house, but a home again, the way I remember it being during my childhood. I have only you to thank."

"I think you exaggerate," she said, hiccupping. "All I have done is smile a little here and there. I'm not very good with formalities."

He chuckled. "My dear girl, when your overworked housemaids take on more work for the pleasure of it, you know you have worked some magic."

"Shelley is singularly talented," she said, lifting her head and looking for her napkin to dry her face with. "If you please, you might personally request Mrs. Campion to reassign her to chambermaid."

"Consider it done," Guy said, placing a handkerchief in her hand. She had to look twice to make sure it wasn't his neckcloth again, but when she turned her head she saw that he still wore the starched linen around his neck.

"Oh, good," she said foolishly, wiping her eyes and blowing her nose. "You didn't have to strip yourself as you did the last time I cried all over you."

"I don't recall stripping," he said, running a finger over his smiling mouth. "Should I?"

Joanna colored. "I meant your neckcloth. You gave it to me Christmas Eve. I—I always seem to be crying on your shoulder, and you always seem to be coming to my aid."

"Look how many times you have come to mine," he pointed out sensibly. "Is Miles not a shining example?" He squeezed her shoulders lightly, then rose to his feet and resumed his seat.

Joanna felt the most enormous sense of emptiness when he moved away. For a fleeting, foolish moment she thought she ought to develop histrionics more often, just for the pleasure of being comforted by him, held tight, for an excuse to breathe in his seductive scent and feel his hard, muscular body against hers.

Deep and low inside her she throbbed at the thought.

She rubbed two fingers against her right temple and looked with enormous concentration at the opposite wall, as if it held the secrets of the world instead of two very nice Van Dyke paintings.

"Joanna? What now? You suddenly look guilty, although I cannot think why."

"It is not guilt. I think I feel the headache coming on," she said in an outright mistruth, ignoring the terms of the evening they'd set. She could only manage so much honesty, and telling him that she wished for him to hold her closer still, to do outrageous things to her aching body just wouldn't do. It wouldn't do at all.

She felt so confused that she hardly knew where to look, although she knew enough not to look at him.

"I have pressed you too hard," he said, now the one looking guilty. "Forgive me. Shall I take you upstairs?"

"I do not need an escort," she replied, her throat so dry

she was surprised the words came out at all. "I thank you for your concern, but I am merely tired. My day starts early."

He stood and pulled back her chair. "Of course," he said, his voice tinged with regret. "We should both have an early evening after a long day. I will see you tomorrow?"

She turned to face him. "You are welcome in the nursery anytime at all. You might even want to take Miles out on his pony tomorrow afternoon, should you be free."

"I will see that I am," he replied. Picking up her hand, he placed a gentle kiss on the back of her fingers. "Good night, Joanna. Sleep well."

"And you," she said shakily as she reclaimed her hand, her trembling fingers now burning with the touch of his lips.

She moved so quickly from the room that she tripped over the edge of the carpet and had to catch the side of the doorframe to keep from falling. Straightening her back, she tried to assume as much dignity as she possibly could, slowing her steps so that she rounded the corner with a semblance of grace, even though her face was flushed with mortification.

Guy, who watched this extraordinary performance with drawn breath but true delight, resumed his seat at the table.

Joanna. He had never, but never in his entire life met a woman anything like her. He doubted anyone like her existed anywhere else in the civilized world.

If asked to describe her he would probably come to a dead halt midsentence. How did one describe a rainbow? Elliptic in shape and composed of the entire spectrum of color, caused by the refraction of light on water. Yet that gave no sense of the joy a rainbow brought, the magic and wonder one felt in its presence.

Joanna was a rainbow in her own right, forever touching him in unexpected ways, the arc of her nature shading from dark to light, as naturally and gently as a rainbow produced its subtle and multicolored hues. But never black.

Never black, not like Lydia, whose moods had swung from the glaring brightness of a noonday straight to the darkest nights hell could produce.

Joanna's emotions were heartfelt and she expressed them without reservation but generally kept them in a balanced perspective.

She did a far better job at it than he'd managed in a long time. His sole defense since marrying Lydia had been to cut off all feeling, and he hadn't been very successful at that either, not since Joanna had come along.

Guy lowered his head into his hands. He was becoming maudlin, that was it. He'd had a long and trying day, and Joanna had simply gotten under his skin. Rainbows? What was he thinking?

"Port, my lord? Or perhaps you would prefer brandy?" Dickson asked, appearing at his elbow.

Guy looked up at him, really looked for the first time ever, and saw a man of some thirty-odd years with a pleasant face, a thin mouth, and gray eyes that seemed kind.

"Dickson," he said, leaning his cheek on his hand, "tell me. You have been here over a year now. Have I robbed you of a family of your own? Have I in any way prevented you from a life outside these walls?"

"No, my lord," Dickson said, his voice and position stiff. "I am content in my position. Most content. Most especially since the contessa arrived."

"Ah. Is it possible you have developed a fondness for the contessa?"

Dickson stiffened even further, a feat that impressed Guy mightily. Dickson looked as if he might snap in two at any moment, especially given the indignant tremors running through his frame. His rather well-built frame, Guy thought with annoyance, wondering if Joanna had admired it. She seemed to be very friendly with him. Overly friendly, in fact, treating him with a warmth not generally conferred on footmen.

"My loyalty is to your lordship," Dickson said, "but my job is to serve those of your guests who live under this roof."

Guy glowered at him. "Just see to it that you serve none too well."

Dickson shot him a look of astonishment. "I—I—never, my lord," he gasped, then bowed and fled the room, leaving Guy to pour his own port and ponder why recently so many people fled rooms when he was about.

14

$\mathscr{G}$uy peered out the window, squinting at the early-morning light. The day, although overcast, looked a far sight more pleasant than he felt after a restless night's sleep, and he decided to take the ride he'd missed the afternoon before, hoping that might clear his head.

Toomsby saddled up Vicar without commenting on much of anything, which suited Guy very well. Toomsby had long ago learned to read Guy's moods and knew when to keep his peace, yet another reason Guy kept the fine man on despite his age instead of pensioning him off—never mind that Guy had known Toomsby from the time he could remember and was inordinately fond of him.

He mounted, pointing Vicar's head toward the east fields, and urged the horse into a controlled canter. Guy relaxed, enjoying the feel of his muscles stretching, the scent of early morning crisp and cold in his nose, the crunch of frost under pounding hooves sharp in his ears.

His thoughts slowly began to focus with the exertion and the need to keep his attention fully on Vicar, who, given the opportunity, enjoyed the occasional bolt.

He smiled softly to himself. As did his master, he thought, remembering Joanna the night before, challenging him over and over, not letting him bolt from anything, save his one request for privacy. She'd accorded him that with an easy smile, although the words that accompanied it had not been so easy.

"Perhaps when you trust me better, you will tell me."

When he trusted her better. If only it was that easy. Some memories really did not bear closer scrutiny any more than they bore being dragged up from the grave, where he'd tried so hard to bury them, along with his friends.

He found it hell enough having to struggle with his memories of Lydia, and speaking of them was like deliberately walking barefooted over broken glass—painful, bloody, and lacking in any common sense.

Still, Joanna had every right to know the truth about the cousin she plainly loved. He felt terrible that he'd upset her so badly, but he couldn't regret the aftermath of that upset. He'd discovered that there was something extremely nice about comforting Joanna, about holding her close to him and smelling that elusive scent of roses mixed with her own unique fragrance, something about the way she gave herself over to him with complete faith, the way she'd burrowed her head into his shoulder, allowed him to stroke her cheek, her hair.

There was only one problem, and it had knocked him nearly breathless when he'd realized it halfway through dinner, somewhere between the turtle soup and the duckling.

He *wanted* her. He wanted her, God help him, he ached for her, had been awake most of the night with his wretched longing, and there wasn't a damned thing he could do about that either.

She wasn't his to have. He was mad to want her at all, a fool, an idiot, a man at the mercy of his loins and his addled brains.

He'd returned to Wakefield determined to see to his son, only to find himself once again captivated by her unexpected honesty, her directness, her concern for everyone's welfare but her own.

Then there was her loveliness. Oh, God, but she was the most beautiful woman he'd ever gazed upon, inside and out. She no more reminded him of Lydia now than the man in the moon did, but she still wasn't his to have.

She'd made that clear enough each time she had pulled away from him, and finally when she'd abruptly left the room, claiming a headache. As if he believed that excuse for one moment. She'd been running away from him.

Still, something enormously important had changed last night between them. He knew it in his gut, and he knew from her flustered behavior she'd sensed it too. The trouble was that he had no way of knowing how she felt about what had become very clear to him: She wanted him too. He couldn't possibly be wrong about that.

Unfortunately, every sense also told him that something, or rather someone, stood in the way—Lydia. Always Lydia.

A flash of movement in the distance caught his attention and jerked him from his introspection. He narrowed his eyes, certain that the horse he saw galloping along in the neighboring field belonged to him—not only belonged to him, but was his prize brood mare, Callisto. Furthermore, he didn't recognize the rider, but his excellent seat declared him an expert, not a mere stableboy out on a jaunt.

Guy's blood quickened in anger. If someone was attempting to abduct his horse, he'd have him think again, and then he'd have him hanged, drawn, and quartered for sheer insolence. This wouldn't be the first time thievery had been attempted on his stock.

The scoundrel was already three miles out, but he wasn't going to go a mile more. Guy leaned forward, shortening the reins, and gave Vicar his head, urging him into a full-out gallop.

Vicar's muscles instantly bunched under him and his head stretched forward, his legs reaching out to take the ground in powerful strides. Guy rode high in the saddle and close to Vicar's neck, his hands moving easily with each long lunge of Vicar's body.

He took the shortcut through the spinney, the trees shielding him from view, then jumped the wide ditch that separated the fields and came around from the top end, cutting off the intruder as he emerged from the far side of the hedgerow.

Drawing Vicar up short, he turned him flank side in and held out his hand in a command to halt.

Callisto, beautifully trained mare that she was, didn't startle, but then neither did the rider. They came to a rapid but smooth stop, both breathing hard.

"What in the name of *hell* do you think you're doing with my mare?" he shouted, so angry he was tempted to break all the wretch's bones. "Who put you up to this?"

"I-I'm sorry. I—Toomsby said I might take her out each day. Have I sinned yet again?"

Guy sucked in his breath, his vision clearing. No. Not possible. "Joanna?" he said in disbelief, moving Vicar closer and peering at her.

"Yes," she said, her face pale. "Whom else? You scared the life out of me."

"Sorry," he said curtly. "I thought you were a horse thief."

"A horse thief?" she said, looking at him as if he was short a sheet.

"Yes. You are riding one of my finest and most valuable mares."

His gaze dropped down to the toes of the boots she wore, then traveled up over the breeches, past the man's saddle she sat on, the back half covered by her cloak, and all the way up to the black velvet hunt cap perched on top of her head. "What the devil are you doing dressed in breeches?" he said, completely taken aback. "And who taught you to ride like that?"

She gave him a tentative smile. "My father taught me to ride, and—and Cosmo had the boots and breeches made for me after I nearly broke my neck when I fell and my skirt caught in the stirrup leather. That is when he insisted I wear the cap as well, probably wise given my propensity for jumping anything that comes to sight."

"Why ride astride at all?" Guy asked, then looked away. "Never mind. Pretend I didn't ask."

She burst into laughter. "I truly am sorry if I worried you—I had no idea you would be out this early, or I would have mentioned my habit of riding at sunup. I try to exercise Callie before Miles wakes."

He slowly nodded, still recovering from shock, and not just at the discovery that it was she riding Callisto. The sight of her slender, beautifully formed legs outlined in the tight breeches and the thrust of her small breasts against the linen shirt only partially concealed by her coat made a sweat break out on his forehead and his groin begin to tighten dangerously. "Where is Boscoe?" he asked, trying to distract himself. "I would think he'd enjoy the run."

"Oh, he's still sound asleep. Neither he nor Miles likes to rise early, so I leave them to Margaret—oh, dear," she said, her hand slipping to her mouth. "There's that cat out of the bag."

"Do not tell me that Boscoe is not only in the house, but up in the night nursery sleeping on Miles's bed?" he demanded.

"Well, not precisely on his bed, but very close to it," she said, lowering her eyes.

Guy reached out with his crop and tilted her chin up with the tip. "There's no point in trying to look sheepish. I worked out long ago that this expression of humility is nothing more than a sorry attempt to win me over to your cause."

Joanna's eyes flashed up to his, her face wreathed in a smile. "You aren't at all the menacing marquess you try to make yourself out to be, are you? I do believe you are nothing more than an oversize lamb at heart."

"Do not make the mistake of comparing me to a lamb," he said, dropping the crop back to his side and drawing himself up. "I am nothing less than a wolf in sheep's clothing."

"Oh, my. How my heart does flutter with fear," she replied, her eyes dancing.

"Excellent. I feel much better, my male pride restored.

Shall we ride up the ridgeway into the woods? I have been curious to see if the snowdrops are out since I returned."

She inclined her head in assent, waiting while he turned Vicar around, then joined him at his side, trotting along comfortably for the next two miles, feeling no need to speak.

He couldn't help his surprise at how completely at ease he felt—here was a woman he'd been longing for in the most basic way possible only minutes before, and yet he felt as if she'd been riding at his side in just such a manner for the last decade.

The idea was perfectly ridiculous, and yet it made more sense than anything else had in nearly as long.

The glade Guy took her to was one Joanna had not yet discovered in her travels around Wakefield, and its beauty took her breath away. The trees stood only twenty feet high or so, their bases surrounded by an entire carpet of snowdrops, their branches reaching in a delicate fashion skyward, bare and entreating, as if waiting patiently for spring to come and clad them again in magnificent blossom and leaf.

"Cherry trees," Guy said, dismounting and offering his hands to help her down.

She shook her head with a polite smile and dismounted by herself, terrified of what his touch might do to her this morning, when she'd shaken with the memory of it, the longing for it, half the night.

"My grandfather planted them," he continued, looping his horse's reins over his neck and leaving him free to snuffle about in the loose leaves. "He said he wanted a place to come to in the spring that made him think of heaven, when the grove was covered in nothing but white blossom and filled with sweet fragrance."

Joanna drank in the sight of Guy standing in his grand-father's cherry grove, looking wistful yet unbearably handsome, not a single glimpse of his usual armor showing. He might have been a farmer proudly showing off a favorite crop. Only his immaculate dress and thoroughbred horse reminded her of the aristocrat he was. The highly desirable man he was.

Trying to push the thought away, she moved over to one of the trees and knelt down to place her gloved hand on the trunk, running it down over the smooth bark. "How shiny and bright it is," she said, "as if you can see the life inside just waiting to wake at the first sign of spring. It makes me think of a young girl's luminous skin."

He came up behind her, so close that she could see his breath in the air as it moved over her shoulder. She stood and turned, her back pressing against the tree trunk, her heart beginning to hammer painfully against her rib cage.

"It is lovely, most especially if you see it through an artist's eye," he answered. "I begin to think more and more that you must be an artist, Joanna. The book I found you reading that day in the library was the first hint—yes, I went and looked afterward," he said at her startled expression. "You have given me clue after clue, but I did not put them all together until last night. All the references you've made, the way your eye sees and interprets, your need for solitude—these are all the marks of someone who not just appreciates art, but practices it. Am I correct?"

She bowed her head, heat staining her cold cheeks. "I wouldn't call myself an artist, just someone who likes to paint."

"And what sort of painting would that be?" he asked. "Watercolors, pastels?"

"I know it is not ladylike or admirable to want to do anything more than accomplished watercolors and sketches, but I cannot help tackling canvases and oils, painting what I see, what I *really* see." She pulled off her hunt cap and hung it on a branch, just to give herself something to do with her hands.

"Why should you apologize for that?" he said with a fierce intensity. "You should be grateful for the talent—I wish I had it. I've never had the ability to manage more than a few badly executed sketches. An appreciative eye is the only gift I have, and I am thankful to have that."

Joanna risked a glance up at his face. "I am not very good, but I do love my work," she said. "It was Cosmo who gave me the opportunity to pursue it properly, offered me the right teachers. I will always be thankful to him for that—that among so many other things."

Guy grasped both her hands in his, gazing at her intently, his dark eyes searching. "Joanna. Will you answer one last question? Here, now?"

Her blood froze in her veins. What now? Whatever now? She had the most dreadful feeling that she knew what was coming, but she still nodded, not able to refuse him even in this.

"Why did you marry him? Why did you marry a man so much older than you, whose life was already largely behind him?" He released her hands.

"Because he was kind," she said, her gaze dropping to the snowdrops springing about her feet. "Because he *understood* about my need to paint, and he understood about solitude. Because he understood me."

She slowly raised her eyes to Guy's. "Cosmo cared for me in a way no one had cared in a very long while," she murmured. She ran her hand over her throat where her pulse threatened to jump out of her skin.

"How did you meet?"

"He had a summer palace not far from my villa. I met him through a mutual acquaintance the year after I arrived in Italy, and we discovered we had common interests. He offered to help me restore my gardens, and as time went by we discovered that we had more in common than we'd first realized, that we had developed a deep and lasting friendship."

She smiled softly, remembering. "I always missed him terribly when he left for his home in Florence, and he missed me too, so much so that he started making flimsy excuses to come to Pesaro whenever he could. In the end he decided it would be easier just to marry me so that he could get on with his life."

"And you had no objection to his age?"

"Why should I? He made me happy and I made him happy. I adored him."

"Adored him?" Guy asked, his voice soft as smoke and just as elusive. He rested his palm against the trunk, just to the left of her head, forcing her to shift away from his towering form. "You didn't love him?"

"Yes, of course I loved him. I would never have married someone I didn't love."

"Yes, but there are many kinds of love," Guy said. "He was old enough to be your father. Was that how you felt toward him, as if he were like a father?"

"He was my husband," she said uncomfortably. "That is how I loved him."

"Tell me then, Joanna, and tell me true—what kind of lover was he to you?"

She pressed herself so hard against the tree trunk that one of its knobs dug painfully into her back. "He was considerate," she stammered. "He was always a gentleman."

Guy reached his hand out and lightly ran his finger down behind the back of her ear, the warm leather of his glove soft and sensuous, causing a shudder to run through every nerve in her body. "A gentleman. How thrilling. Did he say please and thank you and wipe his fingers on a monogrammed handkerchief when all was said and done—if it was said and done?"

She jerked away from his touch, turning her head sharply to the side. "You are being cruel," she said in a low voice. "I am no virgin, if that is what you want to know. Cosmo managed well enough." She glared at him. "Not that it is any of your business."

"Forgive me," he said, looking away. "I cannot think what came over me—I have no right to ask you questions of such an intimate nature. I suppose I wanted to know if it was a real marriage."

"It was a very real marriage," she snapped, walking a few paces away, turning her back to him. "We had only eight months together, but in that time he never gave me a moment's unhappiness or a moment's regret. My heart broke when he died."

"I am sorry," Guy said from behind her, his voice gentle now. "What happened to him? Was he in failing health?"

She turned to face him, determined now that he know the full story and be done with his idiotic assumptions.

"Cosmo was in perfect health," she said, her eyes clouding over as the memory of that dreadful day came back to her as clear and sharp as if it had been yesterday and not over two years before. "His family had come to stay, and we were having a garden party at the palazzo. It was the most beautiful autumn afternoon, warm and bright, the sea shining greenish-blue in the distance, sparkling with sunlight."

Look, cara, *look at the color of the Aegean, exactly the shade of your eyes when you are happy. You will give me a little girl with eyes that color, and I will dote on her as I dote on her mother. . . .*

She ran a hand over her forehead. "Cosmo said he had a surprise for me upstairs and was going to get it. He smiled at me like a little boy with a secret and kissed my forehead."

Wait for me here, bella, *and I will be back in an instant. You are so lovely that I cannot bear to be gone any longer than that.*

"I waited, but after fifteen minutes or so I became anxious, so I went inside to look for him. He was coming down the staircase, but I could see something was terribly wrong. His face was pale, and he looked as if he was in terrible pain. Before—before I could cross the hall to reach him, he clutched his chest and fell, tumbling down the last few steps. I held him in my arms and tried to comfort him as best I could, but we both knew he was dying."

She squeezed her eyes shut. "He managed to speak a few words, but the end was mercifully quick."

Ti amo, cara. Ti amo. Be happy . . . find someone to make you as happy as you have made me. . . .

She wiped her eyes with the back of her sleeve, remembering the feel of his still lips as she'd kissed him for the last time, cold as the marble floor he lay on. "The doctor said his heart suddenly gave out," she said tightly over the hard lump in her throat. "He was only fifty-five years old."

"Joanna—"

"Later I found a box tucked in his pocket. Inside was a butterfly brooch he'd had made of tiny little gemstones. He—he ran upstairs to fetch a present for me, and his heart gave out." She pressed a shaking hand against her mouth as if she could hold back her misery and guilt. "I never have been able to bring myself to wear the brooch. He modeled it on the butterflies that swarm the valley in the spring, knowing how much I loved to watch them—"

She covered her face with both hands.

Hands touched her shoulders, drew her closer.

"Joanna, please forgive me," Guy said, his breath warm against her ear. "I had no idea. You obviously did love him very much, and I was wrong to assume anything else."

"You weren't to know," she said, pulling away from him after a long moment and wiping her eyes again. "How could you possibly have known? Oh, *why* do I never have a handkerchief when I need one?"

He reached into a pocket and produced a square of linen, handing it to her. "I have learned to carry an extra," he said with a smile.

She took it, mopping at her face. "I have never cried so

much in all my life," she said with disgust. "You must think me a regular watering pot, although I assure you I usually am not."

"I doubt you usually have annoying men insisting on delving into the most painful details of your private life," he said, scratching the side of his cheek. "I apologize again."

She shook her head. "I cannot mind most of your questions, for you have a right to know what sort of person is looking after your son, and you were brave to take me on, believing what you did about me."

A horrible thought suddenly occurred to her, and she clasped her hand to her throat. "Oh—oh, no. No wonder you asked so many questions about Cosmo—you heard that rumor too, didn't you? I hadn't realized it had made its way to England, but I suppose I shouldn't be surprised."

"I heard that rumor too," he said gently.

She stared dismally at the ground. "Which means that all this time you've wondered if on top of the earlier scandal, I wasn't also a greedy, manipulative woman who married Cosmo only for his wealth and connections and poisoned him when I had what I wanted. That is how the story goes, if I remember correctly."

His fingers wrapped around her shoulders, holding her firmly. "You had no idea you were marrying into a nest of vipers. From the sound of it, Cosmo was the only decent one among them."

She blew out a long breath, her heart feeling sick at the memory of the weeks and months that had followed. "In the end that was true. I had no idea how they resented me until after Cosmo had died. When his will was read, naming me principal heir to his property and fortune, they all went mad, as only Italians can do, screaming and shouting about my obvious motive for marriage and my even more obvious motive for murder."

His hands slid slowly up and down her arms. "But in

the end you prevailed, so what difference did their appalling behavior really make?"

She stared at him, trying to ignore the shivers running down her spine at his sensual touch. "Surely Lydia must have told you that at least."

"Told me what?" he said, looking puzzled. "She told me about the charges the Capponi family made, yes, but no more than that."

"Guy, I didn't take a single penny from Cosmo's estate."

"*What?*" His hands fell away, and this time he was the one staring in shock. "You cannot be serious."

"I am perfectly serious. I wanted nothing to do with any of it. I didn't marry Cosmo for his possessions or his rank. If his family had been nicer about it, I might have taken a few cherished things that reminded me of him, but as it was, I couldn't bear to deal with their dreadful bitterness and bickering, so I left with my clothes and the things Cosmo had given me himself, small things, like my brooch. They, of course, said I was overcome with the guilt of my terrible misdeed, and they took everything very happily." She shrugged. "I thought that had been an end to it, until now."

Guy reached his hand out and gently, so gently, touched her cheek with his fingers. "Joanna . . . you are an enigma, you truly are. I think one minute that I am beginning to understand you, and in the very next I discover yet another facet to you, and always unexpected."

Chortling, she turned her cold cheek into the warmth of his hand. "Like peeling the layers off an onion, I should think," she said. "In which case it is you who should be constantly crying, not I."

"If I were to cry, I would cry for you, for the hardships you've had to endure, for the falsehoods told about you by people interested only in serving themselves. I do not know how you've borne your trials so well."

She lifted her head, smiling impishly into his eyes. "Do

you not see? As a result I gained all the solitude I ever wanted."

Guy slowly shook his head. "You are the most extraordinary woman I have ever met," he said, in a low, quiet voice.

"I must get back to Miles," she said, abruptly disengaging herself, her stomach queasy, as if a million of her Italian spring butterflies had taken flight directly in the middle of it. "He will be wondering where I am."

Guy gave her a long, enigmatic look. "Yes. You must." He held out his cupped hand, not to her but to the sky. "Look," he said. "Snow. Where on earth did that come from?"

15

$\mathcal{J}$oanna glanced up, amazed that she hadn't noticed the snow before this. The overcast sky had darkened, now gray and filled with snowflakes, hundreds upon thousands of them, coming down in a furious flurry. Both she and Guy were covered in white, as was the ground.

"Oh," she gasped, wiping her wet lashes and hair. "Snow? I haven't seen snow in years!" She held out her arms and twirled in a wide circle, opening her mouth to catch some cold flakes on her tongue, the memory of her last snowfall bringing joy to her heart.

"Just how long has it been?" Guy asked, moving quickly to gather up the horses and leading them over. "You're behaving more like a child of Miles's age."

Stopping abruptly, she grinned. "Actually, I was seventeen that winter, and my parents took me to visit friends in Lincolnshire. The snow didn't stop falling for a week, and drifts piled up everywhere so that we had to stay an extra fortnight before the roads were cleared. I loved every moment of it."

"Up, Joanna, and fast," he said, holding Callie's head. "I'm afraid this is blowing in hard and fast and could turn dangerous quickly if it does start drifting—and believe me, there's nothing amusing about it if it does, since we're riding down into the valley."

Alarmed by the tone of his voice, she put her foot in the stirrup and swiftly swung her leg over Callie's back, taking up the reins in one hand.

He reached up and handed her the cap she'd forgotten all about. "Please, put this on."

Joanna twisted up her hair and shoved the cap over it,

shooting an anxious glance up at the sky. "It does look rather bleak, doesn't it?"

Guy quickly mounted and turned his horse around. "Yes, and it's looking more troublesome by the minute," he said, his expression grim. "We're going to have to ride hard. Stay close to me, whatever you do. We have a good five miles to cover, and there's no clear path." He moved ahead and gestured for her to follow.

She nodded, instantly urging Callie into a fast canter, having heard the stories of sudden winter storms turning deadly.

The first ten minutes were not so bad, although as soon as they left the shelter of the woods the wind blasted straight at them, sweeping off the ridge and swirling the snow so that it blinded her, but at least she could see Guy to her right and knew that he kept her in his vision.

It was after that that the nightmare began.

As they moved lower down into the valley floor, the snow became so thick that she couldn't see more than a foot in any direction.

Guy shouted something at her and pointed down at the ground, but she couldn't make out what he was saying or what he meant, since she couldn't even see what was on the ground. She shook her head, then turned it away, trying to keep the wind out of her eyes and face.

The next time she looked she couldn't see Guy at all, although she thought she could just make out the muffled beat of his horse's hooves close by. Or could she? It might just as easily have been Callie's muffled hooves she heard. She hoped she was wrong, that he was close beside her, guiding them safely home.

She lowered her head against the snow, which blew more fiercely by the moment, stinging her face and numbing her nose, and finally she leaned right down onto Callie's warm neck, speaking encouraging words into her ear, knowing she must be having as much trouble seeing.

The snow blew harder still, obscuring all vision.

For the first time Joanna felt real fear.

Only a mile to go, surely only a mile more now, she thought, praying that Guy was still near. She had ceased to hear anything at all save for the steady blowing of snow and wind.

Callie steadily forged on, her feet slowed by the snow that had begun to drift into great piles, just as Guy had predicted. She stopped as she ran up against one drift and had to turn, and then ran into another and turned again.

Disoriented by the all-encompassing whiteness, Joanna hung on tightly, giving Callie her head, trusting in the mare's instinct to get them home safely, although she began to wonder if Callie's sense of direction wasn't as confused as her own, since they seemed to be going in circles.

She grew colder and wetter and even more frightened as an interminable amount of time seemed to pass. Exhausted, she finally laid down and wrapped her arms around Callie's neck, trying to draw warmth into her shaking body. All she wanted to do was go to sleep.

Sleep—what a lovely thought. If she went to sleep she'd be warm again. The snow would go away, she'd be warm, and she wouldn't have to worry about anything anymore. She sighed and closed her eyes and gave herself over to the urge she could no longer resist. Dying really wasn't so bad at all. . . .

Joanna hazily felt arms coming around her, lifting her off Callie's back, holding her close, something pressing against her cheeks. *Of course,* she thought giddily, *this must be an angel and I must be in heaven.*

"Joanna—Joanna, wake up. Oh, please, God, wake up, sweetheart. You're home, thank God you're home. Open your eyes, Jo. Look at me."

She made an enormous effort to open her eyes and see what an angel looked like and decided that he looked remarkably like Guy. He held her scooped in his arms, pressed hard against his chest, his hand cupped against her face. She could feel the rapid beat of his heart all the way through his coat and her cloak, straight into her own.

A heartbeat.

"Oh," she said, blinking, looking about her and vaguely registering that heaven looked remarkably like the stable yard at Wakefield and that Guy didn't really look at all like an angel now that she reconsidered. "I'm not dead."

"And a miracle that is, ye poor girl. Ye should be thanking the good Lord for it. Take her inside, dunce-head—it's no good holding on to her out here in the blowing cold when ye can see she's frozen to the marrow. I'll look after the horse, bless her good sense. Fools, both of ye be. And get her out of her wet clothing!"

Joanna recognized Toomsby's familiar tones, first comforting her, then definitely letting her know with his lacerating words that life still flowed in her frozen body.

The next sensation she registered was of being carried off as if she were a prize in some sort of tournament.

Guy unceremoniously dumped her on a heap of hay and followed that offensive action by stripping off her wet cap, cloak, and even her shirt, leaving her only in her camisole and breeches. He heaped a pile of horse blankets on top of her.

She weakly pushed the scratchy, suffocating blankets away from her face and chest. "Stop," she mumbled.

"Warmth is one of the primary needs of life," he said, shoving them straight back around her, "and I'm not letting you give yours up just yet."

"Leave me alone," she said, wanting to go straight back to sleep.

"Leave you *alone*?" he cried. "That was precisely what I was trying to avoid!" He shrugged out of his wet greatcoat, then leaned toward her, an expression of intense concern on his face. "Where in the name of Hades did you disappear to? I told you to stay close! You scared the very life out of me—I was about to go back out there and look for you, but Toomsby threatened me with a shotgun, saying that two of us dead wouldn't do anyone any good."

She pressed a hand over her mouth, stifling a giggle. "Toomsby held a shotgun on you?" she said, trying to picture anything so absurd.

He leaned back on his heels and pushed both hands back through his hair. "He did. Somehow it had the desired effect and brought me to my senses."

She grinned, tucking a corner of blanket under her chin, where sensation began to return, and rather uncomfortably, feeling like pins and needles attacking her. "I adore Toomsby," she said mistily. "He's so . . . so *practical*."

Guy smiled reluctantly. "He is that. Joanna, what did happen out there? I had you right at my side. Why didn't you stop when I told you to?"

She stared at him stupidly. "You told me to stop?"

"Yes. I told you to stop so that I could take you up with me on my horse and lead yours behind. You looked straight at me, and then you shook your head and turned away. The next thing I knew you were gone."

She rubbed her hands against her face, trying to think, not an easy task at the moment. "I couldn't hear," she said. "I remember now. I couldn't hear, but you pointed at the ground, and I thought you must be telling me to be careful of something, but I couldn't see what it was. It doesn't matter, I'm here now. You didn't have to wait very long."

"Joanna," he said on a long sigh, "you were missing for nearly two hours. I was going out of my mind with worry."

"Two hours?" she said, wrinkling her brow. "I must have lost track of time. It was so . . . so white. And cold. Very cold. Guy, I'm so cold." She started to shiver uncontrollably.

He immediately stripped off his jacket and shirt and laid down on his side next to her, pulling away the blanket and bringing her back against his chest, his hips and thighs pressing against the backs of hers.

Flipping the blankets over them both, his arms moved fast around her and he held her tightly against him.

She felt too cold to think of anything but the welcome heat slowly seeping into her, warming first her icy flesh and then gradually, as her shivering subsided, starting to thaw her frozen bones. She drifted in and out of sleep, conscious only of the blessed, precious warmth slowly filling her body.

"Mmm," she murmured lazily, "that feels nice. Thank you, Bunch. Much better now."

"Bunch?" a deep voice said somewhere above her ear. "Just what about me resembles Bunch? Perhaps I should be offended."

She jolted awake and flipped onto her back, her eyes flying open only to see Guy raised up on one elbow, looking down at her with lazy amusement, the lower part of his body still pressed against her, his chest bare.

"Ohhh," she moaned, mortified, rolling over onto her side and covering her face with her hand. "Oh, what have I done?"

A smile flashed over his face before he straightened it. "Ruined yourself again?" he suggested nonchalantly.

"Beast." She sat up, clutching the blankets to her chest. "I am sure you amuse yourself, but I find myself in a predicament."

"Feeling better, I see. Good. I think it is high time to get you back to the house and into a hot bath before you catch pneumonia. Do you feel strong enough to stand, or must I haul you over my shoulder?"

She pushed at his chest. "I do not need hauling anywhere," she said, tossing the blankets aside and looking down to make sure she was still fully clothed. She wasn't. She'd forgotten he'd taken her shirt off.

He raised an eyebrow. "I confess that it went against my better judgment to leave you in any way wet but with your modesty intact, when every sensible inclination told me to strip you straight down to the flesh. But then there was Toomsby's modesty to consider, and also Bill Willowsby's— he looked shocked to pieces as it was, discovering us prostrate on a haystack."

Joanna looked at him suspiciously. "You are not serious—are you?"

"Not entirely. Bill Willowsby is rarely shocked at anything, although I do believe he considered such goings-on before noon a bit presumptuous, considering that he does have work to do."

She burst into laughter. "You are a fiend."

"Perhaps, but a concerned fiend, and also a guilty one." His expression sobered and he picked her hand up, holding it close against his chest, his skin hot. "Joanna, forgive me—I should never have risked your life like that. I should have realized that we would never cover the five miles in time and taken you up with me from the start. I was an idiot, as Toomsby has reminded me over and over."

"How could you possibly have known how severely the storm would blow and how quickly?" she said logically. "You told me at the time that you were concerned and wanted to get home as fast as possible, and you made every effort to do so. It was not your fault that I didn't understand you."

"It was my fault that I lost you out there," he said, his eyes darkening. "My fault that you nearly died. If Callisto didn't possess so huge a heart and so enormous an intelligence, not to mention the extraordinary endurance that runs in her veins, you probably would have. Somehow she found a way to bring you home, despite the fact that she's never been that way before."

Joanna smiled softly. "Callisto. You named her after the Arcadian goddess whom Zeus loved. She bore him a son—"

"Arcas," he said, squeezing her hand. "That's right. One of Callisto's finer foals bears his name."

"Zeus turned her into a constellation, the Great Bear, and her son into the star Arcturus," she said dreamily.

"How *do* you know so much?" he said, his fingers running lightly over hers.

"Bunch," she said, "who introduced me to Ovid. And then art—Titian painted two wonderful pictures of Callisto. Do you know them? You have a wonderful book that depicts them both most beautifully."

"Have I," he said, looking down at her hand in his.

"Yes, I cannot remember the title, but they are of Artemis denouncing her—brilliant, but rather depressing from Callisto's point of view. She was about to get turned into a bear, after all. Why did you name your horse after her?"

"Because Callisto means *most lovely* in Greek. Because her constellation has always made me think of a beautiful Arabian horse rather than a bear when I look at it and trace its lines. Because I have always been extremely fond of her." He raised his gaze to hers. "I have even greater reason now for that fondness."

Joanna's eyes shot wide open. "I didn't even ask," she cried, feeling terrible. "How is she? She must be exhausted, poor darling. She was so brave, Guy, trudging on, somehow finding her way back, even though those terrible drifts stopped her at every turn."

"She is in her stall eating hot mash, warm blankets are covering her, and she is basically being treated like the queen she knows she is. As far as Toomsby can tell, she's feeling very pleased with herself." He stood and held out a hand. "Now, please, Joanna, let us both dress and let me get you back to the house. The snow has let up just enough that I can conduct you safely as long as you keep hold of my arm."

She let him pull her to her feet, surprised by how shaky she felt. He shrugged into his shirt and coat, threw his wet shirt over his shoulder, then let go of her for a moment to retrieve a blanket for her shoulders. Her knees nearly buckled.

"That's it," he said, scooping her up in his arms. "You will have to resign yourself to traveling in this style for the next ten minutes."

He carried her all the way up the path that already stood a foot deep in snow, more coming down by the minute, and carried her up the back stairs, shouting commands about hot water and baths and hot toddies as he went. She felt so sleepy yet so safe in his arms. Finally he deposited her gently on the nursery sofa in front of a roaring fire.

Margaret came flying out of Miles's bedroom, her hands pressed to her face, her cheeks and eyes reddened with weeping.

"Thank the Lord," she gasped, "thank the Lord! My Bill sent a message up saying she was safe home at last, your lordship, but he wasn't so sure about the outcome." She knelt before the sofa and clasped Joanna's hands between her own. "Oh, Joanna, dearest, can you hear me? Are you sickening for anything?"

Joanna pushed herself upright. "I am perfectly well," she said, patting Margaret's hand. "Where is Milo?"

"He's downstairs in the back kitchen, making dough with Wendy. I thought it best for him to be busy," she said, mopping at her eyes.

"Oh, good—so he hasn't missed me. How clever of you to think of it, Margaret."

"He hasn't a clue that anything was ever amiss, my dear, I swear that to you."

"For God's sake, will someone get this woman into a bath?" Guy roared. "She's half frozen!"

"You've already made enough noise on that front to wake an army," Joanna said calmly. "Water only heats at a certain rate, my lord, and it will arrive when it arrives. Might I suggest that you take yourself off to your own quarters and do the same? You are just as soaked through as I am."

He shot her a long, cryptic look. "Very well," he said, "I will take myself off then, since I am obviously not needed here."

She turned her face into her hand. Guy seemed to induce this condition of hilarity in her on a regular basis. "I thank you for all your attentions," she said, her shoulders threatening to heave, "but you have already been too kind. Please, Guy, do look after yourself?"

"Your servant," she heard him say as the door shut behind him.

"Goodness gracious," Margaret said, "he did look upset, and little wonder. What got into your head, the two of you galloping off into a storm like that?"

"There wasn't any storm," Joanna said, her head starting to ache. "We accidentally met in one of the fields and then we went off to look at some cherry trees, and then—then the storm came out of nowhere, and then—" She stopped, unable to speak another word, and burst into tears, suddenly overwhelmed.

"There, there, my dear, there now. It's all over, and a terrible time it must have been." Margaret, whose Scottish blood made her eminently sensible and reliable but equally warm and compassionate, sat down on the sofa and gathered Joanna into her arms, rocking her. "Bill told me all about it, he did, the first time he came up to the house to say you were lost out there. You've been through a dreadful time, and his lordship too. We're lucky to have you both safely back, we are indeed."

"Oh, Margaret, it was so cold and I was so frightened," she sobbed, "and I didn't know where Guy had gone or if he was lost too, and—and I couldn't see anything or hear anything, and I thought I might die."

"These winter storms can be terrible things," Margaret said. "Bill was beside himself and so was Mr. Toomsby."

"Guy tried to get us back safely," Joanna said, shivering as Margaret's efficient hands started to strip her of her damp camisole.

"Of course he did, of course he did," Margaret crooned. "In here with that tub, Shelley, and right quick. The poor girl's blue with the cold. Where's the water?"

"Dickson's outside lining the buckets up outside the door," Shelley said, dragging the heavy copper hip bath in front of the fireplace. "I'll fill the tub straightaway. Is she going to recover?" she asked in a small voice.

"Naturally. Her ladyship's just a bit weak right now, that's all. Get on with it, Shelley!"

"Right away," Shelley said, scurrying back outside.

After that Joanna was aware only of Margaret depositing her in the tub and lovingly bathing her as if she were a child, and later, Margaret bundling her into bed with a cup of hot broth that she could barely manage to swallow.

It was the last thing she remembered for a long time.

16

Guy stood, stretching his stiff back. He wandered over to the window and looked out. The snow still fell lightly, but he barely saw it. Five days. Five days, and Joanna's fever still hadn't broken. The doctor had said that a crisis would eventually come, that there was no way of knowing whether Joanna's strength would rally or whether she'd succumb to her illness.

He turned and walked back to her bed, his hand massaging the back of his aching neck, then moving over his tired, scratchy eyes. He couldn't lose her—he refused to entertain the possibility. He'd keep her going by sheer force of will if necessary.

He sat down again in the chair next to her bed and picked up her hot hand, holding her slim fingers tightly. "Joanna. Joanna, sweet, wake up. Miles misses you, the whole household misses you—they're all walking around with long faces, hardly speaking above a whisper, half of them in tears. It seems no one can manage without you, myself included."

She turned her head on the pillow, mumbling something under her breath that he couldn't make out. Little wonder: She'd been delirious for the last four days and nights. He knew—he'd barely left her side since Margaret had sounded the alarm the afternoon of the storm.

He bowed his head into his hands, overcome with guilt. If it hadn't been for him, she wouldn't be hovering between life and death. She'd never have ridden into the woods, never have been caught in the blizzard. He had only himself to blame, only himself.

"Papa?"

Guy looked up to see Miles standing in the doorway of

the bedroom, Boscoe at his side and a large piece of paper dangling from his hand.

Guy smiled at him wearily and held his hand out. "Come in, Miles."

Miles moved quickly to his side and pressed against his thigh, one small hand going out to cover Joanna's. "Is Jojo better yet?" he asked, turning his large brown eyes on his father.

"Not yet," Guy said, giving him a squeeze around his waist. "We have to be patient." He pressed a kiss on the top of his son's head.

"She's still very hot, Papa," Miles said solemnly. "I think you should squeeze more water on her."

"Wendy is just bringing up a fresh basin," he said. "What do you have there?"

"A painting for Jojo," Miles said. "I made it specially for her. I think she will like to see it when she wakes up."

"May I look?" Guy asked.

Miles nodded and held it out.

If Guy could think of anything good that had come out of this catastrophe, it was his developing relationship with Miles. Bound by a common concern for Joanna, they both kept a vigil, Miles surprisingly calm and steady—indeed, more so than his father.

Guy couldn't help but be gratified at how well Miles had come along—he was mostly back to his old self, only without any of the nervousness and excitability he'd shown when his mother was alive. Miles was the most shining example of how easily Joanna reached out and touched lives, touched hearts, never demanding anything in return.

He shut his eyes and covered them with one hand, his throat squeezing tight.

"Papa? You cannot look if you cannot see," Miles said, patting his arm.

Guy collected himself with an effort. "Of course. Here, why don't you lay it on the covers?"

Miles stood on tiptoe and carefully spread out the paper, then stood back.

As carefully as he looked, Guy couldn't make heads or tails of it. Joanna had told him of Miles's myriad paintings and how important she felt they were in depicting his internal progress, but this was the first time that Miles had actually presented one to him.

He couldn't make out what he was looking at, since it all seemed to be white and pink swirls with a bit of purple and blue swirl thrown in here and there, and one yellow blob up toward the top. "It's very nice, Miles," he said with what he hoped sounded like encouragement. "What . . . er . . . what is it a painting of, exactly?"

"It is the sound of snow," Milo said, as if that explained everything.

Guy looked at him, perplexed. "The sound of snow?" he said. "I didn't know snow had a sound."

Milo giggled. "Oh, Papa, everything has its own sound. But," he said, eyes wide and earnest as he held a finger to his lips, "if you want to hear you have to be very, very quiet and listen very hard." He nodded.

"Ah," Guy said. "Can you make the sound of snow for me? Is it like a whisper, perhaps?"

"Silly Papa, you cannot make the sound, you have to imagine it inside your head. Then you have to paint the feeling."

"You paint the feeling," Guy repeated in a daze. *Joanna, oh, Joanna . . . I can hear you now.*

"Yes, you see?" Miles chirped happily. "Like this and this," he said, pointing at the swirls on the picture. Standing on tiptoe again and putting his finger on the blob of yellow, he said, "And here is Jojo, shining in the snow."

"Does she have a sound?" he asked, trying to grasp the workings of Miles's mind.

"Of course," Milo said, looking at him as if he were an imbecile. "Jojo never stops talking—she used to talk to herself all the time, but she's getting better. Now she mostly talks to other people."

Guy smiled. *Like you, sweet boy, like you.* So Miles had been listening all that time he was silent.

"Is she talking in the painting?" he asked curiously.

Milo thought for a moment. "I think she is saying, 'Go beyond silence.' She said that to me lots of times. 'Beyond silence is where you find the songs of the stars, Milo. Everything has its own sound, from the very smallest blade of grass to the biggest, highest mountain.' "

He looked up at his father with a sweet smile. "That's why you have to listen carefully, so you can hear the sound inside, the kind you can't hear with your outside ears. Sometimes it is a song, and sometimes it is just . . . that," he said, pointing at his picture.

Guy stared at his young son, overwhelmed by a flood of emotion so intense and complex that he couldn't speak. A five-year-old child had just reminded him of something that he'd forgotten long ago.

How many years had it been since he'd allowed himself to go beyond silence, allowed himself to experience not just the tangible, but the intangible?

Too long. Far too long. He'd lost his ability to truly feel at some point during the nightmare of the disaster outside Burgos. Somehow—somehow—Joanna had brought it back to him, painful as it was, like the feeling returning to a numb limb, hot and annoying, but a huge relief once the agony stopped.

The only trouble was that the agony hadn't stopped. It kept going on and on, worsening as Joanna lay in her terrible state of limbo.

He looked down at Miles and rested his hand on top of his soft hair. "It's a lovely painting," he said hoarsely, fighting back tears. "Very fine, Miles. In fact, I think it is worthy of framing."

"Don't be sad, Papa," Miles said, patting Guy's leg. "Jojo

will wake up and we will all go riding together, me on my Pumpkin and you on the big horses, and we will gallop and gallop, fast as the wind."

Guy just nodded and hugged Miles with his free arm, trying very hard not to fall apart.

Miles crawled into his lap, reached up to touch his fingers against the corner of Guy's wet eyes. "Jojo knows we love her. She will not leave us like Mama did."

"No," he said with an effort. "She will not leave us."

Miles snuggled comfortably against his shoulder. "Mama is never coming back, is she?"

"No, Miles. She is never coming back. She is with the angels, remember?"

Miles shook his head. "She came back once," he said. "I told Nanny Loppitt, but she said I was a bad boy to say those things and she washed my mouth out with soap."

"Miles—I am so sorry about her. I made a terrible mistake in trusting her to look after you." Loppitt, that was it. The name had made him think of lop-eared rabbits, but there was nothing soft and fuzzy about that shrew.

"Nanny said I told lies, but I didn't, Papa. After that I didn't say anything at all, because every time I did she would hurt me and call me bad names. Anyway, what is the point of talking if no one ever listens?"

Guy stared at him. That was why the poor boy had stopped talking? God, he could shoot himself for his negligence. "Tell me now, Miles, about Mama coming back. I promise you I will believe every word you say."

Miles gazed up at him with trusting eyes that tore at Guy's heart. He didn't deserve the child's trust, but God, he was grateful for it.

Miles fiddled with a button on Guy's shirt. "Mama came in the night when I was sleeping. I think she was a ghost." He nodded hard. "It is true, Papa, she came in through the window and touched my face with cold fingers and she made moaning noises, and then she floated away. I was very scared."

Guy hugged him tight, his heart breaking for his little son. He should have known, should have been there. No wonder the boy had started wetting his bed and wandering in the night. "What a frightening experience. Did you ever see Mama again?"

"No . . . but I tried to stay awake and watch in case she came back. Are ghosts real, Papa?"

"No, Miles, not any more than nightmares are real, but they can seem very real and make you feel very upset. That is what you had, a nightmare, a very, very bad dream. I want you to have happy memories of your mama, not bad ones, and remember her as she was when she was alive."

Miles rested his head on Guy's arm and looked up. "I am glad you brought Jojo to us. I like her much better than Mama."

Guy, startled, didn't know what to say. *I like her much better than your mama too?* He didn't think that would be an appropriate response, as true as it was, but he didn't want to be a hypocrite and tell Miles that he should love his mother above all people.

Miles solved his dilemma. "Jojo makes me feel nice inside. Mama made me feel funny, and she always held me so tightly that I couldn't breathe. When Jojo holds me she is gentle, and she doesn't laugh too loud or cry all the time and say mean things about you."

"I like her too," Guy said, fascinated to hear what had been going on inside Miles's head all this time. And here he'd been thinking that Miles had been missing his mother. "We are lucky that she came to us."

"The very first time I saw her I thought maybe she was the ghost come back in daylight, but then I looked in her eyes and saw she wasn't like Mama at all."

Guy rested his cheek on the top of Miles's sweet-smelling

hair. "How observant you are," he said. "The first time I saw her I nearly fainted. I thought I had seen a ghost!"

Miles chortled. "You are a silly goose, Papa. You just said there was no such thing as ghosts."

"I know I did, but for one moment I thought maybe I was wrong. Thank goodness Joanna set me straight right away and told me her name. Maybe I should have looked carefully into her eyes as you did, clever boy, and spared myself a shock."

"Jojo likes you, Papa. She doesn't say horrid things about you. She says you are a good man and a brave shoulder."

"A brave——oh, you mean a soldier," he said with a grin up at the ceiling. "Well, I was a soldier, it is true, but I don't know about brave." He couldn't help himself. "What else did she say about me?"

"That you were a nice father and that you love me very much. Do you, Papa?"

Guy's chest caught and he pressed his mouth against Miles's hair for a moment, realizing that he'd never told him so—yet another transgression. "Of course I love you," he said huskily. "Very, very much. You are my son and my little boy and more important to me than anything in the world."

"I love you too, Papa," Miles said, sighing with contentment. After a few minutes of silence he said, "Jojo made a drawing of you so that I would remember that you loved me. She made a frame and put the drawing in it and put it next to my bed so that I would see it first thing in the morning and before I went to sleep at night. Would you like to see?"

Guy nodded, incapable of doing anything else. Joanna. She touched every aspect of his life, and for the most part he'd been oblivious.

Miles wriggled off his lap and dashed out of the room, his eternal shadow Boscoe at his side.

Guy leaned closer to the bed, picking up Joanna's hand

again, his thumb stroking over the delicate bones, the tapered fingers, the fragile skin on the inside of her wrist where the veins ran blue. "You have brought a miracle to my life," he whispered. "You've given me back my son, Joanna; you've given me back a sense of myself. Please—please wake up so that I can tell you all these things, so that I can thank you. Please, Joanna, come back to me, to us?"

The chambermaid whom he'd learned was called Wendy tapped at the open door, her capable hands holding a full pitcher of fresh water and clean linens. "Right-o, guv," she said, marching into the room as if she owned it, "you tell her. She'll listen to you if you keep at her. Stubborn as the day is long, that one, but she always listens to reason in the end."

Guy, who was not accustomed to being treated in such an informal manner by his servants—or anyone else's— had become resigned over the last few days to this informal attitude. He didn't know if it had anything to do with his unkempt state, which made him look more like a laborer than a lord, but he strongly suspected Joanna's hand in this as well. They were devoted to her, the lot of them.

Margaret had installed her sister to look after her own family so that she could devote herself full-time to Joanna and Milo—this he knew from Toomsby, who had it from Bill, who of course Guy now knew was married to Margaret. Both Bill and Toomsby spent more time up at the house anxiously inquiring after Joanna than they did down at the stables at their work.

Dickson practically haunted the nursery, and even Ambrose, normally a cool and steady fellow, dragged about, finding all sorts of excuses to join Dickson upstairs. Guy had never been given so many ridiculous messages about nothing.

"Here we go, my lord," Wendy said, parking herself on the other side of the bed. "Shall I start from my end or would you like to do the honors?"

"I will start," Guy said, holding his hand out for the cold flannel. He pushed up the sleeve of Joanna's nightdress and methodically smoothed the cloth over her arm, handing it back to Wendy for refreshing, then lifted Joanna's limp head and ran it over the back of her neck and around to the front, where the sweat gleamed. Once again he gave the cloth to Wendy and she wet it and wrung it out.

He pushed the bedclothes aside and did the same to Joanna's calf, having instantly quashed Wendy and Margaret's initial objections to this immodesty.

"If you think I'm admiring the turn of her ankle or the shape of her calf just now, you're mad," he'd roared at their protests. "I will look after her, and you will do as I ask." That had been that.

"My turn," Wendy said cheerfully, taking the flannel. "If I was you, I'd take myself off for a bit and get cleaned up and rested. Shelley and me, we can look after things here for a bit, can't we, Shell?"

"Right you are," Shelley said. "Get behind the ear, Wendy. It's always hotter behind the ear."

Guy glanced up to see Wendy's comrade-in-arms standing directly behind her, offering her advice as usual. He closed his eyes and gave his head a quick shake.

"Dickson is bringing a tray for you, my lord. He says it's time you eat, and he's right," Margaret called from the door. "Milo is already sitting down to his meal, and he has a picture he's burning to show you."

"Thank you." Guy reluctantly pushed himself to his feet. He had no appetite, but he knew he needed to keep up his strength if he was going to bring Joanna through. And he also knew that Margaret wanted him out of the room for a short time so that the three of them could wash Joanna down thoroughly and change her bed linens, the two things they refused to do in his presence.

They were like hens, he thought sourly, trying to get the

rooster off his roost and out of the henhouse so they could go about their scratching and clucking.

Still, it wasn't as if Joanna were his wife—certain proprieties had to be observed for her sake and the sake of the staff.

How ironic. When he'd been married to Lydia, he'd happily let the servants look after her whenever she took to her bed, which was more often than not. They had done so without any obvious enthusiasm, and he had never even attempted to enter her bedroom.

Now here he was, desperately concerned over a woman who was not his wife, a slew of servants practically fighting each other to tend to her needs, and he was being shut out of the one place he wanted to be.

"Sit down here, Papa," Miles said, pointing at the chair next to his own at the nursery table. "Here is Jojo's painting. I think you look very fine."

He pushed the picture over to Guy and picked up his spoon again. "Rice pudding," he said. "My favorite."

Guy picked up the frame, holding it carefully by the wood. He drew in a sharp breath of shock as his eye took in his own likeness.

His surprise came not from seeing himself so well-depicted: He'd had his portrait painted twice before, and numerous sketches done. Instead, it came from the obvious talent of the artist. Joanna was truly gifted.

The delicacy of detail, the way she'd unerringly captured not just his physical likeness but something much more personal about his character—and all solely from her mind's eye—astonished him. She'd used nothing more than charcoal, and yet somehow she'd managed to convey an expression in his eyes that spoke volumes and told him more than he wanted to know about himself and about Joanna's ability to see inside the heart he'd thought he had kept secret from everyone. How had she known? How could she possibly have known?

He very carefully placed the frame back on the table and rested his forehead on the heel of his hand. Joanna. For all she had been hurt, accused falsely, and despite the loss of so many people she loved, she had let nothing stand in the way of her ability to see truth and her willingness to depict it. For that matter, she'd let nothing stand in the way of her willingness to speak it either, he thought.

"Papa? Papa, don't worry so. Jojo will get better. I know it and Boscoe does too." He slipped off his chair and snuck one hand under Guy's. "You have to believe it too. Jojo always says that you have to believe in the magic of angels, and if you believe hard enough, the angels will listen and they will always answer. Would you like some of my rice pudding?"

"Yes, please," Guy said, blinking back the sting of tears. "I think I would like that very much."

17

Joanna floated formlessly, lost in a world that kept tumbling upside down and inside out. Fragments of images drifted about in her head, as if she'd dropped a glass painting of her entire life and the broken shards were trying to fit themselves back together but not doing a very good job.

Snowstorms blew in her beautiful villa garden, where Cosmo bent over pots of bedding plants, smiling up at her. *Joanna, sweet. Please, Joanna, come back to me.* But it wasn't she who had left, she thought with a frown, it was Cosmo. He'd died and left her all alone again.

Wendy wore a white wedding dress made from flannel. Wet. Why was her dress so wet? It must be the snow, Joanna decided, sighing. Hot. She was so hot. That's right, the summer she'd married Cosmo had been almost too hot to allow her to go outside during the day. She must have poured a glass of water over herself in order to cool down.

Water. What a lovely thought. A glass appeared at her lips as if by magic, but she had a terrible time swallowing and the water dribbled down her chin. If only her teeth would stop chattering.

She must still be out in the snow. Snow. Sleep. That was it, she had to sleep.

Such a lovely bright light shone just in front of her, so compelling. All she had to do was move forward, let herself be drawn into it.

Joanna. Joanna, fight. You have to fight.

She frowned. The annoying voice just wouldn't go away. It seemed to echo inside her head, slipping in between the steady throbs that hurt so much. How was she supposed to sleep with that din going on?

She groaned and rolled over to her side, her body shaking violently. Why couldn't she stop shaking? Anyone would think she had the nervous jitters. Wasn't that what Bunch always said—she behaved as if she was infested with fleas?

Quickly, have Ambrose summon the doctor, Margaret. Tell him to come at once—this instant. I will brook no delay!

Why did Margaret need a doctor? And why was Guy shouting? Oh—surely the doctor was not for Miles? "Milo? Milo?" she cried.

A small, cool hand slipped into hers. "I am here, Jojo."

She sighed in relief. Safe. Her little Milo was safe.

"I love you, Jojo. We all love you. Please come home? You have been gone a very long time, seven whole days. I counted."

She smiled. Home. What a nice thought. If only she wasn't so tired, maybe she could work out where it was and how to get there. . . .

"For the love of God, Lindshaw, you have to be able to do something! Can you not see that she's slipping away?" Guy cried, wanting to shake the doctor till his crooked teeth rattled. "What good are you if you cannot fix her? She's burning up, man, and all your suggestions have been useless to date."

"I am sorry, Lord Greaves," the doctor said, detaching his coat from Guy's fingers. "As I explained to you from the beginning, the fever must run its course. I do not believe in bleeding, I do not believe in interfering in any way, save for keeping the contessa as comfortable as possible, which I have tried to do with the doses of laudanum in her water."

Guy sank back into his chair. "Forgive me. This is not your doing. I am overset."

"And overtired. My lord, if you do not rest properly you

might very well find yourself in the same situation. You are strained nearly beyond endurance."

"I rest very nicely here," Guy said stubbornly.

"That is not the same thing. You have been at this for a week now, and from what your servants tell me, you have eaten hardly enough to keep a sparrow alive."

"Rice pudding," he said with a grim smile. "My son feeds me rice pudding regularly. I think I am rather coming to like it."

"Nevertheless—"

"Nevertheless," Guy said, glaring at him, "Joanna is in desperate straits."

"Then pray, my lord. I am afraid there is little else to be done at this point. She will either make it through this night or she will die." He picked up his bag and quietly left.

Guy, who had not prayed in years, having long ago lost his faith in God, stared angrily at the door. He dropped his gaze to his clenched hands. What did he have to lose? Joanna lay burning in her bed, and nothing else seemed to be working. He would do anything to keep her here where she belonged.

He slipped to his knees next to the bed and lowered his head onto his hands. He released a long breath and tried to gather his thoughts.

"Dear God," he finally said awkwardly, as if addressing a total stranger and not entirely sure of the appropriate salutation, "I need your help. Your—er—your servant Joanna is very ill, and I would appreciate it very much if you would spare her. We need her about the place. At Wakefield, that is. Not just me, but my son, and . . . well, there are a multitude of people here—and probably many others in Italy I do not even know about—who would be very upset if you took her."

Guy lifted his head, suddenly aware of a silent presence at his side. He quickly opened his eyes, only to see Miles standing there, watching him silently.

"Oh. Miles. I was—I was trying to say a little prayer for Joanna," he said, feeling incredibly foolish. "I'm afraid I am not very good at it."

"Like this, Papa," Miles said, kneeling next to him and clasping his hands together on the bed. "Like Jojo showed me."

He bowed his head and closed his eyes. "Our Father, who art in heaven, hallowed be thy name . . ."

Joanna opened her eyes to darkness. Only the flicker of two candles burning on the mantelpiece illuminated the still room. She was in her bed at . . . at Wakefield? Yes. That was right. The faint light of the moon streamed through the crack in the draperies in front of her, the ones that never closed properly. The moon seemed brighter than it should for one that had been only just waxing.

She tried to orient as her eyes adjusted to the dark. She'd been dreaming that she was traveling on a long voyage home but remembered nothing more, only that the seas had been rough and she'd been confined to her cabin.

Moving her hand, she wondered why she felt so weak, as if just lifting a finger required the most enormous effort.

She strained hard to remember what had happened: She vaguely recalled having been put into a tub of hot water, and then something about Margaret putting her into a bed with a warm brick at her feet. Yes, that was it. The snowstorm. She'd been lost and so terribly cold, and then Guy took her inside the stables and warmed her with his body. He carried her to the house and that was when Margaret took over. That was right. Guy had left, looking both anxious and annoyed at the same time.

She must have slept for hours and hours.

Wondering why she felt so terribly wet and uncomfortable, she reached down under the covers with an effort.

Little wonder—her nightdress was soaked through. Hadn't Margaret bothered to dry her off after her bath?

Sighing, she slowly turned her head to the side. Her eyes widened in astonishment. What was Guy doing in her bedroom of all places? He dozed in an armchair he'd pulled close to her bed, his head resting against the back. Even in the dim light she could see that he looked exhausted, as if he hadn't slept in days.

"Guy?" she whispered, her throat feeling as parched as if she'd marched through an Eastern desert in the midday sun.

His eyes instantly opened and he bolted upright.

"Joanna? Oh, thank God. Joanna?" He grabbed her hands and pressed them to his mouth, fervently kissing them as if they were religious relics. "Joanna," he murmured against her skin.

"Yes," she said with a weak smile. "That is my name. Why are you behaving in such a peculiar fashion? And why on earth do you look so bedraggled? I thought I told you to go take a bath."

"That was last week," he said, running his hand over the shadow of beard on his face.

"Last week?" she said, not willing to believe him. A week couldn't possibly have gone by. It just couldn't have. "How is that possible?" she asked stupidly.

"You've been ill. Very ill. I—" He ran the back of his hand over his mouth. "We have all been worried."

Joanna passed her tongue over her dry lips. No wonder she felt so ghastly. "Could I have some water, please?"

"Yes, of course." He instantly pushed back his chair and moved over to the nightstand, pouring her a glass from the pitcher. He sat on the edge of the bed and slipped his arm around her back, helping her to sit. "Sip it slowly," he said, holding the glass to her lips, supporting her head against his chest.

She drank gratefully, the lovely, cool liquid bliss in her dry mouth and throat. "Thank you," she said as he helped her to lie down again. "I feel like a helpless infant, I am so weak."

He stroked the wet hair off her brow. "You are also soaked through. You have been delirious, burning up with fever, but it finally broke tonight, and I thank God for it."

"Oh," she said nervously at the idea that she'd been delirious. "Did I say anything I oughtn't to?" She could just imagine herself pouring out all of her lustful yearnings straight into his ear.

"If you did, I couldn't make it out. You mostly babbled nonsense. I will summon the infantry to come and change you and the bedding—you've soaked that through as well."

She crinkled her brow. "Did you say the infantry?" she asked, thinking she must have misunderstood.

"Yes, commanded by Margaret, Wendy, and Shelley. They are sleeping next door."

Joanna smiled up at him, so tired that even that took effort. "You almost sound as if you might be fond of them," she murmured. "Have you acquainted yourself with your servants in my absence, my lord?"

"I had no choice. They stormed the nursery bastions and essentially took over. I have never been so ordered about in my life. No one listens to a word I say, not even a newcomer like Emile's wife, who has recently moved in and taken over the nursery cooking while Margaret has had her hands full."

"Good." Joanna, well-satisfied, closed her eyes. "How is Milo?" she asked.

"He's as bad as the rest of them," he said, stroking her fingers. "He never stops telling me what to do and how to do it. You have an enormous pile of drawings to admire, by the by—Milo has been busy producing great art. He has told me that when he grows up he intends to be a soldier who paints horses."

Joanna squeezed her fingers around his thumb. "A fine ambition."

"Indeed. It has more promise than wanting to be a horse who paints soldiers." Guy released her hand and stood. "I would stay, but I think you must get dry. I will see you in the morning."

He ran his hand over her brow one last time. "Welcome home, Joanna," he said.

He quickly left before she could answer, softly and firmly shutting the door behind him.

Wakefield Abbey
March 20, 1819

For the first time in her life, Joanna was bored out of her mind. She'd been cooped up for nearly a month now, four weeks, the entire cycle of a moon.

She stared moodily from her chair out at the fine spring day, at the daisies with their white petals and pink tips that ran rampant over the green lawn, and cursed the ridiculous doctor who refused to let her out of her prison and into the fresh air.

"You must rest, contessa, let your body recover from the shock it has been through," he'd said, speaking to her as if she were a woman of ninety years about to draw her last breath. "I prescribe bed rest. Bed rest, as much nourishment as you can take, and nothing too stimulating in the way of company. I suggest you keep your visitors to the immediate family." He took her pulse. "Keep it steady. Your heart has undergone a strain."

Joanna pressed the back of her fist against her mouth, stifling a wicked smile. If the good doctor only knew.

Guy spent a good half of the day with her, chatting,

reading aloud to her, playing with Miles while she watched from her bed. If that wasn't stimulating company, she didn't know what was. Miles had turned into a completely normal, energetic boy of five, and Guy . . . well, he most definitely did not keep her pulse steady. As for her heart, its battered condition didn't even bear thinking about.

Still, she looked forward to Guy's visits more than she could say, and with each passing day she learned more about him. They had become comfortable with each other, good friends, she thought, although she still couldn't help her immediate physical reaction to his presence, as if he were the striking flint that set her to burning.

The first two weeks had been easier: She'd been terribly weak and unable to do very much for herself, let alone feel anything more than immense gratitude for his concern and attention. But as her strength had returned to normal, so had the rest of her, and she discovered to her dismay that nothing had changed. And yet everything had changed.

She still yearned for him, the deep aching so constant now that she'd grown accustomed to it, like a nagging tooth. A bad tooth, though, could be pulled from the gum when the pain grew too great. She had no such easy solution to extricate Guy de Salis from her heart.

How had she allowed him to become such a fixture in her existence? When had he tiptoed past all her defenses and taken her heart captive—she who had been so much on guard? She couldn't put her finger on any defining moment, but that was irrelevant now. She'd somehow become so entangled in his life, in the life of his child, the lives of his staff, that she couldn't imagine living any other way. The thought of returning to her villa, once a constant source of comfort, had become anything but.

Joanna buried her forehead against the palm of her

hand, utterly miserable, as she had been for days, now that her head had cleared and she could think properly again.

Miles had recovered. She no longer had an excuse to stay. Oh, she knew that Guy would not force the issue—he felt so guilty about being the cause of her illness that he'd lavished attention on her. And as absurd and undeserved as his guilt was, Joanna hadn't had the willpower to send him away to look after more important things.

Eventually, though, his guilt would disappear, as would he. Not from Miles's life—never again would that happen. The two of them were bound now as father and son ought to be, and watching them together gave her great joy. Miles had his father to love, and Guy finally had his son.

Now that he didn't need her anymore, Guy would disappear from her life.

She knew him well enough now to know that he would do it gently and quietly, simply by withdrawing, spending his time with his friends as was his habit, hunting, conducting his business, essentially returning to his normal life.

And she would be left with her life at Wakefield, looking after Miles, a child who wasn't hers no matter how much he felt like her own, playing the multiple roles of governess, assistant housekeeper, and erstwhile houseguest, waiting for the occasional crumbs of attention Guy threw her.

Joanna rubbed her hands over her eyes, refusing to cry. She couldn't live like that. She wouldn't. She had her dignity and her pride. She would simply start her life over again back in Italy where she belonged. She hadn't painted properly in nearly six months.

That was exactly what she'd do, she decided, making up her mind, as much as her heart ached with the finality of the decision. She would book passage to Italy as soon as the winter seas had calmed enough to be relatively safe. Until then, she would be the one to gradually withdraw, giving them both a dignified way out. No fuss, no tears, no recriminations.

"Mutiny?"

Her head jerked up. Guy stood in the open doorway, one hand leaning on the side of the frame, his dark eyes alight with amusement.

"Guy . . . I didn't expect you." Her heart sank in her chest. *Not now, please Lord, not now when I've only just made a firm resolution. . . .*

"I hope not," he said, advancing into the room. "Your expression looked as if you were going to throw any comer overboard and toss stones after him to make sure he sank."

She made a halfhearted attempt at a smile. "Forgive me. I am not in the best of temper."

"Ah. I *think* I might have a solution to that. Would you care to wobble downstairs with me? I only ask because I know that your pride does not allow me to carry you farther than I can throw you, if you have any choice in the matter."

She knew perfectly well that he referred to all the times he'd carried her out of her bed when she'd still been too weak to walk and taken her to the nursery sofa so that Wendy and Shelley could clean and air her room. If he'd understood the reasons for her halfhearted objections, he'd have dropped her like a hotcake.

"I will walk, thank you," she replied. "I am much stronger, you know. I have been marching about this—this cage on my own, getting my muscles back in order."

"You sound like a lion in a zoo defending his right to be released because he's feeling very much better after his capture and mistreatment and is now healthy enough to go back to his old habits."

"I will not bite, I promise," she said with a reluctant smile. No matter how hard she tried, Guy always managed to amuse her. "Did I bite before?"

"Rather nastily when your protective instincts came to the fore. Let us just say that Miles was your cub and Lydia a sister member of your pride. Beware the lone male who dares interfere—or, God forbid, neglects his duties. Some of the bites were well-deserved." He took her woolen shawl from her lap and wrapped it around her shoulders, holding out his hand. "Shall we?"

She took it but used her own strength to stand. "Where are we going?" she asked, thrilled at this unexpected escape.

"Aha. You will just have to wait and see. I thought it easiest if we go down the back nursery stairs. Not only will you be spared a loudly cheering audience, but it is a much shorter distance, although aesthetically not very pleasing. Do you mind?"

She shook her head. "I told you, I am perfectly well. That horrid doctor ought to be put to bed for a month and see how he likes it."

"I can assure you he would be screaming and kicking from the first moment on. Doctors are not known for following their own advice. I finally decided I wasn't going to follow it either. You've had enough confinement."

He led her down the corridor to the back staircase, never used by her owing to its steepness, never mind its angles. She couldn't believe anyone would ever have designed such a treacherous thing for children, who might easily have toppled down and broken their necks. She'd bet that Mrs. Loppitt had used it all the time to take Miles out on his forced marches.

"Sorry," he said, suddenly reaching down and picking her up in his arms. "Dangerous territory. I remember falling down the blighted thing when I was about seven. I was lucky I broke nothing more than my arm."

"You read my mind," she said, her arms clinging around his neck as he carefully made his way down. "I was just thinking about how awful this would be for any child to navigate."

"True. You have to remember, though, that this part of the house wasn't built for children. What remains of the original wing was a Cistercian abbey before my ancestor came around in Elizabethan times and rebuilt most everything."

Joanna, who wasn't thinking very hard about architecture at that particular moment—more occupied with breathing in Guy's beloved scent and enjoying his arms holding her hard and fast in his—just nodded dreamily. "What about the chapel?" she asked, trying to sound as if she were paying attention.

"Oh, that's part of the original fourteenth-century structure, as is the gatehouse," he said, finally reaching the bottom of the treacherously winding steps and pushing the door open with one hand. "The de Salis family didn't take the place over for another two centuries, but when we did, the dust flew. The chapel and this wing were nearly the only things left untouched. You will find the remains of my illustrious ancestor in the chapel, his effigy looking remarkably smug."

He gently deposited her back to earth, much to her regret—she'd so enjoyed the ride.

"Come," he said, cupping his hand under her elbow. "It is not far now."

She drank in a deep breath of the fresh, lovely air. "Oh, blessed freedom," she said fervently.

"I hadn't realized you felt *quite* so trapped," he replied, amused. "Did Miles and I not entertain you well enough?"

"You entertained me beautifully, and I thank you for your efforts," she said, admiring a bank of pale yellow primroses. "It is not the same, though, as having the ability to come and go."

"No," he agreed, "it is not. You were very brave."

She didn't reply, coming to a stunned halt as they rounded the corner. There in the middle of the back garden stood an easel, a blank canvas propped up against it. A table with what appeared to be a full set of oils and brushes and all the other bits and pieces necessary to an artist stood next to it.

Miles jumped up and down, waving his hands. "Do you like your surprise, Jojo?" he said, skipping toward her, his eyes dancing with excitement.

She nodded speechlessly, then looked up at Guy, one trembling hand covering her mouth. She wouldn't cry, she absolutely would not.

"Do you like your surprise, Jojo?" he echoed softly, a smile hovering about the corners of his mouth.

"Yes," she managed to say in a choked voice. "I like it very much. I—I do not know how to thank you."

"Thank me by using it, by painting your heart's desire," he said, covering her hand with his own.

Her heart's desire . . . oh, *how* was she ever going to find the strength to leave him?

She disengaged herself and knelt to embrace Miles. "Thank you, my poppet. You and your papa are very, very thoughtful." She kissed his cheek and smoothed her hand over his sun-warmed hair, so silky, so like his father's. As usual, Miles had discarded his hat somewhere along the way.

Miles wrapped his arms around her neck. "Papa said you would probably cry," he whispered.

A laugh caught in Joanna's throat, and she quickly wiped away her tears with her hand before Miles or Guy could see them. "Why would I cry on a day when I am so happy?" she said, leaning back and running her finger down his little nose.

He shot her a suspicious look. "Are you sure?" he said, touching his finger to the corner of her eye.

"I am very sure." She stood and took his hand in hers, glancing up at Guy.

"Shall we walk a little?" she said, thinking she'd better write to Bunch straightaway and announce her plans before she dug herself in any deeper.

18

$\mathcal{G}$uy and Joanna ate dinner that night at the nursery table with Miles, as had become their habit, although Emile always insisted on sending them both up something more elaborate and substantial than the usual light fare that his wife prepared for Miles. For once Joanna was glad for Emile's rich sauces—she'd lost weight during her illness.

Miles, delighted to have their attention while he consumed his boiled eggs, held up a strip of toast that he'd dipped into the yellow yolk. "Look, Papa," he said, "Margaret made me soldiers."

"That's nice," Guy replied absently, then turned to Joanna. "I thought you might paint outdoors when the weather is fine," he said. "With luck we'll have a pleasant spring, but if not we can always have your supplies brought upstairs. Whichever you prefer."

She didn't know what to say. Should she just come right out and tell him that she was leaving? "We will wait and see," she murmured. "One never knows what tomorrow might bring."

"Yes, of course," he said, but looked at her oddly before returning his attention to his fillet of sole.

He waited until Margaret had taken Miles off to ready him for bed before he spoke again. "Joanna," he said, "did I push you too far today? Are you more tired than you are willing to acknowledge for fear you will be shut back in your bedroom?"

"No—oh, not at all," she said, determined that was one thing that *wouldn't* happen. "I am perfectly well, as I told you. I—I feel stronger by the minute."

"Then why the unusual silence? Why do I sense a

withdrawal in your manner? I have felt it since this afternoon—surely you are not offended by your surprise."

"Offended? No! I am grateful, very grateful. I told you how touched I was by your thoughtfulness."

"In that case, perhaps you will tell me what is really on your mind," he said, rubbing his thumb against the corner of his mouth.

She hadn't expected to have to confront the subject so soon, but she didn't see any point in delaying the inevitable, now that he had opened the door.

She summoned up her courage. "I think I am merely a little melancholy," she said, thinking at least that part was true. "With the approach of spring my thoughts are turning to my gardens back home. Planting season is nearly around the corner, and I have so many ideas about what I would like to add this year." She forced a smile to her lips. "I thought that maybe I would try a new strain of roses." She felt sick as the words came out, unmistakable in their intent, impossible to retrieve now.

Guy's expression stayed neutral, but she thought she saw his hands stiffen slightly on his fork and knife. "You are planning a trip back home?" he asked.

"Yes, I thought it time that I leave you all in peace, now that I am recovered. You have been so kind and patient with me, but I cannot overstay my welcome."

"Kind and patient," he repeated, a slight frown marking his brow.

"Yes," she replied, feeling absurdly nervous. "And now that Miles is better and you and he are happy in each other's company, you do not really need me any longer. So I thought I would return to where I *am* needed—I cannot leave my villa unattended for very much longer."

"I see. You miss Italy," he said.

"Oh, I do," she said, warming to her story, desperate to convince him. The last thing she wished for was for him to press her to stay. "I miss Italy, my villa, my friends. Heavens, I've been gone—what—almost six months now? I think it is high time I return, and surely you must agree?"

"I don't recall being consulted," he said flatly.

"You must get on with your life, just as I must get on with mine. And—and I mustn't let Miles grow too dependent on me. One day you are bound to marry again, and then he will have a new mama to love him dearly." She fiddled with her napkin. "It will not do for Miles to grow any more attached to me."

"I can see that you have thought out your reasons for leaving very carefully," Guy said, tossing his napkin down and standing. "You might do me the courtesy of letting me know when you plan to leave so that I might arrange for someone to look after Miles. If you will excuse me, I will say good night to my son before he goes to sleep."

He vanished through the door of the night nursery without another word.

"Papa," Miles said, sitting up in bed, "what do you think Jojo will paint first?"

"I don't know," Guy said, wondering if she'd paint anything at all. She wouldn't have time, not if she planned on returning to Italy so soon.

Leaving. She was leaving.

Her announcement had come as a terrible shock—he'd never even considered the possibility that she might decide to go back to Italy. What was Miles going to do without her, or the staff for that matter? They'd all come to depend on her—Joanna, the sun around which everything else revolved.

More to the point, what was *he* going to do without her? The thought of being without her sent a sharp pain stabbing through his heart.

"Papa? What is the matter? You have a funny look on your face."

He smoothed his hand over Milo's hair. "Nothing. I am tired, that is all."

"You cannot be tired. It is my bedtime, not yours," Miles said with irrefutable logic.

"You are absolutely right," Guy said. "Then I must be wide awake and only wishing I was tired."

Miles giggled. "Sometimes you are very silly, Papa."

"Indeed I am." A damned fool was more like it. When had he started feeling this way about Joanna, as if she were not just part of life at Wakefield, a good friend and interesting companion, but an integral part of his very being?

He hadn't brought her back from the brink of death so that she could leave him, damn her. And yet she had every right to do so. He had no claim on her. Joanna could do exactly as she pleased, although he couldn't help but be upset that she cared so little for Miles, so little for him, that she would just pick up and go back to her bloody villa and her damned gardens, behaving as if that were far more important than what Miles needed.

What *he* needed. Dear God, he wasn't even sure what that was. These feelings had hit him like a bolt of lightning out of a clear blue sky. If he wasn't mistaken, he was head over heels in love with Joanna, and he'd never even realized it.

Miles picked up Guy's hand and toyed with his fingers. "Papa, when I am all grown up like you, can I marry someone like Jojo?"

Guy started. "You can marry whomever you please, Milo, although I do hope you choose someone like Joanna."

Milo nodded thoughtfully. "I know I do not want to marry someone like Mama. Why did you marry her, Papa? She wasn't very nice to you, not like Jojo."

"No, not like Jojo," he said. "I suppose I married her because I . . . because I thought she was pretty and she was amusing. I didn't know her very well. In the end we discovered that we didn't like each other very much. We had nothing in common."

"Jojo is pretty, and she is fun," Miles pointed out. "And you like her and she likes you, and you have lots in common, like horses and me. Why don't you marry her? I think she would make a very nice mama."

Guy stared at his young son. *Marry* her. He could, couldn't he? If he married her, she couldn't leave him. Ever. He could go to bed with her every night—now, there was an appealing thought. Ever since Joanna had recovered he'd been desperately fighting his attraction to her, feeling like a callow youth who couldn't control his physical impulses. Even today when he'd carried Joanna downstairs, he'd felt his groin stir and tighten and had prayed that she wouldn't notice the hard evidence when he put her down.

"I am sure she would make a very nice mama," Guy said, feeling shaken to his core. She would also make a nice wife, a very, very nice wife. Why the hell hadn't he thought of it himself? The only problem was that he didn't have the first idea of how she felt about him. Oh, he knew she liked him, but love?

She'd loved Cosmo. She'd adored Cosmo, he thought sourly.

"He was my husband, that is how I loved him."

Of course, she'd also said that he'd been a considerate lover, a gentleman. That could mean anything, although he didn't think it sounded particularly exciting. Anyway, somehow he couldn't envision Joanna wrapped in a passionate embrace with a man old enough to be her father. He'd bet that Cosmo hadn't even begun to stir the deep passions he was sure Joanna was capable of feeling.

Well, he could fix that if she'd give him half a chance, he thought with determination. He'd just have to work out how best to approach the subject of marriage, because he sure as hell didn't want to get kicked in the teeth, not by Joanna.

He'd have to think the whole thing through very carefully. Logically. That was it. A nice dose of logic would be extremely helpful. Then he could broach the subject with her in the morning, when they were both well-rested.

He bent over and kissed Milo's round cheek. "You are a very, very clever boy, and I love you very much," he said, holding the covers up for Milo to slip under. "Sleep well."

Miles, who looked well-satisfied, beamed up at him. "I love you, Papa. I love Jojo too."

"I know, sweet boy, I do know. Now, go to sleep. I will see you in the morning."

Joanna sat in the recessed nursery window, her knees pulled up to her chest, her arms wrapped around them, her head leaning against the windowpane. The moon, nearly full and hanging bright in the night sky, cast its light over the nursery, but she hardly noticed.

Although the clock had already chimed eleven, she wasn't able to sleep, her thoughts preoccupied with the conversation she'd had with Guy over dinner.

She buried her face against her arms, utterly miserable. Although Guy had behaved in the exact fashion she had hoped for, making no objections to her plans, she secretly wished he might have shown a *little* more reaction.

Perhaps she'd been harboring the foolish hope somewhere deep in her equally foolish heart that he would fling himself to his knees and beg her to stay.

Hardly likely, she thought with a heavy sigh. He probably felt relieved at her announcement but was too much of a gentleman to show it.

Fine. She had said what she had set out to say and would now quickly and efficiently proceed according to plan.

Lifting her head, she rubbed her hands over her face,

trying to force her thoughts into some kind of order. First thing in the morning she would write that letter to Bunch, then another to her man of business, requesting him to arrange for passage and funds. She'd write a third letter to her steward, alerting him that she planned to be home by early summer.

Bunch had taught her well—practicality would carry one through any situation, no matter how painful, no matter how badly one's heart ached, no matter how every nerve felt rubbed raw.

She stared out at the moon, the exact same moon that hung over her villa just now, the moon she took pleasure from watching from her veranda as she sat outside, enjoying the cool of the summer night. Alone.

No—enjoying the scent of the night, she thought with determination, squeezing her eyes tightly shut and trying to conjure up the fragrance. Jasmine. Jasmine and . . . and roses—

"Joanna?"

Her head shot up in shock, her heart thudding to a stop. Guy stood in the doorway, wearing only trousers and a shirt open at the neck.

Moonlight streamed over him, giving him an unworldly appearance, silver catching in a halo around his dark hair as if he were Hades himself come up from the underworld.

Her hand crept to the neck of her nightdress, her heart quickening again, the pace now completely erratic.

"What—what are you doing here?" she asked, lowering her knees and sitting up straight. She couldn't begin to imagine what he could want at this hour, now that she was well again. He surely hadn't come to check on her health?

"I needed to say something and it wouldn't wait." He didn't move any closer, just stood there in the open door, his gaze steadily fixed on her.

"What is it?" she said, bewildered by the piercing intensity in his eyes.

"I am in love with you," he said quietly. "I thought you should know that before you make any more decisions. Good night." He turned and closed the door behind him.

Joanna, so stunned that she could hardly breathe, let alone think, wrapped her arms around herself, forcing herself to concentrate on inhaling in deep gulps.

He was in *love* with her?

Numb with shock, she shook her head back and forth, over and over, her hands covering her mouth, then sliding up over her hot cheeks as if she could cool them.

He had never given a single clue that he thought of her as anything more than a friend—a good friend, perhaps, but nothing beyond that. And yet he couldn't have been more clear just now.

Her only experience of love had been with Cosmo, and he had been forthright about expressing his feelings as they developed. She had known what to expect when he declared himself.

Then again, she'd never known what to expect from Guy—why should this be any different?

And why was she sitting here like a fool? Guy had just told her that he loved her, and he surely expected an answer.

She grabbed her shawl, ran to the door and jerked it open, and without bothering with a candle, navigated by the light of the moon down the corridor, down the stairs, down a further corridor and yet another one, and directly to the door of Guy's bedroom.

She knocked softly.

A moment later the door abruptly opened. Guy stood there staring at her, his shirt now gone, his face and head damp, a towel slung over his shoulder.

"Joanna?" he said, staring at her incredulously. "What the devil are you doing here? I thought we said good night."

"*You* said good night. I came to tell you that I . . . that I—"

She didn't have a chance to finish her sentence, let alone her explanation. Guy grabbed her by the arm and pulled her abruptly inside, kicking the door shut behind him.

He held her by both shoulders, looking down into her face, his expression half pained, half laughing.

"Are you completely mad, coming to my room in the middle of the night?" he demanded.

"No," she replied indignantly. "I am being very logical. I thought you should have the courtesy of a reply."

"And what would that be?" he said, dropping his hands and stepping back, his gaze never leaving her face. "Are you now going to tell me that I should be horsewhipped for my impudence?"

"No, although I could do without the constant shocks you like to give me."

"Is that so?" he said dryly. "I suppose you think you are entirely blameless in that regard."

"Guy, please do not fence with me now. I came to tell you that I love you too, that I believe I have loved you for some time, although I cannot say exactly when my feelings changed. I cannot think when yours did either, but—"

"For the love of God, will you hush just for once?"

His head came down before she even registered the movement, his mouth covering hers in a hard, hungry kiss, his arms moving about her back and pulling her close against him as he fiercely demanded a response.

She had no trouble giving it to him. She'd wanted this for so long, so long. . . . She hadn't ever realized just how much she'd wanted it until now.

Her arms clung around his neck as she drank in his taste, the feel of his mouth claiming hers, the hardness of his body pressed so tightly to her that she could feel every muscle that strained against her.

Without warning he abruptly released her and walked across the room, his back turned to her. "Joanna," he said, his hand smoothing across the back of his neck in a gesture now familiar, "why are you in my bedroom?"

"Because you pulled me in here," she said, trying to calm her rapid breathing with little success. She felt entirely undone in a way she'd never experienced before. "I was perfectly happy giving you my answer from the hallway."

He turned slightly and looked at her, one eyebrow raised. "Really. So anyone who might be passing could hear it?"

"I didn't think of that." She tried very hard not to let her eyes wander over his chest, now that she could actually see the anatomy beneath the clothes. Oh, he really was so beautifully structured, his pectoral muscles asymmetrical, nicely shaped but not overly developed, the ribs beneath ridged all the way down to his flat stomach.

"Joanna? Do you really think it wise for you to be here?"

She lifted her gaze to his, running her tongue over her bottom lip. "Probably not," she admitted.

"How astute of you," he said. "Tell me, are you planning on staying?"

She sucked in a deep breath and stared down at the ground. "If you really do want me to stay here at Wakefield, then I cannot refuse."

"I was referring to my bedroom," he said.

"Oh."

"Oh," he said. "Joanna, as you have pointed out to me yourself, you are no virgin. If you do not leave in the next minute or so, I think you have a very good idea of what is going to happen, as I am no monk. You must know that I have wanted you for a very long time."

"Well, no, I didn't, although I am sure that you would not lie about such a thing."

Guy gazed up at the ceiling. "My dear, sweet love, I think you are missing the point. Perhaps I have been obtuse." He raked both hands through his hair. "If you do not leave right this minute, I will not answer for the conse-quences. Is that clear enough?"

Joanna considered for all of two seconds. "I—I know I am violating every last principle I ever believed in, but if the memories of a few months of happiness with you are what I will have to carry me through the rest of my life, then I am willing to sacrifice those principles."

She forced herself to look up at him.

Guy did not wear anything close to an appropriately appreciative expression at her willingness to become a fallen woman for his sake. Instead, he looked as if he was about to burst into hysterical laughter at any moment.

Joanna drew herself up with great dignity. "Unless, of course, I have misunderstood you and you do not want me for your mistress after all."

Sinking down into an armchair, his hand rubbed up and down over his face. "I believe," he said after a moment, "I believe that you have most definitely misunderstood me."

"Oh," she said, feeling not only horribly embarrassed and humiliated, but for some reason terribly disap-pointed. "Perhaps you meant that you wanted me only for this one night."

He looked away, tracing his finger back and forth over his mouth, staring hard at a point somewhere in the dis-tance, his head turned so far that she could no longer see his expression at all. "If you persist in believing that piece of idiocy, I shall have to shake you till your brains rattle. Did I not mention that I was in love with you?"

"Yes," she said, by now thoroughly confused. "But then, if none of those other things, what *do* you want from me?"

He abruptly stood and came back to her, standing di-rectly in front of her, but without touching her in any way. Looking down at her, he tilted his head slightly to one side, his eyes suddenly gentle, the amusement completely gone.

"I want to marry you," he said.

"To—to *marry* me?" Joanna stammered, taking a step

backward, unable to believe she'd heard him correctly— she'd never even entertained the possibility. "You cannot be serious."

"I am very serious. I want you to be my wife, to be Miles's mother, to be mistress of my house." He smiled at her. "You've already taken on the latter two roles. Why not take on the third?"

"M-marriage? I can't!" she said, bowing her head, her heart breaking all over again. Oh, *Lord,* the sacrifices she'd had to make for the sake of society, and this last one the worst of all.

"Why ever not?" he said, sounding not the least bit perturbed.

"Guy, I would ruin you," she said with exasperation. "You know what is said about me, all the rumors, the innuendoes. I have been accused of entertaining a man in my bed when I lived with the Oxleys, of not having the decency to marry him, I've—I've been accused of poisoning my husband, for heaven's sake. Surely I do not have to remind you?"

"No, you do not have to remind me," he said, looking entirely unconcerned.

"Oh, and what do you think would happen to your good name if you took me on? You would be ruined, that is what."

"Have you finished?" Drawing her toward him, he gently cupped her face in his hands. "I have no concern about my good name, sweetheart. In fact, my only concern is clearing yours, and that I am almost certain I can accomplish, given the right circumstances. I just have to work out what the right circumstances are."

"What about Lydia?" she said desperately, voicing a very real concern. "You were *her* husband. Surely Lydia wouldn't want for us to be married." She couldn't bear to look into his eyes.

He stroked his hands down the sides of her neck in a

manner that threatened to make her knees buckle underneath her. "Lydia is dead and buried, and her wishes need no longer concern us."

"Then what about the rest of society? Surely they would think it most peculiar if you married the evil cousin, especially when it is widely known that your marriage to Lydia was an unhappy one."

"Why are you so concerned with what other people will think?" he said. "You never have been before."

"Because before I only had to worry about myself, and my name and reputation isn't important in society. Yours is. I refuse to drag you down with me."

"Does that mean that I have to give up any hope of happiness, just so you can protect me from yourself? Or are you protecting me from the sharp teeth of the ton? I wasn't quite clear on that point."

"Do not tease me," she said miserably. "I am very serious."

"So am I," he said, his voice heavy with frustration. "I love you, Joanna. I want you for my wife. Furthermore, I am a big boy and can look after myself when it comes to sharp teeth and tongues, so let us hear no more nonsense about that." He held her by her shoulders and looked intently into her eyes. "Please, please will you marry me, Joanna? Marry me and make us both happy. Let me love you as you deserve to be loved."

A faint echo of memory came back to her, dimmer than ever before, but the fragment of phrase remarkably clear, almost as if Cosmo whispered it now.

Be happy . . . Find someone to make you as happy as you have made me. . . .

Cosmo's final wish for her.

Joanna's last defenses crumbled. How could she possibly deny Guy his happiness? How could she deny herself her own? He was right. The ton and their wagging tongues could go hang.

She turned her face up to his, overcome with a happiness she'd never felt before, as if she'd finally opened up all the windows of the dark, stifling house she'd been shut in for so long and let the sunshine and fresh air come streaming in.

"Yes," she cried, "oh, if you truly want me, then yes, I *will* marry you, Guy de Salis!"

Tears spilled down her cheeks as she touched her hands to his dear face, stroking his hair, his lean cheeks, moving her hands down over his strong jaw and corded neck. "I will marry you and—and love you with all my heart and keep you safe always."

"Thank God." He kissed her wet eyelids one by one, then each wet cheek, and finally moved his mouth to hers, kissing it so tenderly that she wanted to cry all over again. "I love you, Joanna Carew di Capponi," he murmured. "I will love you until the day I die."

"And I you," she said, choking on a sob, her heart so full that she didn't know what to do with all that happiness.

Guy did. He took her mouth again, harder this time. His mouth opened against hers, his tongue running along the bottom of her lip, then along the soft inside of her upper lip.

She gasped. Cosmo had *never* kissed her like that.

She couldn't help opening to his demand and took his tongue inside her mouth, quivering deep inside at the sensations he evoked as he toyed with her, plunging in and out of her soft recesses with just the tip, then circling around her own tongue until she nearly collapsed with pleasure.

"Guy," she gasped. "Guy, what are you doing to me?"

"I would think that is mightily obvious," he murmured, brushing his heated mouth down over her neck. "Do you wish me to stop?"

She shook her head, wanting nothing more than for him to continue exactly what he was doing. She'd never experienced such heady, delicious sensations in her entire life. She hadn't even known they existed. "I think I might die if you do stop," she managed to say.

"If that is an invitation to take you to bed, I accept," he said, breathing hard. "I've had enough of your threatening to die."

She wrapped her arms around his neck and buried her mouth against his neck, inhaling his rich scent as if it were the nectar of all nectars and she a besotted bee. "You really will have to marry me after this," she murmured with a smothered laugh.

"The moment I can get my hands on a special license," he said, scooping her up in his arms and carrying her over to the bed.

Somehow he managed to lay her down and come over on top of her in one smooth movement, his weight on his arms as he looked down at her, his eyes so dark, so full of what was between them, his fingers twined in her hair. "Are you sure, my love?"

She nodded, smiling up at him with pure joy, her hands moving restlessly over the hot skin of his back, savoring the shape and breadth of him, tracing the strong, defined muscles with her fingers, her blood thrumming in her veins in quick, hard beats.

He groaned, capturing her mouth with his, ravishing her all over again. Joanna ravished right back, now that she had the way of it, her heart and soul in every single touch and taste and thrust and retreat, a give and take so perfect that she cried out, her body shaking helplessly, the fever of desire so hot and fierce that her breath left her body.

He raised his head, gazing down at her, his eyes filled with banked fire, his hand slipping down to cup one breast.

Her back arched up instinctively under his touch as his thumb slid back and forth over her nipple, teasing it until it stood hard.

"Lovely, lovely Joanna," he whispered, working the

same exact magic on her other breast until she wordlessly writhed under him, wanting him never to stop, her fingers digging into his back. Cosmo had never touched her like that either.

The next thing she knew, he'd reached down and skimmed her nightdress up over her body and over her head, his fingers burning trails on her flesh wherever they touched. Again his head bent, but this time, instead of ravishing her mouth, he lowered his head to one already throbbing breast and assaulted her nipple with the tip of his agile tongue, rolling it over and around the tip until she cried out. When he took it into his mouth and suckled on it, drawing it in between his teeth, tugging with utmost gentleness, she jerked with a surprised cry of intense pleasure.

Guy lifted his head to kiss her again, deep and hard, before he assaulted her other breast in the exact same manner, pulling on her nipple until it stood long and erect.

"You are so beautiful," he murmured, running the flattened palm of his hand in little circles over the tight peaks he'd created. "So lovely, so responsive."

She shook her head. "I didn't know," she murmured with a small shake of her head, smoothing her hands up and over the firm muscles of his chest, her thumbs stroking over his nipples in the way he had hers, delighted to see that they, too, stood hard, that his muscles rippled at her touch. "I never thought I was a passionate person, not really."

"Oh, Joanna," he said hoarsely. "You are the most passionate person I have ever known. You are passionate about life, my love, prepared to meet it honestly, naked¹ never caring about what anyone else might think or w' the consequences of that honesty might be. How c you not be passionate in this most intimate exchang￼ people can have?"

"I—I always thought it was just about being *affectionate*," she said.

"Affectionate." He raised an eyebrow. "Tell me, does this feel *affectionate* to you?"

He moved his hand down over her belly, stroking, caressing in circles that moved lower and lower until she thought she really might die with a hunger that centered between her thighs in the most agonizing ache she'd ever felt. At the same time he took her nipple between his teeth and tugged at it, circling it with his tongue until she squirmed under him mindlessly.

Somehow he managed to roll to his side and strip off his trousers without completely leaving her. He moved back, his hands skimming up over her thighs, her hips, the hard, thick column of his manhood pressing insistently against her belly, turning her blood to fire.

His fingers trailed down again and slipped into her nest of curls at the juncture of her legs.

"Gossamer," he murmured, "gossamer, and below, the delta of Venus."

A long sigh of yearning escaped from her throat as his fingers moved lower still, finding her cleft and skillfully parting it, slowly stroking back and forth, causing shudders to run through her body as unbearable heat pooled just there where he touched, so intimate, so knowing. She felt herself flood with moisture against his hand, could smell the musk of her own arousal mingled with his. She twisted beneath him in irresistible desire, overwhelmed with need.

"Guy," she gasped, "oh, Guy, don't stop—please don't stop?"

He chuckled low in his throat. "Wild horses couldn't ʳg me away," he said, finding her nub of exquisitely sen-
ᵉ flesh and lightly circling one finger over it until she
ˡessly clutched her hands in his hair and lifted her
ᵃ against his hand, seeking something more, some-
ᵈefinable but absolutely essential.

ᶜkly slid his fingers inside her, plunging hard

and deep. The world as Joanna knew it exploded, shattered into a million pieces, shattering her with it, shaking her to her core. She dimly heard a primal cry that she recognized as her own as her body convulsed, contracting in rhythmic spasms that threatened to undo her.

"Oh," she sobbed, as the spasms finally subsided, "oh, Guy—Guy, I've never felt anything like that before. . . ."

Cosmo had certainly not ever touched her like that, she thought hazily. She would have remembered. . . .

"Little love, there's so much more to come," he murmured, his breath warm against her cheek. "Let me take you properly, love you fully."

His mouth sought hers for another kiss, at first gentle, then harder, and harder yet, plundering her with his tongue, lifting and shaping her breasts to his hands, bringing her back to a peak of passion so that her breath came again in short gasps and her legs fell apart to his insistent touch, yielding her innermost secrets.

He rose over her and for the first time she saw his long, thick erection and drew in a sharp breath, unbearably aroused. Her thighs opened even wider, her hand instinctively reaching for his straining penis, guiding it to her hungry cleft, wanting him inside her more than she'd ever wanted anything, some remote part of her astonished at her forwardness, even more astonished by the urgency of her craving for his heavy invasion.

He answered her invitation, pressing his engorged tip against her swollen flesh, and inch by inch he eased himself into her, filling her completely.

A long sigh went through her body as she accepted him, her flesh quivering around him in need, in completion, as if her entire life had been coming to this moment.

He stayed completely still inside her, his eyes meeting hers in silence, his hands moving slowly down her back to her hips and pulling them hard against his. His steady gaze said everything, stabbed straight through her heart to the depths of her belly, where she held him deep inside.

He slowly began to move in her, his eyes never leaving hers, his hips rocking in a careful, controlled rhythm, withdrawing to his tip then plunging in again, over and over until she gasped deeply for breath, her hands pressed hard against his buttocks, asking for more, even more.

He gave it to her, plunging hard and deep, faster and faster, until her hips rose up to meet his with every blow, welcoming and answering his powerful thrusts until they obliterated every other part of her awareness. She knew only that she loved him and he loved her, that time stood still in this one moment and yet stretched out endlessly, held in eternity as he claimed her for his own and she claimed him in return, branding each other, one body, one thought, one heart.

She felt the first ripples start deep inside as he struck hard and held, feeling them too.

Her hands clasped his hard buttocks and gripped, her hips straining up against his as she clasped him inside her, frantically reaching for what she now knew was possible, sobbing helplessly, then crying out as the contractions took hold, a sunburst of ecstasy, a showering of stars.

He groaned loudly and plunged one more time, his body pulsating inside her in release, giving her his life, his love, his very essence.

"Joanna," he whispered a few minutes later, his breath finally slowing, warm against her damp neck, his heartbeat pounding hard and slow against her breast, matching hers beat for beat.

"Mmm?" she murmured, her fingers idly moving through his wet hair, feeling a contentment completely new to her, a quiet, singing happiness that reverberated through every fiber of her being.

"I love you."

She smiled into the darkness. "You took long enough to

say so," she replied, trailing her fingers down over his shoulder.

He turned his head and muffled a laugh against her breast. "I was afraid you might beat me."

"Guy . . . you know I am not a violent sort of person."

"An hour ago you did not think you were a passionate sort of person either. Look what happened there. You practically blew both of us up. Dynamite is not so dangerous."

Joanna rolled up onto her elbow and looked down at him, a smile curving her lips. "If you will light a fire, you must be responsible for the consequences," she said, bending over him and kissing him as he'd taught her, no holds barred, taking no prisoners save one.

19

 uy took a moment to admire the sight of Joanna bending over the nursery bookshelf, her svelte figure revealed as the material of her dress stretched over her shapely derriere, the midmorning sunlight outlining it nicely. How well he knew now what lay under the dress, having spent most of the night exploring every beautiful inch of her extraordinarily responsive body.

He was glad to have been the man to awaken her to her own passion, although he couldn't imagine what kind of lover Cosmo had been if he hadn't managed to fan any of Joanna's smoldering fire into flames—he must have been a gentleman indeed, so considerate that Joanna didn't feel a thing.

Well, all that was behind her. He'd spend the rest of his life making sure that she felt very much alive.

"Good morning," he said, walking into the nursery, thoroughly enjoying the sight of Joanna turning pink as she looked up and saw him. "I trust you spent a pleasant night?"

She straightened. "Very pleasant, thank you," she said, the pink running up her neck into her cheeks.

"I am so happy to hear it," he said, smiling wickedly. "Ah, there you are, Margaret," he said as she emerged from the night nursery, Miles in hand. "Good morning. Did you snore the night away, Milo?"

"I do not snore," Miles said indignantly.

"Indeed? Then it must have been Boscoe I heard when I looked in on you early this morning."

"Boscoe does not snore either. He breathes deeply."

"Oh, I see," Guy said, holding his hand out to his son

and swinging him up into the air. "You are dressed for the outdoors. Are you going somewhere special?"

He nodded. "Margaret is taking me down to the farm for the day to play with her little boy. Johnny is my friend. We play horses together, and we look at the animals, and we climb the fences and make Margaret cross."

"I think that all sounds like lots of fun," Guy said, setting him back down and shooting a smile at Margaret. "Off you go then, and make sure you get thoroughly dirty."

Miles giggled, then ran over to Joanna and held out his arms. She knelt down and gave him a hug and a kiss. "Have a lovely time, poppet. I will see you later."

"Have a happy day with your paints, Jojo," he said, and skipped out the door, Margaret rushing after him with a backward wave.

Guy shut the door and walked over to Joanna, gathering her in his arms. "How utterly innocent you look of any misdoing," he said. "I shall have to fix that." He bent his head and covered her sweet lips with his, savoring the taste of her as he lazily explored the soft inner depths of her mouth with his tongue.

"You are a rogue, my lord," she said with a breathless laugh as he released her. "Do you really think you ought to be kissing the governess in the nursery?"

"I can think of a great many other things I'd like to be doing to the governess in the nursery, but actually, I came to speak to you about something more practical."

"Bunch would be so proud of you," she said, settling on the sofa and looking up at him expectantly, her eyes shining.

God, how he loved her. He'd never known it was possible to love so deeply, to feel *completed* by another person. She touched him in a way he'd never been touched, both physically and emotionally, giving herself without hesitation, without expectation or demand, without artifice of any kind.

She couldn't have been more different from Lydia.

"Guy, why are you looking at me in such a peculiar fashion? Anyone would think I was an animal in a zoo."

He grinned. "Hardly. Actually, I was just thinking about how much I love you and what a very lucky man I am to have found you. You make me happy, Joanna, and that is something I haven't been able to say in a very long time."

She nodded, her face solemn. "You make me happy too," she said. "Very happy. Now, what was this practical matter you came to discuss?"

"Ah. The first order of business is obtaining a special license. I thought about going up to London and taking you with me, but on reflection, I think it best if we both stay here. You are not strong enough to travel—"

"I am strong enough to make strenuous love with you all night, but not strong enough to travel?" she said, both eyebrows raised ominously.

"I worry about your catching a chill. The weather is unpredictable," he said, "and I do not wish to hear any arguments. I also think it best if we are here with Miles. He's had enough of desertion in the last year and a half. Do you agree?"

"You are actually asking my opinion, Lord Greaves?" she retorted, her eyes dancing impishly.

"I am consulting with you. I learned some time ago that I am better served by asking rather than telling you. I certainly save myself a good deal of time, trouble, and aggravation."

"What a clever man you are, to be sure. As it happens, I do agree with you. I'd like to be married here—perhaps not in the chapel, because that might feel awkward, but I would like to be married in church, if you have no objection. I thought perhaps the little church in Pangbourne might do, the pretty painted one with the Norman tower at the bottom of the road."

His heart squeezed tight in his chest. Odd how his attitude toward God had changed since the night his fervent prayer had been answered. Odd how his attitude toward everything had changed since then. "Saint James the Less would do nicely," he said softly. "I used to go to services there."

"Thank you, Guy. I—I was also wondering if we might not be married by Brother Michael. He was so kind to me on Christmas morning when I needed a shoulder."

"Brother Michael?" Guy said, searching his memory but coming up blank. "I'm sorry, but I cannot think whom you mean."

"The monk who sits vigil in the Wakefield chapel every Christmas Eve. I *think* he is also a priest."

"No one sits vigil in the chapel," Guy said, frowning. "It is private to the family."

"But—but he was there. He said it was one of his ministries, and he talked about love and patience and . . ." She paused and gazed toward the window. "And healing wounded souls," she said, looking back at him. "He was so peaceful, so gentle and understanding."

Guy slowly shook his head. "I know no one of that description, certainly not a visiting monk. We are not even Catholic, even though Wakefield once was an abbey."

"Guy, he knew all about Miles and Lydia, her entire story—everything. He even knew about me, that I was Lydia's cousin and had come from Italy and loved art. How could he know any of that unless he was familiar with the family? I thought Lydia must have told him."

Guy was as puzzled as she was. "Lydia was not one for religion, so I cannot imagine her pouring her heart out to a monk, and no one else here knew the details of your life—unless you told them."

"I didn't really know anyone then to speak to. Even since then you are the only person to whom I have confided anything personal. Miles heard me jabber on and on, so he knew quite a lot, but I cannot imagine a boy of five who spent his time in silence telling my life story to a monk in a chapel—in any case, I know he was in bed the whole of the night."

"It is a mystery to be sure. I will ask the vicar if he knows of any such man, but I must confess, if I didn't know you to be so sane and sensible, I would think you imagined it all. Perhaps he was a ghost from the days when Wakefield was an abbey. You do know that the chapel is supposed to be full of them, all sorts of discontented ancestral specters wandering about."

She shuddered. "What an awful thought. No, I swear to you, Guy, everything happened just as I said it did. A single candle burned on the altar, and Brother Michael stood in the shadows. And—then he came and sat next to me and was wonderful to me. I remember now, I was so cold, and when he touched my hands he filled me with warmth. Warmth and a sense of deep peace. I think he was the most godly man I've ever met."

"Well, if he touched you and made you warm, he couldn't have been a ghost," Guy said with a smile. "Ghosts are meant to make you cold and clammy, aren't they?"

"He was no ghost. I do remember thinking that he was an answer to a prayer."

"Hmm. There seems to be rather a lot of that going around," Guy said, moving over to her and sitting, taking both her hands in his. "Maybe that's just what he was, God's answer to your prayer. I have come to believe that we have seen one miracle after another since you came to us, sweetheart. I think you must have done enough praying in those early days for all of us." He kissed the back of one hand, then the other. "There are some things that do not bear too close an examination, don't you think?"

Joanna returned his smile, but she still looked slightly uneasy. "I shall attempt to keep that in mind."

"Good. Now, to my next plan. I thought I would ask my good friend Randolph Cato to purchase the license and bring it down. He lives not far from here at Manderston Hall. Perhaps you have passed it in your travels."

"Yes . . ." Joanna said, biting the side of her lip. "It is the big Palladian house. He is the Earl of Trevelyan?"

"Yes, that's right. We grew up together, always the best of friends—indeed, he is Miles's godfather and is very fond of his godson."

"I should like to meet him," Joanna said.

"You shall." Guy hesitated, knowing his next suggestion would not go down quite so easily. "I also thought I'd ask him to hold a ball for us next week in honor of our engagement and forthcoming marriage. I can kill at least two birds with one stone that way; no one who is invited will want to miss the opportunity to meet you, especially given the gossip that's gone around over the years. That coupled with the fact that you are my late wife's cousin is enough to make the invitation most coveted, so despite the short notice I can count on the key people dropping everything to be there."

Joanna blanched, just as he'd expected. "Oh—oh, Guy, please. I really do not think—that is, I am not prepared. Can we not wait until we have been married for a time before we face down the lions?"

"No. I will have nothing standing in the way of our marriage, and to my mind, your reputation worries you enough that I consider it an impediment to your peace of mind." He squeezed her hands lightly. "I promise you, sweetheart, that I will have not only an answer but an apology from those who did you wrong to begin with."

"I have nothing to wear," she said, and he knew she was desperately seeking an excuse.

"I will take care of that," he replied, waiting for the next objection.

"People will talk behind their hands," she said. "I cannot bear the thought that you will be laughed at."

"Trust me, beloved. No one will laugh; they would not dare. And even if they were stupid enough to try, I can assure you their faces will be not only perfectly sober, but red with mortification by the time I am finished." He reached over and stroked her cheek. "You are the bravest and strongest woman I have ever known, willing to face anything for the sake of the truth. Will you be strong for me now and trust that I can force the truth out of Holtingham and Henry Warnock about the scheme they concocted between them, that I can also convince the small-minded people of the ton that the accusations the Capponis made against you were false?"

She released a long sigh, then nodded. "I will do anything for you, you must know that. I would trust you with my life. What is this in comparison?"

He scooped her into his arms and held her close. "Do you know when I first started to fall in love with you?"

She shook her head against his chest, her hand creeping up to his neck and nestling there.

"It was Christmas Eve, when I came to the nursery to drop off Miles's present and you stood there wearing nothing more than your nightdress." He pressed a soft kiss against her temple. "And then you asked me about Lydia and cried like a child when I told you the truth, not caring in the least what I thought about that either."

She turned her head slightly and gazed up at him, a little smile playing around the corners of her mouth.

"That was the night that I started falling in love with you too," she said. "I didn't admit it to myself for the longest time, but then I didn't care to examine my feelings too closely. I—I also realized something else last night."

"Hmm. I wonder what particular realization that was?" he said, a whole handful of possibilities occurring to him, but curious to know which one she would pick.

"I realized that I was attracted to you from the very beginning, despite what a monster I believed you to be. I didn't recognize the attraction for what it was, never having felt those things, and also because you were Lydia's horrible husband and therefore the very idea would never have occurred to me. Despite that, I do believe I had a strong physical awareness of you from the first time I saw you." She blushed fiercely. "I thought you should know."

He brushed his mouth across her smooth forehead. "Ah. Well, if we're playing at truth-telling, then let me bare my soul in that regard. I believe I felt the same physical pull toward you from the beginning, but because you were Lydia's cousin and bore a resemblance to her, I not only refused to acknowledge the attraction, but I turned it against you."

"I know," she said simply. "Or rather, I know now. That was the only sensible thing you could have done. You no more knew me than I knew you. We only had the distorted filter of Lydia's opinion to see each other through."

"Why do you always make me feel an even bigger cad by forgiving me my faults so easily?" he asked, loving her even more by the moment. At the rate he was going, he'd need a second heart to take up the overflow.

She shifted in his arms, reaching up to kiss him tenderly. "I love you. That is reason enough for forgiveness. I was not particularly kind to you either."

"Joanna, I really do not know how I am going to wait another three weeks to marry you. Are you absolutely certain that your precious Bunch must be here?"

"As I told you at some point last night when you were pressing me on the matter, Bunch has been with me through all of the important times in my life. I couldn't bear to have her miss the best of all."

"Mmm. This is going to require an extraordinary restraint," he said, already feeling himself growing aroused by the feel of her body pressed against his. "I cannot take you to bed every night, lest the servants catch on, but I do not know how I am going to do without you."

"Can we not be inventive, my lord?" Joanna asked softly, brushing her hand up and down his thigh. "I see no one here and expect no one for a good long time. I've been known to take a nap at this hour since my illness."

Guy groaned, then stood and took her hand, pulling her up and practically dragging her toward her bedroom. He closed the door and locked it, pulling her toward the bed, Joanna already yanking at his jacket and shirt, he fumbling with the tapes at the back of her dress, his eagerness that of an adolescent boy's. He managed to pull the top loose and tugged it down over her shoulders, pushing the straps of her shift down as well and baring her beautiful rounded breasts, the nipples already standing hard.

Joanna leaned back against the bed, impatiently pulling him toward her, lifting her skirts, her thighs parting for him, her hips lifting in invitation.

"Now—now," she whispered, her cheeks and eyes feverish as he swiftly unbuttoned the flap of his trousers.

He couldn't wait—he stood at the edge of the bed and plunged into her full length, going out of his mind with his own excitement. He reached down and pulled her hips toward him, knowing this was the way she wanted it, swiftly and deeply, and he gave her all of himself, their bodies meeting, impacting, withdrawing as he met her need with his own in a strong, steady rhythm.

Her legs wrapped around his hips and he reached down to knead her swollen breasts in the way he'd discovered she liked. He bent his head to suckle and nip at her nipples until they grew long and stiff in his mouth, until she writhed under him, whimpering and gasping, begging and pleading for more and more, matching him thrust for thrust.

He moved his hands down to the place they were joined and found the swollen, erect bud, lightly caressing it with his thumb. Her mouth opened in a soundless cry and her hips jerked, her eyes widening.

He felt the beginning of her climax deep in her body, her tight passage opening around him, then the sudden fierce clamping down, the waves of viselike contractions that fiercely milked him, brought him beyond his own endurance until he, too, contracted and burst, flooding her with the searing heat of his release that went on and on, her high, anguished cries mingling with his own groans, both of them shaking with the small aftershocks of orgasm.

He finally collapsed, falling to his knees, lowering his head onto her soft, exposed belly. "Oh, my God," he whispered. "Joanna, my love. Joanna."

She didn't answer at first, still breathing hard and fast, her fingers gripping his hair. After a few minutes he felt her body finally begin to relax, her breathing return to normal.

She lifted her head and smiled. "I think I rather like being the governess," she said, then collapsed in laughter.

He couldn't help laughing as well. Joanna looked like the most abandoned nymph in any painting ever depicted, her hair flowing about her shoulders, the exposed parts of her body covered in a flush of orgiastic satiation worthy of a Bacchanalian ritual, her mouth curved up in the most satisfied smile he'd ever seen on her face.

So much for a person who had branded herself lacking in passion. Joanna had proved her own undoing on that front too many times to ever recant now.

He softly ran his hand over her distended breasts, kissed the base of her throat, her lips, her closed eyelids.

"I will love you always," he whispered, easing off her, moving her sideways and slipping the rest of her clothes off. He pulled the covers up over her. "Sleep. You need it, having had very little last night. I will look in on you later, long before Margaret and Miles are due back."

She smiled sleepily, then tucked her hand under her

cheek and closed her eyes, and even as he watched she fell into a deep, contented sleep.

He paused in the doorway, wondering how he'd ever been so damned lucky, then softly closed the door behind him.

20

As the carriage rolled to a stop, Joanna took in the grand sight of Manderston Hall lit up from top to bottom. More nervous than she'd ever been in her life, throat dry and heart pounding furiously, she decided it looked more like the gateway to hell than a grand house *en fête*.

Wendy, Margaret, and Shelley had all helped her to dress, exclaiming over their brilliant handiwork. Margaret had somehow managed to create the most beautiful ball dress out of rose-colored satin with an over-robe of white tulle, edged with pearls. Shelley had made a headdress woven from a wreath of silk roses and beads, and Wendy had been in charge of the accessories, which she put together from Joanna's meager collection.

Somehow between the three of them they'd made her presentable, although the tears they'd shed when she'd left had nearly undone her and threatened to ruin the entire effect they'd worked so hard to create—that of a happy woman going to her engagement celebration.

Even Dickson had had tears in his eyes as he saw her to the carriage. She'd never seen such a maudlin group as the staff who'd waved them off, handkerchiefs dabbing at eyes and noses. Joanna had been deeply touched, as touched as she'd been by their overjoyed reaction to the news of her forthcoming marriage to Guy.

Miles had been the only one who was at all sensible, looking her over with a critical eye and pronouncing her "the most perfect mama-about-to-be." But then Miles had taken the news of their impending marriage as if he had expected it all along, asking only if Joanna would still be looking after him.

"I will look after you always, my poppet," she'd replied, "and probably long after the time you will wish me to do so."

Well-satisfied, Miles had gone back to riding his rocking horse. Joanna had been the one to force back tears.

"Joanna?" Guy squeezed her fingers, bringing her back to the present. "Are you ready?"

She swallowed hard and nodded. "I—I am a trifle anxious," she said in a massive understatement as her knees knocked together.

"Naturally," he replied. "You are no fool. However, I know you have the aplomb to carry the evening off. Remember that I love you with all my heart and have every confidence that we will succeed not only in bringing out the truth, but also in dispelling all the rumors." He leaned over and kissed her swiftly, and just in time, for the carriage door opened only a moment later.

Dickson, who had recovered his composure during the brief journey, let down the steps, offering her his hand and a broad smile.

She smiled back at him, then turned and looked up at Bill, who sat on the coachman's box, dressed in his fine livery and powdered wig, not looking at all like the Bill she was accustomed to. He winked at her and jerked his head toward the house as if to tell her to get on with it.

For some reason Joanna found his casual attitude immensely reassuring. She winked back and straightened her spine, resting her hand on Guy's arm.

"It is time to breach the stony walls of English society," she murmured to him. "Forgive me if I offend in the process."

Guy chuckled. "I'd forgive you murder under the circumstances. Stay close, sweetheart, and at least try to follow my lead. I am more familiar with the rules of war than you, although you are more than capable of making up your own."

"Which I am sure concerns you above everything else,"

Joanna said, her nervousness easing slightly. With Guy at her side, she felt as if she could accomplish almost anything.

"Ah. Here is Ran," he said, leading her up the steps toward a tall, most attractive man with dark gold hair and the most astonishing blue eyes that regarded her with warmth. His smile held nothing but welcome as Guy introduced them.

"Contessa," the Earl of Trevelyan said, bowing over her hand, "I have been long awaiting this moment. Guy has written so much and so often about you that I can feel nothing but relief to meet you for myself. I am pleased to say that my friend's power of descriptive prose did not go lacking."

"Please call me Joanna," she said, liking him immediately. "If nothing else, perhaps our finally meeting will stem your tide of correspondence—or," she added mischievously, "it might strain it to overflowing, if the evening does not go as Guy has planned. You are very generous to provide the battlefield on my behalf."

"Generosity has nothing to do with it. My mother always did say that I was an overly curious child. Sadly, she encouraged me."

Joanna grinned. "I do believe I would like your mother."

"Let us put you to the test, for she is waiting inside and as curious a creature as I am—she has been just as impatient to meet you, and I feel safe in saying that she will not be disappointed."

Joanna wasn't so sure, but Guy's firm, reassuring hand on the small of her back gave her the strength she needed to cross the threshold and start facing the lions.

"My dear, what a treat this is," the elegant Dowager Countess of Trevelyan said as Joanna curtsied before her. "I do so enjoy hearing nasty rumors, but I *so* much more enjoy exposing them for the nonsense they usually are. In this case I will take very great pleasure doing just that."

"I—I am grateful that you feel that way," Joanna said, amazed that the countess would make such an effort for a complete stranger.

"Nonsense. There is nothing like having the upper hand and feeling morally superior to the fools who tend to populate the upper echelons of this country." She reached her hand out to take Joanna's. "Come along, child. We have very little time before our guests begin to arrive, and I wish to grill you myself. My darling Ran is a very clever boy, as is indeed your fiancé, but men have an unfortunate habit of leaving out the most important parts in matters such as this, and I do like to be fully informed before I bite heads off."

Joanna, who couldn't help but think this magnificently confident and outspoken woman was cut from the same cloth as her beloved Bunch, felt instantly comfortable. She looked over her shoulder to give Guy a backward glance as the countess pulled her away, but he was already engaged in deep conversation with his friend, obviously confident that Joanna was in safe hands.

Fifteen minutes later, having skillfully extracted and dissected every last detail of Joanna's life that she thought necessary, the countess stood and patted at her beautifully coiffed silver hair.

"Thank you for your honesty," she said. "I had no doubt that Guy's judgment would be sound in this instance, and I believe you will make him very happy, my dear. I can already see the difference in his face and manner. The tragedy finally seems to be behind him, and I can only thank the good Lord for that." Her mouth tightened. "No man deserves such torture, Guy least of all."

"I—I feel nothing but sorrow for what both Guy and my cousin suffered in their marriage," Joanna said, trying to be fair to Lydia. "They were ill-suited."

"Oh, that," the countess said, waving her hand. "Guy chose poorly, but we understood, given the circumstances. No, I was referring to his experience in the Peninsula. Ran has always felt so awful that he wasn't there at the time to stop Guy from turning himself into the sacrificial lamb, but then I suppose if Guy had been stopped, so many more lives would have been lost." She gave a small shake of her head. "Still, Guy paid a terribly high price. He lived in his own private hell for a long time, but as I say, I believe that is now behind him, thanks to you, my dear."

Joanna's breath caught in her throat, and a chill ran down her spine. What sort of terribly high price did the countess refer to? And hadn't she just referred to Guy as a sacrificial lamb? Horrifying images flashed through her head—she'd heard the stories of the brutalities dealt out by the French, but she'd never once thought that Guy might have been one of their victims.

As desperate as she was to learn the truth, she didn't know how to respond. The countess obviously didn't realize that Joanna knew nothing of what had really happened to Guy or she surely never would have brought the subject up. On the other hand, she was the perfect person to ask, if Joanna could only work out a clever way to phrase her question so that the countess wouldn't think she'd unwittingly given anything away.

She was just on the verge of trying when Guy appeared in the doorway of the drawing room.

Her heart gave a little jolt, as she realized that she'd just barely escaped being caught in the act of prying. One moment later and he'd have heard her asking about something so deeply personal to him that he refused to speak of it even now.

She felt a deep pang of guilt that she'd even considered prying. Guy was the person to ask, and only Guy, although she began to realize that she might very well have to force the story out of him for his own good if he was ever to liberate himself from the past and truly heal. As much as the countess might believe that he had already done that, Joanna knew better, given his extremely taciturn reaction to the very subject of the Peninsula.

"Forgive me for interrupting," he said, looking extremely relaxed, not like a man who had been to hell and back, Joanna told herself, as if she could erase the appalling pictures the countess had unwittingly invoked. "Our first guests arrive. Arm yourself, my darling, and let us calmly greet those who think to see you tremble before them."

Lady Trevelyan wagged her finger at Guy. "And on your part let them not fall too quickly and too fast, my boy. One must savor the slow march toward victory and the quick final kill. A strategic game of chess is so much more admirable than the predictable sweep of the board."

Guy leaned down and planted a kiss on the countess's cheek. "I do not wonder that you have maintained all of your youthful beauty. Your glorious brain never stops, thereby giving your body no time to age."

"Empty flattery," she said, swatting his arm but looking immensely pleased. "Get on with it, get on with it, both of you. Time is wasting. I look forward to watching your checkmate, Guy. You always were a fine player."

"I learned from you," he said, gesturing for the countess to take the lead, then taking Joanna by the arm and walking her out into the huge hall.

Joanna forced herself to push all thoughts of Guy's horrific experience in the Peninsula out of her mind and to ponder the mystery at a more appropriate time. For now she needed to concentrate with every fiber of her being on the next few crucial hours.

Joanna had prepared herself for the disguised sneers and whispered comments that she knew were inevitable, and for the most part she managed to ignore the looks of scorn and amusement shot her way, along with those of pity bestowed upon Guy—all of these coming after the hearty felicitations and congratulations delivered directly to their faces. She didn't mind so much for herself, but she burned with indignation for Guy, who deserved none of it.

Guy played his part brilliantly, never once giving an indication that he realized anyone might be less than thrilled about their upcoming nuptials.

Joanna nearly collapsed when a certain Lady Neville came down the receiving line and greeted first Guy and then her with barely concealed scorn. "My sincerest hopes for your future," she said to Joanna, slowly looking her up and down in an obviously insulting manner. "My dearest Lydia told me *so* much about you."

"Did she?" Joanna said, her mouth trembling at the corners. It couldn't possibly be—but she would never forget the voice, those drawled tones, not in a million years. Lydia's dearest friend Sally Neville was *Petalfold*? She couldn't believe it.

"Oh, yes," Lady Neville said. "I know everything there is to know about you," and her cold voice let Joanna know that none of it was good.

"You would be amazed at how much I know about you also," Joanna said. "Perhaps we would both be wise to keep what we've heard to ourselves."

Lady Neville tossed her head, then swept away.

Guy shot Joanna a look of sharp curiosity. "What was that all about?" he murmured.

"That was Petalfold of the Sahara Desert, Lambkin's full-bloomed Christmas flower," she murmured back.

Guy tossed his head back and roared with laughter, causing most of the room to turn and stare in open-mouthed surprise.

When Lambkin himself appeared, Joanna had herself

under better control, knowing that he, at least, was a good friend of Guy's.

Lambkin was an attractive enough man, although sadly, given his aspirations, he had not either Byron's looks or his silver tongue, she thought as he made his bow. She found huge difficulty in looking at him with a straight face, but she managed, even though she couldn't help thinking that there were some things one would rather not know about complete strangers.

Oblivious to her wicked musings, he regarded her with curiosity but no malice, murmured a few polite but inarticulate words, and swiftly vanished into the crowd, hardly giving her a chance to form any real impression of him. She'd learned far more from his conversation in the stable than she had just now.

"Lambkin saves his best lines for women he is pursuing," Guy said dryly, not having missed a moment of their exchange.

"I consider myself fortunate," she replied, turning to the next guest.

And so it went for the next hour as Joanna greeted guest after guest, some faces familiar, others not, but she didn't much care. She waited only for the two people who had so affected her past, the only two people who could change her future—and Guy's.

She thought she was prepared, but when Holtingham finally appeared, Joanna's heart jerked hard in her chest. She struggled to keep her composure, to give nothing away.

He looked exactly as she remembered him—perfectly combed dark brown hair and a smug, conspiratorial expression in his gray eyes. She'd been dreading his arrival all evening, but now that he was actually here, something stiffened inside her, an inner resolution that he would not have the upper hand. Not this time.

He greeted Guy, then bowed over her hand. "Contessa,"

he said. "How well you have fared since last I saw you—triumph after triumph, and now this news of your most recent engagement."

She resisted the impulse to snatch her hand away and slap him in the face with it. "Thank you, Lord Holtingham," she said coolly. "As for yourself, I understand that you have successfully managed to stay in an unmarried state."

"To my father's eternal regret," he answered smoothly. "What a lucky man you are, Greaves. Two cousins of lovely and similar countenances, and you claimed them both. My condolences on your first wife's death. Such a tragedy."

"Thank you," Guy said, equally smoothly. "However, let us dwell on happier thoughts tonight. My future wife has been long away from England, as you know, and has many acquaintances to renew."

"Indeed. I do believe I passed Henry Warnock's carriage on the road. He is an old and close friend of the contessa's, as I recall?"

Guy didn't move a muscle at this barely disguised insult, and Joanna wondered at his aplomb. She felt like kicking Holtingham's shins—not the first time she'd had the urge. She imagined that Guy felt like doing something far more extreme.

"An old acquaintance, to be sure," Guy said, "although perhaps Mr. Warnock imagines a closer friendship than existed."

One corner of Holtingham's mouth lifted. "Or perhaps the contessa forgets the details of their friendship after this long time. I believe they were nearly affianced, or so was the case the last time I saw Miss Carew—or the contessa as she is now."

Guy's hand flashed out and grabbed the front of Holtingham's coat so swiftly that Joanna didn't even see the movement coming. He pulled him close, his hand bunched tightly on Holtingham's lapels.

"You have always been a nasty piece of work," he said in a low voice that sent a chill down Joanna's spine, "but I do believe you outdid yourself on that night. Tell me, what pleasure did you gain from whispering your filthy little plan into Warnock's ear? Did you think that by seeing Miss Carew compromised by Warnock you would manage to help yourself that much sooner after her forced marriage?"

Holtingham's gray eyes bulged in surprise and real fear, Joanna saw with utmost satisfaction. "I—I do not know what you refer to," he stammered, passing his tongue over the finely chiseled lips in which he took such pride.

"Do you not?" Joanna said, planting her hands on her hips and leaning her head toward his alarmed face. "Let me make the question clearer, then. Was your idea of amusement to send Henry Warnock to my room that night so that he might be discovered there and therefore force me to marry him? You knew that marriage was what he desired, and you must also have known that I would never assent. So you concocted this ridiculous scheme—what was an innocent woman's reputation to you?"

"I swear to you, I had nothing to do with it," he said, beads of sweat appearing on his pale face, Guy's grip unrelenting. "I am completely innocent of your charge."

Joanna glared at him. "And I do not believe you. You have always been a rake and a—a cad, intent on taking what you please as long as it never compromises you. The last words you spoke to me that night indicated that you hoped to see me married shortly so that you could continue your unwelcome pursuit under what you considered more agreeable circumstances."

"No—no," he said, eyes flashing about wildly at the crowd that had gathered silently from all quarters, mouths agape at this latest delicious scandal. "No, ask him," he cried, one arm reaching out to point toward the door. "I had nothing to do with it!"

All heads turned toward Henry Warnock, who froze in the act of divesting his cloak to the butler. He blanched and smiled uncertainly. "Er, good evening all," he said. "Lovely night, is it not? Rather warm for this time of year. Goodness, what a crush."

Guy abruptly released his grip on Holtingham and pushed him to one side, his hand staying him. "Good evening, Mr. Warnock. How perfect your timing is. Perhaps you would be so good as to step over here. We have a few questions to ask you."

Henry looked about the crowded hall, then licked his upper lip and moved forward, not unlike a man approaching the noose. "I thought I had been invited for an engagement celebration," he said. "This looks a bit more like a lynching. Ha! Rather good, that. Good joke, I mean," he added uncertainly.

"Not as amusing as you might think," Guy replied coldly. "Tell me, Mr. Warnock, on the night of August the thirtieth in the year of 1812, did you not go uninvited into the bedroom of Miss Joanna Carew and there attempt to press on her your uninvited attentions?"

Henry looked frantically about at the assembled crowd, his eyes darting back and forth. "What—what is this? I did not come to be interrogated about events long in the past. Has that trollop been telling lies about me again, trying to defend her name after all this time?"

"I suggest you confine your remarks to my questions," Guy said, his eyes flashing cold fire. "One more insult to my fiancée and I will take you apart with my bare hands. You might recall that I have been known to do it."

Henry Warnock nodded as his face paled even further.

"Good. Then answer me this: Did Lord Holtingham put the idea in your mind of compromising Miss Carew so that she would be forced to marry you?"

"Holtingham?" Henry Warnock said, looking utterly bewildered. "What has he to do with anything? It was Joanna, only Joanna. She came to me in the garden, confessed her deep devotion, told me she couldn't wait any longer to demonstrate the fullness of her heartfelt love. I told Sir Quentin and Lady Oxley all of this." He pointed straight at Joanna. "She knows it for the truth, no matter how fervently she has denied it since."

Joanna passed a hand over her forehead. "You are saying that the idea for your outrageous behavior was yours and yours alone, that Holtingham truly had nothing to do with it?"

"I told you—" Holtingham started to say, but Guy cut him off with one biting look.

"Go on, Mr. Warnock, please. We are all anxious to hear your version of events."

Henry Warnock glowered first at Guy, then at Joanna, his face red as a beetroot, his hand shaking as he continued to point it at her.

"Holtingham had nothing to do with it—everything was your idea and your fault. If you hadn't kissed me with such passion in the garden, your skin and lips so unbelievably hot with promise, pressed yourself against me in the shameless fashion you did, offered yourself to me in marriage, and *then* invited me to your room later, I would never have considered such behavior." He mopped at his brow. "Ever. I am a gentleman. I loved you, or I thought I did. I am sorry to be forced to speak in such a manner in a public forum, but you proved yourself utterly unworthy of my affections."

Joanna looked at him long and hard. She'd promised Guy that she'd be strong, that she'd face down anything thrown her way with truth, but she honestly didn't know how to turn around an outright lie.

She'd been so sure that Holtingham was behind it all, but she now had to wonder if Henry Warnock wasn't either entirely delusional or had completely convinced himself so long ago that he was in the right that his memory of the truth was now set in stone, even though she knew perfectly well she hadn't gone near the garden anytime that night.

"I do not suppose," she said quietly, trying desperately to find a way to help him recant, "that you might have been a little tipsy? That someone else might have treated you to a kiss, and you simply confused the issue and the invitation?"

"I was not tipsy nor was I confused," he said indignantly. "I had planned to propose to you that night, but you took my breath away with your own proposal, and I was overcome along with my judgment. Much to my dismay, instead of your agreement to marry me, all I took away from that unfortunate evening was disgrace. You yourself might have avoided that had you not changed your mind about marrying me when we were discovered."

"I am so sorry for your disgrace," Joanna said with heavy irony.

"I am more sorry for the bad case of measles I came down with afterward," he replied sullenly. "The doctor said I was lucky to live through it."

Joanna's hands slid up to her cheeks as she stared at Henry. "Measles," she said, her voice choked. "How? You—you were only exposed from a distance and for a matter of moments when Lydia came in. . . ."

Guy's arm slipped around her. "That's it," he said, his fingers tightening on her waist. "My God. Measles."

Joanna slowly turned her head and looked into his eyes, seeing that he'd reached the same painful conclusion.

"Lydia," she said. "Oh, dear God, it was Lydia all along."

21

*J*oanna, exhausted but exhilarated as the very last of their guests finally departed, climbed into their own carriage and collapsed into Guy's outstretched arms as Dickson shut the door and Bill moved the horses forward, starting them toward the blessed sanctuary of Wakefield.

"What lovely people your friend Ran and his mother are," she said, snuggling wearily up against Guy as his arm closed tightly around her. "They are so immensely fond of you."

"And now of you, sweetheart. You made an enormous impression on them both. I have to admit, I had a very small worry in the back of my mind that they were being extraordinarily loyal to me by giving this evening in our honor, never having met you. However, I believe the evening was a triumph in every regard." He chuckled. "I did enjoy the way Henry Warnock made a surprisingly swift exit, Holtingham directly on his heels and looking like a chastised dog, even though for once he was innocent in the piece."

"Perhaps he didn't like the way you treated his coat."

"Hmm. I think I actually scared the life out of him. I always did think that beneath the polished bluster he was nothing more than a coward at heart."

Joanna grinned. "The countess assured me that by tomorrow the lapel-lashing you gave him would be the latest on-dit in London, along with Henry's dual case of mistaken identity and measles."

"Let us not forget blasting the malicious rumor the Capponi family spread about your poisoning Cosmo. That will be good for some serious tongue-wagging. By the time we were finished, you looked like a saint. Ran's mother really is an old battle-ax when she wants to be. Do you know that she intends to spend all of tomorrow writing letters to friends and filling them in 'on all the delicious details,' and I quote directly."

"She is the most wonderful woman. I kept thinking how like Bunch she is. And Ran is not unlike you, Guy. He is very warm and kind, but he can be equally cold and curt when he chooses to be. I did enjoy seeing him take Sally Neville down when she tried to insult your choice of wife directly to his face." Joanna sat up straight and screwed up her face, imitating Sally Neville's plum-in-the-mouth voice. " 'One would have thought Greaves would have learned his lesson by now, but perhaps he decided that he actually missed his wife so much that he is willing to settle for a pale imitation—such a shame that her morals are not what one would wish.' "

Guy grinned. "Yes, and Ran replied in his inimitable unruffled-but-deadly fashion, 'You would be wise to learn your own lesson, Lady Neville, and settle for your very real if pale husband before he discovers that you have the morals of an alley cat and tosses you into the gutter where you belong.' Such a fine choice of words."

"For one awful moment I thought that she might slap him, but then the countess appeared out of nowhere and tapped her hard on the shoulder with her fan and a single pointed look toward the front door. I've never seen anyone blanch and run as fast as Sally did. She called for her carriage and left in the next instant."

Guy dropped a kiss on her temple. "I do have to admit that I have yet to see any single member of the ton face down Ran's mother and survive. Lydia never managed more than a stammered greeting before fleeing outright."

Joanna turned her face into his greatcoat at the mention of her cousin. She'd been trying so hard to avoid the subject but knew it was impossible.

"Guy, *why* would Lydia have gone to such absurd lengths to see that I married horrible Henry? She knew I didn't like him. And she was so ill that night—I still cannot believe that she not only managed to get out of bed and dress but also somehow managed to impersonate me."

"And yet she did, sweetheart. She did. There is no other explanation. She'd have been well-enough disguised in the dark, disguised enough to carry out her intention, which was to get Henry Warnock into your bed so that she could then 'discover' you." He shifted and took her face between his hands, gently kissing her. "I *know* how this must hurt you, my love, but for whatever reason, Lydia must have felt threatened by you. I knew her well enough to know how easily she did feel threatened. I do wonder what set her off to do something so extreme, though."

Joanna thought hard, trying to recall the details of the conversation she and Lydia had had that night, looking for a clue to Lydia's bizarre behavior. She remembered Lydia going on and on about the need for Joanna to marry, and then her concern that Joanna would marry Holtingham of all dreadful people. . . .

"Of course," she whispered. "*Why* didn't I see it?"

"Why didn't you see what?" Guy asked.

"Lydia. She wouldn't stop asking me about Holtingham before I went to change. She was sure that I intended to have him, and—and she even burst into tears over the matter. I thought she was concerned that I would marry unhappily; she even tried to shove Henry Warnock down my throat as a more suitable candidate."

"Ah," Guy said with satisfaction. "Well, it all comes clear, doesn't it? Lydia wanted Holtingham for herself, so she made good and sure that you'd be forced to marry Warnock."

"I even asked her if she had any interest in Holtingham, given the way she carried on, and she tossed the question off as if the idea disgusted her. I decided that her tearful behavior was due to her fever."

"A fever that Henry Warnock later mistook for passion,

no doubt. Lucky for Lydia. She never was much inclined toward that sort of thing."

Joanna gazed at him in real surprise through the dim light. "That was all she ever talked about wanting, Guy. Love and passion. She even wrote that—" Blushing furiously at what she'd nearly let slip, she snapped her mouth tightly shut.

"That what? What, Joanna? Come, let us have no secrets between us."

"No—I should have said nothing. That part of your life with her should remain between the two of you."

"I think I see." He touched her cheek with his warm fingers. "She wrote that we had a passionate relationship, perhaps? That she welcomed me to her bed with open arms?"

Deeply embarrassed, Joanna nodded. "Something of the sort."

"Would you like to hear the truth?"

Joanna looked away. "I—I am not sure. I always wondered, and after you and I—well, I thought she was telling the truth about that part because you *are* such a passionate lover."

Guy gently turned her face back to his, his dark eyes meeting hers directly. "One needs to have a responsive and willing partner, my love, to have passion."

"Are you saying that Lydia was neither responsive nor willing?" she asked, shocked to her core. Lydia had always been so full of life that Joanna had automatically assumed she would bring that enthusiasm to the bedroom.

"In the beginning Lydia was as most young women, lacking in experience," he said quietly. "I treated her accordingly. I loved her, or loved the woman I thought she was, and I wanted to have that part of our lives be fulfilling for us both, so I went carefully and slowly." He sighed heavily. "At first Lydia found the process frightening; she hadn't anticipated anything like the reality and felt terribly betrayed."

"Betrayed?" Joanna said with a frown. "Why betrayed, of all things? She had always talked about longing for stolen kisses and—and all that sort of overblown nonsense."

"I believe that what she really wanted was the attention, to be told how wonderful and beautiful she was, to have a man kneel at her feet with armfuls of flowers or, preferably, jewels."

Joanna had to smile. "You have her exactly."

"I was married to her for five years," he said wryly. "The trouble came on our wedding night when she discovered that I was not a prince in a fairy tale, wishing only to adore her from afar and leave her to live happily ever after, but a flesh-and-blood man who had real feelings and desires."

"Lydia always was overly fond of fairy tales and high romance," Joanna said.

"A pity," Guy said. "Unfortunately, she never learned anything about the nature of sexual desire from those tales. She didn't learn a damned thing from me, that is for certain."

Joanna could only imagine how frustrated Guy must have been with a new wife who did not enjoy physical intimacy. "I am sorry," she said. "Did she ever learn to welcome you to her bed?"

"*Welcome* me? When Lydia discovered that I actually expected her to participate, she was appalled—she was prepared to submit dutifully to me in order to provide me with a child, but that was all she was prepared to do. Trust me, Joanna, it is not very exciting to make love to an inert body, however lovely that body might be."

"Oh," Joanna said, her heart heavy with yet another disappointing revelation about Lydia's true character. "But—but then she was so excited to discover she was with child, and so quickly. Even I was surprised by that, since she was still such a child herself. I thought she might be annoyed that she would be restricted from the parties and balls she so adored."

"Oh, but she was thrilled, because she suddenly had a reason to shut her door against the beast she'd discovered I was," Guy said bitterly.

Joanna didn't know what to say. Lydia had made it all sound so different, as if Guy had been the one to turn away, to lose interest, as if desiring an heir had been his only reason for being attentive to her. "I—I honestly didn't know," she finally murmured.

"How could you?" he answered simply.

"Oh, Guy, there is so much I didn't know, so much I blamed you for. I didn't understand what really lay at the heart of the matter."

"You believed what Lydia wanted you to believe."

"*Why?*" She shook her head in puzzlement. "Why do you suppose Lydia wrote me so many letters over the years, telling me all her distorted stories and at the same time professing her love for me, when she was the one who deliberately landed me in trouble to begin with?"

"My beloved Joanna, your heart is so unadulterated that you really do not see it, do you?" He smiled down at her. "Lydia never expected you to refuse to marry Henry. She probably thought in her twisted way that she was doing you a favor by arranging a marriage for you—the last thing in the world she'd have expected was for you to show such an independent streak that you would rather shoulder disgrace and leave everything you knew for a foreign country."

"Yes . . . maybe that was why she started to write. She must have felt terrible about the predicament she'd put me in."

"Probably not—I never knew Lydia's conscience to be of great import to her. I can tell you that your marrying Cosmo did not go down at all well."

"It didn't?" Joanna said, feeling incredibly stupid at her own gullibility. "She wrote to say how pleased she was, and I believed her. . . ."

"Naturally, but I heard the ranting and raving about your marrying a man so much older only for his fortune and title. She went on and on about it for months until I never wanted to hear your name or Cosmo di Capponi's again."

"*Why?*" Joanna said again. "I was no threat to anything she desired by then. She had you, a child, Wakefield, her title, the life she'd always wanted—why would she envy me a quiet marriage to a man I loved?"

"Joanna," Guy said very patiently, "you are still missing the point. She never expected you to marry after you left England, your only purpose in life being to dote on her, preferably feeling envious. You were not supposed to marry the very wealthy and well-connected Conte di Capponi, and you were certainly not supposed to love him and be happy with him when she was miserable."

Joanna wanted to scream with frustration. "If she wanted me to be envious, why would she then constantly write and tell me all her troubles? I only felt sorry for her."

"Darling, I know you loved her, but I don't think you understood her in the least. Lydia liked to be the center of attention, even if that meant having people feel sorry for her. That was your real value to her, your endless sympathy."

Joanna shook her head disbelievingly.

"Then, when Cosmo died," Guy continued, "she suddenly changed her attitude and started saying how sorry she felt for you, being widowed after such a short marriage—that is, until the rumors started surfacing about the poison. I will lay money that you wrote her about the Capponi family's accusations, didn't you?"

Joanna nodded miserably.

"Lydia was probably single-handedly responsible for spreading that lie all over England. You gave her the ammunition her jealous little heart had been looking for. She never bothered to tell anyone that you turned your back on the family and the money and property, but you surely would have written her about that too?"

She nodded again, feeling even more an idiot, her very last illusions about Lydia splintering. "I still don't understand," she said, her voice so painfully tight that she could hardly speak. "I loved her, Guy. It is true that I did not spend a great deal of time with her until I went to live with the Oxleys, since our families weren't particularly close, but after that I thought of her as my sister and believed she felt the same about me. 'Sister of my heart,' she used to call me."

"My sweet love, I wonder who was the real romantic—and in your case I mean that in the best sense of the word." He squeezed her hand. "You believe in everything noble and good in this world and so believe it about other people, always giving them the benefit of the doubt."

"Not always," she said, resting her head against his shoulder, this man who had become so dear to her, so beloved that she would happily lay down her life for him.

He leaned his cheek on the top of her head. "Ah, but then your loyalty for Lydia came first, didn't it? You were prepared to defend her memory and her son against the Charybdis whom you thought threatened to destroy them both, and defend them no matter the cost to you. But it was Lydia who was really the Charybdis, the whirlpool that created chaos in both our lives. I thank God that is all behind us now."

Joanna nodded her head, nuzzling her nose into his neck, drinking in his intoxicating scent, infinitely grateful for Guy's willingness to discuss Lydia so openly and honestly with her, to give her a new insight into the sad, confused woman she really had been.

Joanna wondered if she'd ever known her cousin at all, or if she had believed what she wanted to believe in order to suit her own desperate need to love and be loved after her parents had been killed. It was the only explanation of her own blindly trusting behavior that made any sense, now that she knew the truth. Had Guy not done much the same thing when he first fell in love with Lydia?

With that realization a memory drifted back of something Guy had once said to her that now had an even greater significance.

"I had just come out of a rather bad experience, and when I met Lydia, she represented everything I felt I had lost. . . . She was so full of life, and I wanted desperately to drink in her warmth, her innocence. . . ."

"I suppose . . ." she said slowly, seeing a chance to broach the one subject that still lay unspoken between them, one that was far more important than she'd ever realized until the countess had opened her eyes earlier that evening, "I suppose that I did what you did when you first met Lydia."

"What do you mean?" he replied, lifting his head and regarding her curiously.

Joanna winced, hoping she wasn't about to make a great mistake. She had to gather every last shred of courage to force herself forward, for she intuitively knew that she was entering yet another battle. The difference was that she wasn't fighting this battle for her reputation—their very relationship might be at stake if she couldn't manage to make Guy open up and tell her the truth.

She also knew she would have to be the one to make the first attack and keep attacking, for he would go nowhere near the subject willingly. He'd made that clear to her in no uncertain terms, and he wasn't about to suddenly change his mind, simply because she wished him to.

"Joanna? What were you going to say?" he asked, stroking the palm of her hand with his thumb.

Oh, *God,* she wished he didn't look so trusting, so loving, not with what she was about to do to him.

She took a deep breath, then leapt straight into the abyss, deliberately dragging him with her, praying with everything she had in her that love would land them both safely.

"When I first came to know Lydia," she said, feeling her way through what felt like a yawning, dark emptiness, "my life had been torn apart just as yours was. I'd lost everything, everyone but Bunch, so I think I poured my heart and soul into Lydia, just as you did when you met her. I still do not know exactly what happened to you in the Peninsula, but from the little that Ran's mother said tonight, I gather it was very terrible."

"I'd really rather not discuss it," Guy said. "I thought I had made that clear to you." He turned his head abruptly and looked out the window.

She clenched her hands together in her lap. "I know you would rather not," she said, forcing herself to sound calm, "but we cannot let what happened sit between us, Guy, as if it had no significance in shaping the man you are today. Look at what happened to you and Lydia."

"Lydia?" he asked, turning to glare at her. "Lydia has nothing to do with this! The woman was a spoiled child, and emotionally unbalanced on top of that. For God's sake, if nothing else, didn't you learn that tonight?"

"Perhaps, but from everything I have heard, I do not think that you were entirely in your right mind either, not when you came home from the war." She swallowed through a dry throat. "You made that clear too, when you told me the reasons you chose to marry Lydia. You said you had just been through a bad time. I think it must have been much worse than you let anyone know."

Guy's face went cold as stone. "You know nothing about it. Nothing, do you understand? As far as I am concerned, you never will. The subject is closed."

Joanna dug in her heels, fighting beyond all fair bounds for both of them. "The subject is not closed," she shot back. "Guy, I love you. I love you too much to let it go. You must tell me now and tell me everything if you are ever going to be free. If *we* are ever going to be free."

He glared at her, eyes narrowed, teeth bared, breath coming hard, and for the first time Joanna saw what Lydia must have seen. True, feral anger, a man pushed to the brink of his self-control. She had to fight not to shrink away from him.

"You will leave it alone," he said, his voice low and savage. "There are some things that do not bear discussing. Ever."

Joanna drew in a deep steadying breath, silently asking God to see them both through this. "If that is how you feel," she said, her voice shaking, knowing she had to mean every word, "then we cannot go on. I will not marry a man who can give me only half a heart."

"The other half isn't worth having, damn you!" He closed his eyes and covered them with one hand.

"The other half is perhaps even more important to me," she cried, hoisting herself up on her knees to face him, forcibly pulling his hand away with a strength she didn't even know she had.

"Leave it alone. For God's sake, leave it alone!" he cried, shaking her off. "I have a right to a certain amount of privacy!"

"You have dragged things out of my heart that I have never shared with another soul, and you felt free to do so. Why should that be your sole right? If you love me truly, Guy, then you will trust me with your whole heart, wounded or not—I don't care that you're not perfect! I don't want you to be perfect!" She furiously wiped away the tears that poured down her cheeks. "Can you not understand that I love the man that you are because of everything that has made you *who* you are?"

"I understand only that I do not want your heart tainted with my sins any more than it already has been, any more than I want to share the horrors of war with you. One of us holding those memories is more than enough," he replied, his voice and face raw with undisguised pain.

"Can you not see what you do to yourself?" she cried desperately, trying to find a way through to him. "You have buried something terribly painful deep inside you, so deep that you think you can forget it, that the memory will eventually go away as if it never happened. That never works."

"Oh, and in your infinite wisdom, you think you know what will work? You think you have some cure, some antidote that will make it all go away if you drag a confession to the surface?"

Joanna shook her head helplessly. "My God, Guy, I was accused of poisoning Cosmo, a terrible accusation and hard enough to live with, but that is nothing compared to the poison of the accusation you've been holding against yourself, whatever it is. You as much as told me just now that is what you've done. Don't you see, by letting an unhealed wound scar over, eventually that poison seeps out and infects everything in its path, slowly, insidiously, until it kills. I won't let you do this to us, to our family."

"How many times do I have to tell you to leave it alone, Joanna?" He raised his head and looked at her, his eyes anguished now. "Please," he said softly. "Please. Let it be."

Her heart very nearly broke with what she knew she had to do next if they were ever to get through the crisis that had been waiting for Guy for seven long years.

"Stop the carriage," she said. "I will walk from here."

He stared at her. "Are you mad? You cannot walk home at this hour. It is another mile at least. Joanna, please, do not be a fool."

"I am not mad, nor am I a fool," she snapped. "I can most certainly walk home from here, although as of tomorrow Wakefield will no longer be my home. Please stop the carriage. I will not continue to ride with a man who insists on behaving like an imbecile, refusing to deal with his emotions."

"Joanna. You are being absurd." He reached for her, but she pulled away from him.

"Leave me alone, Guy. I am perfectly serious. How do you think Milo recovered—answer me that? He certainly didn't turn himself around by keeping *his* very painful memories stuffed inside."

"Please do not think to invoke my emotions by comparing me to Miles," Guy said wearily. "He is a child. I am a full-grown man. There is obviously an enormous difference in our experience and our ability to deal with it."

"Is there? I'd be interested to know what it is. From my perspective, Milo has more bravery and fight in his little body than you are showing in yours, grown man that you are."

Guy looked in that moment as if he might go for her throat. "How dare you speak to me like that—you have no idea, no idea at all of what happened," he said, his voice suddenly deathly quiet.

"That is my point precisely—I have no idea, because you do not trust me enough to tell me," Joanna said, crossing her arms against her chest and facing him down. "I will never have any idea until you choose to give up this misconceived idea that I am incapable of bearing the difficulty of hearing about your awful experience—although personally, I think that is a lot of fustian. You don't want to remember, even though you cannot stop remembering. *That* is the crux of the matter."

"Then go," he whispered, his fingers running raggedly over his head. "Go, if it pleases you. I will not be party to your leaving, but I will not keep you against your wishes. God help me, Jo—I love you more than I have ever loved anyone, more than I ever thought to love anyone, but I cannot tolerate your incessant hammering at me. Not about this."

"And I cannot marry a man who does not love me well enough to give me the whole of himself, the bad along with the good," she said, desperately trying not to cry, trying somehow to accept that he had made his decision and she had lost not only the battle but everything else she cared about. The irony was that they'd both fought so hard that night for something as irrelevant as her respectability and won.

She would have given up that meaningless victory in an instant if she could only have saved Guy's soul from the haunting anguish that held him captive. The only problem was that he was both jailer and prisoner of his pain, and each refused to release the other.

Please, God, if I cannot help him, will you find a way? She prayed as hard as she ever had done.

Then, reaching her arm up as high as it would go, she managed to tap hard on the roof with her knuckles in a signal to Bill to stop.

22

The carriage door opened and Dickson's confused face appeared. "Is there a problem, your lordship? It's a mile still to Wakefield."

Guy did not answer, his face turned to the opposite side, one fist pressed hard against his mouth.

"His lordship has no problem, Dickson. He is merely tired." Joanna reached her hand out for the footman's and stepped down. "I, however, will walk the rest of the way. I decided that I need the exercise."

Dickson didn't blink. He grabbed one of the lanterns from the driver's seat. "Drive on," he called to Bill. "I will walk with her ladyship, it being such a fine evening and her wanting to take the night air to clear her head after the festivities and all that."

Bill rubbed the side of his nose, then the other. He finally nodded and urged the horses forward.

Joanna silently blessed his tact, then Dickson's in his turn as he walked next to her, not once asking a single question, not saying a single word. He behaved as if theirs was a perfectly normal midnight stroll along the main road, taken with regularity after long, stifling evenings out.

Joanna didn't know what to do or say when Dickson eventually marched her up to the front door. She wasn't ready to go in, for she knew she couldn't possibly face Wendy, Shelley, and Margaret, not now, not until she'd come to some calmer place inside herself so as not to alarm them.

But where could she go? The chapel was out of the question, since it held Lydia's remains. She didn't have a thing to say to her cousin, not anymore.

An idea struck at the last second. She knew exactly

where she wouldn't be disturbed but would be understood, and by someone who wouldn't talk back.

"Thank you so much for escorting me, Dickson," she said with her most winsome smile that she hoped hid her misery. "I think I'd like to walk a bit more on my own now that we are safely home."

"As you wish, contessa," he said, casting an eloquent look down at her ruined slippers. "Should you need anything else, do call for me."

"I will be perfectly fine," she replied in a blatant lie, then stood waiting for him to leave in as obvious a manner as she could summon.

Dickson cast one doubtful and clearly worried last look over his shoulder before disappearing.

Joanna breathed a sigh of relief and headed for the stables, ignoring her sore and blistered feet and reasoning that Bill would have the horses put away by now—in any case, the carriage horses were stabled in the opposite block, so she had no real worry about running into anyone.

She went straight to Callie's stall, knowing she could pour all her troubles out into her unbiased ear. It wouldn't be the first time, although it would probably be the last. Just that thought alone was enough to send the tears flooding to her eyes and a tight knot to her throat. Tears seemed to have become a constant condition since she'd come to Wakefield.

Callie whinnied in welcome, despite the lateness of the hour. Joanna rubbed her nose and kissed it, then wrapped her arms around the mare's outstretched neck.

"Callie, I'm in the most terrible mess," she moaned, letting her tears come freely now, feeling as if she could die from grief. "I love Guy with everything in me, and Milo too, just as if he were my own, and the idea of leaving Toomsby and Bill, never mind Margaret and Wendy and Shelley and Dickson and Ambrose and everyone else, is breaking my heart. They've become my family, Callie, all of them."

She shifted her wet cheek to the other side of Callie's corded neck. "How will l leave you either, sweet girl? You risked your life for me, and I will always be grateful, and yet how can I stay? I can't, not if Guy keeps himself buried away like this—I never even knew until tonight how bad, how awful it must have been for him, but he refused to talk to me, refused to say anything, Callie, and I told him I had to go." She pushed her forehead into Callie's neck. "Can you believe it, the stupid man actually let me?" she said, trying to sound brave.

Callie blew softly against Joanna's front as if in sympathetic reply.

"I can't live with this deadly silence, despite how much I love him. It will kill us both in the end, kill everything we ever had." She rubbed her face against Callie's soft, warm muzzle, drinking in her sweet scent, Callie's coat absorbing her tears, even if she couldn't absorb Joanna's heartbreak.

The voice came from behind her, soft, quiet, as from a long distance, and yet impossibly close.

"It was autumn, but the day was cold, bitterly cold. The company I commanded had been marching for days trying to get back to the cantonments near Ciudad Rodrigo after the disaster at Burgos. My men were tired. We were bringing up the flank and had no protection."

Joanna spun around, her hand covering the pulse that pounded furiously in her throat, a chill prickling down her spine.

Guy stood a few feet away, his neckcloth gone, as were both his coats. He looked so tired, his head lowered. She wanted to rush to him, to comfort him, but a strong instinct told her to stay exactly where she was, to let him continue speaking. She braced her hand against the stall door to steady herself, Callie's breath warm on her neck.

"A band of renegade Spaniards attacked from behind. They'd been fed and turned by the plentiful pockets of the French. They managed to cut us down from the back end of the ravine we were traveling through. The fog—God, the fog and then the bloody pounding rain that followed kept us from seeing anything, giving us no warning. Over half my men were massacred. There seemed to be no escape for the rest, since the French waited at the front end to finish all of us off."

Joanna kept her gaze fastened on his lowered head, his bowed shoulders, trying to imagine the horror, knowing she couldn't, wishing she could give comfort, knowing she couldn't do that either, but at the same time so relieved he had chosen to come to her. Finally. Finally.

Thank you, God, thank you for hearing my prayer.

"My men were trampled underfoot by horses, bayoneted, gunned down like helpless animals, with no chance to defend themselves. I was their commanding officer, and they'd trusted me. I'd led them into the trap." He rubbed his fist hard over his mouth, looking sick and defeated. "My color-bearer, who had been with me throughout the campaign, fell at my side, defending me from a bayonet thrust. David was a lad of only twenty-one, his whole life ahead of him, and he died defending me."

His body shuddered, and he finally raised his head to look over at the wall with eyes so haunted that she had to grip the stall door hard to keep from running straight into his arms and cutting off the rest of what was to come. The time for comfort would be later. Now he needed to lance the wound, as deeply and as painfully as necessary.

"After that, I decided that the only way to salvage what was left of my company was to create a diversion. I told Malcolm Lambkin, who was my cornet, to get the men out of that hell any way he could once I'd left him. He might be a bit dim, but he's brave and he knows how to obey an order. He managed it in the end without losing anyone else."

Joanna swallowed, feeling terrible about the way she'd judged Lambkin. She should have realized that Guy had sound reason for valuing his friendship.

"Then I took five of my best men and we charged the front of the ravine, screaming at the enemy like lunatics, trying to make it sound as if we were four times that number.

"I'd ordered the men I took with me to save their necks once we got up close—by then I was thanking God for the fog and the rain. I intended to give myself up to the damned French, if I wasn't killed first, thinking that they would be diverted by the officer in charge, obviously a madman, delivering himself directly into their hands. They were diverted, or at least long enough to capture me and let what was left of my men get away."

Guy turned and walked toward the opposite wall, his back to her, his hand rubbing back and forth on his neck. "What happened after that is not important except to say that I was treated with none of the honor usually accorded an officer, never mind the treatment usually accorded a human being."

Joanna took a step forward. "Guy, what do you mean? What did they do to you?"

"The details honestly do not matter. Physical pain is nothing in comparison to the pain of knowing you have left half your company dead behind you. One can survive a bit of torture, Joanna, but it is over when it is over and the body heals. The soul doesn't heal quite so neatly."

"Guy—dear God, why did they treat you so badly? What did they want from you?"

"They were interested only in trying to get out of me where our other companies were and where we planned to attack next, which I wasn't about to tell them. I did not take kindly to my mistreatment, so I decided to escape. I had to break a few necks in the process, but I managed."

He turned around, his eyes so far away, so angry, that Joanna barely recognized him. Still she held her silence, even as her stomach churned with sickness for the horror of what he must have experienced.

"'I was shot in the leg during my escape, but the wound was not serious enough to stop me. The next thing I remember after crawling over a few muddy mountains is waking up in a field hospital. I spent two months there, wondering what the hell I was doing alive when twenty-eight of the fifty men for whom I'd been responsible were lying buried under that godforsaken mud, having died very unpleasant and unnecessary deaths."

He pressed his hands hard against his face, then dropped them. "When I'd recovered from that injury—among some others incurred during my visit with the French—I was sent home to dear old England and commended for my exemplary actions in the field. No one mentioned the lives lost in the process. They all seemed to end up looking like meaningless chess pieces in someone else's game, and I was commended as if I'd actually done something wonderful."

He finally looked directly at her, his eyes challenging, but behind the challenge they were so filled with pain that Joanna could scarcely breathe.

"That was what you wanted to know, was it not? Now that you know it all, Joanna, now that you have all the facts, you can decide if you still want to go. I am sure Bill and Dickson would be happy to take you anywhere you would like, if their behavior tonight is anything to go by. They will miss you, as will Milo, but none more than I."

She didn't bother to reply. Instead, she walked straight over to him and took his hand in hers, looking down at it, already knowing so well its shape and feel, the bones and sinews beneath the skin so familiar underneath the stroke of her thumb, so well-loved, the touch so familiar and loving on her that she could not imagine it gone. Not now. Not ever now that he had opened the last and final door.

"I will go nowhere that takes me from your side," she said, lifting his hand to her mouth and softly kissing its back. "I will stand by you always, my love, always."

His arms wrapped around her so tightly that he nearly squeezed the breath from her body. "Jo," he groaned. "Oh, God, Jo, forgive me."

"Forgive you?" She reached up and touched his face, surprised as her fingers touched wetness on his cheeks. She'd never known Guy to shed a tear before. That had always been her job.

Somehow his tears made her love him even more, for her heart practically cracked wide open. "What am I to forgive you for? I think it is you who needs to forgive yourself, Guy. You cannot have anticipated the ambush, any more than you could have anticipated the weather, or the Spanish traitors, or the French who put them there."

She pressed her cheek hard against his shoulder as she wrapped her arms around his shivering back. "You are not God, you know, as much as you try to assume the job at times. You are a mere mortal who happens to be a deeply caring man, a man who takes his responsibilities very seriously."

He said nothing, shaking his head back and forth as if he couldn't accept the truth she spoke.

Gazing up at him, she took his tear-streaked face between her hands. "You did save those men who were left. You offered yourself up so that they could escape. There is no greater love or sacrifice than that. I can only be thankful that you somehow managed to make your way back." She pressed tender kisses all over his wet face. "Please, my dearest, let it go. Let it go. You are safe, safe at last, home in my heart and in your son's. Let that be enough. Please, let that be enough?"

He lowered his head into her shoulder, trembling uncontrollably in her arms, and Joanna, remembering what he had once done for her, now did the same for him, taking him by the hand and leading him straight to the shelter of the anteroom where Toomsby stored the loose hay.

She pulled him down onto the warm, sweet-smelling pile and embraced him, one knee tucking in between his legs, the other rising over his hip so that every point of her body pressed solidly against his, her arms holding him safe and close, anchoring and sheltering him against the storm that raged inside him as he finally allowed all the guilt, all the torment he'd been holding inside to flow out in a violent explosion of grief.

His tears wet her hair, her face, trickled down her bare arm in cleansing rivulets, his powerful body shaking in great convulsions. She held him close and hard, a safe harbor, the fortification he'd been denied when he'd needed it most, loving him with everything she was worth, hoping it would be enough now, so many years later.

She knew she'd never be able to take away the memory of the men he'd lost, nor should she. That would be with him forever, but at least she had tried to put their sacrifice, and his, in better perspective. Whether he had heard her was a question yet to be answered.

Joanna didn't know how much time had gone by when eventually his body calmed and his breathing steadied. She wondered if he'd fallen asleep, but he shifted his head.

"I love you so very much," he murmured, his arm reaching around her neck. "I do have to wonder how it is that you can love me so well to put up with me. You must be out of your mind."

Joanna hiccupped with laughter, his remark the last thing she expected. "I have never been more in my right mind," she said, smoothing her hand over his cheek. "I cannot help but love you. You have become everything to me, Guy."

He pulled her face toward his and kissed her, both hands moving behind her head as he took her mouth more deeply, then deeper still, his tongue wildly tangling with hers, then stroking over her bottom lip and urgently pulling it between his teeth.

"Jo," he murmured, his hands moving over her back and around to her breasts, stroking over their rounded shape, his thumbs deliberately caressing her nipples back and forth until they stood hard under this touch and she moaned with sheer pleasure. "I need you, my love. I need you now."

"Guy—oh . . .Guy," she moaned, pushing her hips hard against his where she felt his arousal thrusting against her belly. Heat pooled swift and furious between her legs, where she was already wet with desire.

She shifted and fumbled at the waistband of his breeches, releasing him, her fingers reaching for his erection and encircling the velvet skin, the steel directly beneath, with her hand. She felt the pulse beat under her sliding grip in the same moment that he pushed her dress up, his fingers finding the very heart of her need and delving deep, his thumb circling against her acutely sensitive bud.

She arched her back in soundless joy, rocking against his hand, his skilled touch bringing her to an instant climax.

Pushing him onto his back, she frenetically mounted him, driven by desperate need, guiding his engorged length into the most intimate recess of her body. She sank down on him, her hands gripping his shoulders, riding him hard, as if she could somehow take into her body all of his pain, all of his loss, force him to surrender it to her by sheer naked acceptance of her love.

He grabbed her by the hips, his fingers digging into her flesh as he beat furiously into her, meeting every downward stroke with an upward thrust of his own, hard and harder, his breath driven from his body with each brutal thrust, sweat beading over his forehead, his arms, his belly, his groans turning into primal cries.

Rearing up, he flipped her over, forcing her thighs wide open with his knees, so wide that she thought she might split apart, but she answered him in kind, taking each pounding thrust as deeply as she could, her excitement building to a feverish pitch, her legs wrapping around his lean hips to take him deeper still as she thrashed beneath him, all sentient thought lost to a driving physical need to make herself one with him, to lose herself, to be possessed so completely by him that nothing else existed.

Guy groaned, and shoving the top of her dress down, he bent his head, pulling her breast into his mouth, sucking her nipple so hard that she screamed, her nails raking his neck as she bucked underneath him.

He took her hands and raised them above her head, pinning them down, his fingers weaving between hers, his lower body pinning her equally deliberately with his weight as he thrust relentlessly and rhythmically into her.

Shaking uncontrollably, she strained up against the swollen tip that drove so hard and incessantly against the limit of her own control, her body already beginning to break apart, the building sensation becoming unbearable.

"I will always love you," he whispered, his eyes boring into hers as she gave herself over to him, contracting helplessly against his hard invasion, crying out, sobbing, writhing under him, surrendering every part of her being to him as she gripped around him, released him, gripped him again in waves of pleasure that were so close to anguish that she could barely distinguish one from the other.

"And I will always love you," she managed to gasp as the contractions finally started to subside.

"Joanna. Oh, my love." His back arched and he cried out, his eyes never leaving hers as he convulsed into her still-shaking body, throwing her straight back into another climactic frenzy as the smoldering heat of his release flooded her, her inner muscles gripping him so tightly that she thought they would never let him go. She thanked God when they finally did, because she really had begun to wonder if it was possible to expire from too much sexual pleasure.

Guy collapsed against her, silent save for the deep, steady gasps of air that he pulled into his lungs.

Her fingers trailed over his hip and the hollow of his buttock, gently tracing over the ridged scar in the groove of muscle at the top of his thigh. It was the only outward mark of his terrible ordeal. She knew the scars on his heart went far deeper, but with luck they would no longer bind him.

Guy finally lifted his head and brushed his mouth over her neck. "You are a woman to be reckoned with," he muttered. "Dangerous to cross. Remind me never to do it again."

"I think I might have to cross you more often if that is the result," she said, lightly nipping his shoulder through his linen shirt. "I must say, you do a much better job than your friend Lambkin when it comes to rolling about in the hay."

Guy grinned and dropped a kiss on her mouth, then slowly pulled out of her and moved onto his back. "At least I spared you the bad poetry."

"Nothing else, I am happy to say, and indeed you gave me a great deal more, and oh so very much more than that."

He gave her a sidelong look. "Thank you for what you gave me tonight. I may feel as if my guts have been wrenched out, but I do feel better. Odd, that."

He kissed her softly. "Come, we had better get up to the house before we really do scandalize the servants. You know they will be waiting up for us."

"I think we had better," she said, starting to dress. "I left poor Dickson in a terrible state, and heaven only knows what Bill must have thought."

"I pay both Bill and Dickson to think nothing at all," he said, then grinned as she socked his arm. "I was only teasing," he said. "God forbid I should treat my staff like anything but my dearest kin."

"That is more like it, Lord Greaves. You have come a long way in a short time," Joanna said. "Just wait until you meet Bunch next week. She will straighten you out on all sorts of matters in no short order."

"I knew you had to have learned the technique from someone," he said dryly. "Turn around, you're covered in hay." He brushed off her hair and the back of her dress. "I don't know if anyone is going to believe we were out here feeding the horses."

"Really, Guy, haven't you learned by now that you can't keep anything from the servants? They know more about your life than you do. They practically live it for you."

"In that case," he said, brushing hay off himself, "they should all be feeling very satisfied with themselves and can expect to live happily hereafter in wedded bliss."

23

*B*unch held up Joanna's wedding dress to the light, critically examining every last square inch of it, now that it was finally finished, Margaret's clever handiwork in evidence. "I think that will do nicely," she finally proclaimed. "Very nicely indeed. It is simple but elegant, sober enough to be fit for a woman who has been previously married, but not in any way harsh or unforgiving in its lines. I do like the shade of blue you chose—it puts me in mind of periwinkles."

"I am so pleased that you approve," Joanna said, smiling with wry humor. She wondered if Bunch would ever stop treating her like a child who couldn't make a single decision without being corrected.

Bunch leveled an even eye at her. "You have changed, my girl, and I am glad for it. You have finally found your proper place in life, and I must say, you chose the right man to share it with."

Joanna cocked an eyebrow in surprise. "Are you saying that you did not approve of Cosmo? You never said a word against him."

"Why would I do that? He was the man you needed at the time, and indeed a kind, dear man. I was sorry for you both when he died so suddenly." Bunch laid the dress back down on the bed and smoothed her hand over the silk. "I will say that I wanted more for you—much more. I had a feeling that Guy de Salis might suit, and I am happy to have been proved correct."

Joanna gaped at her. "Bunch. Surely you couldn't possibly have thought that Guy would suit after all I told you about him and the way he treated Lydia, and then me—at least in the beginning?"

"That is precisely why I thought he might suit. I never did like that girl, or trust her for that matter. I couldn't be sure, but from the way you behaved once you actually met him for yourself, I felt fairly sure you'd finally met your match." She smiled, looking thoroughly pleased with herself. "I was right, naturally. And *that*, my darling Joanna, is why I went instantly to visit my sister and stayed until you summoned me back with your happy news. You did not need to come running to your old governess every time you and he had a clash—I reckoned it was time for you to stand up on your own two feet and deal with your problems with no help from me."

Joanna, stunned into silence, moved over to Bunch and hugged her tightly. "You always have been so wise. Thank you. Thank you for everything you have ever given me, including the nudge I needed to face my life and my problems on my own."

"My dearest Joanna, you are the closest thing to a daughter I will ever have. Every child needs a nudge out of the nest when the time is right, and this was your time. You made good use of it to spread your wings and fly, and I am proud of you, of what I have seen you accomplish." She squeezed Joanna hard, then released her. "I like him enormously, by the by—he is a charming and intelligent man, and so very practical. Now, let us see to the rest of your attire."

Joanna, about to show Bunch the hat that Wendy had helped her with, turned as Miles came barreling breathlessly into the room, Boscoe at heel.

"Hello, poppet," she said, kneeling to scoop him into her arms. "What brings you down here in such a hurry?"

"I have an idea, Jojo, for you and Papa, for your wedding," he panted. "I just thought now when I was drawing a picture of the big carriage, and I wanted to tell you."

"What is it, my sweet?" she said, touching his cheek, loving the soft feel of his downy skin, loving him.

"You said the horses and carriage would take you away from the church." He nodded very seriously in confirmation of this truth.

"Yes, that's right, Milo. Bill will drive us away. Would you like to come with us in the carriage?"

He shook his head fiercely. "I want to ride Pumpkin. I want to ride Pumpkin next to you. Bill will watch me, but I am big enough to do it, I am, Jojo."

Joanna hugged him tightly, wondering how she could possibly love two men, one large, one very small, with such vast emotion. She'd never known a love like this was even possible. "Of course you may ride Pumpkin. I think you must ride him, or he would feel terribly left out of the celebration. What a very good idea—I wish I had thought of it myself."

"You cannot think of everything," Milo said in a remarkably self-assured fashion, every last drop of his de Salis blood showing.

Joanna gazed at this child viscount, wondering just what he was going to be like in another fifteen years or so, then decided she didn't want to know. She'd find out soon enough.

"Very well, my little man, we will go down together and suggest your idea to your papa. Give me a few minutes to finish up in here with Bunch. Here, poppet, hold my sewing kit for me. . . ."

* * *

Engaged in reading the pile of morning mail at his desk—most of it good wishes for the wedding in two days' time—Guy barely heard the library door open.

"Guy?"

"Joanna, my love," he said, a smile flashing across his face, his gaze fixed with fascination on the page, "you must listen to this letter, for it will amuse you. Lady Valentine writes that she heard from her great friend Mary, Countess of Trevelyan, that of all the marvelous events of the ball, she was most particularly impressed by my masterful squashing of Holtingham's coat. Just as we thought. Let me see, what else does she say—"

"Guy?"

"What is it, sweetheart?" he said, turning the page over and scanning the back for any other tidbits Joanna might enjoy.

The door closed softly. "It is not Joanna. It is Lydia."

Guy's hands froze on the paper, along with his heart. He forced himself to raise his head, thinking he must be dreaming, and having a nightmare at that.

"I am home, my darling, home at last. Oh, *Guy*, I am *back*!"

She stood across the room, her back against the door, tears streaming down her face, her arms held out to him, her face beaming joyously at him.

"*Oh, my God*," he whispered, his scalp prickling with horror as he took her in, seeing the truth. Lydia. It really was Lydia.

He couldn't breathe, couldn't move, his entire world collapsing around him. All he could think of was Charybdis, the whirlpool that pulled everything into its path and destroyed it. He and Joanna hadn't escaped it after all. Blood turned to ice in his veins and trickled down his spine. He sucked in a huge breath, trying to steady himself.

"Guy? Darling? Are you not going to say anything, welcome me home?"

"What—oh, God, Lydia, what in *damnation* have you done?" he said, pushing himself to his feet, his legs barely holding his weight.

"Well, that is a pretty greeting for your long-lost wife," she said, her mouth turning down into a pout that was far too familiar to him. "I haven't done anything except finally remember who I really am and where I belong. You might look a little more pleased."

He shoved his hands against the back of his head, feeling as if he were going out of his mind. "I think you should sit down," he managed to say, forcing himself back into control. "I think we should both sit down." He collapsed back into his chair.

No, he screamed silently, dying inside. *Oh, Joanna, my love, my life, this cannot be happening to us. It cannot be, not after everything we have been through. Dear God, make Lydia go away. Wake me up.*

He felt as if he were back in that moment months before when he'd spotted Lydia up on the ladder, and it had not been her at all but the woman he'd come to love with all his heart. Maybe everything that had come after was a mirage, a long dream of happiness that had never existed at all, for here he was, faced with his worst nightmare come to life.

In a daze he watched Lydia glide artfully across the room and sink with a studied grace into the chair opposite his desk, the chair where Joanna so often sat—the same chair that she had taken that first day, the chair she'd leapt up from when she'd planted her hands on his desk and given him a tongue-thrashing.

"Guy, why are you looking right through me as if I wasn't really here?" Lydia asked, her smile fading. "I am not a ghost, you know, I am flesh and blood, although I suppose I understand your reaction, darling. I felt the same way when I realized the truth, and thank the good Lord it happened when it did, or you might very well have gone ahead and married my cousin, and wouldn't *that* have been the most terrible scandal, never mind a calamity of the worst sort."

He shoved two fingers hard against his forehead. He wasn't at all sure he could tolerate her idiotic chatter, not now, not when he felt as if he were the one who had died. "I think," he said very quietly, "that you had better start at the beginning and explain yourself. Carefully, Lydia. I suggest you explain yourself very, very carefully. You are obviously aware that I thought you dead."

"Oh, my poor Guy," she said, her eyes pooling with tears, her gloved hand slipping to her cheek. "How terrible for you to have thought I perished in that dreadful fire."

"It was not much fun, no." He dug his fingers even harder against his flesh, barely feeling the pressure. This made no sense. Nothing made any sense, least of all Lydia skipping in the door as if she'd merely been away for an extended holiday.

"Well, as you see, I did not die. Not in the least. I am perfectly alive."

Guy shuddered. "Yes, I do see that. However, perhaps you would be so kind as to tell me this: Whose body was found wearing your wedding ring and your necklace? Whose body lies interred in the chapel?"

"I can only think it must be poor Molly, my maid."

"Your *maid*? Why would she be wearing your wedding ring, may I ask?"

Lydia shrugged one shoulder. "I suppose she must have been playing with my belongings. How do I know? Oh, Guy, you must realize that my memory came back only when I read the article in the *Times* about your engagement ball. Suddenly I remembered everything! Such a relief, I cannot tell you—you have no idea what it is like to spend endless months with no idea of one's own identity. It was positively terrifying, like being a piece of lost luggage."

"You are telling me that you lost your memory?" he said

incredulously. Dear God, but this really was happening. Lydia was back in no uncertain terms. "How, pray tell, did that happen?"

"I—I went out walking that night we stopped at the Four Feathers. I borrowed Molly's cloak, as hers was not as fine as mine, and I left all my jewelry behind. I thought that if I looked like my maid I would be less likely to attract thieves. I only wanted to stretch my stiff limbs and clear my head, but I must have lost track of time." She tightly clasped her hands together. "When I returned to the inn, it was ablaze, and people were shouting and carrying on."

"Why did you not step forward and let someone know you were safe? You must have heard them shouting for you?" Guy said, feeling sick to the depths of his soul. How could he have made such a mistake, identifying the wrong body? Granted, it had been charred beyond recognition and he'd barely been able to look, but he should have known. Somehow he should have known.

"That is what I *mean*. I still remember very little of that part, just the fire. I believe the shock must have been too much, and I simply lost my memory. Or perhaps something fell on my head. My next real recollection is of wandering alone in the countryside. A nice French couple visiting the area found me and took pity on me. They brought me back to their home in France and nursed me back to health." She sighed gustily and pressed her hand against her forehead. "After that I went from place to place, finding what work I could, as I could impose no longer on their kindness."

Guy's hand clenched into a fist on the desk. He *knew* she lied, he knew it with every instinct he possessed, never mind what sheer logic told him. She'd been up to no good, he felt certain of that, but he didn't have the first idea of how to start to uncover it.

The grim reality was that even if he did manage to pin

her down, Lydia was alive and well and sitting in front of him, which meant that he couldn't possibly marry Joanna now.

The thought ripped his very heart out. He couldn't begin to imagine what it would do to her.

Standing, he moved to the window, trying to focus on the very real problem before him, determined to get at the truth if it killed him. He turned.

"Why do we not start at the beginning again, only this time at the very beginning. You left here in a rage, as I remember, over some argument or another, saying that you were going to visit friends in Cornwall. Odd that I later discovered that you had sold the de Salis emeralds only days before. Would you like to explain that to me?"

She blanched. "Oh, Guy—I am so sorry. I had incurred a terrible debt that I did not want you to know about, and the only solution I could think of was to sell the emeralds, hoping I would win at the tables later and be able to buy them back, and you would never know."

"I suspected as much," he said, tired to the bone, but at least sensing truth in this one statement. "And then?"

"And then I was on my way to pay back the debt and stopped at the inn for the night. I left the money in a case, along with my jewelry, of course, when I went out for my walk. I—I am afraid it must have burned along with everything else."

"Let us move on to your story about how you returned to the inn."

Her hand moved to her breast. "My—my story? Guy, why are you interrogating me in such a fashion? I have been through so much! Here I am, finally home, and you are behaving as if I have done something wrong—you surely cannot believe that I am telling you anything less than the truth?" Tears welled up and spilled down her cheeks.

"I do not know what I believe," he replied, his voice

tight, thinking that she looked remarkably healthy and well-dressed for someone who had been wandering penniless for seventeen months. "Tell me again about how you returned to the inn. . . ."

Joanna's step slowed, then came to an abrupt halt on the stairs as she took in the alarming sight of Dickson bending over Ambrose, who had collapsed in a chair in the great hall, his face frighteningly pale, his breathing rapid. Dickson fanned the older man with a newspaper, his face frantic with worry.

"Wait here, Milo," she said quickly, releasing his hand and running down the rest of the staircase, terrified that Ambrose might have suffered a seizure of the heart. She had seen it before and had hoped never to see it again.

"Dickson, what happened?" she said, kneeling down next to them, taking Ambrose's limp hand in hers, loosening his neckcloth.

"He's had a right old shock," Dickson said, looking up at her, his own face white.

"A shock? What kind of shock?"

"I don't rightly know, your ladyship, but whatever it was is in the library."

Joanna didn't have the first idea what he was talking about. "In the library?"

Dickson nodded. "I came out to find Mr. Ambrose clutching his chest and doubled over, gasping and babbling, but I couldn't quite make out what it was all about before he collapsed. He just kept saying it was in the library."

"Get him to his room," Joanna said. "And summon the doctor. I will alert Lord Greaves." She stood, intending to send Milo back up to the nursery, but he'd disappeared. Before she'd even had a chance to wonder where he'd gone, a high, terrified cry echoed across the great hall, coming from the open door of the library, and unmistakably Milo's.

"No! Jojo! Jojo!"

"Miles! I am here!" Her heart nearly stopping with panic, Joanna flew toward the library, every instinct she possessed intent on protecting him from whatever had happened inside.

Before she was even halfway across the hall, Milo ran through the door and slammed it behind him as if he were slamming it on the gates of hell.

He flew straight at her, grabbing her around her legs, clinging to her. "Jojo," he wailed. "Jojo, make it better."

Joanna bent down and gently loosened his grip, then dropped to her knees and pulled him close, her heart racing with fear.

"What is it, my pet, my lamb? Not your father? Nothing has happened to him?"

Milo shook like a leaf inside the safety of her arms. "Papa promised," he sobbed against her shoulder. "He promised she wouldn't come back, not ever again."

"Who, my darling? *Who?*"

"Mama."

Milo buried his head in her neck and burst into inconsolable tears.

24

$\mathscr{S}$hock turned Joanna's entire body to stone. "Your mama?" she repeated numbly. "Milo, sweet, what are you saying? You know your mama is dead. Dead people do not come back."

"She did," he sobbed. "Papa promised, but she still did, and she's not even a ghost or a bad dream." He dug his little head hard against her collarbone. "She tried to take me in her arms, but I didn't let her," he said. "Then she started to cry as she always does, and I ran away."

"You—you are telling me that your mama really is in the library with your papa?" Joanna felt as if she might be violently sick then and there, but she swallowed against the bile that rose in her throat and somehow managed to draw in a breath. "You are certain?" she whispered.

He nodded. "Make her go away," he muttered against her shoulder.

Jo stood and picked him up in her arms, holding him tight as if she could protect them both against the tempest that had struck without warning, shaken to the depths of her being. Only minutes before, Miles had been a happy child, skipping about with excitement, his life nothing but sunshine. Only minutes ago she had been coming down the stairs with him to ask Guy if Milo might ride his pony away from their wedding.

Their wedding? They'd never be married now.

Lydia. Dear Lord. It didn't seem possible, but Joanna couldn't see how Miles—or Ambrose for that matter— could be mistaken. She closed her eyes, her heart breaking for Guy, who had to be not only in shock, but in anguish.

"Listen, little darling, little man," she said, leaning back and cupping his chin with one hand. "I think you had better go straight upstairs to Margaret and wait there for me. I will do my best to work out what has happened, and then I will come to you and tell you all about it." She kissed his cheek and gently put him down. "Will you be strong for me now and do as I ask?"

He wiped his sleeve over his eyes and nodded. "Promise you will come soon," he said in a small voice, staring down at the floor.

"I promise. As soon as I can. Be a brave soldier, poppet. We will sort this all out somehow, I promise."

Miles nodded again, then backed slowly away from her, straightening his little shoulders and stiffening his back. She watched as he crossed the enormous hall and marched deliberately up the stairs, taking them one by one, never looking back, as brave a soldier as she could ever imagine. Just like his father.

She nearly fell apart.

Forcing herself to turn toward the library, she took a moment to brace herself, her head spinning with confusion and disbelief.

Lydia was back. She wasn't dead at all; it had been another trick. She'd never been able to leave anything or anyone alone. Trust her to time her grand entrance only two days before Guy and Joanna were to be married. She must have known somehow and come back to stop it. She should have known that Lydia would come back to destroy her life one more time.

She drew in a deep, shuddering breath and went to the library door, her fingers clutching on the handle as she slowly turned it and pushed the door open, her eyes squeezed half shut against what she didn't want to see.

It did no good. Lydia sat slumped over in the chair opposite Guy's desk, her head bent onto her arms, her shoulders shaking, loud sobs ringing through the room.

Oh, yes. Lydia was back.

Sick at heart, Joanna ignored her, her gaze immediately seeking out Guy.

He stood at the window, his head bowed, one hand knotted into the hair at his nape, but his head shot up as he heard the door open.

The ravaged look in his eyes nearly undid her. She had hoped never to see that desolation again, had never expected it for this reason.

"Joanna," he whispered hoarsely, his eyes filled with infinite pain and regret.

"Joanna?" Lydia sat bolt upright, her body whipping around in the chair. "*You.* This is your fault, all your fault! My little boy runs from my embrace and straight into *your* arms?" She pointed a shaking finger at Joanna. "You poisoned him against me!"

"Stop it, Lydia. You should thank Joanna for all she's done for Miles." Guy's voice sounded ragged but surprisingly calm.

"Thank her? *Thank* her for trying to take away my husband, my son, my house, everything I hold dear in life?"

Joanna shook her head helplessly, her gaze fixed on Guy. She didn't know what to say, what to do.

"How is Milo?" he asked over Lydia's ranting. "I'm so sorry—he came charging in with no warning—"

"He is upset, of course, but he is in one piece," Joanna said. "He's gone up to Margaret. He needs an explanation, but he's prepared to wait."

Guy nodded in a gesture of acceptance so like his son's.

"Isn't anyone going to listen to me?" Lydia wailed, pounding her hands on the arm of the chair.

"I think I have heard enough from you for the moment," Guy said. "You are obviously tired from your journey and overwrought. Why do you not go up to your room and stay there until you have calmed down? We can continue this discussion later."

Lydia's mouth dropped open. "You are sending me to my *room*?" she gasped. "I am not a child!"

"You are behaving like one," Guy replied evenly, but Joanna could see that his self-control was stretched to the limit.

Lydia turned her gaze back to Joanna, daggers of hatred flashing in their green depths. "How dare you invade my house and try to take over my life? How *dare* you think to steal Guy away from me? You always were jealous of everything I had."

Joanna had heard enough. She marched straight up to Lydia and stood over her, so angry she could hardly speak.

"You should think twice before accusing me of stealing anything from you," she said, her voice shaking. "Seven years ago you deliberately sent Henry Warnock to my bed. You made certain that my reputation was compromised beyond repair, all because you had the misguided idea that Holtingham wanted to marry me and you had a selfish whim to have him for yourself. I wonder who stole what from whom, Lydia."

The color drained from Lydia's face. "What lie is this that you are telling? Do you think to turn my husband against me with this absurd story? Everyone knows that you invited Henry Warnock to your bed. He said so."

Joanna just shook her head and walked a few paces away, not trusting herself to say anything else.

"Joanna didn't have to turn me against you, Lydia," Guy said, his eyes silently but eloquently conveying his disgust to Joanna. He turned back to Lydia. "You did that all by yourself after I married you. Furthermore, I know that Joanna speaks the truth—but then, she always does, unlike you, who wouldn't know the truth if it fell on you." He folded his arms across his chest. "You are a spoiled, selfish woman who has never put anyone's welfare above your own. You haven't the first idea of what love means, or loyalty, or devotion, or conscience. Normally I would feel sorry for someone so utterly devoid of those qualities, but I haven't an ounce of pity for you."

Lydia stared at him, two angry spots of color burning in her cheeks. "How can you speak to me like that?" she said, her hand clutching at her throat. "How can you, Guy? Surely you mourned me, regretted my death?"

"I deeply regretted the manner in which I believed you had died, but *mourned* you? You must have me confused with someone who gives a damn."

Lydia jumped to her feet. "Oh, you are cruel, horribly cruel!"

"*I* am cruel? I think that word better applies to you, Lydia. You couldn't be content with shattering Joanna's life and mine once before, you had to come back and do it again."

"Oh, I was insane to think you might have changed, that you might actually welcome me home."

"*Welcome* is not the word I would use, no." He pinched the bridge of his nose between his fingers.

"Joanna did this. She . . . came to Wakefield so that she could, she could—"

"So that she could look after the son you begged her to save from his heartless father," Guy finished for her. "So that she could help him recover from the shock of losing his mother. So that she could bring some light and happiness into a house that had held nothing but misery for a long time. And in the process she gave me more joy, more peace, than I have known in more years than I care to remember."

"She seduced you," Lydia said, her eyes widening, her hand slipping to her mouth. "That is it, isn't it? You always were consumed by your baser nature, thinking only of your perverted needs in the bedroom. Joanna knew exactly how to ensnare you, and you, fool that you are, allowed yourself to be enticed, just as Cosmo di Capponi did. You men are all alike."

"That is enough!" Guy roared. "I will not tolerate your

speaking of Joanna in such a manner. You are not fit to be in the same room with her."

"No?" Lydia said, her eyes half-closing in a catlike expression that Joanna knew all too well. "Let me remind you of this, then. You may fancy yourself in love with her, but I am your wife. There is nothing you can do about that, Guy, and I will not tolerate Joanna in my house for a moment longer. You will just have to give up your light-skirts."

Guy looked as if he was going to lunge for her. "Guy," Joanna said, alarmed, quickly moving to his side and staying his arm with her hand.

"Lydia, go to your room," he said through gritted teeth, his powerful body shaking with the force of his rage. "I mean it. Get out of my sight before I really do murder you."

Lydia tossed her head, shot one last hateful look at Joanna, then flounced out of the room, slamming the door behind her.

Guy released a long, shuddering breath. "Thank you," he said. "I really think I might have done her bodily harm."

"Guy—oh, *Guy*," Joanna said, leaning her forehead into her hands. "How did this happen? How on earth did this happen?"

"I have no idea," he said. "She just showed up at the door with some idiotic story that I don't believe a word of, but I have no clue what the truth might be."

"What did Lydia tell you about where she'd been?" she said, looking up at him.

Guy made a visible effort to pull himself together. He quickly and concisely gave her the basic facts. "Tell me, Joanna, does any of that make sense to you?" he asked when he'd finished, looking utterly done in.

"No," she said succinctly. "It sounds like a lot of nonsense. What did she do for money? Why choose to stay in France when her native tongue is obviously English, and her accent that of a gentlewoman? Wouldn't she want to look for her family? Surely she'd have thought that they would be looking for her."

"Anyone with a logical brain would have reached those conclusions, but Lydia's brain never stretched to logic. She said that she'd felt like a piece of lost luggage," he said with a snort. "Only Lydia."

"Wait—wait a moment," Joanna said, her voice sharpening. "That phrase rings a bell, and not because it came from Lydia." She searched her memory, trying to think where she'd heard it before. And then she remembered. "Oh, Guy," she murmured. "I think this might be something—I once read Lydia a book, one of her beloved Minerva Press romances, when she was ill with a bad cold. I remember, because Lydia was particularly taken with the phrase, thinking it profoundly touching for some reason."

"Naturally," Guy said, looking exasperated.

"No, listen to me. The story was about a silly girl who got thumped over the head by highwaymen, or some such thing, and couldn't remember her name. Anyway, for some idiotic reason she ended up in France, having been rescued by two equally idiotic French people. A year later Miss Lost Luggage's memory suddenly returned and she went back to England to her deliriously happy fiancé, a duke as I remember, who had been wallowing in grief, thinking her dead. The village cheered as he carried her off into the sunset to admire her from his rose garden for the rest of his unnatural life."

Guy stared at her. "You cannot be serious. Lydia took the story of her missing seventeen months from a bad plot?"

"Think about it, Guy. Where else would she get it from? She probably got the idea of how to discredit me with Henry from one of the same books."

"So . . ." he said, stroking his thumb back and forth over his lower lip. "I was right. She told me nothing but a pack of lies from the moment she walked in." He gazed at

Joanna, his eyes keen. "Do you think she made up the part about being in France?"

Joanna shook her head, mystified. "I cannot say. If she did use the fire at the inn as an excuse to run away, I suppose she realized she'd have to go far to keep from being recognized, but to go to France? I doubt she'd do anything that brave on her own."

"Lydia has never done anything on her own, including dressing herself," Guy said. "You know that as well as I. If I didn't know her better, I'd have thought that she ran off with an ardent lover in some misguided gesture of high romance, but we both know what Lydia thinks of that side of the sheets."

"But given that, what on earth could she have been up to? Do you think maybe the shock did cause her to lose her memory and she really was taken in by some kind person, but decided to embellish her story to make it sound the more dramatic and heroic?"

He scratched his temple with one finger. "She could not furnish me with any names or places, saying that she'd forgotten all of that as well. I honestly do not know where to begin to track down the truth, if indeed there is any point, other than to be sure there are no more nasty surprises around the corner. With Lydia, anything is possible."

"Guy," Joanna said slowly, "did you not tell me that Ran worked for the government in some secret capacity during the war, ferreting out plots and spies and that sort of thing?"

His eyes flashed with instant understanding. "So he did. Yes . . . I think I might write Ran a quick note and summon him for his counsel. Thank you, my clever Joanna, for that very good idea. I am not thinking with all my faculties at the moment."

"You have had a terrible shock," she said simply.

"Oh, Jo . . ." He gathered her into his arms and held her close and tight as if he could somehow protect them both from the disaster that had struck. "My beloved. I am so sorry, so sorry—" His voice broke. "I feel as if I am in the middle of a bad dream and I'm going to wake up any moment and everything will be back as it was. The real nightmare is that I know I am awake and that we can never go back."

"I know." Joanna gently detached herself from him, feeling as if she were ripping away pieces of her soul as she deliberately moved a few steps away. "I think we had best work out what to do next. Lydia is right—I cannot stay here."

Guy ran his hand over his face. "This is insane," he said. "Utterly insane."

Joanna couldn't have agreed more, but she also knew that from this moment on, everything had to change. Guy was married. She bowed her head, wondering how she was ever going to find the strength to do what had to be done. "I think I had better return to Italy," she said, each word feeling as if a knife were being thrust in her heart.

"*Italy?*" He moved over to her, gently taking her by the shoulders and lifting her chin so that her eyes met his. "My love, there is surely another solution. I need you, God knows, but Miles needs you even more if he is to get through this catastrophe. What do you think will happen to him if you just disappear from his life and leave him to his mother's attentions?"

"I don't know," she whispered. "I don't know, Guy. I only know that I cannot stay here in this house. I cannot bear the thought of seeing you every day and yet not being able to hold you, kiss you, even laugh with you. We can never be that way again." She covered her face with her hands, the tears she'd been desperately trying to hold back for both their sakes flooding over and trickling down her cheeks.

"Jo, oh, my Jo, don't cry, please don't cry," he said, his

own heartbreak cracking his voice. "I cannot bear the hurt this has caused you, that I have caused you."

"It is not your fault," she said on a tight gulp. "You are in just as much pain. The agony is that I cannot soothe it, I cannot make it better for either of us. We cannot change what has happened, Guy. We will have to find a way to live with it." She opened her eyes only to see the deep anguish that marked his face.

He sank into his chair, planting his elbows on his desk and bowing his head into his hands. "How do you find a way to live without a heartbeat?"

Acute pain sliced through her. "Don't, please don't," she moaned, having to force her hands to her sides when all she wanted to do was to stroke through the thick dark hair that curled at his nape just so, to bury her head in the side of his neck and drink in his warm scent that smelled faintly of spice and springtime and fresh linen, so familiar, so familiar, and never to be hers again.

She had lost all right to touch him, all right to love him.

Her feet automatically guided her over to the chair opposite, *her* chair, where she'd spent so many happy hours, her chair no longer. She collapsed into it, feeling weak with emotional exhaustion. "If not Italy, where?" she asked.

He raised his head and looked at her in confusion, his dark eyes blurred with tears. "What?" he said, brushing his knuckles over his eyelids.

"Where do I go that I can be near Miles but keep my distance from you?"

"Why? For the love of God, Joanna, do not cut yourself off from me completely. There is no need."

"Yes, yes, there is," she said, desperate to make him understand, wishing she had the words. "I could not see you without letting my love for you show. I could not lie, could not pretend, even if I wanted to. You and I *have* to stay away from each other, can you not see that?"

He gazed at her for a long moment, his love for her so clear and strong in his eyes that she felt its touch deep inside her, as if he himself had touched her so. She bit her lip hard to keep from crying out.

"Joanna," he said very quietly, "I will do whatever you ask of me save for one thing. I may be forced to let you go—and God only knows how I will manage it—but you will always be my soul's lifeblood. Without you I am only half a man, but I will still be a man who loves you with everything he has left. Do not ask me to stop loving you, for you would be asking the impossible."

She leaned across the desk and pressed her trembling fingers against his mouth. "Please say no more," she begged. "We cannot say such things to each other, not ever again. It is best if we do not speak at all after this, not for some time at least."

He looked at her, the line of his mouth grim. "Then hear it one last time," he whispered. "I will always love you."

"And I you," she choked out. "I—I must leave. I promised Miles I would come to him, although I cannot think what to tell him about where I shall go."

"Tell him that for the time being you are removing to the dower house," he said, looking down at the hands he'd pressed flat against the desk. "Tell him that you will still ride with him every day, that you will not forsake him, that Margaret can bring him to visit you there. It is only just over a mile away, an easy walk. I will keep my distance, I swear it, if that is what you wish."

She pressed her fists against her temples. The dower house? Too close—and oh, still too far. Nevertheless, it was better than nothing at all. Nodding, she stood. "I will tell him."

"Thank you, Joanna," he said softly, a world of meaning in those three small words.

"There is nothing to be thankful about in this whole terrible mess," she said without looking at him, blinded by tears, her heart aching with an unbearable grief that she doubted would ever be assuaged.

25

During the endless days Joanna prayed for the night to come, so that she could sleep and forget, and during the endless nights she prayed for daybreak and a respite from the tortured dreams and tears that soaked her pillow. She couldn't decide which was worse, day or night, but in the end it mattered little. Every moment was equally painful, like drawing breath against the knife embedded between her ribs where her wounded heart stubbornly continued to beat.

The only solace she had were her afternoons with Milo, and he served as nothing but a reminder of what she had lost, for he would never be hers now, any more than his father would.

She glanced over at him. He sat on the ground in the cherry grove.

"Here, Jojo," he said, holding out his drawing pad. She put her own down and examined the sketch. She could make out exactly what he intended to convey: Pumpkin grazing under a white canopy of cherry blossoms, Boscoe lying curled against the trunk of one tree.

"This is very good, poppet," she said, meaning every word. He had an amazingly good eye for spatial proportion, and with time she imagined he would become a fine artist if he chose to pursue that path.

She wondered if she'd ever know.

Three weeks had passed since Lydia had appeared and shattered their lives, three weeks in which she'd really much rather have been dead. She had no appetite, and what little she did eat she had a hard time keeping down, as if anguish had taken up residence and allowed room for nothing else.

She'd finally made up her mind that she had to return

to Italy, to escape from this endless torture, to try to forget. Bunch, wonderful steady Bunch, who had been quietly supportive and surprisingly silent throughout Joanna's ordeal, was packing for them both. They'd leave first thing in the morning.

She gave Milo his pad back, trying to ignore the ache deep in her heart, knowing this was their last afternoon together. "Keep going, little man. You are doing a beautiful job. Do you need any more pastels?"

He shook his head, which was already lowered again in concentration.

She was so proud of him, of the way he was managing with this second difficult upset in his life. From the terrible day when she'd sat him down and explained to him about his mother's return, he had behaved with remarkable equanimity, although he'd shed his share of tears. Hadn't they all?

Margaret kept her well-informed, for Joanna stayed well away from the house and Guy had kept his word to stay well away from her. She had seen him only once, and then from a distance when he'd been riding down the drive. Just that sighting had been enough to send her running to be sick in the bushes.

"His lordship has forbidden his wife access to the nursery," Margaret had said on the second morning, when she brought some of Joanna's belongings around and settled in for a chat. "The whole house is in shock over her return— no one can believe it. The tears being cried downstairs for you and his lordship could fill a lake."

"And his lordship—how is he, Margaret?"

"I've never seen him look so haggard, not even when you were ill—then he was exhausted and sick with worry, but this is different. Bleak is more like it. Mr. Ambrose said that it's how he looked when he first came home from the war, and Mr. Toomsby told my Bill the same. He's suffering hard, that is certain."

Joanna had bit her lip very, very hard. "How is Ambrose?" she said, quickly changing the subject, unable to bear hearing any more. "Has he recovered from the shock Lady Greaves gave him?"

"He has done that, and I'll tell him you were asking after him—he'll be that pleased." Margaret lowered her voice. "He says that now it starts all over again, the hysterics, the arguments, although her ladyship hasn't left her bed since she took to it yesterday. Wendy says she just sits there crying and carrying on and saying such dreadful things that all Wendy wants to do is slap her."

"I know the feeling," Joanna said grimly. "And Milo?"

"He and his father had a long talk yesterday after you left. The poor mite was naturally very upset, but whatever his father said seemed to help." She shook her head. "I don't know what he's thinking, since he's not talking about it. Maybe he'll tell you when you go for your ride later this afternoon. . . ."

But Miles had not said much, then or after. Joanna wondered if he was not still working things out for himself, but she imagined he would work them out just as well when she was gone. He had his father now to talk to when he was ready.

As ever, Miles surprised her, choosing that moment as if he'd read her thoughts.

"My Uncle Ran came to see Papa again today," he said out of the blue, putting down his pastel. "I think he is worried about him. Papa is very sad, Jojo. He misses you."

"I know, my sweet. I miss him too, but there's nothing we can do about it. Your mama is home now, so Papa and I can no longer spend time together." Oh, dear heaven, but she wished it could be any other way.

"I don't see why not," Miles said, looking at his selection of pastels and choosing one that was pink. "I think it is silly. Papa doesn't like Mama, and I don't either, and we both love you very much."

Tears stung behind Joanna's eyes. "I love you too, poppet," she said, her throat tightening painfully. How was she ever going to leave him? How was she even going to tell him that this was the last of their time together? She'd just have to find a way.

"And you still love Papa too, don't you? Don't you, Jojo?"

She swallowed hard. "Yes, of course. You don't just stop loving someone because circumstances change. You see, that is the problem. We cannot change the circumstances even though we do love each other."

"But since Mama doesn't ever leave her room, why can't you move back in? You can live in the nursery with me, and Papa can visit us there, just like it used to be."

"Oh, my little love, I wish it could be like that," Joanna said, choking back a tearful laugh. "I am afraid that the rest of the world would not think very much of that arrangement. We wouldn't want to do anything that would upset your mama, now, would we?"

"Why? She has upset you lots and lots. Anyway, she cannot cry much more than she already does. It is Papa's birthday next week. Maybe you and Papa and I could have a party, just us."

"What, and not invite Margaret and Dickson and Wendy and Shelley and Margaret's children?"

Joanna nearly knocked over her watercolors. She slowly looked over her shoulder, her heart pounding in great, painful thuds.

Guy sat on Vicar, looking down at both of them, a queer, unreadable expression on his face.

Just looking at him felt like taking a precious drink of water after a dreadful thirst. The problem was that it was a thirst that could never be quenched, and the drink was nothing more than a cruel reminder. She felt utterly sick.

"Papa!" Milo jumped up, his eyes shining. "How did you know we were here?"

"I didn't," he said. "I am just as surprised as you. Good day, Joanna."

"Good day," she said unsteadily. He might have been addressing a slight acquaintance, his tone was so casual. The way he was behaving, she'd have thought that he hadn't lost a moment's sleep since she'd left. At least he *looked* terrible, although she could take no pleasure in seeing how gaunt and strained his face had become.

He swung down from Vicar and knotted the reins over the gelding's neck, leaving him free to graze. "The glade has undergone quite a transformation since the last time we were here. It is still as white, but then it was snow that made it so, not the white of cherry blossoms."

She turned her face away. Their lives had been transformed by a great deal more than snow giving way to the blooming of cherry trees, only nothing near as pretty. Why was he talking about something so inconsequential anyway?

"Milo," he said, lightly touching his son's shoulders, "why don't you take Boscoe for a run down the hill? I'd like to speak to Joanna privately, if you do not mind."

Unfortunately for Joanna, Miles did not mind in the least. He instantly obeyed, calling Boscoe and racing off. She had a sinking feeling that he wouldn't return for some time, not when he thought he was furthering the cause he'd just been promoting.

Knowing she was already defeated, Joanna put her sketch pad down and stood, walking quickly away from Guy, her back turned to him.

"I honestly didn't know you would be up here," he said with no preliminaries. "I will not lie, though, and say I am sorry to have come across you. I've missed you, Jo."

She spun around. "Don't," she cried. "It is hard enough just seeing you without your opening that wound."

"Forgive me," he said quietly. "I am sure your life has been as hellish as mine."

"I doubt that," she said, staring down at the ground. "I

haven't had to deal with Lydia. You are in the flames; I am only on the periphery looking in."

The shadow of a smile crossed his face. "Thank you for your compassion," he said. "Fortunately, I haven't had to deal with Lydia much. She is confined to her bed." He hesitated for a moment, then pushed on. "Joanna . . . there is a reason I want to talk to you, other than just the sheer longing to hear your voice."

"What is it?" Oh, how she wished she could draw him close against her, wished that she didn't feel such acute hunger for his touch. It was everything she could do not to throw herself into his arms and give herself to him, offer herself up as his mistress, to the devil with all her principles.

"I—I have been thinking," he said, looking thoroughly miserable. "I cannot go on like this. It is torture, being in the same house as Lydia, knowing you are only a mile away but as inaccessible to me as if you were on the other side of the earth."

"I know," she said, just as miserably. "However, you are married to Lydia, not to me."

"Yes. That unfortunate fact has not escaped my attention." He sighed. "I would immediately start divorce proceedings against her on the grounds of adultery and desertion, but so far neither Ran nor I have been able to come up with anything."

"*Divorce* her?" Joanna said, taken aback. That idea had never crossed her mind. "Guy, that is a very long and very expensive procedure. It could take years in the courts. And what about the scandal?"

He smiled, but without humor. "The scandal? I hardly see what difference that makes if it meant I could eventually spend my life with you. I would do just about anything to make that happen."

"Guy—please don't. I really cannot bear anymore. You just said that you have no grounds."

"Please hear me out, sweetheart." He rubbed the back

of his neck. "As I said, at the *moment* I have absolutely no proof that Lydia did anything wrong, although I have no intention of giving up, no matter how remote the chance. I've had her watched—Wendy and Shelley as well as Dickson and Ambrose have been remarkably supportive and report back to me on everything, but so far, with the exception of a lot of vitriol against the two of us, she hasn't implicated herself in any way."

"She's not entirely stupid," Joanna said. "She must know you are suspicious."

"Oh, yes. Yes, she does, although she's playing her hand close to her chest. She must also know that I can do nothing without proof of her transgressions."

"She has surely contacted her friends, told them her version of events. Can you not speak to them, see where her story differs from the one she told you?"

"She has contacted no one, because I have not allowed it. I've told her that I want her to wait until her memory becomes clearer and she has recovered her strength, that she has been through a long and trying ordeal. I am buying time to discover what I can before she spreads this absurdity about her missing months as a piece of lost luggage, although I don't know how long I can keep her confined."

Joanna frowned. "What about her parents, Guy? Surely they should be informed that Lydia is alive?"

"I made inquiries and fortunately, her parents are out of the country, traveling, so I cannot feel that I am cruelly keeping the news from them. They won't stay away forever, though, and eventually the world has to know that Lydia is back."

"And then?"

"And then I imagine that even if I cannot divorce her, we will separate," he said, regarding her steadily. "I will set her up with a place of her own, for I honestly cannot see how we can continue to live under the same roof."

"I think that sounds wise," Joanna said cautiously, terrified that she knew what he was going to suggest.

"It is as close to freedom as I will probably ever come." He reached out and took her hand, curling her fingers into his palm and covering them with his own, so warm, so strong. "Joanna—you know that I love you, that I want your happiness above all things, and I—I would do nothing to dishonor you. But life without you is a meaningless existence."

She pulled her hand from his, her heart breaking for him, for them both all over again, but she couldn't let him go on, knowing that her will, already weakened, might collapse and she would accept his proposition. Every instinct in her told her that as much as she wanted to be with him, in the end the very love that held them together would be destroyed. If they were ever to have happiness together, he had to be free of Lydia.

"You will find a way to go on," she said, struggling to keep her voice steady, although the effort nearly killed her. She had to convince him somehow that she hadn't understood. "As will I. You must write me in Italy and tell me how it all works out."

The breath left his body sharply, as if she had hit him unguarded in his solar plexus, and he swiftly lowered his head so that she couldn't see his eyes. "So. You are going back," he said, his voice colorless. "When?"

"Bunch and I leave for Portsmouth in the morning. Milo is doing better than I expected, but I think if I stay any longer, he will come to think I will be here always. Better to make a clean break now. I was going to leave you a letter, but perhaps it is best this way."

"Then tell me this one thing," he said, raising his head and looking at her directly, his eyes sharp with pain but also with some other unnameable emotion. "Do you leave so suddenly for the reasons you told me, or do you leave because you carry my child and you do not want me to know?"

She stared at him, stunned. "Guy—oh, Guy, no! Why would you ever think such a thing?"

He looked away for a moment. "Margaret told me that Bunch says you do not eat, that you are often sick. Over a month has passed since we last made love, Joanna. I can count, you know."

Obviously she couldn't. The thought that she might be with child hadn't even occurred to her, but now that it had, she had to acknowledge the very real possibility. When was the last time she'd had her monthly course? She hadn't worried about conceiving, because she and Guy were supposed to marry shortly. Since then she hadn't thought about it at all.

And yet it didn't matter whether she was or wasn't carrying his child. Her decision to leave would remain the same and for all the same reasons. Scandal had nothing to do with it—she'd lived with that for most of her adult years. She left to protect him from creating it for himself, no matter how little he said he minded. She left to protect Miles from the same.

"I do not eat because I have no appetite, and food holds no appeal when I do eat it," she said, frantically trying to count backward in her mind with little success. She would not lie to him, but she didn't have anything to tell him either, since she honestly didn't know. "And I leave now because I must, not from lack of love, but because I love you so much. Neither of us can go on like this. I leave for both our sakes, Guy."

"Then I must believe you on both counts," he said, "for you have never told me anything other than the truth."

She blinked, and hot tears spilled over and trickled down her cheeks. "I tell you the only truth I know, I swear that to you."

He took her face between his hands and ran his thumbs

over her wet cheeks. "Then this really is good-bye," he said, his voice choked.

She nodded, unable to speak, her throat working convulsively for control.

"One last time," he murmured hoarsely, drawing her into his arms and gently lowering his mouth onto hers, kissing her as if he was memorizing every last taste and touch, his lips moving slowly, lingering, his tears mingling with hers.

Joanna clung to him, trying not to sob, drinking him in, memorizing him as well, knowing she would carry this last kiss through the rest of her life.

He finally lifted his head, his wet eyes filled with his heartbreak. "Godspeed, my dearest love," he whispered. "Godspeed and keep you safe." He stepped back, looking at her one last time, then swiftly turned and mounted his horse.

He rode off without looking back.

Joanna watched him until she could see him no more, then fell to her knees, rocking back and forth in soundless grief, her face raised to the sky, her arms wrapped around her waist as if she could somehow staunch the searing pain.

Gone. He was gone and she would never see his beloved face again, watch the slow smile that lit up his eyes, kiss his tears, feel him deep inside her, loving her.

And yet . . . maybe she did carry a part of him inside her. A tiny secret hope bloomed inside her that she might have a piece of him to love and hold close for the rest of her life, God's way of giving her something of Guy while He took everything else she loved away.

She closed her eyes and began counting in earnest.

Bunch closed the last lid of the last trunk and buckled the straps. She turned to Joanna, who watched numbly, feeling as if Bunch had just closed the lid on Joanna's life at Wakefield.

"You look pale," Bunch said. "Did you eat?"

Joanna nodded listlessly. She didn't bother to mention that her breakfast hadn't stayed down.

"This is your last chance to change your mind," Bunch said.

"I cannot, Bunch. You know every last one of my reasons."

Bunch raised her eyebrow. "Including your very latest, which is that since you have finally concluded in your thick head that you carry Lord Greaves's child, you have decided that you are obliged to bring it up as an Italian."

"If he knew I was carrying his child, he would leave his wife in an instant and damn the consequences," Joanna said, her head aching. "I cannot let him do that. If he did manage to divorce Lydia, it would be one thing, but that would still be years away, and the probability that he will ever have the evidence he needs is remote. I explained all of this to you last night, Bunch. Must we go through it again?"

"I merely want to be sure that you have thought the matter through thoroughly. You are inclined to be impetuous, my girl, and raising a bastard child on your own in a foreign country might not be as easy as you think."

"What else am I to do?" Joanna snapped. "I *told* you, I will go away for a few months to some other place and bring back an infant I claim belongs to a friend who died in childbirth. I cannot think of any other solution. I will not give up Guy's child, not for any reason."

"You have the most stubborn head of anyone I have ever known."

"Save for your own," Joanna retorted. "We had best be going. The post chaise will be waiting."

"We are not traveling by post chaise. Lord Greaves has given us the loan of his own carriage and coachman. Apparently he intends to see you to the coast with no comfort spared and all accommodation paid for."

Joanna pressed her fist hard against her mouth. Guy. Even now when she left him he looked after her. "He is very kind," she said thickly, knowing that Guy had sent Bill to guide her and keep her safe all the way to Portsmouth.

"He is more than kind. He is deeply in love with you, Joanna. I have never seen a man with such a broken heart. Yesterday afternoon I took him that lovely oil painting you gave me for Christmas of Camigliano, thinking that he needed it far more than I. He gazed at it long and hard, then politely thanked me, looking as shaken as I've ever seen anyone."

Joanna sat down hard, her hands covering her face. She wondered how many times it was possible for a heart to break.

"He said he'd never seen any of your oils before and thought you immensely talented, but I can assure you that the tears shimmering in his eyes had nothing to do with your talent, nor did his ashen face."

"Enough," Joanna whispered. "Please, Bunch, enough. I can take no more."

"You will be taking a great deal more before all is said and done—infants have a way of growing up, and they are not quiet about it, and any child you and Lord Greaves have conceived between the two of you is bound to be less quiet than most."

Joanna raised her head and glared at Bunch. "One more word and I shall never speak to you again."

Bunch just shrugged. "As you please. I am only an old woman who knows nothing about life. Most of the Wakefield staff is gathered outside, so I suggest you pull yourself together and put on a reassuring face, since they are looking just like you, as if the end of the world has come. Your last act should be to console them and not the other way around."

Joanna rose, knowing her time had drawn down to the last moments of the very last hour and she could not avoid the ending any longer. "Will you ask Dickson and his men to come up for the trunks?" she said, squaring her shoulders, feeling as if she were heading for her own execution.

If she hadn't been pregnant with a tiny new life she'd have welcomed it.

In the end she managed to clear the hurdles of the crowd with relative dignity, speaking a few words of affection to each person, but her composure started to crack when she approached the carriage and Shelley shoved a bouquet of flowers into her hands. She reached up to arrange a lock of Joanna's hair one last time. "Wishing you well," she said. "Think of us from time to time."

"Always," Joanna said through the hot, tight knot in her throat.

Wendy pressed a handkerchief into her hand. "I did the embroidery myself. God keep you," she said, her face crumpling. She burst into tears, which only encouraged Shelley to do the same. Crying their eyes out, they leaned their heads on each other's shoulders in an amazing display of solidarity.

Toomsby stepped forward, hat in hands. "I reckoned I'd better be saying farewell to ye," he muttered, staring at the ground.

"Oh, Toomsby," she choked, leaning forward and kissing his leathery cheek. "Thank you for everything. You will be in my thoughts and prayers."

"Aye," he said, twisting his hat into a tortured shape. "Ye'll be in mine, and his lordship will be too. Go safe, missus. We'll all be missing ye."

Ambrose was next. "Farewell, your ladyship," he said with a formal bow, as if terrified that Joanna would try to kiss him too. "Take good care. You have brightened our lives, which will be the emptier for your leaving."

"Thank you, Ambrose. I will miss you too, all of you."

"Your ladyship."

Joanna turned to Dickson, nearly the very last now.

"Dickson." She took his hand, blinking back the sting of tears. "You will never know how much you eased my way when I first arrived. I can never thank you enough for all the kindness you have shown me, then and ever since."

"Every moment has been my pleasure," he said, his face starting to collapse before he forced it into line, but the sheen in his eyes gave him away.

The highest and most difficult hurdle was Milo, who stood with his back pressed close against Margaret's apron, watching her intently as she approached him, his dark eyes so like his father's and yet so much his own.

Joanna knelt and took his little hands in hers. "I know we talked yesterday about my leaving," she said, "and you were very brave. I need you now to be bravest of all, to be a real soldier for me, but most of all for your father, who will need you very much in the months and years to come. Can you do that for me, little man?"

He nodded, his eyes streaming. "I will. I love you, Jojo," he said, passing his fist over his running nose.

She gathered him into her arms, hugging him tightly for the very last time, drinking in his sweet smell, kissing his soft hair, then both his smooth, round cheeks. "Keep drawing," she said, struggling for self-possession. "Maybe your papa will send me some of your pictures. I love you dearly, my Milo. Be happy in your life and do good things with it."

She quickly stood and pulled Margaret into an embrace. "Look after him," she said, her voice breaking. "Look after yourself too. Thank you for everything."

Margaret didn't speak, her shoulders spasmodically heaving, but she managed to nod.

Joanna climbed into the carriage to join Bunch, then turned and pressed her hand against the glass, looking out at all the people she'd grown to love, Milo above all.

As the carriage started off, Milo raised his hand and saluted her.

Joanna barely managed to raise her hand and salute back, her heart torn to ribbons. She thanked God when the carriage picked up speed and left them all behind so that she could finally give herself over to the anguished sobs that shook her until she finally fell into an exhausted sleep on Bunch's shoulder.

26

*G*one. She was gone.

Guy sat on the hill above the dower house for a good hour after the carriage had carried Joanna and his heart away through the Wakefield gates. The thought of facing anyone was really too painful to contemplate.

Nothing he'd experienced at the hands of the French came anywhere close to the torture he felt now. He had meant it when he'd told her that life without her was a meaningless existence, but until she'd actually physically left him, he didn't understand just how meaningless, or how cruel.

From now on he would have to learn how to move from hour to hour, day to day, week to week, until eventually the weeks and months and years mounted up and he died.

Oh, how he'd wanted to call her his wife, to go to bed with her at night, to wake up with her in the morning, to argue and laugh and share all the small details of life with her, and the large ones too. He'd looked forward to watching her belly swell with their first child, to see her wonder, to hold her close with an infant in her arms, and then another and another, to watch their children grow into adults, to grow old with her.

Gone now. All of those hopes and dreams, gone. And in their place was nothing but cold ashes. Even the tiny hope that she might have been carrying his child, as difficult as it would have made their lives—even that hope had turned to dust.

He thanked God for Milo, his precious son. Without Milo he thought he might truly have lost his mind, but for Milo's sake he would go on, he would do his very best to be a good father. He and Milo would always share the memory of the months they had with Joanna—nothing could take that away from them—not even Lydia. Least of all Lydia.

Exhausted to the bone and beneath to his very soul, he pushed himself to his feet and called Vicar, who'd been grazing nearby, every now and then drifting over to blow on Guy's neck as if that might lend him comfort. Heading down the hill, he tried to turn his mind to the work that waited for him on his desk, but the effort proved futile. When he thought of his desk he thought of his library, of Joanna, of all the hours she had spent with him there, deep in discussion on every subject imaginable. All that was left of her now was the oil painting Bunch had so kindly given him. That was all he had of her—reminders, constant reminders around every corner, in every mournful face.

He looked up the drive where he'd last seen her, empty now. Only it wasn't empty. Ran rode at full speed toward him, his mare's hooves tearing up the gravel.

Guy pulled Vicar to an abrupt halt, hoping against hope that Ran rode with such haste because he had good news from London, but his hopes were dashed when Ran pulled up short in front of him.

"Joanna?" he panted. "She's not at the dower house—am I too late?"

"I'm sorry," Guy said, passing one hand over his tired eyes. "She's already gone. You missed her by an hour."

"I cannot believe it! I had no idea she planned on leaving so soon—on leaving at all, for that matter."

"Nor did I," Guy said, not wanting to revisit afresh the wrenching pain of Joanna's departure. "She said nothing until yesterday afternoon."

"Yes . . . my mother told me over breakfast this morning that she'd had a letter from Joanna explaining her reasons and thanking her for her kindness. Mama was quite undone, having become very fond of Joanna."

"Your mother was very good to be a source of comfort to Jo these last difficult weeks. As were you, Ran. I feel sure that your visits meant a great deal to her."

"It was the least I could do. I felt terrible for both of you." He banged his fist against his thigh. "Damnation! I did not return from London until late last night, but to hear this news . . . I'm so deeply sorry, Guy. You must be devastated."

"I am not feeling particularly happy to be drawing breath at the moment, no."

"Were you—did you have a chance to say farewell to her? I know she felt it was best if you didn't see each other, but surely before leaving this morning . . ."

Guy dropped his gaze. "I saw her yesterday and said my farewell then. In any case, she had enough to deal with this morning. You should have seen the staff, Ran. I watched the whole thing from the hill above—one would have thought the troops were turning out for Wellington." He attempted a smile. "I suppose in a way they were. She did battle for all of us and managed to achieve a massive victory on all fronts. And then Lydia reappeared and shot us all to hell, where it seems we are doomed to stay. Did you make any progress in town?"

"I wish I had better news," Ran said. "Not one of my contacts has come up with a damned thing, not a single reference to a woman of Lydia's description, either in France or anywhere else. The trail is cold, but I refuse to give up." As his mare skipped sideways, he shifted his weight and brought her back in line with his legs. "Settle, girl, settle," he said, stroking her neck. "You have to get over this skittishness."

"Justine is still jumping about, is she?" Guy asked, momentarily diverted. He knew how hard Ran had worked over the last year to rehabilitate this particular mare.

"A bit, but she is coming around. As I told you, her last owner used her ill, stupid woman, and Justine still expects to be kicked half to death and have her tender mouth sawed at like a piece of meat. She'll never trust women again, but she'll learn to settle eventually." He grimaced with disgust. "Amazing the damage that spoiled women of limited intelligence can do, your wife being a case in point. Do you know, I really am astonished at how well she's managed to cover herself, given her general lack of brain."

Guy shrugged. "She took a bad plot from a bad novel and managed to make it work in her favor, Ran. How can you argue with a woman who says she has no memory, let alone divorce her?"

"You cannot, not unless you poke a hole in her story, and so far she has been consistent."

"One would think she'd been trained to resist interrogation by His Majesty's own troops," Guy replied dryly.

"Guy, as much as I hate to say it, her story is so implausible that there really might be some truth to it. Either that or she has the luck of the devil, starting with poor Molly Rathbone. Wouldn't you just know that Lydia's maid would turn out to be an orphan with no family to notice her missing and raise the alarm? Just think how different things might have gone if we'd realized sooner that it had been she who died in the fire." Justine started to dance sideways, and Ran straightened her and stroked her neck again. "Did you take care of that matter, by the by?"

Guy nodded. "Molly is now buried in the graveyard behind the chapel. Moving her from the crypt was a grisly business, but I feel better for having her in a more fitting place, with a marker of her own. I asked the vicar to say prayers for her, explaining that she was buried here because she had once been in service and had no one else, so at least I feel she has been properly laid to rest at last—despite how long it took, poor woman."

"It is a devilish business all around. What was Molly doing in Lydia's room, dressed up in her jewels? Odd, very odd."

Guy snorted. "The whole damned thing is odd. Why would she want to wear Lydia's wedding ring? That was just a simple diamond band. She had a whole jewelry case full of other far more interesting things to play with."

Ran just shook his head helplessly. His gaze suddenly narrowed and he raised his hand, shielding his eyes against the sun. "Look there. I wonder whose carriage is coming down the drive at such a clip? I don't recognize it, or the team, do you? Perhaps we should remove ourselves from its path. Justine isn't much for fast-moving vehicles." He guided her off the road into the trees.

Guy followed, then turned and watched as it went tearing by, sending up clouds of dust. "Obviously it is someone with something to say. Someone with very bad timing. Never mind; I've told Ambrose to say I am not at home."

"Pity, since I haven't anything better to do," Ran replied. He idly added, "By the pricking of my thumbs, something tells me . . ."

Guy looked at him sharply. Ran's intuition was infamous, having saved his neck many a time when he was in the spying business. "Does it indeed," he murmured, urging Vicar into a trot.

They watched from the shadow cast by the west wing, which had a convenient view of the loop of driveway in front of the main entrance. A gentleman emerged from the carriage, well-dressed, if on the foppish side, slight of build, and entirely unfamiliar to them both.

Ambrose took his card, read it, and murmured something. The gentleman appeared dismayed. "I will wait for as long as I must," he said loudly, and in English that was strongly accented. "I have traveled a long distance to see Lord Greaves, and I do not intend to be put off now."

"Do you often have agitated strangers who come to see

you all the way from France?" Ran murmured, examining his fingernails.

"Not often enough," Guy replied in a low voice. "I do believe Lord Greaves might be at home after all."

"How very obliging of you," Ran said. "I was just beginning to feel a touch of ennui."

"We cannot allow that," Guy said. "Wars tend to break out when you become bored." He dismounted and tied Vicar to the hitching post, and Ran followed suit with Justine. For an odd moment Guy felt as if they had gone back to the carefree days before the war when they used to get in and out of all sorts of scrapes together. They'd long since perfected a silent understanding of exactly how to go about these matters.

Guy mounted the steps, pitying Ambrose, who was valiantly trying to bar the insistent man from entering.

"Never mind, Ambrose, the gentleman does not seem inclined to go away. Let him in before he wakes the dead."

The Frenchman turned abruptly. "Lord Greaves?" he said, his fingers fumbling nervously with his hat.

Guy inclined his head. "And I have the honor of addressing . . ."

The man drew himself up to his full height, which was a good six inches below Guy's nose. "I am the Baron de Broussy. Pierre de Broussy?" he added, as if that might mean something to Guy.

"I see. And what may I do for you, monsieur?"

"We—we have something—or someone—in common, I believe."

"Have we?" Guy said, the hairs on the back of his neck prickling, his blood quickening with excitement. Ran was right—something was definitely afoot here, and every instinct told Guy that it was going to be the most pleasing piece of nasty business he'd ever dealt with. "I do so enjoy finding that I have things in common with people I don't know."

He glanced over at Ran with the raise of an eyebrow. "Allow me to present Lord Trevelyan, monsieur. Shall we go inside?"

Ambrose opened the door and stepped back. "Will you be needing anything, my lord?"

"I think only privacy, thank you." Guy led the way across the hall into the library, tapping his riding crop against his boot rhythmically as he walked, thinking hard about how he was going to play his hand. He had a very nervous gentleman who had come for a very specific reason, and Guy had such a happy feeling that he knew exactly what that reason was. He was more than willing to accommodate the little baron.

"Please, make yourself comfortable," he said, gesturing expansively. "May I offer you sherry, cognac? The cognac is an excellent vintage."

"Cognac would be much appreciated," Pierre said, visibly relaxing at his pleasant reception, which was exactly Guy's intention.

Pierre took the snifter Guy poured and settled down in the chair Guy indicated. Guy poured two more glasses and handed one to Ran, although he knew perfectly well that neither he nor Ran would touch a drop. Not until all was said and done.

Ran silently accepted the glass and took up a position lounging against the bookshelf, facing the baron.

"So, monsieur," Guy said, leaning his hip against the desk, flanking the baron on the other side. He casually crossed one booted ankle over the other. "What is this urgent business you have come to see me about? Have we a friend in common, perhaps? Or would it be a distant relative?" He needed to tread very carefully until the baron brought the subject of Lydia up himself, if indeed the subject had anything to do with Lydia at all.

Pierre glanced discreetly toward Ran. "It is a private

matter, monsieur. Perhaps you would prefer to wait until we are alone."

"Ah." Guy said. "Consider Trevelyan invisible if it makes you more comfortable, but I assure you, he knows all my secrets. Please, continue. Or should I carry on guessing?"

"The matter concerns your wife." The baron took a quick gulp of cognac.

"I see," Guy said evenly, although his heart nearly leapt out of his chest. "And what business could you possibly have with my wife? Do not tell me she owes you money. Lydia forever owes people money."

"Well, now that you mention it, she does," he said, pulling out a handkerchief and dabbing at his forehead. "Quite a lot as it happens. In a roundabout sort of way, for services rendered."

"Really," Guy said, uncrossing his legs and straightening. "And what would those services be?"

"I—I am not sure that I should say, monsieur. I do not wish to be indelicate."

"Come, come," Guy said. "We are all men here. You needn't be concerned about your health, as I have no intention of playing the jealous husband and calling you out for pistols at dawn. I would merely like to hear your side of the story."

"Then Lydia—er, Lady Greaves—she told you everything?" he said, his eyes darting around the room, the tip of his tongue delicately touching his upper lip. "I did not know if she would."

"I wouldn't say she told me everything, and I doubt that very much of what she did tell me was the truth. She used no names, so I had no way of knowing to whom I might apply to discover what had really happened. Perhaps you would be so kind as to fill in the bits and pieces she neglected to mention."

"Well, monsieur, I would *like* to oblige you, but . . ." He shrugged in a Gallic fashion that spoke volumes.

"But you would oblige me so much more easily if you knew you were to be generously compensated for your trouble. Indeed, I will be happy to do so, as you will be making certain areas of my life a great deal easier. I am prepared to be very generous if I am assured that you will tell me everything truthfully, leaving nothing out."

"In that case, monsieur, I would be delighted to oblige."

Guy shot a triumphant look at Ran. "Would you mind writing down the baron's statement?" he asked.

"Not in the least," Ran said, as if Guy had asked him to do nothing more important than to jot down a musing or two.

"Thank you. I shall refill the most-obliging baron's glass. Anytime you are ready, monsieur," Guy said. "And please, do start at the very beginning. . . ."

Two hours later, exhausted, sweat pouring from his brow, the little baron came to the end of his story. "And that is when she left," he said, slumped low in his chair. "The same morning she read of your engagement in the papers. Such a rage she threw. And to leave me with nothing—nothing—after everything I went through. . . . Those were the worst seventeen months of my life, I can tell you that. I kept her on only because I was nearly penniless and needed the money." He mopped his forehead vigorously.

"My most sincere sympathies," Guy said, dipping a quill in ink and offering it to him. "Would you be so kind as to sign here?"

Pierre de Broussy leaned forward and took the pen, scrawling his signature on the page Ran pushed across the desk. "I had not expected you to be so reasonable," Pierre said.

"No, I imagine not," Guy replied, regarding him benignly. "I imagine you thought you might have to threaten to blackmail me, such an uncomfortable sort of business."

Ran stood and moved away, and Guy sat at the desk and pulled out a bank draft from the drawer, which he then filled in. "And as we are gentlemen," he said, "I trust that you will take this as a gesture of my appreciation—a one-time gesture, of course. I also trust you will not speak of this matter to anyone again?" He pushed the draft across the desk.

Pierre de Broussy picked it up and glanced down at it, then choked. "Monsieur—monsieur, you are very generous!" he gasped. "Extremely generous! I never expected—far more than I ever hoped—thank you," he said, with all sincerity. "All my problems are solved."

"I understand what it is to endure my wife's company," Guy said. "I, too, once fancied myself in love with her and suffered the consequences. And now, my dear man, I think it is time for you to be leaving. So kind of you to have come."

He practically ran the little Frenchman out the door, down the steps, and into his hired carriage, watching silently as it disappeared into a speck in the distance, just to be sure he was really gone.

He turned to Ran, threw his head back in the air with a great shout of joy, and leapt straight into Ran's arms.

27

"Where the blazes is the damned woman?" Guy paced up and down the library, about to go out of his mind with frustration. Now that he actually had the proof he needed, he wanted to get on with the business of confronting Lydia.

He couldn't afford to waste much more time. Joanna was already hours ahead of him.

"This is Lydia you are referring to, Guy," Ran reminded him. "Perhaps you have become too accustomed to Joanna, who not only knows how to dress in a matter of minutes, but also knows how to answer a summons in a timely fashion."

"Yes. Forgive me my impatience. I cannot afford to waste much more time. Joanna is already hours ahead of me."

"Once Lydia appears you should be able to take care of the matter fairly quickly. After that you can leave her to me, Guy. She's bound to have strong hysterics, and there's no need for you to stay around for that."

"You are a true friend," Guy said, with deep gratitude that anyone in his right mind would offer to stay and cope with Lydia's hysterics.

"I know," Ran said. "Tell me, where do you plan to send her? She cannot stay here any longer, not after this."

"No . . . I thought I would make her a gift of one of my other estates."

"Perhaps London would suit her better," Ran suggested. "You might offer to buy her a house of her own where she can start over. In the meanwhile she can always stay at your other town house, the one in Mayfair that belonged to your mother. I can make arrangements to have her leave today—I think it's best if she is well away from you and Miles and certainly Joanna."

"Yes—yes. Thank God you're here, Ran. I'm afraid my mind is not entirely on the matter at hand, and I confess, I do not trust my temper."

"Understandable, given the circumstances. Never mind, my friend. Life is looking a great deal brighter than it was three hours ago, although I do not envy you the next part of the process of divesting yourself of Lydia. Divorce is such a messy, tedious business."

"I'd go to hell and back for Joanna," Guy said, stiffening. "Listen—I think I hear Lydia coming."

A tap at the door, and then Dickson opened it. "Lady Greaves, my lord."

"Oh, stand aside, you stupid man, you do not have to announce the mistress of the house." Lydia marched in, cheeks flushed with annoyance. "What is it now, Guy? You know I am feeling weak and must keep to my bed. You might have had the courtesy of visiting me in my room instead of insisting that I come downstairs. Oh. Hello, Trevelyan. What are *you* doing here?"

"Good day, Lady Greaves," Ran said with a polite bow. "I am here on your husband's behalf."

Guy walked over to the door. "Dickson," he said quietly, "clear the great hall, will you please, and keep the servants away. I do not wish anyone to overhear, and I have a feeling that it might become a bit . . . loud in here."

Dickson bowed and closed the door, and Guy breathed a sigh of relief, knowing he could trust Dickson to see that no one would be about. He moved over to his desk but did not sit down.

"What I have to say to you, Lydia, is fairly brief and to the point, but I wished Ran to be present as he has been very helpful."

"Very well. Get on with it, Guy. I am sure this will be

another of your tedious interrogations that never goes anywhere."

She sat down in Joanna's chair, Guy noted with irritation. Never mind, he told himself, she wouldn't be sitting there much longer. "I have good news for you, Lydia. I am sure you will be delighted to hear that the distress you have suffered at your loss of memory can come to an end. I have all the details of your missing seventeen months."

She sat bolt upright, the color draining from her cheeks. "What do you mean by that?" Her hands clutched at the arms of the chair.

"As I said. I can give you a full account, starting with the night of the fire. Ran and I have worked very hard to try to retrace your steps, but in the end it proved not so difficult after all. Shall I begin?"

"Do not be absurd, Guy. You cannot possibly know what happened to me if I do not know myself!"

"Oh, but I am resourceful, my dear. I know it all."

He walked over to the window and gazed out, giving her time to absorb the full impact of his words, then turned around. "You left Wakefield with your maid, Molly, in a post chaise, as you did not wish to take one of our carriages or use one of our coachmen. You were on your way to Cornwall with a case of money you had obtained from selling the de Salis emeralds to Olivia Crankishaw. You intended to pay your enormous debt to Frances Astrey, but you will remember all that."

"Yes, of course," she said, her fingers toying with the ribbons on her dress, a cross expression on her face. "I do not see why you bring it up again. I already apologized."

"Oh, I was just setting the scene for you," he said. "You then changed places in the carriage with Molly, giving her your jewelry—your wedding ring—and exchanging hooded capes. When you arrived at the Four Feathers, you appeared to be the maid and she the mistress. An hour later you came back downstairs and went out—with the case of money, I suppose because you did not trust it with anyone."

"That's—that's ridiculous. I *told* you, I went out with Molly's cape, yes, but I did not take the money. I even left my jewelry behind for fear of being robbed!"

"Please, do not interrupt me," Guy said, holding up his hand. "You may speak when I have finished. You were met by Pierre de Broussy in his carriage, who drove you three miles down the road to the inn where he stayed—the Angel, I believe it was?"

Lydia's hand crept to her throat and her mouth opened, but no sound came out.

"You went up to his room, where you spent the next three hours in his bed, putting on a good act, I am sure, for his benefit," Guy said, pressing his advantage. "He was, after all, your illicit lover, who pined deeply for you, and you for him, so you must have risen to the occasion."

"I . . . I—" She snapped her mouth shut again, as if to keep anything else from coming out that might incriminate her.

Guy pinched the bridge of his nose. "When he returned you to the Four Feathers sometime after midnight, you discovered it burned nearly to the ground."

Lydia half-rose, looking frantically around the room as if she might find some escape, then dropped down in the chair again, her head lowered as if she knew there was no point protesting.

"Pierre de Broussy decided that it was an act of God," Guy continued, satisfied that he had her exactly where he wanted her. "Since everyone believed that the poor woman who had been dragged from the wreckage burned to death was the Marchioness of Greaves, he suggested that you take the money—a monumental sum—and escape to his château in France, leaving behind your dreadful life. You agreed, romantic fool that you were, and off you went to Arras, where you stayed in hiding until you read of my forthcoming marriage to Joanna." He ran his fingers through his hair. "Then, of course, you decided to come home and ruin our lives. Again."

"The marriage would have been bigamy!" she cried, not bothering to deny the rest, seizing on the one opening she saw left to her. "I couldn't let you do that, Guy—how could I! It would have been a sin in the eyes of God! I loved you too much to let that happen, even though I knew how dangerous it was for me to return."

"You know nothing of God," Guy said with disgust, walking back toward her, "although you are certainly conversant in sin. You came home because you couldn't bear the idea that I'd fallen in love with Joanna and wanted to spend the rest of my life with her."

He placed his hands flat on his desk and leaned over them toward her, grateful that a large expanse of wood separated them. "You were jealous, pure and simple, and furthermore you were fed up with Pierre de Broussy and your tedious life shut away at the château. So you took your ridiculous story about losing your memory straight from a book you'd read, and you came marching back in the door, having convinced yourself that I would be delighted to have you back."

"And you should have been," she cried. "If you weren't such a heartless brute, you would have been glad that I hadn't burned to a crisp!"

"What about Molly?" he said softly. "Did you ever spare her a single thought?"

Lydia looked away. "Of course I did."

"Of course you did. Well, Lydia. Here we are, the truth finally out. Did you really think you could get away with this?"

"Pierre must have told you," she said sulkily. "I do not know how you found him, but if he hadn't opened his big French mouth, I would have gotten away with it."

"Pierre came to me. His conscience troubled him and

he felt the need to confess." Guy heard Ran's soft laugh from behind him.

"I hate him," Lydia said. "And I hated living there."

"I am not surprised," Guy said. "You hate me too, and you never liked living here."

"And I still do hate you *and* living here," she said, sticking her chin out defiantly. "I shall go straight to London when I have recovered."

"I am afraid that you will never recover, Lydia. You are afflicted with a permanent case of infantilism. However, you shall have your wish and go to London, and there you will stay, for I intend to buy you a house of your very own."

She regarded him uncertainly. "Do you tease me?"

"Not at all. You will have your own house and your own servants and your own carriage and you may do as you please whenever you please and for as long as you please."

"I may?" she said, looking like a child who had just been told she could have Christmas every day of the year.

"You may, for I intend to divorce you," he said, thinking that he really must have been deranged ever to have married her.

"D-divorce me . . . oh—oh, no, Guy, you cannot do that!" she said, jumping to her feet. "That would be scandalous."

"Really," Guy replied dryly. "Nevertheless, that is what I am going to do, if it kills me, if it kills you, if it kills us both. Staying together would kill us that much faster, Lydia. It's already destroying me, and I will not let you destroy me again—once was more than enough."

"You *can't* divorce me," she wailed. "What will people say?" She put her face in her hands and started to sob.

Guy shot a look of complete frustration at Ran, who just rolled his eyes. "I don't give a damn what people say, Lydia. I want my life back. I want Joanna back, and however long it takes, no matter how much scandal I have to endure, I am going to marry her."

"Oh, it's always *Joanna*," she howled, lifting her head

and glaring at him with hatred through swollen, red eyes. "Everything is always *Joanna*. How clever she is, how well she paints, how beautifully she rides. And now you think she will make a better wife and mother than I could ever be. You want to replace me with *her*. I hate her—I have always hated her! I can do all those things, and better if I care to, and—and even in bed if I put my mind to it."

In that moment Guy actually felt sorry for Lydia. He hadn't realized just how deep her jealousy ran or where it had sprung from, that she must have always compared herself to Joanna and discovered that she was the one who had come up lacking.

"Lydia," he said gently, "you must take responsibility for your own actions. Joanna is not to blame for what you have done. You have brought all of this down on your own head."

"You cannot do this to me," she wailed. "You simply cannot be so cruel. My life would be ruined."

"I will be as discreet as I possibly can," he said. "However, I must prove adultery and desertion, so both those things will come out, as well as your feigning your own death."

"Adultery?" she said, looking outraged. "I only went to bed with him once, that time at the Angel Inn. I never let Pierre touch me again after that, I swear it."

Guy pushed back his coat and shoved his hands onto his hips, his head lowered. He didn't know what to say to her—she obviously didn't grasp the seriousness of the matter.

"Once is enough, Lydia," Ran said, stepping into the breach for him. "We have a signed deposition from Pierre de Broussy, who says that there were also witnesses at the inn who can testify to your being there that night. Furthermore, the fact that you lived with him as his supposed wife for the next seventeen months is statement enough, no matter what you say happened—or in this case, what did not. You left your husband and child to run off with another man and pretended to be dead."

"No!" she shrieked. "No, I will not allow this! It isn't fair! I came back, didn't I? I came back." She fell into another torrent of tears, thankfully this time weeping silently. Guy turned his back and scratched his cheek, wondering what the hell to do with her.

"Time for you to be going," Ran said. "I do not think there is anything more you can do here. Oh, no," he said, his gaze flashing to the door.

"Papa? I waited for you. Did you forget about our ride? Oh—is Mama crying again?"

Guy spun around, his heart sinking as Miles came hesitantly into the room. "I'm sorry, Milo," he said softly, quickly crossing over to him, trying to shield him from Lydia's view, "but now is not a good time. Your mama is very upset about something. We will go tomorrow."

"Miles—my dear darling baby," Lydia cried, turning in her chair and reaching her arms out for him. "Come to your mama, who loves you more than anyone."

Miles backed well away, one arm curling around Guy's leg. Guy rested his hand on Milo's head in an attempt to reassure him.

"No! Oh, no!" Lydia wailed. "You will take my son away from me as well as everything else? How can you, Guy? How can you do this to me, strip me of everything I hold dear?"

"To answer both questions, Miles will stay with me, and for very good reason, Lydia. Look at you. Get hold of yourself in front of your child. You do your cause with him no good."

"Papa, why does Mama always behave like a baby?" Miles asked, looking up at him. "She makes me afraid. Jojo never behaves like that, even when she is sad."

"I know, Milo." He bent down and spoke quietly in his

ear. "Speaking of Joanna, I think I must leave right now and see if I cannot catch up with her and bring her back to us."

Miles's mouth opened in astonishment, and his eyes lit up with joy. "Really, Papa? Really? You will bring her home? Right now?"

"I will do my best, although she has to agree," he said. "I have to hurry."

"No! *No no no no no!*" Lydia screamed, stamping her feet, getting ready for true hysterics.

"Ran, for God's sake, get Miles out of here," Guy said. "Take him to the nursery and briefly tell Margaret what is happening, then come back and look after Lydia. I should think a good dose of laudanum might help. I'll try to calm her down in the meantime."

"Come along, young fellow," Ran said, swinging Miles up into his arms. "Let us get you upstairs." He looked at Guy. "Do you want me to have a carriage brought around for you?"

"No," Guy said over Lydia's piercing screams. "I'll take Vicar, since he's already saddled and just outside. It will save time, and also that way I can go cross-country and cut about twenty miles off the journey. Vicar is up to the job."

Ran nodded and quickly left the room, firmly closing the door on Lydia's howls.

Guy scrubbed his hands over his face, then walked over to Lydia and knelt down beside her. "Lydia, please stop shrieking. Listen to me. You cannot change anything by this behavior, and you will only give yourself the headache."

"Go away," she said, flailing at him with her fists. "Go away and leave me alone—you are a cruel monster and I never wish to see you again. Go ahead—go to your precious Joanna. See if I care!"

She kicked his shin hard.

"Very well," he said, wincing. He stood and looked down at this pathetic, sobbing woman-child, feeling nothing except a desperate need to get away. "Stay here and wait for Ran. He will look after you."

"Get out, I say!" She turned her head away.

"Good-bye, Lydia," he said softly. "I am sorry I couldn't be the husband you wanted."

He swiftly made his way out of the room and across the hall, wrenching the front door open and running for Vicar, his thoughts now only on reaching Joanna. He mounted him and turned his head toward the path that led past the chapel to the southern fields and the general direction of Portsmouth.

Randolph frowned when he found the library empty. He'd been gone no more than ten minutes at the most.

"Dickson," he said, poking his head out of the door, "did you see where Lord Greaves went?"

"Yes, my lord. He left the house not four minutes ago, looking as if he was in a tearing hurry."

"And Lady Greaves?"

"Well, my lord," Dickson said with a troubled frown, "she came out of the library about three minutes ago, crying and carrying on, and ran out the door after him. I thought I'd better leave them to it."

"No," Ran said in disbelief. "Don't tell me she thinks she's going to run after his horse, the silly fool."

As the words came out of his mouth he heard Justine give a loud, frightened whinny and then another. "Oh, dear God," he said, his heart stopping. "Not Lydia? Surely she wouldn't—" He didn't finish the sentence, racing for the door, Dickson racing right behind him.

"Lydia, no!" he cried as he took in the appalling sight of Lydia climbing up on the mounting block next to the hitching post.

He ran for all he was worth, shouting for her to stop as she threw herself onto Justine's back, but he was too late, for she grabbed the reins and frantically kicked the terrified mare into a canter, taking off in the direction of the south fields, where Guy had just jumped the first stone wall.

"Lydia, stop!" Ran shouted again.

She tossed a defiant look over her shoulder. As she turned around again, she shrieked, "Guy, Guy!"

Justine, panicked, raced forward, her head low, aiming straight for an oak tree with a low-hanging branch. Ran knew the mare well enough to know that she was determined to rid herself of the devil clinging to her back who kicked her and pulled at her mouth with the reins, and he also knew that Lydia didn't have a clue, nor did she have a chance.

There wasn't a damned thing he could do—it all happened in a split second. Ran watched in horrified silence as the branch caught Lydia in the throat. She screamed once, a terrible strangled sound, as the force of the impact swept her off the saddle and flung her up in the air. She came down hard, landing with a great crack. Then there was only silence.

Randolph, sickened, ran forward, but he knew in his heart that there was no rush. He was more concerned for Justine at this point, who stood a short distance away, pawing the ground, her eyes rolling wildly so that the whites showed.

Guy had heard the scream, too, and turned Vicar around, and he arrived just as Ran and Dickson did.

"Oh, God," he said, dismounting, looking down at Lydia's inert body, her head lying at the wrong angle, her eyes staring skyward. "What the hell happened?" he whispered, dropping to his knees. "What was she doing on Justine? She hated horses."

"She must have decided that she was going to be just as good as Joanna in this too," Ran said in a low voice. "She decided to go after you, Guy."

"I think her neck's broken, my lord," Dickson said, swallowing hard.

"Yes, Dickson, her neck is indeed broken," Guy said, his face ashen. "I should never have left her in such a state."

"Oh, for the love of God," Ran roared, "it had nothing to do with you—for once will you stop trying to take responsibility for everyone else's stupidities? How were you to know she was going to get on a skittish mare and chase after you, when she could hardly ride a rocking horse?"

Guy picked her up in his arms and cradled her. "Still, Ran, I drove her to despair. She never would have mounted a horse if she hadn't been desperate."

"You drove her nowhere," Ran said more gently. "She was unbalanced from the start, and you know it. In a way this is a blessing, Guy. Once word got out about what she did she'd have been censured by the very people whose attention she most craved. Her life really would have been hell."

Guy stroked her hair. "Perhaps you are right, perhaps she will finally be at peace."

"Perhaps you will finally be at peace as well." He touched Guy's arm. "Enough. You have done enough for her. You have the future to look after. Give her to me now, and I will take care of her. Just tell me what you would like me to do, and I will see to it."

Guy closed her eyes with his hand, then handed her over to Ran with a sigh. "Best put her in the crypt, I think."

"You—you want me just to put her in the damned crypt?" he said, startled by this abrupt transition on Guy's part, from guilt and self-accusation to cold logic.

"I want you to lay her in it, respectfully," Guy said reasonably, "and put the top back on. The crypt is now unoccupied, after all, and already has her name on it. What does it matter if the dates don't match up? Who is to know the difference?"

Ran frowned. "You are saying that you want me to put

Lydia in the crypt, and we're all going to behave as if she's been in there all along."

"That is what I am saying, yes. Don't look so shocked, Ran. It's not as if anyone but my staff and you and your mother knows she ever came back—oh, and Pierre de Broussy, of course, but he won't be talking." He looked up at Dickson. "The staff has said nothing about my wife's return to anyone outside the house, have they?"

"No, my lord," Dickson said, back to his usual poker face, now that he was over his initial shock. "They would never think to disobey your orders."

"Why, thank you, Dickson. It is good of you to say so. In that case, they will understand that as far as the world is concerned, Lady Greaves has been lying there since November of 1817."

"Yes, my lord. I can see the sense in that, indeed I can."

"Good," he said mildly. "You see, Ran, Dickson understands that there is no point in revealing the truth, thereby creating a scandal that would only upset Joanna and Miles and taint Lydia's memory. And Lydia herself would far rather be remembered as a martyr who died in a fire than the silly girl who ran away from home with an effete Frenchman and broke her neck falling off a horse she had no business being on while chasing after the husband who was going to divorce her. If you see my point."

Ran couldn't help grinning. "I beg your pardon for being so dull-witted."

"Never mind, I am sure you won't do it again," Guy said with an answering smile. "I mean no disrespect to Lydia, for she was a sad creature who has now gone to God, and I truly hope she finds more happiness in heaven than she ever did on earth."

Ran shook his head. "Joanna has done you more good than even I realized. Speaking of which, I do think you had better get on with fetching her home."

"You are fetching her home, your lordship?" Dickson's

face broke into a wide smile. "Well, it's about time. I gave you until lunchtime, and you disappointed me."

"Don't be impudent," Guy said, grinning. "I'll leave you both to it, then. Oh—Ran. Gather the staff and explain. You can help, Dickson. Tell them that if they love Joanna as much as they say they do, they'll pretend none of the last three weeks ever happened. Oh, and Ran—is that license still good?"

"It is valid for three months, so you have until the end of June to use it."

"Excellent. I think we should be married as soon as the vicar can reschedule us at Saint James's, if you don't mind making the arrangements. I'll have to give Joanna a chance to catch her breath once I chase her down, of course, so tomorrow is probably too soon, but anytime after that will do."

He stood and brushed himself off, then started back to Vicar. Ran stood, adjusting the weight of Lydia's limp body in his arms.

Guy stopped abruptly, turned around, and came back. He leaned down and gently kissed Lydia's brow. "Rest in peace, dear girl, and thank you."

"*Thank* you?" Ran said incredulously. This definitely was not the same Guy de Salis who had come back from the Peninsula. Ran hadn't seen this Guy de Salis since his mother had fallen ill of a wasting disease when Guy was eighteen. Lord, but it was good to have him back.

"Why, yes," Guy replied. "If it hadn't been for Lydia and all her machinations, I never would have met Joanna, and then where would we all be?"

As Ran carefully laid Lydia's body in the crypt and crossed her hands over her breast, arranging her to look as if she were peacefully sleeping, he reflected that Guy was right. Where would they all be? Joanna had brought sunshine into all their lives.

"Some flowers, your lordship," Dickson said, reappearing at his side. "I thought they should go in the crypt with her." He tucked the little bouquet he'd gathered between Lydia's cold hands, and then together they slid the heavy marble top back over the base.

Randolph turned to leave, in a hurry to finally see to Justine, but Dickson stopped him.

"I thought you might say a little prayer, your lordship," he said, pressing his palms together in front of him and bowing his head, and Randolph, feeling ashamed of himself for not having thought of it, did the same. He cleared his throat.

"The Lord is my shepherd, I shall not want, He maketh me to lie down in green pastures . . ."

"*I* don't know what you are standing there looking at," Bunch said in an acerbic tone. "It's been dark for a full half hour now. You surely do not think Lord Greaves is suddenly going to appear out of the blue, not after the way you gave him his marching papers?"

Joanna turned from the window of the private back parlor that the innkeeper had provided, mercifully quiet and removed from the hubbub of the rest of the inn. "Bunch, please. Show a little mercy?"

"Ha," Bunch said. "You are one to talk of mercy, tearing the hearts out of a small boy and his father."

Joanna sank down into a chair and rested her forehead on the heel of her hand. "If you think for one moment that I am going to change my mind, you are quite mad, Bunch. What would you have me do, become Guy's mistress?"

"I would have you not run away from your troubles, that is what I would have you do. How are you to know what God has planned? I doubt He would have taken you this far without having something up His sleeve."

Joanna stared at Bunch. "And *you* are the one always telling me to be practical?" she retorted.

"All I am saying," Bunch said, assuming an expression of infinite patience, as if Joanna were a very small child who was short on understanding, "is that you never know how circumstances might work out. You certainly are not going to find out if you've buried yourself away in the backwaters of Italy. With a child, I might add."

"If you don't like my choice, Bunch, then why don't you go back to your sister's house and stay there?"

"And leave you to your own devices? I think not," Bunch said, bending back to her embroidery. "Heaven only knows what you would get up to—and in any case, someone has to look after that child you're going to have. The problem with you, my girl, is that you are too proud and too fond of your high horse."

"My *high horse*? What is that supposed to mean?" Joanna was so annoyed that she'd forgotten she felt sick and utterly miserable.

"I mean that you think you have a corner on morality. You are no better than the next person, you know. You wouldn't be pregnant with Guy de Salis's child right now if you hadn't been carrying on in his bed before you were married, and yet now that you cannot marry him, you refuse to let him provide for you and his child on the grounds that it wouldn't be right." She poked her reading spectacles up on her nose and made a dainty stitch. "Ha! is all I have to say to that."

"You know nothing about it," Joanna said.

"Don't I just. It just so happens that I heard from Lady Trevelyan—who happens to be a third cousin of mine on my mother's side, by the by—who heard it from her son Randolph, who heard it directly from the lips of Guy de Salis himself, that he was prepared to set you up in a nearby estate of your own, just so that you could continue your relationship with young Miles."

"And how long do you think it would have been until I completely fell apart or gave in to him altogether?" Joanna snapped. "How much do you think I can take, Bunch? And now with this child on the way, that would have looked just splendid, wouldn't it? Guy would have become a laughingstock. His wife in one house, his presumed mistress in another. How cozy."

Bunch just pursed her lips and took another stitch.

Joanna went bleakly back to staring out the window.

She turned a few minutes later as a commotion started outside, the sound of someone pounding on the outside door, the innkeeper's voice, then a rapid exchange of conversation.

"Oh, no," she whispered, her hand creeping to her breast, where her heart had started beating like the wings of a wild bird trying to escape. "It's Guy. Bunch, it's *Guy!*" she said, half panicked, half exhilarated.

"Yes," Bunch said imperturbably as the door flew open and Guy appeared framed in the doorway, his breath coming hard and fast, his hair windblown. He looked done in.

"Joanna," he gasped, trying to catch his breath. "Thank God. Thank God I found you."

She pressed her back against the windowsill, not knowing what to do, what to say. "What—what are you doing here?" she finally managed to stammer idiotically.

"I came," he panted, "I came to tell you—" He stopped and blew out a long breath, then took in two more quick ones.

She watched him in an agony of confusion.

"I came to tell you that Lydia is dead," he finally managed to gasp, then collapsed into a chair, his head lowered as he made a serious effort to recover his breath.

She stared at him. "Wh-what?" she stammered, waves of shock tearing through her body. Lydia, dead? "You— you didn't—"

"No, I didn't, although I cannot fault you for asking. She broke her neck falling off Ran's mare."

Joanna sank to the floor in a daze, unable to absorb the implications. She couldn't believe it. This was worse than anything she could have imagined—as much as she'd come to dislike Lydia, it wasn't supposed to end like this, not like this. . . .

"That silly girl never could ride," Bunch said. "What was she doing on Lord Trevelyan's mare? Lydia hated horses."

"She was chasing after me," Guy said, moving over to Joanna and kneeling in front of her. "I told her I wanted a divorce. I learned the whole truth, sweetheart, not long after you left. I'll tell you about it later. The point is, I was leaving to find you, and Lydia got some insane notion in her head that she could stop me. She managed all of a hundred yards before she ran into a tree limb."

Joanna shut her eyes as if she could shut out the waves of guilt that washed through her. If it hadn't been for her, Lydia would still be alive. If it hadn't been for her, Guy would never have asked for a divorce, never come after her, and Lydia would never have been driven in desperation to mount a horse she couldn't possibly control.

Guy reached out and took Joanna's cold hands. "Joanna? Do you understand what this means?"

She opened her eyes and looked at his beloved face through a mist of hot tears. "Yes," she said, her throat so constricted that she could hardly speak. "It means that you have lost a wife and Milo has lost a mother."

"It means that we are free to marry," he said gently.

"No," she said, her already bruised heart squeezing so tight in her chest that she could hardly breathe. She couldn't believe the irony—she'd left him because he wasn't free to love her, and now that he was, she couldn't have him. "I cannot marry you, not now. More than ever it is impossible."

"Why?" he said, a deep frown scoring his brow. "Joanna, for the love of God, *why?*"

She pulled her hands from his and covered her face, trying to stifle the sobs that came from so deep inside that she felt as if they tore straight from her soul. "Because—because to marry you now would be to create the worst wrong of all."

"Why would you think that?" he said, sounding perplexed. "Lydia's gone. She cannot hurt us anymore, Jo. The scandal would have been in the divorce."

Joanna dropped her hands and met his eyes, desperate for him to understand. "Guy, don't you see? *I* am responsible. Lydia would still be alive if it hadn't been for me. I took from her the only thing she ever wanted, I made her life impossible when she returned—all she asked for was your love, the love of her child, and I stole those things from her, just as she said." She pressed her hand hard against her mouth, stifling a rush of nausea, trying to catch her breath. "For the love of me you asked her for the one thing she could not endure, and she died as a result."

"Joanna. Joanna, my love, you must listen to me now," he said, his fingers tenderly stroking her wet cheek. "Please listen."

"No," she moaned, turning her head away. "No. There is nothing more to say. If I had been strong enough to stay, to leave things as they were, none of this would have happened."

"You are wrong, sweetheart. I understand why you feel as you do, since I've done the same thing to myself, but you really are wrong."

Bunch stood. "I will be outside. Listen to him, Joanna."

Joanna heard the door softly close. Here she was with Guy, the man she loved above all else in this world, his growing child nestled inside her, and yet she felt more alone than she ever had in her life. "Please, Guy," she whispered, "I think it is best if you leave. Nothing you can say will change the facts. Lydia is dead, and we cannot marry now, not if we have any honor." She bowed her head, tears dripping steadily onto the tops of her hands.

Guy didn't speak for a long moment. "Joanna," he finally said, his voice very quiet. "Not so very long ago you taught me that one can poison oneself with misguided guilt. I realized then that I had used that guilt as a way to flagellate myself for the senseless deaths of people I cared about, people who had counted on me to see them safely home. I blamed myself for having lived, believed that my own death would at least have been honorable."

He picked up one of her hands and smoothed his thumb over her palm. "You forced me to see where the real senselessness was, that my guilt would not bring those men back and that the greater dishonor was in not valuing at all the miracle that had kept me alive. I realized that God's will was not mine to command, that whatever He gives us in life as well as what He takes from us is all part of His plan, and we are not meant to question it, only to accept it and do our best with what we are dealt."

Joanna drew in a sharp breath, Brother Michael's words drifting back to her.

"God's will is not for you to understand, my child. It is only for you to accept."

She ran shaking fingers over her eyes, incapable of speech.

"Lydia died today, it is true," he continued. "But you are not responsible for that any more than I am. She made her choices, my dear love, each and every last one, from the moment she decided to falsely implicate you up to the moment that she chose to mount a horse she must have known she couldn't possibly ride. Never mind all of the other foolish things she did in between." He sighed heavily. "I cannot feel anything but sorrow for her death. I cannot even find it in myself to hate her for the misery she inflicted on all of us, for if she gave me nothing else, she gave me Milo, and she inadvertently gave me you, the two most precious gifts of my life."

Joanna turned her cheek into her shoulder, her face contorting with pain. "She—she's gone, Guy."

"Yes, she is, but as Ran pointed out, maybe she has finally found peace, for God knows she didn't have a moment in this life. I thought about it long and hard as I was riding here. I do honestly believe that Lydia was eaten up inside with jealousy of you from her very early years." He folded his fingers around hers, his voice calm and steady, infinitely reassuring.

"Think about it, Jo. She was a little girl who was indulged in every whim and told how perfect she was in every way; she was given the single-minded adulation of her parents, told that she was fit to be no less than a princess. I believe that any person who did not treat Lydia according to her unrealistic expectations was immediately considered the enemy, which is where you come into it."

"But—but I was devoted to Lydia," Joanna protested, lifting her head and looking at him in confusion. "I was as guilty as anyone else of pampering her. Why was I the enemy?"

"Because you were a threat by virtue of your very existence. You were not just a cousin, you were cast in Lydia's own image, only even more beautiful, certainly more accomplished."

Joanna shook her head, mystified. "But Lydia was so much more fun, so impish. Everyone adored her—she knew I paled in comparison to her."

"Can you not see it even now, Joanna? Lydia was like a butterfly, gaily flitting about, but never lighting on anything for more than a moment. Her head was full of light chatter but no substance. You, on the other hand, had not only a good brain, but you had heart and wisdom and the talent to use them to real effect."

"Lydia had no time for those things," Joanna said, hiccupping. "She put no value in anything beyond social ritual and position, and she mocked me for my uselessness in that regard."

"Of course she did. She would find anything she possibly could to denigrate you. She felt diminished by you, sweetheart. Her only defense, her only way to make herself feel better, was to diminish you in turn. She didn't care that you always treated her with devotion—that only made you more of a fool in her eyes. Silly, gullible Joanna." He smiled softly. "And yet you were the one who could hear the sound of snow."

Joanna looked at him blankly. "The sound of snow?"

"Yes. You remember the watercolor Milo did for you

when you were so ill? He painted his feelings, his perceptions, the way you'd taught him. I probably learned more from that one sheet of paper than I did over the last twenty years." He lifted her hand and kissed her fingertips. "How could someone as shallow as Lydia not be jealous of you, of your quiet beauty, your gentleness, your innate sensitivity? She was the pale imitation of the original, my love, and she knew it."

"Guy," Joanna choked, "I *hurt* her. I hurt her terribly. Can you imagine how she must have felt on her return to see Milo run to me, not to her—how she must have felt when you came to my defense against her and let her know just what you thought of her? And finally in her last hour of life to have you put her to one side because you wanted me—is it any wonder she did something so unbelievably stupid and died as a result?"

"As I said, Jo, she brought all of this down on her own head. We'd be fools to forsake our own happiness, never mind Milo's, just because we feel bad about Lydia's dying. I need you, Joanna. Milo needs you. God knows the staff at Wakefield needs you—I've never seen such a sorry-looking group as when you left."

Joanna leaned her head back against the wall, exhausted. "You still have to mourn Lydia for the next year. I cannot be anywhere about, Guy, or there really would be scandal."

"I have no intention of going back into mourning," Guy said. "Once was enough."

Joanna stared at him, shocked. "You cannot mean it! Even if you don't mourn from your heart, you have to observe the proprieties."

"I don't have to observe a damned thing," he said tightly. "Ran and Dickson have already put Lydia in the crypt, where she's supposedly been eternally resting for the last seventeen months. The staff has been sworn to secrecy, and as far as I am concerned, that is the end of that.

We do not need the rest of the world knowing that Lydia spent those seventeen months disgracing herself. But that is another story, and one I will tell you on the way home." He paused, his hand tightening on hers. "You *are* coming home?"

Joanna didn't have a single argument left. With his usual thoroughness Guy had countered every last objection she could possibly think of. She wiped her streaming eyes with both hands, then looked into his beautiful, dark eyes, anxious with his unanswered question.

"Yes, I'm coming home," she said shakily, her heart welling with a happiness she had thought never to feel again. She smiled mistily, her gaze falling to her stomach, still flat but burgeoning with new life. "Bunch was so worried that I was going to bring this child up as an Italian."

He stared at her. "Jo? Jo, my sweetheart? You *are* with child?" His throat worked hard and he passed a hand over his eyes. "Why didn't you tell me when I asked?" he said, his voice hoarse. "I prayed for this."

She pressed her forehead against his beloved chest, although there was too much coat in the way for her liking, so she impatiently shoved it aside and found his jacket and his heartbeat and rested her cheek against that. "I didn't know, I honestly didn't, not until you put the thought in my mind, and then when I did realize, I thought that I couldn't bear to complicate your life any further, not when you had so much to deal with as it was, and I couldn't tolerate the thought of any more scandal heaped on your head, so I thought it best if I left after all."

Guy kissed her hard. "Never mind," he said, lifting his head. "We'll talk it all over in the carriage, if you feel strong enough to travel."

She nodded, then burst into tears and sobbed against his jacket for a few moments, while he quietly stroked her hair and let her get it all out.

"Better now," she finally said, lifting her face, only to find a handkerchief at the ready in Guy's hand.

She smiled up at him. "I love you."

"I should damn well hope so," he said, wiping her eyes and nose and cheeks, then presenting it to her so that she could blow. "Let's go, sweetheart. Miles is waiting."

That was all the incentive Joanna needed. Miles and Wakefield. Dickson and Margaret and Wendy and Shelley and Ambrose and Toomsby, they would all be there, and Bill would see she and Guy and Bunch got back safely.

Home at last.

Despite the lateness of the hour when they finally arrived, half the staff was up and waiting, and the emotional greeting Joanna received was enough to send her back into floods of tears.

"Anyone would think I'd been gone a year instead of a few hours," she said, wiping her eyes with Guy's already sodden handkerchief. "Is Milo up?"

"He finally fell asleep," Margaret said, wiping her own eyes. "I imagine he'll be pouncing on you first thing in the morning."

"Are you ready to retire?" Wendy said, looking as if Joanna had never left. "Shelley and me, we aired your room and put fresh linens on the bed and flowers on the table and all when we heard the news."

"Thank you," Joanna said, "but if you do not mind, there is something Lord Greaves and I must do first. You might see to Miss Fitzwilliam's comfort, though, and then go to bed, all of you. It is far too late for you to be staying up any longer on our behalf. We're back safe and sound, and all is well."

They slowly dispersed, and Guy turned to take Joanna's arm. "Are you ready?"

She nodded. To her surprise, Dickson appeared at her

elbow, a lantern in hand, the fresh candle burning brightly inside. "I thought you might need this," he said. "There is a cloud cover tonight and a ground mist. You will need a light to safely guide your way."

Joanna bit her lip as her breath caught in her throat. Dear Dickson. He always knew. Always. "Thank you," she said simply.

Together she and Guy walked down the path to the chapel, neither speaking, each wrapped in their separate and private thoughts.

"Shall we go in?" Guy said, pausing in front of the chapel door. "I will arrange a memorial service for Lydia with the vicar, but this seemed important for us to do ourselves tonight."

She smiled and nodded, feeling no sense of trepidation. She needed this time to make her peace with Lydia.

He pushed open the heavy door, then halted abruptly, releasing a quick breath of surprise. "Who in the name of—"

Joanna squeezed his arm hard, her heart lifting in joy.

Brother Michael stood beside Lydia's crypt, a simple white stole around the neck of his black cassock, his cross hanging in the middle. In his hands he held a vial of water raised high above him. He'd covered the top of the crypt with a white cloth, on which sat a cup of wine and piece of bread, along with a single candle.

He lowered the vial and sprinkled it over the top of the crypt and around the sides. Next he took the bread and held it up in offering, murmuring quietly to himself in Latin. He broke the bread and ate a piece. Then he held up the cup in the same manner and murmured again, sipping from the cup and reverently putting it down.

And then, as if he'd known they were there all along, he looked toward them and smiled in invitation.

They moved toward him without speaking, drawn by his very presence.

"*In nominus Patri et Filii et Spiritus Sancti,*" he said, making the sign of the cross over them as they knelt, giving them each a piece of bread and offering the cup for them to sip from.

"Unto almighty God we commend the soul of our sister Lydia," he said, "and we commit her body to the ground; earth to earth, ashes to ashes, dust to dust, in sure and certain hope of the resurrection unto eternal life, through our Lord Jesus Christ. Amen."

He gestured for them to stand.

"Guy, this is Brother Michael, whom I told you I met here at Christmas," Joanna said.

"How did you know to come?" Guy asked, his voice shaking.

"I only come when I am needed," Brother Michael said with a gentle smile, tucking away his cup and the vial of water inside his cassock, then folding the cloth and finally his stole and doing the same.

"But—but how did you know what happened here today?" Guy said, looking thoroughly shaken.

"God guides me, as He guides us all," he said. "If you will excuse me, I have other ministries, and I am sure you will want some time alone. May the blessing of God be on you and young Miles, and on your coming child. I foresee great happiness for you all."

He turned as he walked down the nave and looked over his shoulder at Joanna. "You listened well, my child," he said. "Perhaps you will paint me the next great pietà."

He chuckled as he drifted out the door and vanished into the mist as if he'd never been.

Guy turned to Joanna, his mouth parted in a question she saw he couldn't even formulate. "That was no ghost," he finally managed to say. "I don't know who—or what—that was."

"As you once said to me, there are some things that do not bear too close an examination," she replied softly. "All that matters is that Lydia has been properly laid to rest and we are free."

Guy drew her close and held her tight. "Ah, Joanna, I think God really has answered all our prayers."

He released her, then took her by the hand and led her out into the night, leaving the single candle burning on Lydia's crypt.

Epilogue

Villa di Camigliano
Pesaro, Italy
August 30, 1822

 *J*oanna paused, paintbrush in hand, and gazed out over the rolling landscape punctuated by tall spikes of cypress trees. Breathing in a deep breath of the balmy summer air, she savored the rich, heady fragrance of flowers mixed with herbs and a hint of lemon that drifted over from the gardens to the south.

Peace, such incredible peace.

She gave up a silent prayer of thanks for her beloved Villa di Camigliano—House of the Camelias—once a place of refuge, now of simple sanctuary. It was ten years to the day since the night of Lydia's birthday dance, the night that her destiny had been set into motion, a destiny that had eventually led her to Guy.

She had no regrets, although she could not help the sorrow she always felt when she thought of Lydia and her short and tragic life, but as Guy always said, without Lydia they never would have found each other. They had long since laid the past to rest, starting the day that Lydia had died—she still remembered so well how that night had ended. Guy hadn't even bothered to pretend. He took her straight to his bed and spent what was left of the hours before dawn letting her know exactly how much she meant to him.

Just after daybreak she'd crept upstairs to her bedroom in the nursery so that she'd be there when Milo awoke.

The joy of that reunion had been immense, no less than the joy of the days that followed as she and Guy were married in St. James the Less, Milo proudly riding Pumpkin alongside the carriage as they left, Toomsby walking alongside.

Life had held nothing but happiness since, just as Brother Michael had promised.

Joanna wondered if Milo would ever read Lydia's letters that she'd saved, her locket safely stored inside the chest. She'd kept them to give him when he was older, thinking that one day he might want to have a better insight into his mother and the chaos of his early years, but she didn't have any idea if he would ever be interested. As far as he was concerned, his mother was a closed chapter, a subject that never came up.

Joanna sighed, returning to the present, to the lovely misty light. She stood back, examining the canvas, pleased with what she saw. It was no pietà, but rather a mother holding her infant son and looking down at him with adoration. She didn't think Brother Michael would have been too disappointed.

The sound of merry laughter came from the veranda, and she looked over to her right to see Guy appear with one very wet baby Florentina on his hip, Milo pulling along two-year-old Michael, and both of them just as wet as Florentina. Boscoe trailed behind, his tail splashing water everywhere.

"What have you been doing?" she asked, her face breaking into a smile.

"We, my darling, have been down to the river," Guy said, running a hand through his hair and spraying water around just as effectively as Boscoe.

"And Boscoe went in, so I had to go in after him," Milo said, "and then, since Michael wants to do everything I do, he had to come too, and Papa came in to drag Michael out."

"And since Florentina felt so terribly left out and started

to howl, we decided we had better all go swimming," Guy finished. He dropped a kiss on her head. "Don't worry, it's not nearly as dramatic as it sounds. We were only in the shallows."

"I wasn't worried," she said, turning her face up to his. "I never worry anymore. I leave that to Bunch, who worries enough for everyone."

"Oh, Lord," Guy said. "I had better get the children clean and dry before she comes back from the market, or there will be the very devil to pay. I sometimes think I'm better off when we're in England on my territory, where at least she gives me nominal respect."

"I'll be right in to help," Joanna said. "I'm finished for today."

He peeked a look over her shoulder. "It's coming along beautifully," he said. "And yet somehow I don't think the painting had your attention when I first saw you. You looked as if you were in another world. What were you thinking about, sweetheart?"

"Nothing," she said, reaching behind her for his hand, holding it tightly, loving him with everything she was worth. "Nothing at all."

If you're looking for romance, adventure, excitement and suspense be sure to read these outstanding romances from Dell.

——— ❋ ———

Jill Gregory
☐ **CHERISHED**   20620-0 $5.99
☐ **DAISIES IN THE WIND**   21618-4 $5.99
☐ **FOREVER AFTER**   21512-9 $5.99
☐ **WHEN THE HEART BECKONS**   21857-8 $5.99
☐ **ALWAYS YOU**   22183-8 $5.99
☐ **JUST THIS ONCE**   22235-4 $5.99

Katherine Kingsley
☐ **CALL DOWN THE MOON**   22386-5 $5.99
☐ **ONCE UPON A DREAM**   22076-9 $5.99
☐ **IN THE WAKE OF THE WIND** 22075-0 $5.99

Joan Johnston
☐ **THE BODYGUARD**   22377-6 $6.50
☐ **AFTER THE KISS**   22201-X $5.99
☐ **CAPTIVE**   22200-1 $5.99
☐ **THE INHERITANCE**   21759-8 $5.99
☐ **MAVERICK HEART**   21762-8 $5.99
☐ **OUTLAW'S BRIDE**   21278-2 $5.99
☐ **KID CALHOUN**   21280-4 $5.99
☐ **THE BAREFOOT BRIDE**   21129-8 $5.99
☐ **SWEETWATER SEDUCTION**   20561-1 $4.50

Connie Brockway
☐ **ALL THROUGH THE NIGHT**   22372-5 $5.99
☐ **AS YOU DESIRE**   22199-4 $5.99
☐ **A DANGEROUS MAN**   22198-6 $5.99